Praise for

The Pinstripe Prisoner has received a nur
Listed for the Exeter Novel Award 20ῑ
erary Prize 2017, Shortlisted for the PENfro First Chapter Competition 2018, and Number one bestsellers position on YouWriteOn.com, funded by UK Arts Council.

At turns insightful, disturbing and wrenching. *The Pinstripe Prisoner* is a deeply psychological portrait of one young man's attempt to cope with a horrific event and its aftermath. While the present moves at a catastrophic speed, the narrator's touching memories allow the reader to pause, reflect and find peace.

Judge's comments, Yeovil Literary Prize

This collection has a timeless message that lends itself to the current generation … painting a picture of a fierce warrior who is both strong and protective, an advocate of fairness when there's none, and a multicoloured messenger of truth and hope worthy of any urban wall.

Dannielle Line, Author and Editor

Kelly Van Nelson's website is titled with the description: EDGY STORIES FROM INSIDE THE MIND. I find this an apt description of her poetry. It's very edgy, an unfiltered musing on the darker elements present within society. The hidden, the insidious, the things people want to hide from. Her prose is powerful, and rather impressive. Kelly Van Nelson is a talent to watch for those interested in the Australian poetry scene.

Theresa Smith Writes

This book is packed with heavy themes and raw, unfiltered poetry that speaks directly to the poet's experience of violence, abuse and bullying. The author's working-class upbringing informs her perspective, lingering in the corners of most poems, sometimes with nostalgia and sometimes with powerful, bitter resonance.

Holden Sheppard, Author

This poet's work began with themes gathered in her early days as an underdog on a council estate in Newcastle upon Tyne. Using simple powerful language, she offers the reader a very personal perspective about life on the gritty side. With honesty and heart, Van Nelson tackles concerns such as discrimination, corporate and playground bullying, domestic violence, mental illness and other important social justice issues. Her collection speaks of hard yards and heartbreak, but there is also a sense of hope and courage.

Writing WA

To keep your truth in sight you must keep yourself in sight, and the world should be a mirror to reflect your image and to reflect upon. This is exactly what Kelly Van Nelson conveys. It is her journey, the good the bad, and the ugly. By putting it to paper she turns her experiences into a way to bounce back from her underdog world and help others in the process. We are thrilled to have her collection of poetry in our Hollywood Swag Bags honouring Oscar Weekend.

Lisa Gal Bianchi

The beauty of poetry: when it is written exceptionally well it takes you to a place of vulnerability. It gets your heart beating and your thoughts branching out to question, to wonder, to connect, to understand, to break the barriers of judgment. Kelly Van Nelson is one such poet that takes you one step further than this, diving into a world that hits so many relevant topics in today's world. It's not just poetry. It's hardcore magic. This masterpiece touched my soul.

Micky Martin, Author

Graffiti Lane swaps rose-coloured glasses for grit, dirt and shadow. There's a rawness and simplicity to the language that evokes feelings of empathy, 'I've-been-there' understanding, empowerment, sadness, tenderness and even smiles. One minute you're wincing and the next you're nodding your head – it's that kind of poetry; poetry that gets people, that reveals the poet's heart, poetry that packs a punch.

Monique Mulligan, Author

Poetically written, the rawness of the words immediately drew me in from the first page. Written in an utterly honest fashion, Kelly Van Nelson skilfully explores both the darker side of human nature, as well as the hope and resilience within every one of us. Profoundly moving and emotionally charged, I loved reading it.

Yu Dan Shi, Author of **Come Alive**

Great collection of poems showcasing deep insight into the human psyche as it deals with life's challenges. The author has a natural talent of capturing the raw feelings and artistically playing it back in beautiful language. Highly recommended for anyone interested in diving into life's emotional roller-coaster.

Omar Alim

A well-written and thought-provoking book that leaves the reader reflecting on the emotional intensity of the words and message through them. Highly recommended.

Danielle Aitken, Author

This collection of urban poetry is just incredible. Sometimes challenging to read, because of the emotions it invokes or the fact you think on it for a while. Some beautiful moments too. The author has an incredible voice and her works in this book have something for everyone.

Jacie Anderson, Author

Dark and distressing themes are laid bare, yet accomplished poet Kelly Van Nelson manages to imbue a sense of hope, rather than hopelessness, approaching every topic with unwavering honesty, unafraid to venture into harrowing territory to reflect on a myriad of challenges. Using the vernacular of the street, the boardroom and the domestic front, Van Nelson reveals a keen sensory perceptiveness, an acute awareness of injustice, a deep-rooted empathy and the life-altering potential of resilience.

Maureen Eppen, Author and Blogger

This collection provides a raw, eclectic mix of poems relating to many of today's issues. What I liked most about it is the accessibility of the writing, which is understandable and highly emotive.

Lisa Wolstenholme, Author

Graffiti Lane is an engaging collection of poems that revolve around the concept of being the underdog, bullying and finding ways to bounce back. The poet's angst and fear will help readers perceive the broader effects of discrimination and bullying as they bleed into teenage bullying, corporate bullying and harassment, gender inequality, domestic violence and suicide. The poems are raw, dark and intense, and will take readers to a dimension where they realise that there is always hope.

Mamta Madhavan for Readers' Favorite

Punch and Judy explores the horrors of relationship breakdown in graphic detail, yet, for me, anyway, it was not so much a horror story as one of growth and resilience. Even in her darkest moments, 'Judy' asserts her right to be; she is an everywoman, a heroine who we feel deeply for, willing her on and applauding her efforts to extricate herself from the toxicity in which she finds herself enmired. A rollicking tale in verse, with an economy of words that really pack a punch with every line. Make yourself a big pot of coffee, sit down and enjoy the ride!

Julia Kaylock, Poet

What a ride *Rolling in the Mud* is, from the sly humour of a cheeky widower getting payback to the desperation of bullying and abuse, this collection takes you through the gamut of emotions. I had intended to pace myself and read just a couple of stories at a time and instead found myself reading it all in one day. Thoroughly enjoyed it and well recommended.

Karyl Treble

I am such a huge fan of this authoress! *Retrospection* is full of spunk and grit. I couldn't get enough of it. Loved each one! A must to add to your bookshelf and makes a sensational gift to those who welcome adventure in short bursts of poetry.

Rosa Carrafa Publishing

Punch and Judy is an expressive, hard hitting and intense form of contemporary poetry from Kelly Van Nelson. Although deeply serious in tone, this is a creative and theatrical collection that will draw in both fans of the poetry field and new readers to this emotive form of writing. It is clear Kelly Van Nelson is quite the figurehead in terms of contemporary Australian poetry. Her writing is powerful, moody, targeted and emotive. Every word has been carefully selected and each separate poem thoughtfully produced. In this world of increasing domestic violence, continual images of toxic relationship breakdowns, unacceptable attitudes in relation to sexism and negative behaviours, it is high time a progressive collection such as *Punch and Judy* is released in the public sphere. Keynote literature such as *Punch and Judy* can help lead the way in terms of breaking down barriers and can work to change public perceptions with regards to relationship challenges.

Amanda Barrett, Mrs B's Book Reviews

The
Pinstripe
Prisoner

To Dot

From a northern girl to
a Southern lady, thank
you for your support!
" Make every second count!"
Kelly
xx

Also by Kelly Van Nelson

POETRY

Graffiti Lane
(MMH Press 2019)

Punch and Judy
(MMH Press 2020)

Graffiti Lane Collector's Edition
(MMH Press 2020)

Retrospective
(MMH Press 2021)

Globalisation: The Sphere Keeps Spinning
(Compiled by Kelly Van Nelson and MMH Press 2021)

LITERARY FICTION

Rolling in the Mud
(Ginninderra Press 2020)

Content Warning:

This book contains themes that some readers may find troubling and/or disturbing which include:

Violence

Incarceration

Death (involving firearms)

Self-harm

Suicidal ideation

Miscarriage

Reader discretion is advised.

The
Pinstripe
Prisoner

KELLY VAN NELSON

Lusaris

Typeset in Adobe Garamond Pro 12/17pt by Chelsea Wilcox
Cover Design by Dylan Ingram
Edited by Eleanor Narey

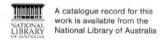

A catalogue record for this
work is available from the
National Library of Australia

National Library of Australia Catalogue-in-Publication data:

The Pinstripe Prisoner/Kelly Van Nelson

ISBN:
978-0-6454564-5-5
(Paperback)

ISBN:
978-0-6454564-6-2
(Ebook)

For Shaun,
who took me to see the sunset at
the Meisho Maru

Meisho Maru

Chapter One

The Ace of Spades is tucked behind a queen and king of the same suit, and I know I'm in with a chance. My eyes blink once, an uncontrollable reflex, but every other muscle remains still. The back of my throat is dry, but I hold back from gulping to avoid my Adam's apple giving the game away. My hand is kept close to my chest. That's pretty much the way I like to live life.

Always one for pulling my weight around the house, I've stocked the *braai* with *rooikrans* wood and we're sitting out back enjoying a lazy afternoon with the fire crackling away. Pa has a *potjie* simmering over glowing coals he's piled to one side. He has a knack of pulling coals from the heart of the flames when they're the perfect temperature for his cast iron pot. Oxtail stew has always been my older brother's favourite. Jaco likes to suck the bones to get every bit of flavour out. He's driven home from Cape Town for the weekend, enjoying time off from medical school.

Every so often Pa lifts off the lid with his tongs and Ma gives the pot a stir with her wooden spoon. It's impossible not to smile at her looking so happy in a brightly coloured floral dress, with the apron I bought her last Mother's Day tied over the top. It says, 'Dad's the boss, unless Ma is home.'

Between the synchronised stirring, my parents sip their wine and take turns at cards; both in their element since Ma loves rummy and Pa loves red wine. A second bottle of Pinotage is opened. Wine doesn't hang around in our house long enough to catch dust.

'Remember the first time you drank this stuff, Simon?' Pa asks me.

'It was a few years ago now.'

'You were underage,' Jaco points out.

'Only just. You were barely old enough yourself.'

I recall Pa pouring me a glass, only half full. I took a swig and spluttered while Jaco slapped me on the back to help clear the pathway for another mouthful. Then I gulped down the rest and tried not to grimace.

'You pair haven't looked back since I introduced you to the finer things in life.' Pa swirls his glass and sniffs it. 'Heavenly.'

He likes to think he's a connoisseur, but he just knows what he likes. Keeping a straight face, I put down triple spades and take the game.

'No way,' Jaco grumbles, as Ma shuffles the deck and deals another round. We trade duplicates and start quickly, since the family are keen to redeem their losses. Occasionally I question Ma's rules of the game, but she doesn't budge an inch.

'In my house, we play rummy my way,' she says.

Her apron did warn us.

I play a joker hand and thrash them again, fist-pumping as I get up from the table. Ma gives me a hug, and Pa applauds.

'That's my boy,' he says, taking a sip of red.

'That's it, Simon,' Jaco declares, 'we're off to Maxwell's and you're buying.'

I clink his glass, delighted to have beaten my older *boeta* at something.

'You boys have already had a wine,' Ma warns. 'Don't be drinking and driving.'

'I've not had much. I'm fine to drive there,' Jaco says, as I clear away the dishes to save Ma a job. 'Pa, will you fetch us later if we leave the car there?'

'As long as it's not too late,' Pa replies.

***

We swagger into Maxwell's, an old warehouse converted to a bar in Struisbaai Industrial Estate, or rather, Jaco swaggers and I stroll. His social skills far outweigh mine.

It's dimly lit inside, but a brunette's face lights up the place when Jaco catches her eye at the bar. She's not a local. Everyone knows everyone around here, but this place attracts tourists too. It's the only joint around with a late-liquor licence.

'See how chicks dig the dishevelled look of a hardworking doctor,' Jaco says, staring at the brunette again as he pays for our drinks.

'Two problems with that statement, boeta. First off, shouldn't you be trimming the hair now you're a city boy? And second, you're off the market, so put the charm back in your wallet.'

My brother shakes his overgrown locks. 'Gotta keep the surfie good looks.'

'I'll beat you riding a barrel wave even with my short back and sides. Remember I'm surfing the uncrowded break every day while your nose is stuck in textbooks.'

I rub my hands over my head as Jaco rises to the banter. 'We might have to test that before I leave tomorrow. I haven't lost my magic.'

'Sunrise it is,' I say, even though Jaco's love of the swells means he glides through a tube better than most in the Overberg region. I relish the fact we spent our whole childhood at the southernmost point of Africa here in Struisbaai, where the Atlantic clashes with the Indian Ocean.

Maxwell's isn't crazy busy, but it's still early. A few couples twirl each other around as they dance in traditional Afrikaans *langarm* style to the latest *sokkie* tune by Juanita du Plessis. We sit on stools around a fat barrel for a while, gulping down beers. Jaco is chasing his with *Springbokkie* shots of crème de menthe layered with Amarula.

'I don't know how you can drink that stuff,' I grimace as he knocks one back.

'So, get us a brandy and Coke,' he says, as the music changes to contemporary beats.

'I need a leak first.' I get up and head to the men's room, but on the way out I accidently clip the cue of a newcomer playing pool with his pals.

'Prick, you messed up my shot.' He squares his shoulders inside his flannel shirt.

'Sorry, buddy.'

'You two think you're everyone's buddies.' He glares towards Jaco, then at the brunette who has taken my seat.

'Don't worry about him. He's spoken for,' I tell him, as Jaco throws me a look that tells me he's enjoying the attention.

'Then he's an even bigger prick. That's my ex,' the pool player slurs.

'Dude, seriously, he's got no interest in her.'

He steps towards me. 'Are you saying she's not good enough?'

I flip over possible responses in my head like it's a game of rummy. If I reiterate Jaco's disinterest, it devalues this guy's ex to a useless duplicate card nobody else can pair with. Answering to the contrary, he encroaches on his hand, confirming Jaco is trying to steal his joker from under his nose. So, I drop my head and attempt to pass, but he lands a coward's punch on the back of my neck that hurts like hell.

Jaco is off his seat, quickly moving into the thick of it, but he's outnumbered: three to one.

Crack.

This idiot has whacked the cue on Jaco's skull, and he falls. The burly figure comes straight at me. I try to back away, not wanting to get dragged into the mess, but a punch hits my cheek.

Adrenaline pumps as my fist swings back towards his bristly jaw and connects.

'My mama tickles me harder.' He clips me under the eye with another hook, then grabs a bottle and smashes it against the table.

'Stop it, you tosser,' the brunette screams at her ex, as he waves the jagged edge of the bottle neck in my direction.

I duck from sheer reflex while another of his chums charges full force. My opponent's head slams into my guts, knocking me, winded, to the ground. My body spasms. Disoriented, I curl into a ball as a pair of workman's boots come towards me. I pull my hands up to protect my head, but mercifully Jaco is on his feet and throws a pool ball to ward him off.

The wooden floor is covered in a layer of dirt, the slats capturing remnants dragged in from the outdoors between the cracks. Some finds its way into my mouth and I try to raise my head to spit, but heaviness overcomes me. The timber floor is comfortable, like sinking into a mattress after a hard day's work. I remain there, vaguely aware my brain is checking out. Just Jinjer is pumping a killer track through the sound system: 'Father & Farther'. I think of Pa and wish we'd stayed home.

'Get the fuck up,' Jaco hollers, so I push my body into a crouch position to take in the scene. My brother is up against it, still swaying as the dickheads swing at him. Manoeuvring myself from all fours feels like an insurmountable task, but I wrench myself from the floor and stagger towards them, managing to throw a wobbly punch. Against the odds, it connects with the dude's teeth and blood drips from his mouth, before two bouncers finally step in to break up the brawl. They stink of smoke. Must've been on a break. One of them pins Jaco's arms behind his back while the other grips me by the shoulders to shove me towards the door.

'Out,' the bouncer orders Jaco.

'Fuck you,' Jaco snarls, looking back at the group who waylaid us. 'What about them?'

'They're next when we're finished with you two.'

'Let's go,' I say to Jaco, staggering into the night.

He looks back again towards the bar. 'Boeta, this is bullshit!'

'Just leave it. Let me phone Pa to pick us up.'

'Leave him out of this. Fucking government should sort out public transport.' He heads towards the car on the far side of the car park. 'I'm fine to drive.'

'You're not. Just wait on Pa.'

Jaco unlocks the car, so I grab the keys from him. 'Give 'em here. I've had less than you.'

Jaco climbs in the passenger seat; I jump in and pull out of the car park turning towards the main road. A vehicle travelling in the opposite direction flickers its headlights at us in warning.

'Shit! The cops must have a roadblock up,' my brother states, as I quickly do a U-turn.

'You okay?' I sneak a glance at Jaco. He has a cut to his forehead and blood is trickling onto his eyebrow.

He ignores me as I double back through a partially built housing estate, dusty from construction. I take the back roads and we make it home in one piece to a house veiled in darkness. Ma and Pa would have retired to a book and bed long ago.

Jaco is still fuming. 'I bet those idiots are still going to sit in Maxwell's for the rest of the night, drinking their beers and trying to rule the place.' He opens the pantry and pulls out a half bottle of olive oil and dumps it on the bench. 'Where's the Klippy?'

'You don't need a brandy.'

'Might need this though.'

He takes out the gun from the top shelf. It's been there as long as I can remember, fully loaded and gleaming from the old man's meticulous maintenance regime. Ma hates the thing. She made him move it there from his bedside cabinet to keep it out of the way. He used to store it next to his reading glasses.

Jaco grabs the weapon and waves around the 9 mm pistol like we're still boys playing with our lightsabers.

'This mean motherfucker can inflict revenge.'

'*Moenie kak praat nie, poephol,*' I reply.

'I'm not talking shit!' he roars.

'You're totally talking shit, and you are being a *poephol.*'

'Who do you think you are, calling me an arsehole?'

I scoff, like he's asked me to sing the New Zealand anthem ahead of watching the Boks dive into a scrum with the All Blacks. It fails to quell his temper.

Chapter Two

The sun is rising over the cluster of whitewashed cottages as I'm hauled from the police vehicle. If I could crawl inside one of them now, to shut out the horror of what happened after Maxwell's a few hours ago, I would. The smell of gutted fish would be an improvement on the acrid stench of dry blood clinging to my nostrils.

Officer Nick Boshoff, who is a good friend of Pa's from church, places a hand on my shoulder and steers me silently towards the *Suid-Afrikaanse Polisiediens*. 'We'll question you when you sober up.'

The last place I want to be is in a corrugated-iron pressure cooker, but I'm manoeuvred into a shack attached to the main police station, where two coloured men sit slumped against the wall, emitting an overwhelming waft of stale body odour.

'Leave those *takkies* on his feet,' Boshoff warns in his thick Afrikaner accent, nodding his mop of red hair at my new Nikes before slamming the door. I panic inside as I suddenly realise they should have been removed and placed in evidence.

The pair get to their feet to face me. One is wiry like me, but the other is built like a rugby prop.

'Dumb fucker. Take them off.' The prop shoves me against his friend who pushes me back, like I'm a ping-pong ball.

I bought designer labels just to dress as well as Jaco, but now I really want them gone. I used to be like the rest of the fifty-nine million South Africans all chasing a new pair of takkies; they'll have to seek their materialistic possessions without me now. I remove them and hand them over.

'Socks too.' He kicks off his tattered flip-flops and pulls on my Nikes, which are enormous on him.

'Nice,' his friend admires.

'*Boer* trash,' the heftier of the two sneers once he's tied his new shoelaces. He straightens up and grabs my cheeks with a sweaty palm. Tattoos cover his hands and arms. His sneering lips almost touch mine as he squeezes until my nose feels at risk of bursting open, spilling blood, like egg yolk dripping down the sides of a breakfast roll. I love eggs, but the thought of one now brings up bile which I quickly swallow.

'Just leave me alone!'

The man laughs.

'We've a hard man here. Maybe some of this will soften you up.' He lets go of my face to cup his own balls.

My blood runs cold. It's violence that put me here in the first place. I think of the tooth I might have knocked out in the brawl. Even if I were to replicate the move on this man, his two front fangs are already gone. 'I don't want any trouble,' I say, terrified.

'Too late.'

'Take him for your *wyfie*,' his friend *cajoles*.

My hooded eyes watch his every move. No goddamned way are

11

they laying a finger on me. It's impossible to comprehend how my life has spiralled so quickly. Deep down, I regret not handling things differently. I deserve to be carted off to Pollsmoor and locked away in maximum security, but although I deserve the degradation of being locked up with the worst of South Africa's criminals, I don't want to spend every waking moment trying to avoid being sodomised.

He comes at me and lands a hook on my eye. 'Take your best shot.'

'Help!' I yell, hoping for someone to come in and put a stop to what's happening rather than being baited into yet another fight.

His hands are on my pants, tugging them down.

'Help!'

He tugs again. I hesitate, petrified, then nut the prop in the face with my head. It catches him unaware, and he reels backwards onto his wafer-thin mattress. His friend swarms in to take his place, chest puffed beneath a stained white vest. My elbow connects with his face, before both reload and come at me. Terror rips through my entire being as my arms are pinned behind my back. I psych myself up for the violation, but the door swings open and my adversaries back off as Officer Boshoff's bulky frame appears in the doorway.

'You've enough problems without this. Out,' Boshoff says, his glare shifting to the brute about to jump me.

'Next time.' He blows me a kiss as he's led away in my takkies, literally walking critical evidence out of there.

There are just two of us now; me, skinny and unassuming, and the wiry sidekick, which evens the odds. I hope my pulling a decent defensive move shocked him as much as it did me. A day ago, I'd have run a mile from violent conflict, but now here I am in this incomprehensible mess, struggling with the penitence of having to defend myself.

'You're a dead man,' he says, running a finger slowly across his neck. 'My friend is 28s.'

I try not to flinch at the mention of the notorious numbers gang, infamous for controlling South African communal cells with extreme violence. They use inmates as sex slaves, brutally exhibiting their manhood as a display of power to ascertain status and to climb the ladder. They rape and recruit to dominate the weak.

I am weak.

The roof of my mouth is coarse and rough. The hangover is kicking in and I need to brush my furry teeth. I want to squeeze out the guilt like toothpaste from a tube, but it's blocked inside, the narrow opening covered by a tiny piece of foil. The pressure is so intense, I could split apart with such toxic intensity; the truth splattering its minty breath on everything around it.

Cause of death: Traumatic aortic rupture.

I regret listening to my brother reeling off all manner of medical conditions when he still lived at home and was studying for his exams to become a doctor. He used to make me test him every day using flashcards. Potential causes of my own death are now much more real than a line in one of his textbooks.

Although we're coming into the summer season, the wind howls outside as loud as I'm howling on the inside. A draught swirls around the cell, caused by the glass from the high slim window being smashed out. Only a metal grid attempts to keep the elements at bay. If I had a rope it would be simple enough to sling a noose through the bars. Checking out this way would be easy, but this animal would probably screw my dead body, so I begin to pace because a moving target is far more difficult to hit.

Shuffling does nothing to distract from the fact I badly need the toilet. Three steps across the room, the silver bowl stares back at me, splattered with radioactive stains that make me wish for incurable constipation. A patch of corrugated iron has been replaced above the toilet, after someone creative must have unscrewed the plumbing fittings to try to escape. There's no longer a way to flush away waste, but I assume someone figures the logistics out later otherwise I'd be wading in sewage, not just living with the human version of it.

Before being banged up, I was the kind of man who would take the newspaper into the bathroom. I'd sit on my throne reading headlines filled with accusations about people in situations just like the one I'm in now. There's no privacy for such luxuries in here, but it could be a whole lot worse. Judging by the pile of filthy green sleeping mats and mottled grey blankets, this hellhole is equipped to contain half-a-dozen prisoners.

Despite the feral conditions, my stomach is cramping so intensely it wins the dilemma of shitting myself versus fighting off a rapist. Mushy Face is dozing, perhaps not so brave now his partner has gone, so I grab one of the blankets to screen myself. The blanket is coarse, the type you find in pet stores. I'd rather be in a dog kennel than in such a vulnerable situation. It prompts me to finish my business as quickly as possible and tug my trousers back up with haste.

'You white boys reek,' my cellmate mumbles, his eyes still closed.

I'm surprised he's able to smell much through a bust nose, but I throw a spare blanket over the pan when I'm done in an enterprising move to contain the offensive odour.

He seems content I've shown him some respect and returns to dozing. I hunch in a corner and fight back the tears, watching my sleeping cellmate for signs of movement until a sudden bang on the door startles me again.

'Breakfast,' Boshoff announces, the door swinging open.

I recognise the lady behind him handing out plastic cups of lukewarm coffee and chunks of bread. She's a stick of a woman with an out-of-proportion backside, which Jaco once told me during one of his many medical overshares, is sometimes an indicator someone has steatopygia, a condition that triggers a high degree of fat to accumulate around the buttocks. She lives in Struisbaai North, the coloured area nearby also known as Molshoop. Mbali is another churchgoer, always volunteering to rustle up an incredible banquet for congregation social events. Pa reads at mass every Sunday and has been spending more and more time there since he lost his job. The church community come from all walks of life and are like extended family. The last thing I feel like doing is eating, but I don't want to offend Mbali and figure it might soak up any remaining alcohol and help clear my head. Before I take the food offered, I wipe my hands down the front of my jeans and give her a nod of thanks. In return, she smiles. As there's no running water to rinse them of germs, the conditions make me think of getting a bout of gastro so intense that there's no comeback from the ravaging dehydration.

Cause of death: Infectious gastroenteritis.

It's the first time I can truly imagine how it must have felt for the South African's subjected to apartheid laws before Mandela was released. For years, basic human rights were stripped away from millions. Freedom was the pot of gold sought at the end of a rainbow for a nation struggling to reinvent its identity. I don't think I can cope without mine.

'Where's the hot breakfast?' Mushy Face mumbles with a mouth already stuffed with bread. He can still shovel in grub even in his wounded condition.

'We're short-staffed, Nolizwe,' Boshoff replies, clearly familiar with the prisoner. 'What happened to your eye?'

'I walked into the fridge door,' Nolizwe answers before I get a chance to respond.

'There's no fridge.'

'You should be a detective,' Nolizwe chuckles, causing his coffee to splash onto the floor. 'Motherfucker! Will you bring me another cup?'

Mbali shakes her head. 'What do you think this is, room service?'

'Yah, why don't you bring us both a beetroot smoothie while you're at it.'

My eyes widen to saucers. Everyone knows the rumour that the former health minister, unofficially dubbed 'Dr Beetroot', was in denial of the AIDS epidemic and rebuffed antiretroviral drugs in favour of natural beetroot remedies. If I'm raped by an HIV positive prisoner, the damage will go way past physical injuries from forced penetration.

'Not a finger on him, you hear me?' Boshoff warns.

'What's wrong with giving the white boy a slow puncture?' Nolizwe sticks his tongue out and flicks it.

'How much longer are you gonna keep me in here?' I beg.

'As long as it takes, I'm afraid, Simon,' Boshoff tells me, clanging the door closed again.

Chapter Three

I 'm relieved it's not too long before Officer Nick Boshoff comes back, but unfortunately, it's to cart Nolizwe away, not me. Once I've the place to myself, I succumb to a screwed-up state of overwhelming guilt.

I've ample time to dwell on my life and lack of achievements; a job repairing PCs since leaving school, still living with my folks. Jaco has always compensated for it with his photographic memory that rocket-launched him straight to the top of medical school. We shared a room for two decades, until he left home, every inch of the bedroom wallpapered with surf posters. Even now, our lives are inextricably entwined. I'm here while he too is confined like an animal, and although I can't speak to him, I'm quite sure he's regretting what he did as much as I regret what I did not.

Tired brain cells fumble to recall happier scenes from our carefree childhood, but my memories are clouded, as compressed as Table Mountain beneath a tablecloth of clouds settling over the summit on a stormy day.

Eventually, Mbali comes back to serve a hot meal; congealed *mieliepap* on a plastic prison tray. It's so bland I lift the blanket off the toilet and add to the rancid contents of the bowl. There is no intentional game going on of denying myself nutrition; a warped stance on some premeditated hunger strike in a petition for tasty prison food. My stomach just repulses the morsels I'm trying to shove in there. Until I can hold down meals, it'll have to make do with devouring my own surplus fats, then the excess, before it moves on to attack the muscle tissue, like a cannibal feasting away at the human body. My feeble existence is part physical, from my metabolism grinding down from lack of sustenance, but for the most part it's mental. Thoughts once filled with all life has to offer have shrunk to the skin and bones of what it does not. Perhaps the silver lining is if I'm in here long enough, unable to keep down a bowl of mieliepap, then I'll eventually chew off my own tongue, leaving me unable to answer any more questions from the cops about what happened after my brother and I were drawn into the Maxwell's brawl.

Cause of death: Starvation.

It has a befitting ring to it.

I try to replace my morbid thoughts with coherent thinking. I've always leaned towards being a rational thinker. Even in my job, I've a tendency to ponder on every move I make while dismantling computer equipment piece by piece, before putting it back together in systematic order.

I should have logically thought through the Maxwell's incident and found a better way to deal with the situation afterwards. Hindsight … it's too late for lessons learned. Retrospection is merely guilt in a jester's costume.

My body convulses, triggering a temporary cessation of breathing, then a brief blackout.

When I come around, I'm confused, unsure of whether I'm dreaming or awake, alive or dead. My brain opens and closes the filing cabinets, throwing memory snippets from the drawers like there's a poltergeist inside my head having a tantrum over blood, guns, police, slow punctures.

The accessibility of so many memories being reinstated at once causes a rush of stress hormones. My heart palpitates. Sharp pains upsurge in my chest and the rhythm of my breathing changes. This could be the moment I cross from this life into the next.

Cause of death: Shock.

That has a befitting ring to it too.

I curl on my side, frail and drooling. I don't know how I'm able to drool when my mouth feels so dry inside. My eyes are dry too, then wet. Wet then dry.

Sleep evades me, even though I always sleep in a ball on my side.

I think of home and my comfortable bed that smells of fabric softener. Ma always uses copious amounts of fabric softener. She's a good mother and I've let her down. Pa too.

I don't know if I let Jaco down or if he failed me. He's only older by a year, but isn't the eldest sibling supposed to lead by example? I've always been more sensible than him and should have known better. We both should have known better. A bongo-drum beat echoes in my head.

We should have known better.

We should have known better.

We should have known better.

I press my hands over my ears, but the beat doesn't stop. Perhaps I'm now criminally insane. With certainty, I know I'm a criminal. The fact I'm lying on the floor in jail reaffirms this.

Am I insane?

If I'm not insane, it won't take long to get there in a place like this.

I reach out my arm and grasp one of the pet blankets, pulling it over my body so it cocoons me, prickly and harsh on my skin. When I resurface, I hope I'll have sprouted wings to fly out of here.

***

The young black officer who was with Boshoff when I was arrested eventually swings open the door to dump a bucket of watered-down bleach, a scrubbing brush and a toilet plunger next to me.

'Shut the hell up,' he says, even though I haven't said a word.

I poke my head out from underneath the pet blanket.

The officer smooths his moustache. A clump of bumfluff is forming on his chin. 'You need to clean this place before we let you out. Kill the lice, you know.'

It isn't worth arguing over sprucing up a few square metres, so I get to work and Bumfluff leaves me to it.

When I'm done cleaning the floor, I pour the filthy water down the toilet pan. It fills it to the brim and I plunge until it gurgles and the waste gradually trickles away.

Bumfluff comes back to escort me to a section of the station with 'Detective Branch' chalked on the wall. It looks amateurish, no better than the scrawls of a kindergarten kid, but my hands shake all the same, so I shove them deep in my jeans pockets.

The interview room I'm ushered into is sparse; a window behind iron burglar bars, a table and two chairs on opposite sides. The sound of chirping birds in the distance cuts through the silence. It's still light outside. I've been incarcerated for less than twenty-four hours, but it feels like a lifetime.

Bumfluff formally introduces himself as Officer Peterson, then sits down opposite me and reads me my rights. Peterson and Boshoff both missed this step until now.

'Where's Boshoff?' I ask, wishing the Afrikaner were taking things from here. This cop has stony eyes that don't seem to move from me, not even for a second.

He ignores my question. 'Name?' he fires.

'Simon Coetzee.'

'Middle name?'

'Ronald, after my Pa.'

He scribbles down my answer with a chewed-up pen. 'Address?'

I've no problem answering another undemanding question.

'Now tell me what happened from start to finish.'

'Like I've already said, Jaco and I were dragged into a fight with a bunch of imbeciles in Maxwell's.'

He makes me recount the whole night. I give him a blend of the truth about the bar brawl and fiction concocted to avoid the ramifications.

'Tell me about your cuts and bruises.'

'They're from the fight.'

He thumps the desk. 'Last chance. Do you want to tell me what really occurred?'

This interview is going down the old-fashioned way, with a hint of brutality. Despite the shortcomings of Peterson and Boshoff, I'm royally fucked. Anything I confide in this interrogation brings risk of contradicting what I originally told the pair of them. Pa told me not to utter another word if I wanted to have the best chance of avoiding being charged, and if I change my original statement and tell the truth now, I'm still a liar. Can I ask the audience? Improve my odds to a fifty-fifty chance of staying out of jail? Maybe I can phone a friend before I'm sent off to endure forced anal sex.

Who wants a bowl of mieliepap?

Who needs more takkies?

Who wants to be a millionaire?

I take Pa's advice and assert myself; pumping air back into my tyres instead of risking an answer that might lead to a slow puncture.

'I've told you what happened.'

'For your parents' sake as well as yours, I hope it's the truth.'

Peterson sucks on his pen and then pushes it across the table with a piece of paper.

'Sign it,' he demands, leaning so far forward I can smell his breath.

I turn the paper the right way up. 'Can I read it again first?'

'Sign it,' he roars, this time whacking the desk with his fist so near to my fingers I draw both hands back into my lap. 'I don't have time for this.'

There's no good cop, bad cop. Boshoff is now off-duty, so I take the gnawed pen. It's damp with his saliva.

Cause of death: Infectious disease.

I scribble my signature.

He takes the statement from me as my mind races. I look around to check for a tape recorder or camera capturing the inter-action, but there's nothing. All there is bearing witness to my story is a one-page statement signed under duress.

My heartbeat suddenly malfunctions. With its pumping action severely disrupted, chaotic flutters mount inside my chambers, like a monarch butterfly is trapped inside, its freedom confiscated. Its wings flap with increased velocity, panicking, unable to catch enough wind to escape the tiny enclosure where it's detained. I know from Jaco and his textbooks, this rhythmic disturbance may be a sign of an undetected heart condition rather than something necessarily brought on by shock.

Cause of death: Cardiac arrest.

But my heart regulates, the fluttering subsides, and I live.

'So that's it then?' Peterson asks.

'That's it.'

He leans over the desk to scribble something in his interview notes, then peers at me, frowning as he notices I still have his pen. Rather than ask for it back, he feels about his person and eventually reaches into his shirt pocket to pull out another. He tries to write something down, but the ballpoint pen fails to leave a mark.

'It's new,' he informs me as he licks the ink-end to soften it up.

When he's finished writing notes to himself, he gives the pen a click and the nib disappears, then he places it back in his pocket and folds his arms.

'You're free to go.'

My jaw drops: relief mixed with a twinge of angst at the injustice of being let out so easily.

Maybe the post-apartheid government and police force want to be seen to be cleaning up the streets when all they're doing is shovelling shit under the carpet, but it's not the moment to be cynical about the integrity of the establishment. Placing both hands on the desk, I lever myself on to unsteady feet before turning towards the exit.

'Not so fast, boy.'

Peterson points at my chair and I sit again.

'Something isn't right.'

'Am I free to go, or not?' I ask, realising he's not as incompetent as he led me to believe.

His stare doesn't waver from mine. 'Just don't stray too far, in case we need to bring you in again.'

I trade his pen for the clear bag he offers me containing my watch and cell phone, then bolt outside where I immediately call Pa.

On paper, I might be a free man, but there's always a price to pay.

Chapter Four

P a looks older than his sixty years and his skin has a dull grey pallor to it. It makes me feel beyond my twenty-six years too. I aged us both.

Cause and effect.

He picks me up from outside the station in the *bakkie*; a twin-cab HiLux relic, pale blue, spotless inside, rusting on the outer shell from the sea air. He's had it since my primary school years, washes and polishes it every week while Ma makes the Sunday roast. I climb inside, and when he starts up the engine it gives a shudder. I give one too.

Neither of us speak as he shifts into first gear. I grasp the handle and wind the window down to hear the waves pounding on the shores close by. It's always been a soothing sound that usually cheers me no matter what the mood. Today, it fails to ease the tension.

The weather has turned again and it's hot and storm free. The cusp of summer is usually my favourite time of year: a time for swimming, snorkelling and fishing for snoek. To have one incredible ocean on the doorstep is amazing enough, but I'm lucky, I've lived my whole life enjoying the spot where the two oceans meet. One is warm and calm, the other cold and wild, but they fuse together seamlessly into something inseparable, like me and my brother.

Pa pulls down the sun visor and lowers his speed, even though he could ride blindfolded and only hit air. Struisbaai is a tiny fishing village on the road to nowhere. Rush hour is when the boats come into the harbour filled with the day's catch and the odd soul pulls up to get fresh seafood straight from the source.

He continues along the coast road as dusk creeps in, past the campsite where holiday-makers from Cape Town and Johannesburg make merry during school holidays. Desolate just now, but it packs out in peak season since it's the only one in the municipality. We ordinarily veer inland, winding uphill towards our home which enjoys foreshore views.

'Where are you going, Pa?' I ask, as he misses the junction.

He ignores me, either because he can't speak, or perhaps he simply has nothing to say. My own larynx tightens. The silence is worse than the explosion ringing in my ears from the last time I saw him.

Staring out the window, I attempt to relax my limbs, stiff from jail time. People say there's nothing around here but the lighthouse and a seagull, but they're not looking closely. A bok stands rigid for a moment before darting into the fynbos. It's fast but my eyes are accustomed to spotting nature. Sometimes puff adders slither in the dust and rare black oystercatchers soar above the ostriches. Despite South Africa's problems, I've always felt blessed to live here.

We go south-west, beyond the old lighthouse onto the dirt road cutting through L'Agulhas National Park into Suiderstrand. I know where he's going now.

Despite bumping over uneven terrain, I don't bother fiddling with the seatbelt hanging limply at my side. It's been broken for years. Now and then the traffic cops collect dividends for not being buckled in, but local law enforcement won't be around today. They're still relishing in the excitement of my case, shuffling paperwork as they contemplate whether or not they need to talk to me again.

Pa nudges the HiLux into four-wheel drive and we trundle towards the Meisho Maru shipwreck. The metal structure that ran aground in the eighties looks ethereal in the evening light. The silhouette is upright but tilted on one side; a drunken sailor trying to maintain some dignity.

The sun disappears, leaving an orange blaze above the swell. I've taken in this view in all kinds of weather, and it's always made me feel grateful to be alive. Gale-force winds and unruly currents have wiped out numerous vessels along this stretch of coastline, like the Zoetendal, Arniston and the Birkenhead. The elements ruthlessly scattered their cargo and left many condemned to a lifetime without closure after having their loved ones lost at sea. Although this is a maritime graveyard, no other shipwreck has left such beauty still visible above the surface as the Meisho Maru. I love the place. It's the first spot Jaco and I went to for a picnic on our own as kids, and I remember the day clearly.

Pa drops us off in the bakkie. 'Be careful, boys. I'll be back in an hour.'

Jaco has been bossy lately, probably because he's just turned double digits. 'Come and paddle in the rock pool,' he orders.

I wade in, not because I want to let him be in charge, but because I want to soak in the warm rock pools too.

'Arrrgggghh,' I scream, as my eyes well up. Lifting my leg, I clutch my foot with both hands and crane my neck to see what's causing such throbbing agony.

27

'It's a stinger. It's left red streaks. I'll pee on it if you like,' Jaco offers.
'Gross.'
'It's the best thing for it.'
'I don't care. I'd rather live with the sting.'
'Suit yourself,' Jaco kicks sand over the bluebottle.
'Do you think it'll help?' I hop on my good foot as the sting's intensity increases.
'Everybody knows pee helps jellyfish stings.'
'What if someone sees?'
'Like who?'
I look around, but rocks obscure everything but the shipwreck. 'Okay, but make it quick.'
I lower my foot while Jaco unzips his denim shorts.
'I can't believe I'm letting you do this,' I tell him, as the tepid liquid hits my skin.
'Does it feel better?'
'Yah.'
'You see. Aren't I the best boeta ever?'
I nod my agreement and we both laugh.

We never told anyone about the stinger. Between us, we thought we could handle anything.

I know better now.

Pa turns the engine off and grabs a screwdriver from under his seat. He prises the centre console until the whole plastic lifts out, then reaches inside the cavity and takes out my blood-splattered clothes, tightly wrapped in Ma's sunflower tablecloth.

I'm surprised at both the size of the gap beneath the console and Pa's ingenuity.

He grabs a box of firelighters from the back seat before we get out of the bakkie, then we clamber over the jagged rocks. I pause to gather several smaller rocks in my arms and then we stop before it starts to get too slippery. I construct the stones into a makeshift firepit and then Pa piles on the firelighters and clothes and sets them ablaze.

We sit side by side, silent as the flames toast our skin, watching the waves rise and fall up the sides of the wreck. Bit by bit they're eroding layers of history. I want to wade in and have the saltwater wash away the last few days of my own past.

The thought of drowning myself makes me want to cry, but I can't. Not while Pa is weeping.

He does it quietly, wiping away the tears with the sleeve of his woollen jumper, but I catch it from the corner of my eye. It slams home the fact I've crushed every hope he ever had as a father. I run my shaking hands through my hair in angst, then tell him everything.

The details make him flinch. When I'm done the silent tears have been replaced by great wracking sobs.

They belong to me.

'*Maak elke sekonde tel,*' Pa says without looking at me.

Make every second count.

As he reaches into his pocket, I don't ask him what I should do next.

It's obvious when he pulls out two flight tickets.

Chapter Five

T he fitted sheet is soaked, one corner completely off the mattress from tossing and turning. A combination of regret and fear has taken my sleep hostage, no negotiation or ransom demands, just sheer conviction. Over and over again, I constantly question the decisions I've made and the ones I'm having made for me. I want to decline the ticket because I don't want to leave, but after what I've done, there's no way on earth I can disagree with Pa's desire to have me gone.

As the sun sifts through the gaps in my blinds, I get out of bed and traipse downstairs.

Ma is scrubbing the kitchen floor; hair straying from her usual neat bun, hands red raw. I bend to help her.

'Leave it!' she snaps.

I hesitate, wanting to push the matter and stay, but her lip quivers and she gives a small shake of the head. I retreat and go to find Pa, who is on the phone in the front room. He's sitting in his favourite chair made of olive-green velour; soft and comfy, contoured where his body has sunk into it over the years. I listen at the doorway at him arranging for us to visit the local *shebeen* and it's certainly not to check if they are open for us to pop by for a casual pint.

'Thanks, Pa,' I rasp when he hangs up, despite my uncertainty about the arrangements he's just made.

He pinches the bridge of his nose.

'You okay?'

'Just be ready in an hour.'

I head back upstairs to take a shower and let the hot water run over my body for what seems an age. After a while, I turn up the temperature until my skin is unable to bear it, then adjust it to icy needles. The faucet is dispensing with full, uninterrupted pressure and I turn my face into the powerful jet. It's hard to cry when you're drowning.

Cause of death: Waterboarding.

I lather my hair with shampoo, once, twice, a third time, rinsing until it squeaks, but it still feels dirty.

When I'm done, I pull on a tracksuit and lie back on my bed, staring at the ceiling until Pa comes to get me.

He gives me an envelope. 'This is for you.'

Inside is a wad of crisp British pounds.

The ability to form a cohesive sentence fails me and all I manage to mutter is, 'Thanks.'

***

Pa and I travel past holiday homes with multimillion-dollar views of the longest coastal stretch in the Southern Hemisphere. I avert my eyes as we pass the Suid-Afrikaanse Polisiediens and quaint Hotagterkilp fisherman's cottages, then just before the town entrance, Pa turns into the grid system of Molshoop.

The houses here don't have floor-to-ceiling windows facing the waves. Molshoop is an old apartheid dormitory suburb with cost-effective, low-rise properties. For many years, the wire-enclosed blocks have been populated by local fishermen and their families, and although out-of-town settlers have also made their homes here too, there's still a sense of space in an area crammed with character. We pull up at a pink painted shebeen, the low-key African version of an American speakeasy. It's lopsided, as if the builder ran out of bricks part way through construction and shoved the roof on the tipsy structure anyway. Sheets of corrugated iron make up the roof, and the door looks like it's been pilfered from a decaying stable. Many shebeens are now legal in South Africa, but this one, well-known by everyone in the area, is illicit and isn't somewhere I'd frequent after dark. A male *tik* dealer manages it rather than friendly Shebeen Queens – who brew and distil their own alcohol and provide safe havens for free conversation – so when we enter, I'm not surprised to see three men puffing from light bulbs that have been hollowed out and taped up with an inserted straw to inhale the drug through. Two of the men are coloured and one is white, although his face is covered with scabbed-over red spots. Drug addiction has no race.

One of the coloured men stands on shaky feet and offers me the light bulb. 'Hit?'

I consider how much tik it will take for me to become as gaunt as this man; how many rocks I'll have to melt and inhale through a straw in a light bulb to no longer care about what I've done. I'll be energised enough to keep on living for a short while on a blissful high, building up tolerance until the drug kills me at its leisure. Unless, of course, I skip the light bulb and slam a double-dose syringe straight in the vein. It's tempting.

Cause of death: Overdose.

'Simon!' Pa glares at me.

'You always listen to the old man?' the pusher asks.

'Pretty much,' I answer, unable to recall a time when I defied a man who has all my respect. Perhaps this is the moment to break one habit to gain a new one.

'They're not here for drugs,' the shebeen owner says to the men from behind the bar before turning to Pa. 'You back for your papers?'

'You've been here before?' I ask Pa as he walks to the bar and exchanges money for a British passport.

He nods. 'The minute you went to jail.'

This shocks me more than watching the trio of addicts slowly kill themselves in a prohibited shebeen. In South Africa, making underworld contacts is easy, but I never expected my father to be so resourceful in such a short period. He's planned my exit and bought me a new identity for the same price as a day pass to Ratanga Junction Theme Park, to ride the death-defying Cobra roller-coaster. I suffer from motion sickness and am not looking forward to the ride.

Chapter Six

Ma has made yellow rice and bobotie with almonds and raisins added to curried mince. I reach out to lift the dish from the counter and one of her hands covers mine. It's ice cold and trembling. Even though it's what Pa wants, I'm ashamed to be running from South Africa when she's in so much anguish. She touches my chin gently with her other hand and lifts my head. My heart breaks at the streaks of mascara under bloodshot eyes.

She looks like she's about to say something but then her eyes fill with fresh tears.

I want to apologise but words cannot undo her anguish, and in any case, the lump in my throat renders me speechless. Instead, I place my hand over the one she has placed on my face and give it a gentle squeeze. I carry the dish to the table once decorated with a sunflower tablecloth but now bare.

In a ploy to try to keep some level of normality in our home, Ma tells me about an incredible book she's reading, *Fingersmith,* by Sarah Waters, which is about a deceitful plot of interwoven lives and jumbled identities. Sometimes fact is far more unimaginable than fiction. I'm ashamed I've forced my own father to tell lies to get me out of a hole. He's always been a man of honour.

Sunday mass' late morning session is packed to the rafters, mainly with residents from the surrounding area. Several familiar faces say hello as we all shuffle in and take a seat. Ma rolls her eyes when Pa causes a traffic jam from chatting too long. Jaco and I are still small enough to go right up to the front to shake Father's hand after he says, 'Let us offer each other the sign of peace.' I feel important, spreading peace. The Rite of Communion forces us to interact with others, so nobody ever feels alone, and as I walk back to my place, families are still hugging and kissing, which makes me happy.

It's like a game of 'Simon says' as we all listen for instructions to kneel, sit and stand, but I copy Jaco's moves to do the right thing at the right time until it's time for communion to be ministered. When I get close to the altar, I cross my arms and Father blesses me on the forehead. I'm too young to take the thin round unleavened wafer to eat, and the sip of wine is off limits, but I still feel special in those few moments.

I rush back up the aisle and am about to squeeze into the pew when Pa steps in front of me, trying to grab the tithing collection off a man with wild eyes the size of saucers. They grip a handle each and play tug of war for a split second, then Pa lets go of the velvet offering bag.

'Stop him,' someone shouts across the church.

Pa doesn't move. 'He needs it more than we do,' he says, as the thief climbs onto the pew and jumps over several rows to run from the back of the church.

'You did the right thing, Ronald. You could have been hurt,' Ma says, clutching her chest.

'Pa was stupid to let him go,' Jaco whispers to me as we sit back in our seats.

'He's not. I think he's a hero for letting the man go if he needed money that bad,' I whisper back.

'Then you're also stupid,' Jaco whispers.

As Father continues addressing the congregation, I silently thank the Lord for blessing me with sensible parents and for keeping Pa safe.

I've never thought Pa stupid; he's always been my unsung hero. Still is.

He's applied for a job on my behalf. It's working for a Scottish friend of his, Donald, who Pa met a few years back when he took Ma on a Mediterranean cruise for their silver wedding anniversary. I've a telephone interview with Donald for the position in Edinburgh already scheduled, so I leave Ma alone at the table. Pa's fast thinking pushed me into a quandary somewhere between gratitude for him going to such great lengths to keep me out of jail, and anger he's so adamant on getting rid of me so quickly. There's no scale capable of measuring how much he must hate me, so I can only judge it by how much I hate myself. My chest tightens just thinking about all the hurt I've caused as I remind myself over and over again how much of a trooper he's been since our lives imploded and he made plans not just for me, but Jaco too. Plans for me to go to one place, my boeta to another. It's beyond comprehension we will be separated like this, but no matter how much I scrape around the bottom of the barrel, I'm out of choices.

I dial in for my interview with Donald McMahon. He tells me all about the opening with the recruitment firm in Scotland in the IT industry, and then gets me to tell him all about my customer experience. With an injection of surface-level enthusiasm, I play up my technological experience from fixing PCs.

'We've got one position available at the moment and it's been difficult to recruit in the UK. Everyone with experience seems to prefer larger competitors. We're independently owned.'

'I'm your man,' I say with enthusiasm, not wanting to let Pa down.

'Give me a call as soon as you land, and we can have a chat about the salary and go through the role expectations in more detail.'

'Will do,' I say, winding up the call.

When I'm done, Ma is nowhere to be seen.

'Getting ready for church,' Pa replies when I ask where she's gone.

It's my cue to go sort my own unkempt self out, but as I stand ironing, the absurdity of caring about pressing seams down the front of my trousers is not lost on me. The steam rises and my face is damp when I'm finished.

It is to be a day of goodbyes. Jaco and I have spent our whole lives in this town, growing up hanging out behind the post office run by an old teacher of mine and praying with a priest we consider a family friend. There are so many people being left behind, the thought of not being able to readily see those closest to me is unbearable. I sink into a heap beside the ironing board and wipe away a tear. I contemplate yanking out the iron and sticking my damp finger in the socket.

Cause of death: Electrocution.

After a while, Pa fishes me from the laundry room, much like he hauls snoek from the ocean. He baits me first, telling me how much he and Ma need me to hold it together for the rest of the day so we may say our goodbyes as a family.

When that doesn't get a nibble, he hooks me under my arms. I don't wriggle. I've always been a good kid, the compliant type. Jaco is the bad boy everybody loves.

Saying goodbye to him will be the hardest.

Chapter Seven

At the end of the day, Pa and I head for Cape Town, taking the route through Bredasdorp we've travelled a thousand times. I've a fondness for the historical buildings in the *dorp*. Most of them service the agricultural industry around here. As a kid, I loved when Pa took me and Jaco to the Shipwreck Museum, to see the exhibit of artefacts from the one hundred and fifty sunk ships peppering the Agulhas reef, including the Meisho Maru. However, we drive straight past it this time, slicing through town towards Caledon.

Some of my best holidays have been at the Caledon Spa and Hotel, a gem of a resort with mineral-rich hot springs. The water of the Victorian bathhouse has a brown tinge due to high iron content. On leisurely breaks, Ma immerses herself in the therapeutic waters until she flushes redder than her hands turned while scrubbing the kitchen floor. Our family has swum in every spot around the resort. The lazy river pool was always Jaco's favourite as a kid. We would drift for hours at the current's disposal, bums lodged inside a rubber tube. Caledon Spa is also where Pa taught me and Jaco casino rules when we were old enough. Pa likes to play two chips per spin, one placed across several numbers to give him a higher chance of success, the other on a single.

The bakkie is crammed with luggage under the canopy and the old lady groans as Pa pushes past Caledon. A vehicle of her age would not still be roadworthy if it weren't for Pa treating her with the same tender loving care he's always shown his guns. He slows down and drops gears when he gets to Sir Lowry's Mountain Pass, cutting through the steep Hottentots Holland Mountain Range. It's a hairy drive. If I were at the wheel, I'd push the gas to the floor and take the corners with such abandon my misjudgement would cause the old lady to topple over the edge.

Cause of death: Car crash.

'I remember when the government evicted the coloureds from District Six and relocated them here,' says Pa as we exit the winding pass and merge onto the N2. Khayelitsha township spawns the Cape Flats either side of the highway.

'I'd hate to live in the middle of all that conflict.'

'No different from the conflict in our neck of the woods,' Pa replies as I feel the weight of his words. 'Most people want a peaceful life. It's not their fault they have to live like that. There are so many refugees pouring in.'

I let Pa ramble. Most people see the Cape Flats as a racial dumping ground with a radically expanding gang culture; a legacy left over from South Africa's turbulent past, but he sees the good in everything. 'The residents are getting more creative and resourceful. They don't waste a thing,' he says as we pass the shacks. 'It's a shame it's getting too dark to properly see their unique incorporation of materials in all the different colours, textures and shapes.'

He accelerates past the township towards the international

airport, right on schedule for my late-night departure. Then we hit a bump and Pa slows to a crawl. Even though it's too dark to see in the wing mirror if we're trailing shreds of tire, my instincts flare up. Criminals frequently place obstructions on the road to force vehicles to halt so they can be hijacked.

'I have to pull over,' Pa says after covering a short distance at snail's pace. He glances in his review mirror. 'Keep your wits about you. Someone's approaching.'

The car grinds to a halt just before the exit ramp and Pa flicks on his hazards. Outside, a mist swirls around our stationary vehicle. In the hazy conditions we're a soft target.

My heart races. 'I don't like this, Pa.'

'Just stay calm and give him whatever he wants, Simon,' Pa instructs.

'Why don't you keep a gun in the glove compartment like everyone else?'

'Never needed to, and now it's in police evidence, isn't it?'

There's no time to reply as a black guy in a baseball cap shatters Pa's window with a brick and leans in to wave a knife in Pa's face.

I wind down my window. 'Here! My wallet is here.' I toss my wallet onto the road to get this man away from Pa. He takes a step back, but then hears the sound of sirens slice through the air and bolts towards the township.

An unmarked car, with only a blue LED glow indicating they're the law, screeches to a halt. A pair of plain-clothes officers jump out.

Although I should feel a sense of euphoria at their presence, there is a good chance I'm now in even deeper shit.

'Are you okay?' the driver asks, arriving at my side of the bakkie.

'Been better,' I reply, stepping on fragments of glass as I get out and go around the vehicle to help Pa out.

'And you, sir?' He peers at my father.

'You arrived just in time,' Pa replies. 'How come you got here so fast?'

'Ghost squad. We patrol these roads most nights. Another motorist called it in, and we were already on this stretch.'

The second officer comes to Pa's side and shows us a makeshift device made from a plank of wood infused with nails he's lifted from the hard shoulder. 'You're lucky this wasn't a concrete block. They're using all kinds of foreign objects now to puncture wheels. Have you got a spare tyre?'

'There's one in the boot.'

'We'll help you change it, then I need a statement from you.'

'My son will miss his flight,' Pa replies.

'Where are you going?' the driver asks.

'Europe,' I say, purposefully vague.

'If your father covers the statement with my colleague, I'll run you to the airport?' he offers. 'It's only a few minutes away. We need to sight your ID though.'

'I'll grab it from my bag in a second. I just want to get my wallet off the road.'

I climb out of the car and retrieve my wallet, then get my backpack from the bakkie and place it on the bonnet. I carefully manoeuvre it so the zipper faces away from the officer. My own South African passport and green identity book are inside by the name of Simon Ronald Coetzee, along with my new fake British passport under the name of Graham Coetzee. Although I'm a suspect in a crime, there's no warrant yet for my arrest. My plan is to travel to Amsterdam on my own passport, then abandon my old self as I continue on to the UK using the fake identity procured in the shebeen. Pa changed only my first name. He had his reasons.

41

Given the time small window of time, he figured it was easier all round and would still be enough to get me off the grid. He even split my flight into two separate tickets for each leg of the journey so the first names match up with my two passports.

I hand over my identity documents which he scans. 'How long are you going to Europe for, Simon?'

I wipe a bead of sweat from my forehead. 'I'll be backpacking for a few months.'

He hands my documents back. 'Bet you'll be pleased to leave all this behind.'

'Absolutely, except for the family.'

'That's the tough bit. Let's go then,' the ghost squad officer says.

Pa looks white as he helps me haul my larger bag into the boot of the unmarked car.

My voice cracks as we hug. 'I'm sorry.'

'Maak elke sekonde tel,' he replies.

'I'll try.'

I climb in the car next to the officer. The close proximity of the law is an invisible pillow over my face, restricting ventilation. My windpipe feels blocked and my lungs crushed.

Cause of death: Asphyxiation.

As he pulls away, Pa gives a farewell wave. I return the gesture, but it's lacklustre and filled with immense sadness as dark as the night sky.

The officer weaves through the traffic. 'In future, try to drive in the right lane. They always target the left, close to the hard shoulder.'

'I'll remember that next time.'

'I'm not sure if you were brave or stupid to distract him with throwing the wallet. Last week a lady was hit in broad daylight. She didn't survive what they did to her.'

'Lucky you were close by.'

'These cars are modified to quickly respond to hijackings.'

'Good to know our taxes are being well spent.'

We fall into silence, my mind drifting back to the identity documents in my backpack. They're burning a hole in my conscience, making it difficult to maintain concentration on what's being said.

'Europe?' he prompts.

'Sorry?'

'What's taking you to Europe?'

'British heritage on my mother's side, mixed with a bit of Dutch,' I reply as the airport lights appear ahead. 'Have you any other road safety recommendations?'

'After hitting an obstruction, drive on as far as possible and contact the Western Cape traffic office as soon as you can.'

'Not the most foolproof plan, is it?'

'It comes down to how you react in the moment.' He pulls into the drop-off zone in front of the departures terminal. 'Your father might have been dead if it weren't for you.'

The irony of the compliment is not lost on me.

Chapter Eight

S chiphol Airport in Amsterdam is packed, so it takes a while for my bag to trundle around on the carousel. I don't mind. Plenty of time to collect my luggage and check in for the flight to Edinburgh.

New airport. New name on arrival. Same incompetent idiot.

It's an odd feeling, transiting through an airport carrying identity documents in a name that's not my own. Passing through immigration sends me spiralling back to those bleak hours spent in a cell. Trying to combat a gnawing fear of being pounced upon at any time by staff wanting to search my bags. The official with the sniffer dog comes so close my limbs start to freeze up, but then they walk on. Unseen eyes burn into me from behind a two-way mirror. Sweat pools under my pits. Paranoia mounts until even the air hostesses appear to pose a threat. I leave Amsterdam feeling as guilty as a radicalist with a bomb hidden in my shoe.

But I land in Edinburgh a new man.

***

My taxi pulls up at Gilmore Terrace, an inconspicuous street a few kilometres out of town. Both sides of the narrow street are packed with bed and breakfasts with enormous bay windows and tiny front gardens. I spot the pre-selected two-star option I went for which was advertised in a backpacker's magazine I grabbed in the airport. The garden is overgrowing with weeds and the bell doesn't work so I rap on the door with my bare knuckles. The landlady greets me in beaded slippers. She's an elderly Indian, with dark hair thinning on the top and a lopsided face, indicating a stroke. One eye is sealed shut, but she stares at me hard with her good eye. In return, I offer a smile, hard cash and a glimpse of my fake passport, all three of which she accepts graciously.

'Thanks, Graham,' she says.

My brain turns over the weird sound of my new name being spoken out loud. Any cop worth their salt could connect the dots and track me down, but that takes time, money, resources, and Pa is counting on the local station in Struisbaai lacking in all three.

'Your room is at the top of the stairs on the third floor. There's no lift, but you look fit enough.' She gives a crooked smile. 'I should charge a premium for the penthouse.'

'Only the best. Do you by any chance have a phone I can use to make a call?' I ask. 'I haven't had a chance to pick up a new SIM card.'

She wiggles her head and hands me her cell phone from her pocket. Her hand lingers as she places it in my palm and I place my other hand on top of hers. It's warm and wrinkled, filled with kind generosity that I never want to let go of.

'You're booked in for three nights. What are your plans after that?' she asks.

'I'm hoping to find something more permanent close to the city. I start a new job on Monday.'

'My nephew, Luckraj Rampal, has a place not far from here that was just vacated. He likes to be called Lucky. If you like, I'll call him and arrange for you to view it?'

She launches into a property inventory, giving an animated description of everything from the floor space to the brand-new toilet brush.

'I'll take it,' I say, knowing I'd rather snap up the offer of a private landlord than go through a real estate broker who'll want to know everything right down to my inside leg measurements.

'You don't want to see it?'

'I'm happy taking your recommendation.'

I place a call to Donald, and we go through another lengthy chat about the job vacancy. I do my best to convince him to take me. 'I'm a fast learner. I won't let you down.'

'I'll remind you of that one day,' Donald says in his Scottish drawl, before formally offering me a position.

I hand the phone back and head to my accommodation on the top floor, happy that I've managed to sort out at least one of my problems.

My room is antiquated, with a single bed, freestanding rickety wardrobe and a tasselled lamp resembling an accessory in a seance. The lamp gives me the creeps. Makes me think the dead are trying to connect with me. I imagine a voice saying it will always watch over me as I tuck into a bowl of cornflakes and drink concentrated orange juice included in the continental breakfast package.

I wash my face in the small basin in the corner of my room and give my cheeks a slap. Once freshened up, I go for a walk to sink myself into the guts of the place.

***

My legs take the compact city in their stride. The castle is incredible. It provides a focal point for the city, towering over me, casting its enormous shadow over me as I walk from west to east, cutting through the shops to locate my new place of work. The handsome building is a triple-storey grey mid-terrace townhouse that wouldn't look out of place on Downing Street. Black double doors are adorned with a brass doorknocker, shiny enough to see my own reflection staring back. I look away, not wanting to be reminded of the fact I now have two identities.

Simon can be as fucked up as he likes, but Graham needs to pull his shit together real quick if he's to fit into the elite end of the professional recruitment market.

Chapter Nine

T he British seasons are the polar opposite to South Africa's, and even though I've been here a few days now, the deep chill of winter still shocks the hell out of me. I suck in oxygen, then expel carbon dioxide into the air. Every breath is visible, announcing that I'm alive.

Ahead, a woman is battling the winter elements. She's holding a soft brown leather briefcase in one hand and is grappling with a golf-sized umbrella in the other. Her auburn curls are billowing like a fiery halo. A huge gust suddenly turns the brolly inside out, bending it out of shape. She halts next to a bin to try to shove in the disfigured umbrella, but the metal spikes stubbornly stick out at contortionist angles. It reminds me of the Meisho Maru jutting from the ocean in Suiderstrand.

Maak elke sekonde tel.

It was the last sentence Pa said when we were sitting in front of the shipwreck and again when I left him stranded on the hard shoulder of the N2.

'You need a hand?' I say, hurrying to her side.

She jumps. 'I didn't see you there.'

Catching her unawares is to be expected. I'm camouflaged with the other suits, all beautifully synchronised in our quest to be at our desks well ahead of the morning bell. I should be thrilled to be in Edinburgh amongst them, shuffling in our black-and-white garments like giant barcodes along the conveyer belt of Scotland's capital.

But I'm not thrilled.

Although I've replaced being locked behind steel bars to hide behind the stripes of my suit, I don't feel free.

I'm the Pinstripe Prisoner.

'Let me have a go,' I offer.

She moves aside while I use brute force to bend the rest of the umbrella inside the bin.

'Done.'

Her hair is covering much of her face. A strand sticks to her lip gloss which she hooks away with her little finger. 'Thanks.'

'You're welcome.'

'Argggh,' she exclaims, hands flying to her head. She rubs her fingertips together, reminding me of Ma making rhubarb crumble topping. I love Ma's fruit crumble.

'Argggh!' the woman yelps again, prompting several other passers-by to give her a wide berth as if she has an invisible force field deflecting them.

'It's not rain, it's pigeon poo.'

Flicking her wrist, she tries to dislodge the white gunk that's transferred to her hand.

'Do you have any tissues?'

'No, sorry.'

'I need grass or something.'

There's an expanse of lawn enclosed by wrought-iron fencing opposite, in the centre of St Andrew Square, but it's off limits. A pair of topiary trees in terracotta clay pots catch my eye, symmetrically placed to frame the entrance to the building nearest to us.

'Wipe it on one of those trees.'

She moves to the greenery and wipes her hand down the miniature leaves covered in dew.

'They're plastic,' she yells as the rain pelts us.

'May I help you, young lady?' an elderly man asks as he exits the building and springs open an enormous golf umbrella. He has a Jagger pout, and a tartan scarf wrapped around his neck.

'I'm good thanks, just a little poo on me.' The man steps back in alarm as she raises her hand to give a full-frontal of her palm. 'From a bird.'

He grimaces like he's sucking the life from a bitter lemon, then retreats into the building he came from.

'How embarrassing.' She gives her hand another token wipe on the topiary tree. 'I'll wash my hands once I get inside.'

'Inside where?

'There,' she nods towards the Georgian structure further down the street.

'You work there?'

'Yep.'

'I'm starting as a recruiter there today.'

'No way. You must be a glutton for punishment joining our team. We're a right bunch of misfits.'

'I'll fit in nicely then,' I reply as we pick up the pace for the last few metres to the office.

'I'm Cassie.'

'Si ...' I pause. Her head is low, so rain doesn't pound her in the face. 'Graham,' I say. 'I'm Graham Coetzee.'

We reach the entrance, the brass signage glinting despite the dull weather.

Talent-IT Services.

'You want to help people secure their dream job?' Cassie asks. 'We're the best technology specialists around.'

'Absolutely.'

Maybe I can do something good for someone else.

Maak elke sekonde tel.

I smooth my jacket lapels from nerves rather than a desire to iron my pinstripes into straight lines, then step over the threshold. My shoes sink so deep into the plush blue carpet they get a full polish. An intricate internal banister is ahead, winding up a stair-case, as well as spiralling into a basement. Framed pictures line the walls depicting Edinburgh scenes. I recognise a few places already from long lonely walks I've already crammed in: Arthur's Seat, Holyroodhouse Palace and the Scott Monument commemorating Sir Walter's writing. History seeps from Edinburgh's pores as cold sweat oozes from mine.

Cassie leads me into the reception area where a middle-aged lady behind the desk glances up from an edition of *Good Housekeeping*. 'Nancy, this is Graham. He helped me win a fight with a brolly and a pigeon.'

I give Cassie a nod of thanks as she tries to flatten down red, chaotic hair.

The receptionist offers a handshake, her magazine firmly held in the other hand. 'I'm Nancy McDougall. Let me show you to Donald's office. He's been expecting you.'

'I'll take him,' says Cassie. 'I'm heading that way.'

She takes off her overcoat, revealing a skirt and blouse hugging curves in all the right places and looks at me. The intensity of her emerald eyes is startling.

My heart pumps so loudly Nancy will surely put down the housekeeping magazine to fetch the office defibrillator.

'Are you okay?' Cassie asks.

'Sure, he's okay,' Nancy scoffs, looking at me. 'You're one of the lucky ones, managing to escape South Africa. Bet you can't wait to wear a kilt and eat a haggis supper.'

I should feel affronted by the suggestion I wanted to flee my home country, but she's right. I'm eternally indebted to Pa for getting me out of a terrible situation.

I follow green eyes. They're as green as the grass at Newlands Cricket Ground.

At home I mostly watch rugby with Pa and Jaco, but I'm fast becoming a fan of cricket too. Pa has brought me and Jaco to our first game at Newlands and I feel all grown-up, part of the crowd in the cricket cap he's bought me.

India bat first. Pa says there's a hint of brilliance when a ball is bowled to look like a boundary can be hit, but instead gets the batsman out for a duck. I vigilantly watch for the Indian man coming back with a duck, but he doesn't return.

'Where are the ducks, Jaco?' I ask.

He hoots and tells Pa what I said.

Pa laughs too, then explains a duck means out with no points. Then he nips to buy us all a boerewors roll and I happily munch away until the rest of the Indians are out and South Africa get to bat.

'You realise this is one of the biggest One Day Internationals ever played,' Pa says as the ball disappears amongst the spectators. He raises his hands in the air and wiggles his two fingers, even though it's not cold.

'What are you doing, Pa?' I ask, since he's done this a few times today.

'It means he's scored a six which is the maximum possible off a ball. Copy me.'

Jaco and I mimic him, waiting eagerly for a big hit again. I'm desperate to do the finger move so all the other fans know I understand the cricket rules.

Then one of our batsmen is out. Something to do with his leg being in front of the wicket. The South African batsman marches off in his spotless white clothes and a replacement arrives to take his place.

'Dammit, this place is a breeding ground for world-class spinners,' Pa mutters, when India throws another fastball the batsman can't get to. Lots of other fans swear too.

I'm not angry. I love this unpredictable game. Sometimes the batsman misses the ball, and other times it soars through the air like a rare blue crane and we all go wild.

The whole day is brilliant. Table Mountain and Devil's Peak tower above the stands. Because we live in L'Agulhas, seeing the mountain is one of the other benefits of Pa bringing me to the cricket. We are like tiny ants at the bottom of its huge mound.

Pa makes another move with his hands like he's playing the piano. 'This means he's scored a four, boys.'

'Thanks, Pa,' I say, glad he's still patiently explaining the rules to Jaco and me, even while the momentum is fizzing into a final frenzy of overs.

'Maak elke sekonde tel,' Pa shouts at the top of his voice while I play the piano harder and harder until South Africa beat India and everybody claps at my tune.

We wind our way upstairs to Donald's office, my hand gripping the banister.

'I've Graham for you,' Cassie announces, stepping to one side for me to enter.

A silver-haired gentleman is facing a monitor; the flat screen at an angle visible to me. He frantically clicks his wireless mouse, shuffling a virtual deck of cards. 'Come in. Let's have a blether.' He pushes the mouse to one side and gestures towards a blue swivel chair several shades brighter than the carpet fibres. His office is filled with modern kit: a metal filing cabinet, an MDF desk, plastic in-trays crammed full of paper. The oldest thing in the room is Donald by at least half a century.

I take a seat as Nancy appears with a jug of water and glasses for us. She places them on the desk, before adjusting her chiffon scarf so it covers the majority of her neck.

'I'll leave you both to it,' she tells us.

I smile. There is something homely about her that calms my jitters. She's no doubt heading back to her magazine to absorb the latest advice on growing chrysanthemums and cooking pot roast.

'I wouldn't normally offer a position during a telephone interview, but your father is a jolly good fellow. Kept me company a few nights in the casino on the cruise we did a while back. I hope you won't let me down.' Donald's grey hair flops over his forehead just like Pa's does.

'I won't.'

'Have you given Nancy your bank details? She'll need to onboard you for payroll.'

'Not yet.'

Donald turns back to his online card game. He grabs his mobile and attempts to use it to play the Queen of Spades. 'Let's get you shadowing Cassie. She's only been here a few months herself, but she's doing a great job.'

'Perfect.'

'Pop your head into the sales room next door to my office and say hello to the mob.'

'Will do.'

My new boss gives the mobile a bash against the desk. I leave him to realise in his own good time that it's not his computer mouse, and cross the hall into the sales room.

'Folks, this is Graham Coetzee, our new recruitment consultant,' Nancy broadcasts from where she's standing next to a corner desk. 'Graham, this is Graydon Vernon, our top biller, and Janine, one of the best recruiters in the country.'

A good-looking bloke with skin a touch too orange for a cold country like Scotland gets up. He's short. I once borrowed *Charlie and the Chocolate Factory* from the local library where Ma works, but have never met a real-life person who resembles an Oompa Loompa. Janine is sitting on the corner of his desk. She gets up to walk away.

'A pleasure to have you on the TITS team, mate. You know, Talent-IT Services.' He chuckles and raises a hand in what I expect to be a handshake. Instead, he gives Janine's departing bum a whack. 'Can't resist a peach.'

Janine swats his hand away. 'Do that again and it'll be your face next time.'

'Oh, come on, Janine. I was only messing about.'

'Some of us like to call him Graydon Vermin, not Vernon,' Janine tells me.

Vermin winks at her. 'My name is a mouthful, just like me.'

I contemplate telling him it's not cool behaviour, but it's my first day and Nancy is already introducing me to a different woman who has cropped blonde hair and serious eyes looking at me from behind oversized glasses.

'Lorraine recruits for government and Graydon covers our prominent banking clients,' Nancy elaborates.

'I've the monopoly of IT business with Scotland's financial companies,' says Graydon. 'You know, a keyboard can be bought on a debt and a debt can be paid on a keyboard. Money doesn't physically change hands anymore. We don't even need bank cards anymore. Everything can be done from the mobile or with some kind of technology.'

'And that's Kevin Beaumont,' Nancy says, pointing towards another cluster of pods divided by partitioning in the same electric blue colouring as the chairs.

A man of around my age smiles in acknowledgement. His phone is cradled against his ear and he's busy selling the benefits of working for a touchpad tablet manufacturer to someone. We hover next to his bombshell of a workspace. A half-eaten apple lies atop the morning newspaper, browning where a bite has been taken. 'He's a great recruiter, but he's been battling it a bit lately to be honest,' Nancy adds from the corner of her mouth, which gives her the appearance of an amateur ventriloquist.

Kevin finishes his call. 'Nice to meet you. Sorry I was caught on the phone. You have to work hard to succeed in this place, like a *kaffir* in your country, right?'

My blue eyes widen. Kevin has dark skin himself. One would think he'd be more politically correct. Despite being born in a country in constant racial conflict, most people I know try to expunge prejudiced terms from public conversation. Even folk from older generations, like my Afrikaner father, who lived most of their lives in the Apartheid era and might not be the biggest fans of African National Congress legislation, do their best to avoid using racist labels.

'Gotcha!' Kevin gives me a smile packed with sincerity. 'Pretty tasteless, I know, but just winding you up, mate.'

Everyone laughs as I dwell on the fact I've rarely seen people from different races and colours working in such relaxed harmony. Back home there was a lot of pushback from locals in applying quotas to employ people formerly racially disadvantaged. Kevin Beaumont, with his tailor-made suit and cheeky grin, doesn't look at all disadvantaged. I'm the one who is disadvantaged with a backward mindset that has been insulated too long.

I enter Kevin's cube and shake his hand, disgusted at my own underlying prejudice. I'm a white man, but I'm the one here with black ink on my fingertips, not Kevin.

My mood darkens at the thought of never being able to put out of mind everything I've seen and done, so I try to distract myself by taking another look around at my surroundings. The spaghetti junction of computer wires and the ancient chandelier, both pulsing with electricity beneath the corniced ceiling. Old mixed with new. Above an original ornate fireplace hangs a modern reproduction print. It's a portrait of an ancient Mother Teresa.

'Yesterday is gone.
Tomorrow has not yet come.
We have only today.
Let us begin.'

It seems wrong to question Mother Teresa's words, but it's beyond me how I'm supposed to move on from yesterday. I turn to the whiteboards dominating the opposite wall. Colourful scribbles fill them with information about live jobs, placements and pound signs. There's a line with my name on it, void of any substance. I suddenly long to have something happen in my new life that can be written on a whiteboard in colourful markers.

'Hi again.'

I meet Cassie's stare. She gives me a friendly nod and sits down in her swivel chair. 'Officially, welcome to the cube farm.'

'The cube farm?'

'You'll get cabin fever in your first week of being boxed in.'

'Thanks for the warning.'

'Take plenty of breaks, because if you sit on these seats too long, you'll sink so low you get carpet burns on your backside,' she adds.

I laugh, then Nancy steers me to the opposite side of the cube farm to properly introduce me to the raven-haired girl, Janine. She's a plump woman, pretty, with cerise lipstick matching her knitted jersey.

'I hope you're not some hot shot expecting to beat me in the upcoming competition,' she says.

'What competition?'

'The top recruiters from every office are getting sent on a trip to the highlands. All expenses paid with a self-awareness course thrown in for good measure.'

'I'm sure you guys have it all sewn up.'

'Nothing is over until the fat lady sings,' says Vermin. 'Hey Janine?'

Janine stands, hands on hips, glaring at him. 'When I sing, honey, you won't know what hit you. That goes for the rest of you too. Accessorising with that briefcase to look the part isn't going to help you win the comp either, Cassie.'

'Whatever,' Cassie replies.

'She's like Paddington Bear with nothing in there but lunch,' Janine smirks. A streak of her lipstick has rubbed off on her teeth.

There's a click as Cassie opens the clasps on the old-fashioned case to pull out a polystyrene bag. She drops it over the partitioning onto Janine's desk. 'Cheese savoury on Mighty White.'

'Looks good,' I say, attempting to ease the tension.

'Have it then, new boy.' Janine flings the sandwich my way.

I catch it with deft hands, wondering how someone like me is going to fit into somewhere like this.

'I'll show you the ropes, then maybe we can go to the local at lunchtime,' Cassie offers. 'The sandwich has lost its appeal.'

I smile, grateful Newland's green eyes has bowled me a six at the beginning of a gruelling five-day test match.

Chapter Ten

T he local is the Anvil, a short walk away on the corner of Rose Street. It's packed with lunchtime customers.

'I'd go for a beer but then I'll be no help to anyone back at the office,' Cassie says as we queue at the bar.

We settle on a couple of Cokes and some nachos to share, before sitting at a scuffed wooden table.

A screen above the bar is airing prerecorded highlights of a football match: Hibernians against Hearts. The people in the bar groan as the Hibs keeper dives in the mud to stop a goal. He leaps to his feet quickly, his green and white humbug of a strip filthy.

'Do you have a team?' she asks as we watch.

'I'm more of a cricket and rugby man. You?'

'I've lived here a long time and still hate the football sectarianism.'

'What sectarianism?'

'Hearts and Rangers are Protestant clubs and Celtic and Hibs Catholic. Fans make it all about the religious path you walk and what pub you drink in.'

'Sounds like South African apartheid,' I reply as a waitress, skin like wizened leather, delivers our order to the table.

'D'ye youngsters wanne wee dram in yer Coke?' she asks putting the glasses of Coke down.

'Not for me, thanks,' I reply.

'Not a whisky drinker then?'

'Not a drinker, full stop.'

The waitress shrugs and turns her attention towards more lucrative punters.

Cassie leans straight in to scoop salsa on a nacho. She's pretty in an unusual way, with curls framing a pixie face and those amazing eyes with a slight slant to them, feline and fearless.

'Where did you live before you were here?' I ask Cassie.

'Australia.'

'Which part?'

'Fremantle in Western Australia. I moved here when I was seven.'

'Do you remember much?'

'I remember our house. It had uneven floorboards with rugs scattered everywhere. The whole house was filled with mismatched knick-knacks Dad collected on his travels.'

'What does he do?'

'He used to work on the oil rigs back then, first in Australia, then at BP in Grangemouth, but I've no idea what he does now. I never heard from him again after he split from my mother.'

'That sucks.'

She shrugs so I don't pry further. It's awful losing someone important. Having my brother drop out of my everyday life feels like I've lost a limb.

'What about you. Are you a city boy?'

'Nope. I grew up in a small fishing village just outside Cape Town.'

'We also lived not far from Fremantle port. I used to go for fish and chips and watch the cargo ships loaded with all these colourful shipping containers.'

'Sounds nice.'

'It's better than where I am now, on the underbelly of the Fitzroy Estate.'

'Where's that?'

'Way out past Wester Hailes. It's pretty rough. The weekend entertainment is watching the police helicopter locking a search-light onto joy-riders.'

'Sounds rough.'

'We've never had our car stolen because we never had one in the first place.' She laughs as we tick into the food. 'What brought you to Edinburgh?'

'My mother was born in the UK so I'm lucky I have a British pass-port. I figured it would be a sin if I didn't use it to see more of Europe.' The lie tastes uncomfortable as it rolls off my tongue, so I divert the conversation back to her. 'Have you got brothers and sisters?'

She pops another nacho in her mouth, so I wait for her to finish chewing. It's nice to meet a girl who doesn't pick at her food like it's a bowl of cold mieliepap dished up by Mbali.

'No, it's just me and my mum.'

'Where does your mum live?'

A flush snakes up Cassie's neck. 'With me. She had a meltdown years ago after Dad left and never got over it.'

'Don't worry about it. I was still living with my parents until I moved here. It was just more affordable.'

'Are you also an only child?'

'No, one older brother.'

'You must miss them?'

'Yah, loads, but I don't mind being on my own. You get used to it.'

'If I'd known you were a loner, I'd have eaten my cheese savoury sandwich in my cube instead of sharing nachos.'

'That sandwich was intense. What's with Janine?'

'She's always prickly, but she's an amazing recruiter. Is your first day what you expected?'

'Some of the office vibes are weird. Graydon's a bit out there.'

'He thinks he's being funny, especially with Janine, but sometimes it's just not, you know. They're a pretty good bunch to work with overall though, considering the job can be full on.'

'It's selling people by the hour. It is going to be intense sometimes.'

Cassie laughs. 'I never thought of myself as a pimp.'

'What's the story with this competition?'

'Luigi runs a league ladder to win a trip somewhere.'

'Luigi?'

'The chairman. He's based in London and owns the whole company.'

'Do you think you'll make the grade?'

'I'm doing okay even though I've not been in the job long. If you dig deep in Benny, there's always someone in there who's right.'

'Benny?'

'The database. It's so cranky you would never guess we work for an IT company. Someone named it after Benny Hill, the dead comedian. I'll show you how to navigate him properly this afternoon. If you learn to treat him well, he'll throw you the punchline.'

'Thanks.'

She's already shown me so much this morning. Searching social media, advertising on career sites, how to calculate the profit margins. I'm shocked how much money a recruiter can charge a company in desperate need of niche resources.

'Stick with it. You never know what Luigi will have in store for the winners somewhere up in the Highlands.'

'A mystery holiday, huh?'

'For all we know it could be a cheap mini-break in a tent. Have you ever been camping?'

I nod, memories flooding my thoughts.

The household is in a frenzy as we prepare to leave for the great outdoors. Ma opens and closes cupboards in the kitchen like her sanity is inside one of them.

'Where's the meat Tupperware?' she asks for the fifth time. 'The one with the blue lid.'

Pa ignores her. He's too busy trying to ram the cooler box closed by sitting on it.

'We need the meat Tupperware,' Ma repeats, grabbing a chair from the dining table and dragging it to the larder. Ma is not the tallest, so she climbs onto it to reach the top shelf.

'Ronald, how many times have I told you to get rid of this thing?' She lifts out Pa's pistol.

'That's where it lives,' he replies.

'Why does it have to live anywhere? Get armed response on the house instead.'

'I don't want to rely on anyone else to protect my family if someone breaks in. Put it back.'

They've had this argument before over Pa keeping firearms in the house. Ma never wins. She places the gun gingerly back on the top shelf and resumes her cupboard slamming.

'Can I take my skateboard with us?' Jaco asks, already wearing his Tony Hawk helmet.

'Me too?' I add, as Jaco jumps on his board and performs an ollie. The move is quick, a blend of popping, kicking and jumping on the skateboard which makes the wheels hit the tiles with a clatter. He's good for an eight-year-old.

'Jaco!' Ma shouts as she wobbles on the chair.

'Sorry.' He grabs his board and I follow him into the backyard where we practise our moves in peace until Pa has filled every last inch of the HiLux cab, and Ma is satisfied we've not forgotten anything.

But as soon as we get to the camp site we realise we've missed something. The hammer for the tent pegs and the gazebo.

'Oh, Ronald,' Ma shakes her head. 'Boys, this is what happens when we let Pa pack,' she tells me and Jaco. We all laugh, even Pa.

'Good job the Van der Merwes are here.' Pa wanders off to borrow suitable tools to nail the tent to the ground.

It's the first time we've been on holiday with the neighbours from a few houses away and I'm quite excited. They've brought their daughter, Erin, a girl from school who's in Jaco's class. She plays with us in the street most days. She has a bell on her bike which she rings twice whenever we get in her way on the skateboards, but she's nice, with blonde plaits. What I like most about her is she never cries. Even when she fell off her bike once and burst her knee open, she kept it together.

Erin wanders back over with Pa, hammer in hand. Our tent is tiny in comparison to theirs. Tall and thin, like a Dr Who Tardis, but I don't want to be transported anywhere other than here.

Camping is awesome.

We play until sunset, then get our torches out and play spotlight, hiding from each other in the dark. Erin is clever. She climbs a tree and Jaco and I only find her when she eventually giggles.

Later, we cram into the luxury of the Van der Merwes' gazebo and eat cowboy food. Baked beans, sausage, potato and tinned tomatoes cooked in one pot. It's the best dinner ever.

Afterwards we toast marshmallows on the fire burning in the tin kettle weber while we admire Erin's father's handiwork. He's wired a solar panel to his tent and their makeshift home is lit up like a beacon. To top it off, they have music too.

The adults play the Bee Gees until the camp manager instructs us to keep the noise down because people are sleeping. Jaco laughs at him, but I say goodnight to Erin and shrink into the Tardis.

The football match on TV turns to a blur. The Tardis was roughly the same size as the jail cell I was thrown in. I can't shake off the flashback.

'We should head back to the office.' I pull out my wallet and throw a note onto the table before making a beeline for the exit. 'I'll see you back there.'

I knock my hip against the corner of an empty table in my mad dash out of there. No doubt I've just bruised way more than Cassie's ego.

It's been an unexpected surprise to meet someone who's genuinely open and nice, but I can't return the gesture.

Chapter Eleven

I don't recall ever tasting such glorious nachos, but all afternoon regurgitated guacamole threatens to erupt all over my cube as if I've washed it down with enough tequila to swallow the worm. I'm thrilled when the day is over and I can head to the number five bus stop. Hollow mannequins draped in patterned fabrics stare out from the shop windows. Their faces are sterile of any emotion. Mine probably looks much the same.

I shove my coiled fists deep into my pockets. Although it's only early evening, it's already getting dark and the temperature must be close to zero. Most evenings growing up, Jaco and I would hit the surf, so this whole atmosphere feels alien. I pine for the African sun on my back.

The bus queue snakes along the pavement, and I take my place behind a couple of 'neds'. In my short time here, I've learned neds are a small cohort of troublemakers, who rely on the British welfare system supplemented with the odd mugging. One of them nudges his pal, eying the pensioner in front of me who is gripping the handle of a floral-patterned bag on wheels.

'What the fuck are you staring at?' he snarls, catching my stare. He throws a half-finished portion of hot chips my way and the wind blows the greasy mess over my shoes. I kick it away with the stub of my toe.

'Nothing,' I reply.

'Fuck you, pal.'

'He's not worth it,' his friend says as a parting shot, as the two neds wander off up the street.

He's right. I'm not. Turning away, I concentrate on the silhouette of the bus approaching from a distance.

If I jump in front of it now, the bus driver will have time to hit the brakes and maybe avoid impact.

I could wait. Wait. WAIT.

Then leap.

The bus will slam into me hard. Propel my body so it's airborne until I land somewhere, a mangled mess of lacerations and fractures. The impact may be so severe I could suffer immediate haemorrhaging, or it could give me a spinal cord injury that could put me in a coma or leave me unable to walk again. If I'm lucky I might be immediately snubbed out. *If* I'm lucky.

Cause of death: Road traffic fatality.

I doubt anyone would miss me.

The bus pulls up and I climb on. As it passes the hooligans, one gives me the finger through the window. Around me, everyday sounds muffle the screams inside my mind. The engine purring, people shuffling in their seat, a carrier bag rustling. Nobody on the bus seems to notice anything is amiss. An unbearable wave of self-pity washes over me. Talent-IT Services need me, or rather I need them. Without my job there, I can't send funds to Erin back in South Africa and I promised to support her no matter what.

***

At the far end of Gorgie Road, I hop off the bus. A drainpipe coming from a wall beside the bus stop is spouting dirty water onto the pavement, replacing chip fat with sewerage on my shoes. In more ways than one, I'm knee-deep in shit.

A neon sign blinks, advertising The Taj Mahal restaurant. A few letters are broken so it reads 'The Taj aha'. I've taken the flat above it and have grown used to the lurking stench of curry spices consuming my living space like an airborne virus. I decide to give the grub a go.

Parting a curtain made of strands of beads, I enter and spot Luckraj Rampal.

'Lucky.' I politely nod to my landlord.

He wipes his hands on his trouser legs and shakes my hand, before taking my order. A stream of patrons come and go while I wait, which is a good sign considering the dilapidated restaurant exterior.

Carry-out in hand, I let myself into the tenement. The scrawny tabby who seems to permanently live in the stairwell meows and I pause to rub it behind the ears. It gives a satisfied purr. I check my post in the row of metal postboxes and find a small package with colourful stamps in the corner. I'd have preferred to have found anthrax spores in my mail rather than an international package.

My hand shakes as I fiddle with the temperamental door lock to my tiny flat and stumble inside. I toss the parcel in the bin on top of yesterday's leftover two-minute noodles.

The sparse cream walls of my flat close in as I pace the lounge. If they creep in any closer I'll be able to touch either side of the room with my fingertips, my back against the third, nose touching the fourth wall. I will be trapped upright in a coffin, unable to breathe.

Cause of death: Buried alive.

I want to break free. Be free. Live free. Beside the ancient russet couch, which came with my lease, is a coffee table with a glass top. I kick it in desperate rage.

The glass shatters onto the beige swirls of the rug underneath. I regret damaging Lucky Rampal's property instantly. The man gave me a roof over my head when I needed a place. No questions. Only trust. I'll pay him back, but it's such a disrespectful thing to do and only adds to my guilt from what I've left others to cope with back home. I'm such a waste of space. Leaving Cassie sitting in the Anvil today was also bloody rude. The glass on my floor is enticing; fragments with the capability to end it all. Sharp enough to prise me from this coffin forever.

Cause of death: Slit wrists.

I won't slash across my wrist, which will maul the tendons and make it impossible to hack the other arm successfully. Instead, I'll use a shard on the artery between my wrist and elbow, slicing straight down towards the wrist quickly so I've time to do the other arm before unconsciousness takes over from the blood loss. It's a horrible way to die and could easily go wrong. To do it properly needs preparation. The artery should be enlarged to accommodate increased blood pressure, by drinking more water the day before committing suicide. This makes it easier to bleed out, but apart from a coffee and a Coke in the Anvil, I've been a camel today. A decent razor would be a better blade than using glass from the coffee table, but mine are cheap disposables, undoubtedly leading to severe pain and scarring. Soaking in a bathtub of hot water might help relaxation long enough for my blunt instrument to do some real damage, but my bathroom only has a shower. To see it through, a wuss like me will need to numb the pain, and I've no painkillers. Everything is stacked against me. I'm chickenshit, unable to go through with such a hideously painful death.

I sweep up the glass into a handheld dustpan from under the kitchen sink and head downstairs to dispose of the glass in the outside recycle wheelie bin. The garbage area smells rancid, a reminder of the decaying process going on around us all. My thoughts are decaying too. Maggot infested and putrid in their ability to wriggle into my day and fill their guts with what good there is left. My skin crawls as the glass shards hit the bottom of the bin with a tinkle.

Back in my bedroom, I tear off my suit and pull on a creased old T-shirt. *The Doors* is emblazoned across the front. When I was a teenager, I used to think Jim Morrison ruled the planet while the Lord above ruled heaven. Now I wonder which of them speaks the truth; Jim crooning 'this is the end', or God who promises no end, only resurrection.

Remembering my takeaway, I start to eat. It's delicious but I feel sick at the thought of what I was contemplating doing tonight. If this were my last meal, I'd want one of my mother's desserts. That mouth-watering malva pud of hers. She makes it with twice as much apricot jam than anyone else I know and adds an untraditional twist of chopped preserved ginger. Makes all the difference.

I cover my leftovers and stick them in the fridge. It's empty except for some milk, which I sniff. It's not as sour as me so I gulp down the last few dregs and toss away the empty carton. The brown package is in there, decaying my mind along with the rubbish. I take it out and fumble to open it with my stumpy fingernails. Inside is a note on thick cream stationery that threatens to bring both milk and curry back up.

I thought you should have this,
Erin

The note drops to the floor. How can one woman bring back memories I want to supress yet stimulate so many others I want to treasure?

Erin's head bobs above the water, her blonde wet hair slicked back making it easy to see the excitement on her face, goggles propped on her forehead.

The turquoise water enclosed in the secluded lagoon in Suiderstrand is clear and still. Erin lies back and floats. She's begun to fill out her bikini with perky breasts, perfectly complimenting her trim figure.

'Erin, watch out,' I yell, spotting a stingray swim inches away from her, its tail swaying.

She lets her legs drop towards the ocean bed and treads water.

'There are two of them,' she says, as another smaller stingray goes past. 'And there I was thinking we were alone out here fooling around.'

Jaco splashes her, then she splashes us both back. I tackle Jaco and dunk him, making Erin laugh so hard she swallows water and has a coughing fit.

We get out of the ocean, and I give her my can of cream soda to stop her from turning purple and she gives me the best smile ever.

The stingray were a pair that day, but we were three. Always a third wheel present.

I retrieve the note, flattening the creases as if it's a worthy document of historical note. In some ways, it is. I check the rest of the package contents. There's a leather-cord necklace wrapped inside a square of bubble wrap. I stare at my gift for an eternity before touching the sharp white tooth threaded onto it. Eventually, I lift it and pull it over my ruffled hair, then over the lump in my throat. It's the only tangible object I have from the good old days, and I'll cling onto it with all my might.

Chapter Twelve

As I enter the office with an espresso in hand, Kevin narrowly misses knocking it down my pinstripes as he charges past to invade Janine's cube.

'I've just checked John Fullerton's record, Janine.'

'So?' Janine retorts.

'I spoke to him yesterday about a project management role and the comments I logged in Benny have been changed from my initials to yours.'

'What's your point?' Janine asks.

'He's my guy and you've tampered with the record.'

'Maybe I accidently entered the wrong record.'

'Bullshit. You know how many times I've spoken to John Fullerton. Why would you even be in his record, Janine?' Kevin demands.

'Who gives a shit?' Janine bellows.

'I do.'

'Calm your jets. If he calls again, I'll pass him back to you.'

'You're a cheat.'

'Are you going to let him speak to me like that?' Janine says to Graydon who has just walked in.

'I'm not getting involved in World War Three.'

'Thanks a bunch. I thought you would have my back,' says Janine.

I stay out of it. I'm hardly qualified to be judgemental about anyone's tendency to tell lies. Wiggling my mouse, I attempt various unsuccessful login combinations. 'Hey Janine, I've locked myself out of the system. Any ideas?'

'You should call The CAD,' she suggests.

'The CAD?'

'Our IT guy in London. Give him a bell.'

She scribbles the number on a Post-it Note and passes it to me, then resumes her argument with Kevin while I pick up the phone.

'Press control, alt, delete,' the support guy tells me.

'Done and it didn't work.'

'Are you sure you pressed control, alt, delete?'

'I'm sure.' I get now why the troubleshooting guy is called The CAD.

'It must be your keyboard,' he informs me.

'My keyboard? Why?'

'Check your keys are in the right place.'

I look at my hovering fingers and it registers.

'Someone's swapped the letters around.'

'Classic,' The CAD chuckles. 'First week?'

'Yah, I should have guessed since I used to take apart broken PCs and put them back together again for a living. Thanks for your help though.'

'You're lucky they didn't superglue your coffee cup to the table,' The CAD says before ringing off.

Kevin and Janine high-five.

'At least you pair are smiling,' I say.

'All part of the induction program, big fella,' Kevin replies.

They laugh and the tension eases.

Vermin suddenly appears. 'Donald wants you in the board-room, Graham. Cassie's in there already. They're waiting on Charlie Rivers arriving, the bank's CIO.'

'What does he want me for?' I ask.

'I've won an exclusive project and need you and Cassie to help find the right candidates.'

'Why those two?' Janine asks. 'They should be finding their own clients.'

'It's too much work to manage on my own and Donald thinks it will be valuable experience for them since they're both the newest.'

'That sucks,' Janine protests.

'Does it?' Vermin grins.

'Vermin is such an accurate name for you,' she retorts, yanking her scooped-neck jersey down.

'Christ, Janine, you could store your umbrella down there for a rainy day,' Vermin ogles at her chest.

'Screw you.'

'Feel free,' he retorts before strolling out.

'You shouldn't talk to her like that,' I say, following Vermin downstairs.

'Why? She likes it,' he replies as we go into the boardroom.

Donald is sitting next to Cassie with a bakery box in front of him. He opens it and offers the choice between chocolate eclairs or apple turnovers. 'I've been waiting on you to get stuck into these cakes.'

'Sorry, Donald. I might skip …'

He holds up a wrinkled hand, pausing me mid-sentence. 'It's compulsory to have a cake. So, you're settling in with the team?'

'Yah, thanks.'

Cassie tucks a curl behind her ear and passes me a napkin to catch my flaky turnover pastry.

'Wonderful, because Graydon has the perfect opportunity for both of you, working with him on servicing the Royal Celtic Bank account.'

My energy levels soar with a combination of the sugar hit and the word opportunity. Maybe it's possible to make a bigger financial impact on Erin's life than I anticipated.

'I've so much demand coming out of the bank I can't get across the volume of open roles. While it's busy like this, I'll split commission on any positions you help fill,' Vermin tells us. 'I'll introduce you to Charlie when he arrives. He's the head honcho of the bank's entire technology department. I can get you up and running quickly on sourcing the type of people they hire.'

'You're both going to London for extra system training too,' says Donald to me and Cassie. 'If you snooze you lose, so the training will help you pick up ways to work smarter. You have to make every second count.'

The comment punches me in the gut, triggering thoughts of Pa and his no-nonsense approach to obstacles.

Maak elke sekonde tel.

Nancy suddenly enters the boardroom with a stout man in tow; a woollen tartan scarf wrapped beneath his craggy features.

I do a double take. It's the topiary tree witness.

'Charlie, this is Graham Coetzee and Cassie Walker,' says Vermin. 'They're assisting with recruitment to give us additional bandwidth.'

'Nice to meet you again.' Cassie rises to offer her hand, but rather than grasp it, the CIO recoils.

'Oh, I've washed it since we last met,' she blurts, ignoring the confused look passing between Donald and Vermin.

'Pleasure to meet you.' He gingerly accepts the handshake. 'Shall we head for that coffee, Donald?'

'Sure.'

Charlie's lips protrude as he walks stiffly out of the room.

'What are the odds?' says Cassie when they've gone. 'He seems really grumpy.'

'Even with that Jagger pout I bet he never gets any satisfaction.'

Cassie laughs. 'We'll just have to sweat Benny's assets to find him every last candidate out there. As soon as Donald and Vermin are back, we can find out more.'

'Donald won't be back for ages,' Nancy says, taking out a nailfile to saw off the tip of a talon. The motion is fearsome, with more muscle than a lumberjack hacking down a tree, particles flying everywhere. 'They're grabbing a brew with Charlie, but then the racing is on at Goodwood. Donald loves the horses more than poker. He thinks I don't know about it, but the man can't wipe his own nose without me requisitioning the toilet paper and tearing off an appropriate number of squares.'

'Sounds like you know him well,' I say.

'I love him dearly, but the gambling, well … you know.' Nancy shakes her head sadly, her styled hair moving in such perfect sync it could be coated with superglue. 'So, you're both off to head office next week for advanced training on Benny?'

'Looks like it,' I reply, wondering how news of the head office visit filtered from the boardroom to Nancy in a matter of seconds. If the Central Intelligence Agency had asked Nancy for a tip-off, they would have found Bin Laden much sooner.

'You'll be away a couple of days. It's a domestic flight but take your passports for ID,' she tells us both. 'And before I forget, we need a copy of yours for payroll to get you set up, Graham.'

'Yah, no problem,' I answer, pasting on a smile. 'I just need to nip out and open a bank account for my salary though.'

'Do what you've got to do,' says Nancy.

***

Back upstairs I grab my backpack. Inside, my documents beckon me to sort out the complex logistics of living in a different country with a new name. I head out towards the nearest high street bank. Bright orange and black letters surround the entrance. I go inside, feeling I've been caught in the jaws of a great white with strips torn off my integrity.

The teller inside is an elderly lady who seems extremely thorough, judging by the queue moving at a sluggish pace. Nerves get the better of me, so I step aside to grab a plastic cup and gulp down some water from the cooler, then bolt down the street to an alternative bank.

Inside the second branch, there's no water cooler and the queue is short, so I quickly find myself in front of a different teller: young, with shiny gold jacket buttons and enthusiastic words of welcome.

'Freezing out there, isn't it,' I say, handing over my passport and a copy of my lease which Lucky Rampal drew up.

'Sure is,' she replies, completing the paperwork swiftly with me. 'Lots of Christmas shoppers. Are you organised?'

Palpitations mount. I can't think straight about the purchases I should be showering on my family. I'm more worried about remembering who the hell I am right now and how to correctly sign my name on the dotted line of a bank form.

'You … you worked here long?' I stammer.

The bank clerk replies with some insights to the graduate program that helped her get a foot on the ladder. The inane chatter is soothing, and I scribble my signature with a flourish.

I offer my brightest smile. 'I'd have popped in sooner if I'd known how efficient this bank is.'

She rattles off some detail about the perks of the current account I'm opening while I use the time wisely to review what I've written, before handing back my flawless paperwork.

She gives me a smile. 'Your card will be with you in the next few days and your pin will come out in a separate letter, Graham.'

I breathe so easily I don't even leave the steamies on the glass partition between us. Committing fraud gets a lot easier with practise.

Chapter Thirteen

In Edinburgh airport, Cassie and I leverage the amazing technology used for domestic departures, offering passengers the ability to check-in from a computerised terminal and bag drop without human interaction. The transport industry is going through an overhaul. I've read about mining sites implementing driverless trains carrying iron ore from the mines. It's not unreasonable to think aeroplanes could be pilot free one day, although I don't know how passengers would feel about that.

The system spits out my boarding pass without any issues and we proceed to the security gates.

'You okay?' Cassie asks as we pass through the full-length body scanner and wait for our belongings to come through in cat litter trays.

I'm not okay. There are officers everywhere, hoping for someone to pose some kind of national security threat so their shift will become more interesting than removing hairspray aerosols from passengers who have zero intention of using them as a blow torch on a 747.

A barrel of an officer pulls me over to swab my armpits, inner thighs, shoes and backpack, then runs the sample through an explosives trace detection test.

I'm given the green light and pick up my bag. I need to keep moving before I coil into a ball and rock myself to comfort, but my feet have lead weights anchoring them to the spot and my limbs have stiffened in protest.

'Are you okay, sir?' the officer asks, gleefully rubbing his hands together.

'Fine, thanks.' My voice is hoarse and foreign to me.

Perhaps the muscle rigidity is a symptom of an early onset neurological illness. It could be the cause of my fumbling fingers and haphazard coordination, introducing debilitating complications to my wellbeing that will affect my future mobility and reduce life expectancy.

Cause of death: Parkinson's disease.

My bag drops to the floor and one of my passports peeks its ugly head out. It's my South African one, Simon Ronald Coetzee, different from the name printed in capital letters on my boarding pass. With enormous mental strength, I force the neurological symptoms to oppression as I shove the passport back in my bag, seal up my belongings and move along.

'Are you a nervous flyer or something?' Cassie asks as we walk through the terminal.

'I just need the loo. Back in a minute.'

I hurry to the men's room and make for the nearest sink to douse myself in cold water. Someone flushes a toilet, and the occupant comes out of the cubicle. He takes one look at the reflection of my bloodshot eyes in the mirror before making a quick exit without washing his hands. At twenty-six, I should be bursting with energy, but I'm a lethargic, deadpan disaster with the zest of life zapped out of me.

I need to calm the fuck down. The airport presents nothing to be apprehensive about. London will be a thrill. A buzz from learning how to make deals and reaping financial rewards that will make recruitment addictive, like a tik addict. As I get one score under wraps, I'll crave the next. My quest for success will eclipse my failures.

I'm kidding myself to think I'm adapting to my new humdrum life, but even though I'm no deal-making junkie, I'll give the job all I have. It will be nice to spend time with Cassie. She's easygoing company and might help me keep a cool head. With renewed determination to stop living in the past, I grasp the steel tap and turn it off. It's time to make the most of my future. I lower my hands into the latest Dyson contraption on the wall to blow them dry. Shame someone hasn't invented hygienic technology sizeable enough to stick sweating armpits in.

A beep in my pocket notifies me a message has arrived.

Cassie: *Boarding!*

The text reminds me I can always be found. The mobile phone is too damned smart. It rips to shreds the simple pleasures one takes for granted, like privacy whilst in the privy. I type back: *On my way.*

I've a plane to catch and important lessons to learn on acquiring new clients and winning candidate turf wars. This is the nature of being a recruitment consultant. One way or another, it takes over your life.

It beats the one-dimensional life that could be imposed on me back in South Africa.

***

The flight from Edinburgh is packed with executives travelling south. We pass through business class, filled with suits who have orbited earth enough times to accumulate air miles for a free domestic upgrade. They're already glugging bubbly while I'm bustled along into economy. I'm the lucky sardine who got a middle seat next to a well-dressed woman who slips off her shoes the minute we leave the runway. I could follow her lead, but I was running late this morning and pulled on dirty socks from my floor. Offending strangers with an offensive whiff of my feet isn't my concern, but Cassie is in the aisle seat to my other side and I'd like her to think I'm reasonably hygienic. She's always immaculately dressed; the only dishevelled thing about her is the unruly mane, but the curly locks suit her. Like her, they have a mind of their own. Every so often her elbow brushes mine as we wrestle for the armrest space. I tuck my arms in to give her the extra inch. The closeness is unnerving, so I grab the airline magazine and skim read recommendations for gadgets for the frequent flyer. A stylish pen with a powerhouse torch, straighteners with a built-in travel adapter, a voice-activated waterproof music speaker that bluetooths playlists. The advertisements satisfy materialistic consumer demands, making the world a better place if you need the light on when you write, your curls ironed out while abroad or a tune to sing along to while taking a shower. Then something catches my eye. The latest fitness watch that captures lifestyle habits. Devices for the health-conscious are becoming commonplace but this new model has advanced functionality around monitoring of sleep patterns, heart rate and anxiety levels through a mood tracker, then giving you the right advice on what needs to be adjusted.

'It'd be cool to invent something like this,' I say to Cassie. 'Something with the potential to stop a person from going to an early grave.'

'Why don't you?'

'I wouldn't know where to start.'

'Sometimes you have to go after what you want.'

'Maybe. What's your dream?'

'I'd like a place of my own one day. I don't have much freedom living with my mother.'

'That bad, huh?' I say, suppressing the image of my own freedom being ripped away.

'I'll save enough to get there eventually. That's why I joined Talent. Vermin makes thousands in commission each month but I'm going to work my arse off until I pass him on the sales ladder.'

'You'll make it.'

'I know.'

I should set myself some goals. Growing up, I always hovered below the radar. My brother, straight-A student, med school, the town success story. The guy who cut loose from local life to build a career as an orthopaedic surgeon. Me, on the other hand, I'm pretty sure nobody even knew my name. If I do ever make tabloid headlines, it will be for all the wrong reasons.

'You seem like you enjoy the job,' I say.

'I couldn't believe my luck when Donald hired me. I'd been working a decade at this place called Enviromentech refilling ink cartridges.'

'How come?'

'When I finished school, my mother pushed me into work to help with the rent, but ever since Dad left, I wanted a chance to prove myself.' Her lips take a tiny downturn.

'Do you miss him?'

'I used to, but I never fully forgave him for checking out. It was hard on me and Mum. Do you know what I mean?'

84

A wave of anguish bubbles under my skin. 'Sometimes these challenges make us stronger.'

'I want to win that competition. Don't you?'

Obtaining pole position to take out a sales prize has been completely absent from my radar, but her enthusiasm is contagious. I recall the coloured markers on the whiteboard. 'I suppose it would be cool.'

Cassie reaches over and grasps my hand nearest her. 'So, take your best shot. Punch above your weight, you know.'

Take your best shot.

Take your best shot.

Take your best shot.

I visibly flinch.

'What happened?' She runs a thumb over a scar on the knuckle of my forefinger.

'I got sucked into a bar brawl in South Africa. It was nothing.'

'Then let's shake on giving it our best shot.' She pumps my hand, then lets it go again as the air hostess leans in to hand me a plastic tray.

The food is compartmentalised into mini portions, accessorised with a pack of disposable cutlery and a plastic cup of orange juice plonked on a paper doily. My serving of mieliepap from Mbali was served on a similar plastic platter, less the paper doily. The stomach clenching returns.

'No thanks.' I pass the tray back to the air hostess and stand as she reverses her trolley. Cassie moves to let me shuffle out.

'You alright?' she asks.

I nod as the red man turns to green at the back of the plane. 'Back in a minute.'

Entering the tiny area, I pull the door closed and slide the lock across. The bowl is empty and the toilet is reasonably clean, a far cry from the basic cell amenities that plague my thoughts. It takes several minutes of retching until I'm only able to deposit bile in the pan. I flush, delighted there's a well-designed lever to pull and automate the process. The engineering of the aircraft is quite remarkable and the rush of air is as powerful as the one I exhale. Pa was right to help me flee. No matter what I've done, I never want to be put back inside with a toilet that has no illuminated green man who turns glowing red to shut out other inmates.

'Are you sure you're okay?' Cassie repeats when I get back. My body tenses as I wiggle past her lap to squeeze into my designated space.

'I'm just not a fan of airline food.'

'Would you like something else, sir?' the air hostess asks, hearing me from behind her mobile restaurant cart. Before I answer, she thrusts an oat and raisin flapjack my way and moves on down the line.

I eat it, thinking of the hunger across South Africa. Millions of squatters would kill for complementary snacks, a choice of beverages served on a paper doily and hot food dished in a compartmentalised prison tray.

Everyone is capable of killing someone for something.

Chapter Fourteen

With overnight bags by our feet, we slowly weave through London in a black cab, heading towards Chancery Lane. It's gridlocked, but Cassie is agreeable company and the change of scenery provides a welcome break from an otherwise mundane existence.

Eventually we pull up outside head office. It differs from the architectural splendour of Edinburgh. The modern frontage has full-length windows covered with professionally produced adverts. Oversized signage screams the presence of TITS in the capital city.

Inside though, there is an air of familiarity. Electric blue paint covers every inch of wall and glazed blue pots house a mass of plants.

'Alan Titchmarsh would have a field day in here,' Cassie whispers.

'Who?'

'TV presenter of gardening shows.'

'There's no garden in my tenement.'

'You don't know what you're missing.'

'I guess not,' I reply, envisaging Ma treating her plants with the same care an accomplished orthopaedic surgeon would show a patient on the operating table.

Ma is pruning the roses in her gardening gloves. We've rows of bushes planted along either side of the path leading from the gate to the front door. Every year they sprout stunning flowers, attentively planted in alternating colours of red and yellow to ensure the garden is symmetrical. It's early August, and although it's still winter, it's balmy outside which Ma says she's to exploit if she is to generate grander blooms than last year. I'm playing with my new set of Swingball I got for my seventh birthday against Jaco. We're not keeping scores, but Jaco is easily more skilled. He hits the ball in both directions, left on his forearm, then on the back of his bat so it comes back at me the opposite way. Our longest rally is twenty hits and Ma still has six more bushes to clip.

'Do you want a bunnilick?' I ask Jaco.

'If you'll fetch them.'

'Ma, can we have a bunnilick?'

My mother looks at us from under her floppy straw hat and smiles. 'Only one each, otherwise you'll spoil lunch.'

I toss down my racket and run inside to the freezer. It doesn't matter if it's spring, summer, autumn or winter, Ma always makes sure there are bunnilicks because she knows we love the ice poles. There are all kinds of flavours to choose from, but I pick two tropical ones. Ma sometimes likes to buy Jaco and me the same outfits. I never used to mind, but lately I've started to hate dressing the same as he does. It's better to be different, except with bunnilicks. With bunnilicks it's better to be identical so Jaco doesn't take the nicest kind.

I run back outside, sucking on mine already so it doesn't melt. Jaco has started playing Swingball with Erin, but he stops to come and take his bunnilick.

'Get Erin one, Simon,' he says.

Erin is nice so I go back inside and grab the last tropical bunnilick. I don't want her feeling left out.

We sit on crates, eating the icy pops in the wooden garden shed Pa made into a den. We don't talk much as the bunnilicks are too tasty, so I finish mine quickly just as Jaco jumps up.

'Hold this.' He passes me his bunnilick and moves over to Erin.

'Sit still, Erin.'

'Why?'

'You have the biggest grey spider on the shelf behind you I've ever seen.' He grabs a jar filled with nails, tips them out, then puts the jar upside down on the shelf behind Erin. Then he slides the jar to the edge to puts the lid back on.

'Urgh, thanks, Jaco.' Erin does a jig, even though the spider isn't on her, then we all go outside so Jaco can call Ma to show his catch.

'It looks like a rain spider. It's that time of year,' Ma says, peering at the spider in the jar. She's used to Jaco and his bugs.

'Where can I set it free?' Jaco asks her.

'How about in that bush? It's got the best branches for the biggest roses to sprout from,' Ma answers.

'Won't it prickle my spider?'

'No, spiders are clever navigators. I think it might be an interesting obstacle course for it.'

Jaco gently releases the spider on one of the lower branches. He watches it for so long by the time it's moved along the obstacle course into the middle of the bush, all that's left of his bunnilick is melted tropical juice pooled in the bottom of the wrapper.

A perky receptionist, who doesn't have reading materials about chrysanthemums and pot roasts anywhere in sight, gives us a warm smile and tells us to take a seat for a few minutes until Jonathan Travett arrives.

'Hi, I'm The CAD,' says Jonathan when he appears. He massages his ginger goatee, possibly because he's in pain from wearing trousers so tight he would have a camel toe if he were a woman. His bulging groin is so close I risk being poked in the eye, so I stand to get out of its way.

'It's a pleasure to finally meet you.' Cassie extends a hand. 'Don't you mind the nickname?'

'Let me tell you, those three little words solve all kinds of weird and wonderful issues. I could be a marriage counsellor if a reboot could be applied to dysfunctional couples. There's an unknown user accessing the system, press control, alt, delete. There's too little action causing a malfunction in the hard drive: control, alt, delete. Catch my drift?'

Cassie and I grin and follow him for a tour of the server room.

'You know pigeons work a treat for communicating without any bugs. They eat theirs instead,' he says.

I egg him on as he regales bad jokes of worms in the system and Trojan Horses riding the network, marvelling at the spaghetti junction of wires until we circle back to reception.

'Hi, I'm Revis, Luigi's assistant,' a striking oriental girl with high cheekbones and cherry-red lips interrupts. 'Luigi is ready for you now.'

The assistant is smartly dressed in a red jacket and black trousers. Her long jet-black hair is piled high on her head, reminding me of one of the much-photographed sentries guarding Buckingham Palace in fuzzy helmets.

'We should go see the changing of the guards while we're here in London,' I say to Cassie as we get to the CEO's office. Revis raps on the door and leaves us to it.

'Come.'

The Chairman is mid phone call but gives a curt nod to a pair of carved Louis XV chairs that look older than Donald. I settle on the claret velvet padding and realise the rest of us have mass-produced office furniture because all the profits of a lucrative technology recruitment company are being spent here.

'Do you think I've got the IQ of a carrot, you Scottish imbecile?' Luigi rants. 'Stop fudging the figures. You should send your report to me with a London Underground warning. *Mind the fucking gap.*'

It doesn't take a Mensa IQ to figure out he's talking to Donald, but I'm not fazed. People with a loud, foul mouth tend to be all talk and no action. It's the quiet ones to watch out for.

'Time is money.' Luigi rubs his fingers and thumb together.

We're all his worker bees, churning honey while he sits back, rolling in the sweetness of it all.

The mounted TV behind Luigi's head is tuned in to the stock market. Just as I am on the edge of my seat about fluctuating bank share prices, the chairman winds up the conversation. Ignoring Cassie, he throws me the kind of look you give when you tread in something sticky and have to turn up your shoe to find out exactly what it is.

'Hello sir, I'm Graham Coetzee.' As we shake hands, a glint draws my eye to his Swiss watch. Silver and expensive looking. The TITS founder grips me in a vice capable of leaving nutcrackers redundant, but I grip back, matching his force.

'I might have been on the dog and bone, sunshine, but I know who you are. The South African, yes?' he asks, pronouncing 'Saaf African' in a thick East London drawl. Only in the big smoke will you find an aging Italian with good looks and a Kray's mob accent.

'That's me.'

'You'll earn your keep if you stay focused and put a decent plant on your desk. That office north is a dodo.' He notices my confused frown. 'Extinct. Get Nancy to order some shrubs to bring it back to life.' He gestures his jungle of plants. 'The leaves keep oxygen and carbon dioxide levels steady and optimise brain power. And speaking of brain power, make sure you get your tickets from Revis for the dinner tonight.'

'What dinner?' I ask.

'We've a round table networking event. Since you're from out of town you might as well join us.'

'Sounds good.'

'The guest speaker is the former head of MI5.'

I blanch. Since I'm avoiding the law in South Africa and am not exactly an asset to British society, mingling with the homeland security service isn't something I'm overly enamoured about.

'I don't care how you do it but next time we meet make sure you've done a deal. You too, treacle.' He turns his attention to Cassie for the first time. 'Now get out.'

As we're dismissed from the lavish office like low-life picciotto in a well-oiled Mafia organisation, stress washes over my body. The thought of hanging out with MI5 makes my calf muscles tense, and I bump a delicate table standing on curvaceous legs against a wall lined with gilt-framed paintings.

'Be careful with my stuff or you'll be in Barney Rubble,' Luigi chastises.

I manage to escape without causing any damage to an antique collection that could give Queen Elizabeth a run for her money. Closing the door behind us, I take off my blue silk tie and shove it into my jacket pocket. I don't fit in here. My blond hair has grown an inch too long over my collar line and I refuse to carry a black leather compendium embossed with the TITS logo.

'What was that?' Cassie mutters under her breath.

'He's what I believe the Cockney's call chicken jalfrezi.'

'What?'

'Crazy.'

'Crazy … but genius. The Oracle could have warned us.'

'The Oracle?'

'Nancy. She's the Oracle of information in the Edinburgh office.'

'Yes, that she is, treacle.'

Cassie gives a throaty laugh. 'Does everyone in the recruitment business have to have a pseudo-identity?'

I contemplate this and nod.

Perhaps I'll fit in after all.

Chapter Fifteen

D inner is in Hyde Park in a vast marquee draped with fairy lights. It's a twinkling beacon beside Speakers' Corner where a scruffy man is spouting tales from his sacred Bible.

'Go ahead, I'll be there in a minute,' I tell Cassie.

'Don't take too long.'

I listen to the religious rant. Our family have always been churchgoers, always in our Sunday best, well-known in a close community full of faith. This peaceful existence, where the congregation looked out for one another, disappeared in my last few days there. People no longer looked out for me, they looked *at* me.

'There are no saints, only sinners,' the preacher continues his sermon. 'Your day of reckoning will come.'

The truth hurts. I'm so far astray from my religion I turn and walk away.

Climate warming is thriving inside the marquee from patio heaters dotted strategically around to counteract the winter chill. Round tables are spread with crisp white linen, set with enough cutlery to open a silverware factory. From between the bow ties and evening gowns, Cassie gives an animated wave. Neither of us packed clothing for such a glamorous occasion. I'm in the usual boring pinstripe suit. Cassie looks stunning though, in a simple red corporate dress that clashes magnificently with her auburn hair.

'We're on the same table as Dame Stella Rimington,' Cassie gushes when I reach her.

'Who?'

'She's the first female director general of MI5 Luigi was talking about. She's retired now, but what an honour. Can you believe it?'

I can't.

Of all the dining tables in London, Luigi had to put us here.

Cassie sits on a white chair that has been dressed in a white pullover with a purple bow around its middle. Reluctantly I follow cue as people gradually drift in. I can't breathe. Where are Luigi's plants when a man needs to balance the atmosphere's carbon dioxide and oxygen to stop hyperventilating?

With only a small amount of exposure to excessive CO_2 my breathing will become laboured and my eyes may water. I'll develop a headache, be overcome with dizziness and develop weak muscles. Eventually, if the toxic gas exceeds more than its normal percentage of the air, I'll vomit, pass out, and eventually, the respiratory distress will no longer be tolerable. I'll convulse and die on the chair that is wearing the white pullover and purple bow.

Cause of death: Carbon dioxide poisoning.

A judge introduces himself and sits across the table with Luigi. A strapping fellow in a sombre suit jazzed up with spotted bow tie takes his place next to me and informs me he's the Commissioner of Police for the London Metropolitan Police Service. On my other side, the Dame settles between me and Cassie, sandwiching me in.

The domino of lies I've told tumble in my head. One by one, I lay out each black tile, connecting the dots, knowing how important it is I'm not left knocking, clean out of moves. When my story is straight in my mind, I look at Cassie. Her skin is glowing as she rubs shoulders with the leaders who represent public safety and protect law-abiding citizens.

'I'm Graham Coetzee.' It's a struggle to pronounce every letter and syllable with precision when you have a mouth scratched with sandpaper.

The police chief asks me what I do. The judge asks where I'm from and why I left my home country. Sitting still is excruciating. It takes every ounce of energy to give acceptable answers without flinching.

Confidence radiates around the table as people make small talk and build a rapport. I smile at appropriate moments in-between eating an appetiser I don't taste and a main course I don't want.

Then Dame Stella takes to the podium. She's a formidable figure, with short, no-nonsense grey hair, a confident posture and assured delivery of her words. Silence falls in the tent as she shares insights into her days in the lower ranks of Britain's domestic intelligence agency. I start to relax. Her speech is saving me from more complicated questions from the police commissioner and judge.

Back in the sixties, Dame Stella Rimington became the first female director of MI5, working in a male-dominated environment and dealing with government figureheads. Her strength of character shines through as she talks. It's easy to see how she made it to the top of her game. She was in the thick of the action during the height of the IRA bombings, coming into the leadership seat a few years after Pan Am exploded over Lockerbie. It's humbling, being in a room with someone who has served her country for most of her life, saving countless lives through foiling sabotage, counterterrorism and counterespionage threats.

She talks about her husband and children, of work-life balance and the endless compromises made over the years. Of a crucial decision she had to make between getting informants out of the country alive or tending to one of her sick daughters in hospital. Of a classic Bond moment where she travelled through Russia in a limo after years of spying on them during the Cold War. Each tale is action packed as she elaborates on how she evolved from being a person to whom things happen to, to being someone who makes things happen.

Here's a lady who understands the impact decisions can have on others. She's used a fake identity, lived covertly, hidden parts of herself from friends, neighbours and colleagues.

I'm perversely fascinated and more than mildly terrified. We're so different, yet I too know what it's like to experience the impact of a split-second decision. There's so much to resonate with around the amount of intricate planning needed to assume another identity and what it takes each day to live with such a big lie. I'm enjoying her presentation as I sip my sparkling water and crack through the caramelised top of a crème brûlée with my silver spoon.

'Isn't she amazing?' Cassie whispers.

I nod as Dame Stella Rimington looks around the room. 'It's hard to be amidst a crowd of strangers and not evaluate everyone,' she says, sharing insights into her inability to break the habit of assessing everyone she meets. 'I have a knack of identifying the people who are having an affair by the clothes they're wearing or the watch on their arm,' she says to an enraptured audience. 'And I'm trained to notice someone who is hiding something, pretending to be someone they're not.'

I wipe my face with my napkin, mutter something about popping to the gents, then bolt.

Chapter Sixteen

Waiting staff dash from table to table, clearing plates and pouring coffee. Despite the early hour, the hotel breakfast room is packed with guests shovelling the most important meal of the day into their bodies.

'Two poached eggs, with bacon and toast, thanks,' I order.

'Same,' Cassie adds.

Her hair is tousled and even though an office relationship is out of the question, I can't help wondering what it would look like on the crisp white hotel bedding after a night's rest, or without any rest, for that matter.

Talent-IT Services are offering me a new life. Although I can't redeem myself for mistakes made, at least I can make every second count by helping ease the financial strain I've caused others. Jeopardising my job over Cassie isn't an option, and besides, she probably would never be interested in a messed-up bloke like me, and even if she was, I don't deserve someone so upbeat with everything going for her.

'That's twice you've left me in the lurch,' she says after our food arrives.

'Sorry. Sometimes I get huge panic attacks and need fresh air.'

'Yeah, I covered for you with Luigi after I realised you weren't coming back, but you could have text me about it.'

I take a bite of my toast.

'Something cool happened at end of the night.' Cassie fishes a paperback from her handbag. 'It's *Open Secret,* Dame Stella's autobiography. There was an auction after dinner to raise money for a charity she supports. I was the winning bid.' She passes the book over the table. 'It's for you. Not that you deserve it.'

'Seriously?'

'I thought you'd like it, what with your parents being librarians.'

'I can't believe you remembered that.'

'I'm a good listener.'

I read the blurb on the back of the book. 'Sounds a good read.'

'Anyone with secrets should try and be more open about them. It always works out better in the end.'

I wither under her stare. 'I can't take the book. It must've cost a fortune.'

'No choice. Look inside.'

I open the cover. On the inside page, the former director-general of MI5 has scribbled a note.

Graham,
'Remember, you only live twice.'
Dame Stella Rimington

The toast sticks in my throat.

It's not true.

When you're dead, you're dead.

Then I remember the faith instilled throughout my upbringing and the words we said as a family in church. The Nicene Creed talking of the resurrection of the dead and the life of the world to come. I give Cassie a smile which is genuinely grateful.

Open secret.

You only live twice.

***

After we complete the database training in head office, I take Cassie to Buckingham Palace to repay her for the book. We deserve some downtime now we're considered recruitment subject matter experts, equipped with all the critical skills needed to scavenge around Benny's complicated inner sanctum. He's our ancient candidate management system, but he's a beast. Benny chews up hundreds of applicants each week and spits out a select few when the keyword search is implicit in its instructions. To find that one magic candidate for the job, we've to treat Benny with respect.

I'm determined to treat Cassie with more respect too. I shouldn't keep leaving her stranded just because I'm swaying on the edge of a cliff, contemplating a jump into the abyss. It would be a sure way to join the afterlife. Although there are many variables effecting survival odds, when plummeting from an elevation of greater than twenty metres or so, death is inevitable. To have the best chance of death on impact I'll find a quiet spot somewhere to take a leap of faith from the loftiest of heights. I'll do my utmost to land headfirst. When falling at speed, with an abrupt halt, blood vessels tear, cells burst and the aorta from the heart will generally rip loose. The heart may beat for a few final seconds, massive internal bleeding will occur and death will transpire.

Cause of death: Falling from a height.

Allowing this psychotic mental state to thrive is exhausting. It would be so easy to check out. The alternative is to focus on Cassie's green eyes.

They make an effective harness, clamping me to the here and now.

***

We walk to our hotel in the heart of Bloomsbury, past the well-established gardens of Russell Square. Inside the revolving doors, Cassie and I separate to swap the pinstripes for jeans, then head for the tube. The journey along the Piccadilly Line is an experience, starting with the option of queuing for the lift or braving one hundred and seventy-five steps. We take the steps.

'Crikey, I'm unfit,' Cassie puffs as we wind down the concrete staircase into the earth's core.

'The air is thin and horrible down here.'

'It's the stairs. There's a lot!'

I remember the seventy-one steps winding through L'Agulhas Lighthouse.

Being a teenager in L'Agulhas is unique; a far cry from the mobile device and video game addicts who rarely leave the house. In this corner of South Africa, we have the Meisho Maru to braai at, the tidal pool to swim in and the lighthouse to ascend, all at the southernmost tip of Africa.

The red-and-white-striped lighthouse is in sight; standing tall since being commissioned in 1849, the second oldest still in operation in South Africa. It was originally fuelled by the tail fat of sheep, but these days it's powered with modern technology.

We cycle up to it and boeta pulls a wheelie before jumping off to chain up the bike. There's a serious problem of bike theft in our area as bicycles are such a common form of transportation for township residents.

'You look like you've stuck your finger in a socket,' I tell Jaco. The breeze in the air is picking up and since nobody around here wears helmets, his hair is long enough to be windswept. Mine is cut sensibly short, the same as Pa's.

He's already weaving up the path through the twenty-thousand-hectare L'Agulhas National Park to the entrance.

'Hurry,' he shouts. 'You've got the money.'

I catch up, eager to reach the ancient lighthouse. It's a vital sea beacon in this area, once condemned in the sixties for demolition after the crumbling sandstone walls were deemed unsafe. It was the locals who pleaded with the municipality to save her stripy skin. The government took over the upkeep and opened a museum, visitors gift shop and a restaurant inside her circular skirt to enjoy an espresso.

Once inside, we check the maritime displays with tributes to a bygone era of sunken ships. My favourite exhibits are of the ancient stone fish traps used centuries ago by the indigenous Khoisan people.

'Khoisan often retain genetic elements of the most ancient Homo sapiens. It's evidenced in their DNA and what gives them their first-people status,' Jaco says, rattling off a bunch of distinctive anatomical characteristics.

'Why are you so obsessed with health conditions?' I ask.

He shrugs and when we're done in the museum section, we ascend the twenty-seven-metre-high tower, bursting out next to the rotating optic that flashes every five seconds after dark. The three-hundred-and-sixty-degree vista is spectacular. We do a few circuits to take in the ocean, national park and our house.

'Look, Ma is hanging the washing.' Jaco looks into the distance.

She's in the back garden, pegging our clothes upside down, by the corners. She complains about how they take ages to dry when I throw them, folded in half, over the line.

'You can see Erin's house as well,' I tell Jaco.

'Spying on her is creepy,' he says.

'I wasn't spying on her. I was just saying you can see her house.'

Jaco ignores me as we watch activities on our street for a while longer, then wind back down through the circular interior where the air is thin and there's not much natural light.

Exhausted, we make it onto the Underground platform. Being this far below ground creates claustrophobic conditions, reminding me of being locked in a cell. It's easy to understand why many of the stations were great air-raid shelters during the World War.

Thankfully the train pulls in and we clamber on, only to find there are no seats. Gripping the nearest pole, we race through an aging warren of tunnels connecting Greater London and parts of the home counties of Buckinghamshire, Essex and Hertfordshire. We stop at busy central landmark stations such as Covent Garden and Piccadilly Circus. I'm reminded of Luigi's fudging conversation with Donald as commuters are instructed to *mind the gap* as they squeeze into every inch of carriage space on one of the busiest rapid transit systems in the world.

'Tell me more about the work competition,' I ask, squashed against Cassie. Our faces are so close I spot freckles peppering her nose I've not noticed before. They're pretty cute.

'There's some mystery around the prize. Nobody knows where it'll be yet, but I don't think anyone cares. Everyone gets a bit ruthless trying to protect their clients and carve out more new business to win a space. It's the prestige of being recognised as the top performer in the company.'

Cassie is right; defending your turf in the recruitment business is like protecting a rabbit from a circling flight of vultures. Given a chance, the scavengers will suck dry every last *hare* of nourishment.

It's even harder for newcomers like me to make a name for themselves in a saturated market. Boutique agencies in serviced office space and one-man bands operating from their garage are constantly opening. You don't need any formal qualifications to become a recruiter, so the industry attracts all kinds, good and bad; seasoned salespeople, used-car salesmen, people running from their past.

'Let's make a pact to win this thing,' Cassie says. 'We can beat Vermin.'

'Have you seen his Porsche? He paid for it in cash from placing a load of CIOs into their new gigs.'

'He only drives a car like that to hide other shortcomings.'

I laugh. 'You don't think he's in it for the love of the job?'

'There might be some agents fulfilled by helping someone take the next step on their career journey, but Vermin's not one of them.'

We arrive at Green Park Station and step out into an old platform with curved tiled walls.

'Urgh, speaking of Vermin, there's a rat,' Cassie baulks as the train pulls out. The rat scuttles along the track, following the throngs of people moving towards freedom.

Out in the street, we stop to listen to a busker playing 'One Love' on an acoustic guitar. He holds a note worth paying for, so I pull my own note from my wallet and drop it in his guitar case.

'That's pretty generous,' Cassie says.

'I love Bob Marley. Anyway, you can talk, splashing out on that book for me.'

'Consider me thanked,' she replies as we follow the foot traffic. 'Check out the palace up ahead.'

'Wow. South Africa has nothing remotely resembling a monarchy.'

We sit at the top of the Queen Victoria Memorial steps in front of the Palace gates. It's a vast marble monument commemorating Victoria's death in 1901, topped with a gilded bronze winged victory standing on a globe. The additional personification statues around the central pylon represent courage, constancy, motherhood, and confrontationally for me, truth and justice. I don't deserve to be next to this centrepiece, surrounded by intricately sculpted gardens, with a clever and radiant woman by my side.

We watch the wooden sentries on either side of the gates in their red and black outfits.

'They definitely look like Revis, Luigi's assistant,' I say. 'They must get fed up standing still for so long. Wonder if anyone ever does stuff to make them flinch?'

'I suspect it would be a quick way to wind up arrested.' She nods towards a couple of police officers patrolling the area on horseback.

I try not to flinch at the sight of them. 'You ready to go? There's only so long we can sit in the cold here.'

Cassie agrees so we double back and climb back on the Tube. 'Shall we grab something to eat?'

'Yah, let's get off now and walk to find something,' I reply, as the train pulls into Leicester Square. 'It's better than staying down here with the rats.'

We get off into an area brimming with energy. Slow-moving vehicles hoot their horns, neon billboards blink and street artists entertain on every corner. A mindless assault on the senses is exactly what I need.

I grab a map from a tourist information booth and figure out our route back to Bloomsbury. We pick up takeaway noodles and eat as we walk down Charing Cross Road. All manner of goods are for sale along the way. Second-hand books, vintage platform boots, hand-crafted jewellery. A lady, surrounded by wooden statues, catches my eye on the pavement. She's sitting cross-legged in front of her merchandise, her hair wrapped under an ethnic print scarf that matches her long traditional orange and brown African dress. Her dark face is kind, but behind the eyes is a vacuum. There are many African expats who have experienced trauma even more incomprehensible than mine.

'You want to buy?' she asks, noticing my interest.

'Where are you from?'

'Mozambique.' She points at her wares. 'I carve these by hand.'

'They're great.' Cassie hands me a small elephant. 'You should buy it.'

'This one too,' the seller urges, showing me a smooth figure void of features. 'It's the thinking man. You have to buy it for the man who knows what he wants in life and who executes on everything he does.'

I'm holding both statues now. The thinker and the elephant. One represents my brother with the brains, the other is me, the man who never forgets.

I pay for both inanimate objects and allow the African lady to bag them for me.

'Where are you going to put them?' Cassie enquires, as we come onto Shaftsbury Avenue.

'I've no idea. It's the first time I've bought anything like this for the flat.'

'Do you miss home?'

'Yah, I miss it. South Africa is a stunning country, but the history here is something else,' I say as we stroll past the British Museum.

The Greek revival style of the architecture provides an appropriate backdrop for an exhibition on Greek mythology that's the drawcard for the month ahead. The place is locked for the night, but it commands pride of place on Great Russell Street. This is a building far more forthcoming about making sure the past is visible than I am.

We cut a trail through the arctic air, eventually arriving back at the hotel.

'I'm glad we walked,' says Cassie as we enter the lobby.

'See you tomorrow.'

Cassie's cheeks are rosy; two strawberries nestled in a creamy complexion. I cast my eyes down to admire the marble flooring. 'We've an early morning start.'

'We have. Goodnight then.'

I'm rooted to the spot until she disappears into the elevator, then retire to the confinement of my own room to wallow in my own depression.

A card has been placed in the middle of the crisp white linen. It informs me I'm in the presence of a firm Heavenly Pillow that'll make me float into a divine slumber.

Perched on the edge of the bed, I open the bedside table. Inside is a Gideon Bible, so I gently close the drawer again without touching the holy book. I cried out to God for help in the moments that changed my life forever and he repudiated the miracle I asked for.

The only thing left to do in my room to kill the boredom rather than myself is browse through the leather-bound hotel directory. Telephone call prices are extortionate. It's lucky I've nobody to call.

Options exhausted, I collapse on the bed. It doesn't take long to realise a complaint with hotel management is justified.

The Heavenly Pillow promise of a restful sleep is false advertising.

Chapter Seventeen

T he empty tank is refuelled. Spending time in London with Cassie has been the gasoline needed to get me going again, to reconnect with gratitude and appreciation, even if it's clinging to the simpler things in life, like learning how to be an expert recruiter from The CAD. It's time to return to Edinburgh to put my new skills into action, propelling me forward into new earning brackets where I can capitalise on the Talent-IT commission structure. Sending funds back to South Africa gives me a sense of purpose. Of worth. Of hope.

Cassie wanders around the departure lounge shops while waiting for boarding to commence. She's carrying an oversized, bright pink handbag. Quirky like her.

I fixate on it to promote my good intentions to be more positive, doing everything possible to distract from the stomach cramps ravishing my gut. The bongo drum reverberates inside my skull.

We should have known better.

We should have known better.

We should have known better.

I sit hunched in a chair screwed to the floor, wondering if the airport planner got the design idea from a mental asylum. Crazy as some of us might be, who would steal a chair from the departure lounge? Not the kind of thing you can stash into the hand luggage rack with your bottle of duty free.

Am I crazy?

We should have known better.

We should have known better.

We should have known better.

A couple of seats away, a toddler with golden pigtails spills the belongings of her Dora the Explorer case on the floor. I jump to help her repack crayons and a teddy bear.

'Thanks,' says the girl's mum, cradling a baby in her lap.

'I can draw you a picture if you want?' says the little girl.

'That would be amazing.' The tug on my heartstrings is unbearable. She reminds me of the family I turned my back on. As she adds a plethora of colours to a rainbow with the wildest abandon, drifting outside the lines more often than she stays inside, she gives me much to be hopeful for.

***

'Dammit. I think I've locked myself out,' I say, rummaging in my backpack once we are off the flight and safely nestled in the back of a black cab. 'The CAD gave me a TITS keyring in London and I've gone and left my house keys on his desk. I'll have to get him to post them. I think my spare set is on my desk at work.'

'I've got office keys if you want to take a quick detour,' Cassie replies.

'Oh, what a relief. Do you mind?'

'No, let's go.'

The cab sets off, the heat of Cassie's thigh melting the fabric of my trousers to my skin.

As we pass Murrayfield Stadium, it's impossible not to think of the rugby tackles made over the years with my brother. At school he played fly half. Joel Stransky became his childhood hero in 1995 after his famous drop goal during the Springboks versus All Blacks final helped the team become world champions. Jaco, always on target. Me, I played hooker. Always in the scrum between the props, trying to intervene, getting in the way of play.

'How stunning is Edinburgh Castle at night?' Cassie says as we approach the city.

'It's pretty amazing. Now we've also seen Buckingham Palace, maybe we should take in a few more heritage buildings here.'

'Stirling is an option. There's another castle there and the William Wallace monument is also there. You've seen *Braveheart*, right?'

'Yah, weird how some people like William Wallace inspire multiple generations through history.'

'Nelson Mandela is like that,' says Cassie. 'Nobody will ever forget him.'

'True. The whole world was watching South Africa when he was released from custody.'

'Must've been good for the country.'

'He was revolutionary during my youth. When he was in charge, the government dismantled apartheid and began trying to stamp out institutionalised racism. There's still a massive gulf between the *have* and *have nots* though.'

The ferry to Robben Island is so bumpy a handful of tourists hang over the side to hurl at the fish.

'Watch your hat doesn't go overboard,' says Pa. He has one arm around Ma's shoulders, and she snuggles into him.

I cling onto my favourite Tony Hawk cap. It's old and scruffy but I'm invincible when I wear it.

When we reach the landmark island, we disembark and are shepherded onto a tour coach with all the other families doing the daytrip. Once we are all seated, it pulls off and trundles past the old wardens' living quarters and an area where the guide on the bus tells us Robert Sobukwe, the prominent South African political dissident, was kept in solitary confinement because of his radical anti-apartheid profiling.

Then we're escorted inside the prison by an ex-inmate. He talks of his riveting life as a political prisoner behind bars. Rather than bitter, he's factual about the severity of the conditions endured and I'm filled with empathy at the barbaric behaviour humans sometimes inflict on one another.

'Check it out.' Jaco pushes me into Mandela's cell. 'It's awesome.'

I shiver. It's damp inside with sparse furniture. Feels eerie. Ghosts everywhere, I bet. 'It would be hell to live in here.'

Jaco laughs. 'Yah, no TV to watch the rugby.'

I bolt from the cell as the tourists snap away with their cameras to capture the moment. Don't know why anyone would want to capture the 'have nots' of a dismal place like this.

The cab stops outside the office and the driver agrees to wait.

'I might as well grab my jacket while you fetch your keys. It's on the back of my chair.' Cassie climbs out and lets us into the office. 'Someone must be working late. The alarm's switched off.'

Leaving the lights off, we head upstairs to check the sales floor. Except for a flickering monitor, it's dark and devoid of life.

Bang.

'What the hell was that?' Cassie asks, grabbing her jacket.

I mentally remind myself this is not South Africa where you would get out of the place as fast as possible if you thought there were intruders around. Wanting to make sure there is no danger for Cassie, I refuse to allow myself to be intimidated as I grab my house keys before prowling around the office to locate the source of the noise. All manner of scenarios run through my mind. If it's a burglar, the police will end up getting involved and I'm doomed.

Cassie is following a few steps behind me when a grunt stops us in our tracks at the bottom of the stairs. I peek around the door leading into the boardroom reserved for internal and external meetings. A strong smell of perfume wafts up my nostrils and the glimpse of Vermin with his trousers around his ankles means tonight's session is categorically *internal*.

I stand stock-still, relieved there are no balaclava-wearing menaces to contend with. The room is dim but both silhouettes quickly come into focus. Vermin's naked backside is pounding his partner. The second dark-haired female is lying on the boardroom table, her legs snaked around Vermin's waist.

'Arghh, Marianne, Marianne!' Vermin hits a high note.

Welcoming the diversion, we exit undetected, leaving one full moon behind as we head back outdoors to stand under the light of another.

As we clamour back into the taxi, Cassie says, 'Was that who I think it was?'

'Marianne De Nunes, the Brazilian HR manager from Royal Celtic Bank. She's been into the office once or twice for meetings with Vermin. Only he would screw one of our biggest clients.'

'He's misinterpreting his obligation to provide a personnel service with a *personal* service.'

It feels good to laugh, even if it is at Vermin's expense.

Chapter Eighteen

'Do you know who was in here last night?' Nancy asks the minute I arrive at work the next morning. 'I was first in, and the alarm wasn't on.'

There's a reluctance on my part to get caught up in gossipmongering about last night's escapade, not least because news of such magnitude will have The Oracle tearing away at the details with more intensity than a piranha stripping it to the bare bones.

The bite of a piranha is one of the most forceful to be found in bony fish. The mighty power of their jaw muscles and finely serrated, interlocking teeth, enable them to not only nip the flesh, but to dilacerate strips off their prey. They viciously disarticulate soft tissue from hard bone, scavenging and skeletonising their victim to a bare carcass. The Oracle is a predator, able to work alone or in a shoal, hunting to satisfy an insatiable hunger.

Cause of death: Eaten by piranha.

'Sorry, I've no idea.' I walk past and take the stairs two at a time. I don't want the last vestiges of privacy torn away by Nancy, leaving me or any of my colleagues mauled and decaying before I've even had my morning coffee.

When I enter the cube farm, the team are playing a quiz. Vermin is sitting on his desk firing trivia to his rapturous participants who are sitting on their swivel seats in front of him.

'Marilyn Monroe!' Janine shouts.

'Not fair,' says Kevin. 'No man worth his salt would know that.'

'Don't undermine the quizmaster just because you're thick,' Janine fires back.

'It isn't you who will have to make the coffee for losing,' Kevin replies. 'It's muggins here, although maybe there is hope for me since we do have a latecomer.'

They all twirl to stare, judgemental of my unpunctual arrival. I pull up my own swivel and work hard to recoup lost ground, recalling my knowledge of sports, music and anatomy.

Kevin loses.

'See, even the new boy can beat you,' Janine gloats. 'It won't be long and he'll have overtaken you on the sales ladder too.'

We all look at the whiteboard. Vermin is still perched up top, but Cassie is catching up. Me, I'm in the gutter on all fronts, but although my personal life is irrecoverable, at least there's a chance I can crawl out of the professional sewer.

I enter my cube, grateful for the flimsy partitioning providing the illusion of seclusion. My walls look less blue from my collage of paraphernalia wallpaper, mostly CVs pinned up submitted by zany candidates.

Most recruitment agents won't entertain a wacky CV; the ones with five different fonts, multicoloured tables and bordered pages, mainly because they're too hard for Benny to digest. They're like sinew to Benny who chews them over and spits them out, all mushed up. He prefers processing candidates he can parse with ease, made up of ingredients of plain old Times New Roman and peppered with familiar buzz words.

I'm an SAP consultant.

I'm an SAP guru.

I used SAP yesterday, SAP today, SAP tomorrow.

SAP, SAP, SAP, SAP, SAP.

Submit.

My own technique when it comes to filtering applicants is to pay attention to the interests people disclose on their résumé. They provide different indicators of what their characters are like, not what degree has been obtained or what elite university they may or may not have attended. I've pinned the profile of Gustav Manfron on the partition between me and Cassie; he's a website designer who thinks collecting memorabilia from famous massacres is a hobby. I could send him forward for a position with the Ministry of Defence, but he's too macabre even for them. Then another who has blood donating under his favourite pastimes; perhaps an NHS job for him. Their technical skills are amazing, but whereabouts on the employment landscape I'm going to successfully place them is anyone's guess.

On my CV it should say resourcefulness as my top skill. It takes ingenuity to fool others into believing I'm someone I'm not. Reads better than deceitfulness.

I check on a candidate from the other side of the Firth of Forth who had a phone interview scheduled with Marianne De Nunes this morning.

'How did the interview go?' I say when the candidate answers my call.

'It didn't.'

'The bank didn't call you?'

'Dunno. I had to take my sheep to the vet.'

'A sheep?'

'Aye, one of them was sick, ye ken. It couldn't wait.'

'Erm, nope, I don't ken. Shall I reschedule?' I ask, regaining composure.

'Aye, anytime, except not t'day. I've to fetch Dolly at four.'

'Dolly?'

'Named after that cloned sheep in Edinburgh Museum.'

I got it wrong with this guy. His CV noted a love of animals under hobbies and interests, so I assumed he'd get on with Marianne who appears to be something of an animal herself.

'I'll get back to you.'

I put the phone down, knowing I've told the sheep lover a lie. He won't disappoint me twice. I might work in IT, but this guy takes *rams* to a whole new level. His brain is crammed full of Dolly's stuffing.

Cracking my knuckles, I wander to the window to glance over the manicured lawn of St Andrew Square. The resplendent Dundas House is visible from here, occupied by the Royal Celtic Bank. The building must be worth millions of pounds; an investment by the bank to portray their discernible age to the outside world. Inside, they crave an application modernisation face lift to introduce faster, smarter, smaller machines. Legacy hardware will go in the skip next to the retired chequebooks. Information will be routed to a place where 'the cloud' means something other than water particles in the atmosphere and 'Amazon' is quantum leaps away from the Brazilian rainforest. Banknotes are obsolete. Money is invisible. Credit cards are phasing out as 'pay pass' from a mobile device becomes the shiny new penny and crisp new pound. Marianne De Nunes is hiring people with first-class digital technology skills to automate business processes and make transactions contactless and more efficient. My candidate was going to be interviewed for a position to work on analytics, using big data and artificial intelligence to predict customer spending patterns before they even know what they want to purchase themselves.

'What's with the trance?' Cassie asks from behind me.

'I was trying to figure out how to tell Marianne why my candidate was a no-show.'

'Everything for a reason.'

I search for the silver lining in my *cloud,* but my brain is as stuffed and useless as Dolly's.

***

It's past dusk as the office winds down, rush hour long gone along with most of Scotland's workforce. Working late is part of the assignment brief of a recruiter, much like working early is a way of daily life for a baker. Candidates are more readily available to talk to their agent out of hours without worrying their boss might overhear them talking about bailing for a better gig.

A snoring body is lying in the doorway as Cassie and I leave. His grubby feet are bare and it's bitter outside. Although poverty is an issue in Scotland, local authorities seem to have a focus on preventative approaches. This is the first time I've witnessed homelessness firsthand since leaving South Africa where the housing deficit runs into the millions. I pull my wallet out and pass him a note.

'Buy food with it, mate.'

'That's the second time I've seen you be kind to a stranger,' Cassie says as we continue past him.

'Everyone has to eat.'

'Do you want to come back to mine for dinner then? Guessing you might be sick of eating alone.'

'Why not?'

***

We take the busy double-decker number five bus, full of workers in their office wear. Some are in suits. Plain black, navy, grey, pinstripes, some garishly thick and others discreetly thin. I'm part of the pinstripe scene now; a regular corporate citizen.

'You'll have to ignore my mother,' Cassie warns as we take up two seats at the back.

'Why?'

'She's a bit eccentric. I don't ever invite people over, to be honest.'

'I'm sure she's lovely.'

'Don't bank on it. Speaking of banks, how did you go in the end with Marianne and your no-show?'

'She sucked it up.'

'I bet she did.'

We both laugh at the innuendo.

'I see you made a placement today.'

'Two,' Cassie confirms with pride. 'I'm telling you; I'm going on that trip.'

'I know you will.'

I've seen that sense of drive in my brother too. After he smashed his Matric exams, Jaco sailed through medical studies and built up his medical accreditations. I never had that type of accolade or had a big flag on the hill like becoming a surgeon. Until I moved to Scotland, I was content repairing PCs in a place where everyone knows your business and it didn't occur to me to mind.

***

The high-rise block of council flats is an eyesore; its roughcast exterior peppered with boarded-up windows. The interior stairwell is covered in graffiti, more tagged vandalism than street mural art. Two teenagers ignore us, their eyes glazed as they inhale something from a plastic bag.

'It's not quite Buckingham Palace, but still, it's home,' Cassie proclaims. 'I got mugged a few months back coming home from work. Nothing serious.'

Her upbeat attitude is sobering. I've been so caught up in my own self-absorption I've rarely stopped to consider others might have problems.

We take a lift to the fourteenth floor and pass several identical front doors on the walkway before we reach her entrance.

'I'm home,' Cassie calls as she lets herself in.

There's no answer as she leads me into a small front lounge where black-and-white footage of Ella Fitzgerald crooning is on TV. Glued to the set is a scrawny lady sipping on a cup of tea in a tracksuit and velvet slippers.

'This is Graham from work, Mum.'

She jumps and slops her drink over herself, before glaring at Cassie. 'You should have said you were bringing someone home.'

'It was last minute.'

'Nice to meet you, Mrs Walker,' I say to break the ice.

'It's not Mrs. Just Margarita. There's no man in this house.' She offers a thin smile that doesn't quite reach the sadness of her eyes. Her head is topped with the same lovely natural auburn of Cassie's curls.

We hover beside an electric fireplace transmitting a surprising amount of heat, its lights flickering over fake lumps of coal. There are no family photos on the mantelpiece above it, just a small gilt clock ticking loudly, despite Ella trying her best to drown it out with her jazz.

My own mother has hundreds of family snaps lovingly presented in albums. Several, blown up and framed, adorn our lounge walls, each one capturing a moment in time from our childhood. Me on the first day at school, Erin on prom night, Jaco holding his medical school acceptance letter.

'We're going to grab something to eat. Do you want something?' Cassie asks Margarita.

'Another cup of tea since this one spilled.'

Cassie and I back out of the room and cover the few metres to a long kitchen with tiles patterned with country baskets filled with fruit.

She puts the kettle on, rummages in the cupboard and gives an apologetic shrug. 'Beans on toast?'

'One of my culinary favourites.'

She pours a tin into a pot and passes me a wooden spoon. 'You can stir while I sort the drinks.'

She finishes making the tea and disappears to deliver a steaming mug to her mother. Although I don't mean to eavesdrop, it's impossible not to overhear them.

'Why are you dressed up to the nines?'

'I'm hardly dressed up,' Cassie says.

Ella Fitzgerald begins to sing another one of her classics, *'I'm gonna wash that man right outta my hair ... '*

'You don't want to be washing ne' fella out of your hair, Cassie.'

'He's a friend from work, that's all.'

'Watch out for those fancy work people and big work ideas.'

'There's nothing wrong with doing something more with myself.'

'I'm just saying, no good ever came from having airs and graces.

I've been packing supermarket shelves for thirty years and it's done us alright.'

Cassie appears again in the kitchen, sombre as her navy-blue suit and court shoes.

'I'm not the only one with problems with my ma then,' I say. Cassie turns red and I instantly regret tactlessly verbalising my realisation. 'Sorry, I didn't mean to put my foot in it. I just meant I've a few problems of my own back at home.'

'You want to talk about it?' she asks.

'Not right now.'

'Me neither.'

We take our plates to her bedroom. 'Tuck in. I mean to the food.' She indicates the single bed.

I chuckle and shuffle against several plump colourful cushions. They provide a padded safe haven in an otherwise cold house.

'You going to the Christmas party tomorrow?' she asks.

'Obliged to, I suppose.'

'I'll be there.'

'Good.'

'Sorry about my mother.'

'No need to apologise.'

Cassie is next to me, our backs against her bedroom wall. She looks forlorn amidst the ethnic cushions. Buried in their eclectic brightness when she deserves to shine with life.

I plough through my beans on toast. 'You're a good cook.'

She smiles. 'I'm glad you came over.'

'Me too.'

I don't add it's the best night out I've had in a long time. In fact, if the truth be known, it's the *only* night out I've had since moving to Scotland.

Chapter Nineteen

T he venue of our Christmas party is a thirteenth-century for-
tress set in several acres of wooded parkland on the pictur-
esque banks of the River Esk. The stone walls of Dalhousie Castle
tower in splendour and are covered in moss. Slats of light glow
from narrow rectangular windows. I'm glad they look welcoming as
centuries ago people were sometimes ruthlessly tossed from castle
windows in punishment for wrongdoings. The act of jumping from
a window has continued to grow in trend as a popular modern
suicide method, and I don't want to dwell on such morbid thoughts
this evening.

Cause of death: Self-defenestration.

'Wow.' Cassie gasps as we disembark the minibus that transported us from the office. 'I can't wait to see the rest of this place.
I'm like The Little Match Girl, used to nothing.'

'Stunning.' It's impossible not to stare at Cassie who looks
incredible in a floor-length halter-neck black dress that cuts low on
the chest. The image of that prom picture of Erin that hangs on the

lounge wall back home rears up in my mind. Black dress, corsage tied to her wrist, huge smile.

Ma painstakingly surrounds the white rose she clipped from the garden with baby's breath and ties the bundle together with white ribbon. She trims the ends of the ribbon and dabbles the edges with clear nail polish.

'Stops the corsage ties from fraying,' she says. 'It needs to last the whole night on her arm.'

When she's done, she sweeps the trimmed leaves and a few loose rose petals into the kitchen bin and stands back to admire her handiwork.

'You only get one prom, so we need to get lots of photos of Erin wearing it,' Ma says as I pack away the scissors in the top kitchen drawer and head outside with Jaco to toss the rugby ball for a while.

'You're shivering,' says Cassie. 'It's freezing isn't it, but do you mind if we have a quick look at the market before we go inside?' She looks at a row of stalls set up in the gardens selling all manner of Christmas wares.

'It would be rude not to. You look great, by the way. New dress?'

'No, it's just something I had hanging in my wardrobe.'

'Shame you forgot to remove the price.' I reach behind her and swiftly snap the offending tag off her gown.

'How embarrassing,' Cassie laughs.

'Here, take this. You need it more than I do.' I remove my jacket and wrap it around her shoulders as we stroll around the market. Several stalls are under a huge wooden A-frame roof, showcasing everything from Christmas stockings to mulled wine spices. 'Do you think it might snow?'

Cassie picks up a brightly painted bauble to admire the snowman on the front, then looks up at the early December sky. It's unusually clear and filled with stars. 'Nah, it's too cold to snow.'

'What the heck does that mean?' I ask, perplexed.

'It's too dry even though it's well below zero degrees. Trust me; it's not going to snow today.' She places the bauble back again.

'I've never seen snow.'

'It's not all it's cracked up to be. Once the powder has gone, all that remains is grey slush to wade through.'

'Sounds bleak.'

'You know, some people in Scotland suffer from SAD? It's depression from the cold.'

'I suppose there's not always that much to laugh about, is there?'

'No. There's not.'

The bluntness of Cassie's response is out of character with her usual chirpy persona.

'You okay?'

'Nothing to do with the weather, but I just find Christmas a bit depressing.'

'How come?'

'Dad left us on Boxing Day. He accidently stood on my new baby doll he'd given me for Christmas the day before and my mother lost the plot with him and me. I copped a black-and-blue backside off her for leaving it on the floor and Dad told her to back off, so she threw the doll at him. It somehow cut him under the eye. I'll never forget it.'

'That's heavy, Cassie.'

'She never got over him.'

'Where's he now?'

'My mother heard from someone that he went back to Western Australia to work offshore somewhere.'

'How come she didn't go back to Australia after they broke up?'

'There was nothing to go back for. Her parents are dead now

and she's an only child. She was probably worried her old friends would judge her, or that she might run into Dad with another woman.'

Transfixed, I stare at her, looking to see if my own reflected pain is muddled with hers. It's not. Her green eyes convey a strength I want to channel back my way so I can replenish my own resilience. The wind picks up and I catch a whiff of her perfume mixed with the intoxicating scent of roasted chestnuts.

'The smell of this market is awesome,' I say, needing the diversion of turning to the nearest stall. I lift a hand-carved angel from the stand. 'Look at this.'

'That's a pretty special piece.'

'I have to buy it,' I say, not elaborating any further.

I know just the girl to give this to one day. It's simply a matter of timing.

***

The tartan-kilted bagpiper beginning to belt out 'Scotland the Brave' is our cue to leave the market behind and make our way along the red carpet, through the grand arched castle entrance. We're ushered inside by a hostess who directs us to the 'secret bar' hidden inside the library and offers us a pre-dinner bubbly.

'Could I order a glass of milk, thanks?' I ask.

'Pardon, sir?'

'Would it be possible to have a glass of milk? I'm not a champagne drinker.'

'Erm, of course,' the hostess stammers, hurrying off.

'What are you, a bloody cow?' Janine jibes.

'I just don't drink anymore.'

'Moo la la.'

'You coming to sit at the restaurant table?' Cassie intervenes.

'You read my mind,' I reply. 'Let's get our drinks though.'

We wait in silence until the waitress reappears with my milk.

'He'll drink that until the cows come home.' Janine hoots at her own wittiness.

I walk away with Cassie. Janine can stab at me all day, like a fork trying to prod through the crispy jacket of a baked potato to encourage steam to escape. I won't give her the satisfaction of knifing her back.

***

Christmas dinner is a surreal affair, held in an ancient, vaulted dungeon only accessible by passing several worn flags hung in an ancient stone stairway. Dramatic shadows heighten the atmosphere, casting darkness across the burnished steel knight's armour standing in the corner of the room.

I google the castle's history and am not surprised to find several Kings and noble Earls have all stayed within its thick walls. The dungeon here is notorious too. A rope was used once to lower prisoners into the confined space which has a ventilation shaft but no window, ensuring they were deprived of an escape route.

On top of feeling enclosed, I have to contain my irritation as Vermin's phone vibrates several times on the table. A headshot of Marianne De Nunes pops up and he eventually picks up the device to message.

We're the generation of repetitive stress injuries to thumbs as we ask each other *WhatsApp?* Facebook removes the need for verbal conversation to stay in touch with friends. Smiley emojis replace the sound of real deep-belly laughter.

LOL – I'm bucking the trend. The only way to contact me

is by post, and letterboxes are going out of fashion as fast as red telephone boxes. Not a soul in this country even knows my real name. I sip my milk but it's already turning warm, slowly curdling with my thoughts.

'That's what I'm talking about,' Vermin gloats. 'I've made my whole monthly target from one sale.'

'Do you have to rub our noses in it?' Janine asks.

'I'm the early bird that caught the worm.'

'Go tweet somewhere else,' she tells Vermin.

'You look like a canary yourself in those yellow shoes.'

'You dig these shoes,' Janine retorts.

Donald turns to Kevin. 'What about you? Have you kicked any goals this month?'

Kevin shrugs. 'No placements yet unfortunately.'

'I'll give you some match-winning tips if you need them,' says Vermin. 'I'm better than Beckham ever was on the ball.' There's a united groan so he stands and takes a bow.

'I hope some of his confidence rubs off on you.' Donald gives Kevin a stern look. 'I'm expecting a visit from Luigi soon.'

Kevin splutters on his pint. 'To Edinburgh?'

'So it seems.' Donald's grin doesn't quite reach his eyes.

'When?'

'Anyone's guess.'

We all fall silent as our food is delivered to the table in alternate servings.

'What's this?' Cassie whispers to me.

'Tuna.'

'But it's raw.'

'We can swap.'

'You don't have to do that.'

'I love fresh fish.'

'This isn't fresh, its gills are still flapping. But if you're sure, I'll do anything not to have to eat this.'

'Anything?' I raise an eyebrow.

'Depends.'

'On what?'

'On whether you'll be stinking of fish.'

I chuckle as we change plates.

***

After dinner there's music and ceilidh dancing with various diners weaving between partners as if navigating a landmine site.

If a bomb were concealed beneath the floor, it would be dangerous for every one of us. I could say the wrong thing. Do the wrong thing. Put my foot in it. Feel the pressure beneath my sole before the explosive detonates, ripping me into fragments.

Cause of death: Primary blast total body disruption.

I'd have preferred to watch the whole tricky business from the sidelines, but Cassie drags me up by both hands.

'All I can manage is a little langarm,' I say.

'*Langarm?*'

'Afrikaans for barn dancing.'

'Then you should have rhythm.' She hooks an arm through mine, swinging me around as one song blends in to the next. We go faster and faster and I pause to loosen my bow tie. Cassie tugs it off and hurls it across the floor. I thank her by standing on her toes.

'Sorry, I'm two left feet in a rented tuxedo.'

'Keep practising. I need a quick break to make a pee.'

'Too much info, but I also need to go.'

Despite not being the most coordinated dancer, I don't want to part from her. She looks sublimely wild, hair pinned up, with a few damp curls loosely framing rosy cheeks.

'I'll meet you back here in a minute.'

Cassie heads off towards the bathroom with me lagging a minute or so behind. When I get to the facilities, Cassie is hovering outside. She beckons me to follow her into the ladies.

'Come in here and listen,' she whispers.

'Why?'

'Just come in.'

When I get into the bathroom, I hear a grunt from Vermin coming from inside one of the cubicles. 'Go baby, go.'

Cassie bends to peer under the gap between the door and the floor. When she straightens up, she motions for me to leave.

'Marianne?' I ask once outside of the bathroom.

She shakes her head. 'Yellow shoes. I honestly don't know what women see in him.'

'Ah, that explains why he's always throwing weird remarks at Janine,' I reply as a passing lady accidently knocks Cassie into me.

Cassie grasps me to steady herself and her face is inches from mine. She softly runs her thumb down the side of my forehead, wiping away a bead of sweat. I swat away her hand and jerk back.

Cassie turns to walk away but then stops and looks back. 'Now I know why you swapped the tuna. You're a cold fish.'

She flounces away, taking her dignity with her because I cannot offer her anything else.

***

Keen to avoid both minibus and peers, I call a taxi and do a runner back to my flat. I needed to put some distance between me and Cassie, and now I'm home I yearn to be back at the Christmas party. What a tosser I am, encouraging mindless flirting one minute and shutting her down the next.

You're a cold fish.

You're a cold fish.

You're a cold fish.

The radiators are off, so I rub my hands to get my blood circulating, then flick on the television that came with the flat inventory. A blurred re-run of *E.T.* is on. The aerial bares a strong resemblance to an outer space contraption, and I fiddle with the wire frame. E.T. comes into focus, appearing larger than life as he tries to phone home. I know I should do the same but the television, like me, protests with a crackle.

For a split second I thought Cassie was going to kiss me. A huge part of me is disappointed not to have let her, but disengagement is best for everyone. Distractions at work wouldn't be good for either of us. I don't want to be the emotional baggage wearing her sunny disposition down. An image of what she would look like peeled out of that dress pops into my head. She would be like hot buttery toast in the morning, waiting to be devoured, but I'm burnt goods. I'm the damaged black bits of overdone toast you want to scrape off with your knife because they leave a bad taste in the mouth.

Stripping off my clothes, I take a shower. There's not nearly enough power in the water jets to wash away my desire for her. I don't fantasise about women all day. There are no naked Playboy Bunnies taped to my wall or porn flicks stashed under my spring mattress. I can count my past girlfriends on one hand. Cassie just seems to constantly play havoc with my testosterone. Despite the temperature in my flat being sub-zero, I turn the shower to the coldest setting and try not to imagine screwing a beautiful girl from work in a cubicle shouting, 'Go, baby, go.'

Chapter Twenty

Monday morning in the office, Vermin pats his knee as if he's Santa Claus beckoning a child to share their Christmas list.

'Come here, Cassie.'

'What do you want, Vermin?'

'I'll settle for a cup of tea. Go, baby, go,' Vermin says.

Cassie looks at me and grimaces, before pushing back on him. 'What do you think I am, a teapot?'

'No, two jugs.'

'Cut it out,' I pipe up.

'Who rattled your cage?' Vermin asks.

'You know where the kettle is, that's all.'

Vermin straightens the knot in his tie. 'I work seven days a week to keep you all in a job.'

'Yah, right. There's more chance of seeing you coming over the threshold with a Russian bride over your shoulder than coming into the office to work on a weekend.'

'Graham, is it you who took it?' Janine suddenly bellows from her cube.

'Took what?'

'It's the third time this month it's gone from my desk.'

'What are you carrying on about, Janine?'

'My pencil sharpener. I'll find it myself.'

She appears in my cube and tips over my desk tidy.

'This is my sharpener, Graham.'

'How do you know it's yours?'

'That.' Janine points to the blob of red nail varnish on the sharpener, glowering like the X on the door of a plague-infected home. 'Thief.'

'I must have borrowed it,' I shrug. I may be a criminal but I'm not a thief.

She stomps off, pencil sharpener clenched in mitt, while I feign superficial shame and begin the methodical job of searching Benny for potential candidates.

I place a few calls and try to build a rapport with some candidates to raise the bar on my performance ratios. Simple mathematics apply to lodging enough CVs with clients to generate interviews, that in turn result in offers. It's like churning through enough Wonka Bars to win a golden ticket to the chocolate factory. Some agents throw so much chocolate at the wall something eventually sticks, but I prefer to peel off the wrapper to check the flavour, texture and ingredients, ensuring it will stimulate the taste buds of the client. Even though it's time-consuming, I also like to book appointments for candidates to meet me face to face, to make sure they're not going to melt along the way.

One such Wonka Bar is shown into the boardroom. She dabs at an everlasting-gobstopper-sized red nose with a handkerchief, as she debriefs me on the outcome of her interview with the bank.

'Sorry, I've a stonking cold.'

'I didn't realise you were sick. We could have rescheduled.'

'I had to come in and tell you myself. I got the job!'

'Fantastic.'

Her eyes well up. 'I needed this. My husband's gone and I'm trying to put the kids through university.'

The candidate hugs me and against the odds, I feel like a winner. Like Charlie.

***

The cork bounces off the ceiling and Donald pours champagne into flutes, which Nancy passes around the team. I grab my mug of black coffee instead.

'To Graham and his opening placement,' Donald toasts, raising his glass. 'How does it feel?'

'I'm thrilled I found a single mother the job she wants.'

The compliments fly as I mark my first tally on the whiteboard in green marker.

'How about dinner tonight to celebrate?' Cassie asks. 'You pick the place.'

Our friendship has felt strained since Dalhousie Castle, so I'm glad she's asked. 'You're on. I'll take you to my local Indian.'

'Oops, my bad. I've just remembered it's my mother's birthday. Another night?'

'Bring her too.'

'I'm not sure how she'll go with Indian cuisine.'

'Try her. She might love it.'

***

For the first time since joining TIT, I've accomplished something, by getting a woman a job which will help her navigate through a tricky spell in her life. It prompts me to think about my Pa's words as I begin the stiff walk from St Andrew Square to my flat on Royston Street.

Maak elke sekonde tel.

The lights are already on across town; lampposts ablaze with wattage, shop windows brightly lit to entice buyers, headlights glaring from cars packing the roads in rush hour. We take so many things for granted. Some of the townships in South Africa don't even have running water, let alone electricity. It gets dark quicker here than there during winter, partly as a result of human intervention – tampering with the clocks to implement daylight savings. I wish I could tamper with time and flip it backwards and forwards with such ease, but I can't and it's high time I make an attempt to stop wallowing in my own pity and practice more gratitude. I'm right here, right now, outside a public phone booth.

As I open the door, the stench of urine is overwhelming and I quickly close it again. It's a shame my flat doesn't have a landline, and my mobile package covers local calls only. One can assume Luigi is as fanatical about reviewing itemised company phone bills as he is about personally checking and signing off on the detailed breakdown of monthly commission statements, so I can't risk making the call from work either. Besides, it's not something I want to do with colleagues within earshot. So, I try again, stepping into urine fumes because I cannot put the call off any longer. I drop all my change into the slot, each coin deafening as it jangles through the system, then I press each familiar digit slowly.

Pa answers after two rings. 'Hello.'

I'm relieved it's not my mother. Seeing her crumble before I left was unbearable. I'm ashamed I did that to her.

'It's me, Pa.' I fiddle with the cord, wondering if the prevailing pause is a result of the long-distance nature of the call or the pro-longed deeper tension.

Finally, he speaks. 'It's been so long.'

'I should have called sooner. How are you?'

'I'm okay. How's Scotland?'

'Cold, but the city is beautiful, and work is okay.'

'I'm glad.' There's another silence, neither of us knowing what to say.

'How's Ma?' I ask eventually.

'She doesn't talk too much but she's back at the library now. She's working today.'

'Tell her I wish her a merry Christmas.'

'I will.'

'Have you heard anything from the police?'

'Officer Peterson stopped by a couple of times wanting to talk to you, but I said you were out.'

My blood runs cold.

'I called Nick Boshoff and he told me not to worry about it.'

'That's good, I guess.'

'Be careful.'

'I will.'

And he's gone with a click.

Walking the remainder of the way home, I dissect the conversation line by line until there's nothing left but the hollow vacuum accentuating the things I should have said.

I didn't have a chance to talk to him about Jaco, and I should have asked after Erin, but it would have upset Pa who's always loved her like the daughter he and Ma never had. I contemplate calling back, but it's easier to leave my backbone at large.

Chapter Twenty-One

Margarita sniffs the air with a tinge of disdain as she and Cassie are escorted by Lucky Rampal across the gaudy patterned carpet to where I'm sitting. 'I don't know if I can eat anything from here.'

'Don't worry, madam. You will like.' Lucky hands Margarita an open menu.

'You serve goat? I've never seen goat on a menu before.'

'Will you please just give the food a try?' Cassie asks, cheeks glowing.

'Perhaps madam would like to try a vegetarian dish, yes?' Lucky suggests. 'We have a chickpea curry.'

'I don't know about chickpeas. I like processed peas.'

'So sorry, madam. We do not have processed food on the menu.'

'In that case, just chips please. And maybe a plain chicken curry.'

He bows and scurries off.

'I should have wished you happy birthday by now, Margarita,' I say.

'This is for you,' Cassie presents her mother with a small giftbox.

Margarita peers at the silver earrings inside. 'Thank you,' she says, before snapping the box closed and dropping it in her handbag.

'Graham is also celebrating making his first placement today,' Cassie tells her. 'He'll be catching me up in no time.'

'You know, Cassie was once fired from her job at McDonald's,' Margarita throws out of nowhere.

'I was sixteen!' Cassie exclaims. 'It's not as bad as it sounds, Graham. A lady came in with no shoes on, looking ragged, so I donated a burger to her on the house. The manager watched the whole episode on CCTV and that was the end of that job. Refilling ink cartridges came after McDonald's.'

I smile. 'I'd make your toes curl if I told you about the mistakes I've made.'

'You should tell me about it sometime. You know, I'm determined to make something of myself at Talent.' Cassie turns back to Margarita. 'I was thinking of saving so we can take a break somewhere, maybe the Lake District.'

'It's probably not good timing. I've been meaning to tell you, I've met someone. His name is George Lauren-Baxter and he owns Philatelic Pennies. It's a rare stamp auctioneering company.'

'What happened to the no men policy?' Cassie asks her mum.

'Don't be cheeky. I was stocking the shelves at work and met him in the aisle. I could see his groceries in the basket were all the things I like.'

'Quite compatible then,' Cassie quips.

'He's offered me a job managing their mailing list and distributing auction catalogues and the items people buy.'

'Be careful dating someone you work with,' Cassie cautions.

'My sentiments exactly,' I add, instantly regretting it as Cassie gives me a wilting glare.

'George is coming over for Christmas lunch.'

'I could invite Graham to even the numbers?'

'Fine, as long as you chip in extra on the rent. Turkey doesn't come cheap.'

Cassie's jaw drops open.

'I thought you said you were having Christmas lunch with me this year?' I give Cassie a disarming smile.

Cassie's eyes well up. 'That's right. I am.'

I want to reach out and squeeze her hand, but Lucky arrives with steaming dishes of food.

Erin cried the day I left South Africa, mascara streaking down her cheeks.

So black.

Everything so black.

Chapter Twenty-Two

'Luigi's in the boardroom with Donald,' Nancy hisses the next morning.

'So?'

She looks at me like I'm insane, which is potentially the case, but not because the boss is in town. 'We weren't expecting him yet.'

Upstairs, the place is busy for such an early hour, with Cassie and Janine on the phone loudly negotiating with candidates and Vermin scribbling his latest deal on the whiteboard.

Lorraine grabs a bunch of corporate brochures under her arm the second Luigi strides into the room. 'Clients love this marketing material. Got to go. I'm trying to squeeze in a deal today.' She breezes out.

Luigi stares at the whiteboard results, then shifts his glare to Kevin. 'With those results, why are you not out at meetings like Lorraine?'

'It's been a quiet month,' Kevin replies.

'What do you think this is for?' Luigi lifts Kevin's phone and tugs it from the socket. 'I might as well stop paying the bill, *capisce?*'

'I did make a placement, but it went pear-shaped.'

'What happened?'

'My candidate took a counteroffer.'

'And you didn't have a backup ready?'

'I'm hopefully—'

'Hope is not a strategy. You need to play it safe with using reliable candidates, otherwise you let customers down. Go for a walk to clear your head and start thinking about how to get back on target.'

Kevin darts for the door.

'And you again.' Luigi shakes Cassie's hand as she finishes her phone call. 'Thankfully your placements are not too bad. You'll do better if you look after your foliage. This palm is thirsty, no?' He rubs a dry leaf on her desk plant between finger and thumb. 'I told you, plants generate oxygen and feed your brain.' He turns to me. 'And what good news have you got?'

'I made my first placement yesterday.'

'Great. You're finally getting past the gatekeepers. Do you know how I made it to where I am today?'

'On a business class flight.'

Luigi bursts into laughter. 'You Saaf African, you're funny you are. I was eighteen when we came to London from Italy. My parents opened a restaurant.' Luigi pulls Kevin's empty seat into my cube and sits. 'I worked hard to keep my father happy. He was a proud man, you know.'

The Godfather's decapitated horse head scene pops in my head. Sometimes a father will do anything to protect his family and a son will do anything to keep him happy in return. Pa burned my bloodstained clothes at Meisho Maru to protect me from Dr Beetroot and I fled without question because he asked me to.

'Let me google the old restaurant.' Luigi pulls out his phone and taps away. 'What's wrong with the internet in here?'

'The wi-fi plays up all the time.'

'Get The CAD on the dog and bone!' He picks up my landline and dials. 'What kind of a technology specialist are you? I'm sitting here in Edinburgh and there's no wi-fi. Are we supposed to send messages via pigeon?'

I feel sorry for The CAD who is no doubt giving excuses down the line.

'I've had enough of this place for one day.' Luigi gets up to storm out but throws a parting comment. 'Keep making placements with those perfect candidates. No mistakes. Only you can spread your wings and fly.'

I've already flown the nest, but I get his point.

'Poor Kevin,' Cassie says, coming into my cube.

'How are we supposed to play it safe when searching for the perfect candidate match?' I ask.

Vermin pipes up. 'Better put a condom on before entering Benny.'

'Ignore him,' Cassie says. 'We just need to use harsher interrogation techniques. Play bad cop a bit more to weed out any applicants telling us porkies.'

'Maybe their lies aren't malicious,' I say. She gives me a quizzical look and I realise how defensive I sound. 'I mean, they could just be trying to smooth over challenging circumstances.'

'I guess. Anyway, there's drinks after work if you want to come. I've been meaning to say thanks for offering to bail me out from an expensive turkey lunch with my mother. I've a bit of a weird relationship with her.'

'Haven't we all.' Her heady scent of old-fashioned soap is wafting around my cube.

'What are your parents like?' she asks.

'My mother is normal. You know, clapped too much at every school play.'

'And your dad?'

'Pa loves fishing but sometimes throws his catch back in the water when he thinks nobody is looking.'

'He sounds nice. No skeletons in your closet then?'

'The opposite. There's no space for linen.'

'How come?'

I shrug and she retreats to her cube, taking the smell of soap with her.

***

Donald buys the first round of wine by the bottle in Wolfie's, a minimalist new venue on George Street. 'Luigi was impressed with you all.'

'Hardly,' Kevin retorts.

'The chairman just likes to keep you on your toes.'

'I wasn't on my toes. I've been on all fours trying to sort my phone cables out.'

'He's old school, that's all. Likes you to make use of the phone. He approved funding for a stand at the Scottish Recruitment Fair before he left. It's a while away but we'll also be attending the Grand National.'

Vermin cheers and orders a round of Irn-Bru and vodka. I stick to the tutti-fruity flavours of plain Irn-Bru.

The floor space begins to fill with Edinburgh's yuppies who are perhaps attracted by the appeal of dual-sex bathrooms and transparent furniture. A DJ has set up at one end of the bar, mixing eighties trance and sending lasers beaming around the place.

'Let's dance,' says Cassie.

'Not in my repertoire of skills.'

'I know this music is cheesy, but you had a few moves at Dalhousie.' Cassie holds out her hand.

'I said no.'

She flinches. 'It was only a dance.' She moves off to pull Kevin up instead.

I gulp down the rest of my Irn-Bru. 'See you all Monday.'

'Never mind seeing us on Monday. Have you seen them?' Janine flicks her head towards the dance floor.

Kevin's fingers grasp Cassie's curls as he moves his lips towards hers.

The room blurs into a kaleidoscope of colours. I stumble into the labyrinth of the Edinburgh night to find snow drifting onto the wet pavement where it disintegrates.

I should run inside and grab Cassie so she can share the moment I see snow for the first time, but I'm rooted to the spot, head upturned. Soft flakes land on my face, in my eyes, in my mouth.

I tell myself I'm only uptight because of my insulated upbringing. Where I'm from in South Africa, even all these years after abolishing apartheid, it's unusual to see mixed-race couples. In our small community, most people marry a flame from the immediate community; someone from school, a friend of the family, the girl next door. Erin, three doors down from our house.

I'm kidding myself. Pa always taught me and Jaco that we are all equals in God's eyes. Race is not the issue. I don't care a hoot that Kevin is black and Cassie is white. He's a good guy. The truth is, I like her. Cassie is not the girl next door. She's not Erin. But she is the girl that's too good for me.

I wanted to dance.

I wanted to dance with her.

How can I dance when all I want to do is die?

The snow picks up momentum and turns into a blizzard. I rub the snowflakes from my head and stroll on, angry for not hanging around to see if Cassie reciprocates Kevin's advances.

I should have danced.

I should have danced.

I should have danced.

Chapter Twenty-Three

S lush is piling up outside the double black doors on Christmas Eve as we eat sweet mince pies and listen to Bing Crosby on the radio.

'Sink or swim,' Vermin shouts, nagging us all to ask Benny for a Christmas bonus.

'I've been swimming with a snorkel on all year.' Kevin picks up the phone to call another applicant.

'It's a miracle you haven't drowned,' says Janine, pinning plastic mistletoe to her jersey.

'Happy to do breaststroke with you anytime,' Vermin tells her.

Nancy waddles in, her head poking out from the top of an over-sized gold Christmas cracker costume. 'Merry Christmas.'

'I always knew you were a cracker,' Vermin chuckles.

'You've no chance of pulling me,' Nancy quips, gaining raucous applause from the rest of us.

'You want to borrow some mistletoe for you and Kevin?' Janine asks Cassie.

'It's more like poison ivy you've got,' Cassie snaps.

'I'm just saying, you and Kevin were cosy on Friday.'

'Ditto you and Vermin,' Cassie retorts.

Janine's head springs back. 'Why don't you use that spoon of yours to stir me a cuppa instead?'

'Make your own.'

An email pings which distracts me from the mud wrestle.

Cassie: *Fancy a proper coffee?*

I ignore the email and get to work, opening and closing CVs, hunting for options to fill several senior positions for Marianne and Charlie at the bank. I work fast in case the best candidates register with competitors who might try to submit them first. Despite it being Christmas Eve I already have one interview scheduled today.

Maak elke sekonde tel.

Having the power to represent the best candidates while relegating others to the belly of Benny is tricky. I rule out serial applicants who don't come anywhere close to the brief, then work methodically through the rest. I want to give them all a chance. Upskill them to overcome any competency gaps. Instead, I play with lives, resuscitating some, killing off others.

I email a couple more CVs from interested applicants to Marianne, before Nancy calls from downstairs to advise I have a candidate waiting. Someone I'm briefing before they head to the bank for an interview.

'On my way,' I tell her.

'No need to rush like a mad woman.'

Baffled at the cryptic remark, I head downstairs. Michael is hovering in reception wearing an A-line dress and a blond curly wig on his head. I offer a welcoming handshake.

'I'm Michael, but my friends call me Michaela.'

'Excellent, Michaela. If you could take a seat for a few minutes, I'll grab my jacket.'

I sit her in the boardroom and head back upstairs to grab my jacket. 'Just letting you know, it's Michaela who's going for an interview, not Michael,' I tell Vermin. 'He is a she.'

Vermin slumps forward on his desk, head on his hands. 'We need to cancel.'

'No way are we discriminating. You need to get with the program. Marianne won't care. I'll take her over and do the introductions.'

'Marianne is going to have my balls, much like this Michaela person.'

I glare at him.

'Too far?'

'You need to learn to shut up sometimes.'

'And you better know what you're doing.'

'I'll walk with you,' says Cassie. 'We'll grab coffees on the way back.'

'Fine.'

We head back downstairs to fetch Michaela and Cassie tags alongside as we enter the bank for formal introductions. I shouldn't feel apprehensive, but between the tension fizzing in the air with Cassie and wanting my candidate to do well in the interview, I'm a pile of nerves. When Marianne appears, I babble with inane chatter. 'Don't you love this brisk winter weather? It's colder than South Africa where I'm ...'

Marianne stretches her neck to a length I only thought possible of a giraffe and spots my candidate.

I do the introductions. 'This is Michaela. She's here to see you and Charlie.'

'I'm aware of that. Charlie's waiting. Let Graydon know I'll call him later.' She disappears into the bank with Michaela.

'You look like you really need that espresso now,' Cassie suggests.

'I'm not fussed.'

'Well, I'm going to get coffees for the team and need help carrying them back.'

'Glad I'm useful for something.'

'About the other night … nothing happened. If you'd just …'

'You're not my property, Cassie. You can do what you like.' I stomp towards Café Kamani.

A bell jingles as we enter the cosiness of a coffee shop buzzing with laughter. One corner is dominated by a tinsel-covered tree with fake presents underneath and the barista has flashing reindeer horns on her head.

'Do you want to sit in?' Cassie asks as we join the queue.

'Takeaway is better. I've work to do.'

We're side by side, shoulders inches from touching. There are knots in mine. Tying up my stomach too.

'You did the right thing giving Michaela a chance. South Africans have a reputation for being a bit narrow-minded.'

'Gee, thanks.'

'It's a stupid generalisation. I'm saying you're *not* like that.'

Cassie orders the coffees and we hover while beans are ground and milk is frothed. 'The Anvil is open Christmas Day. Does lunch with me still stand?'

Her green eyes stare at me, set within a face flushed from the cold. The colour combination is perfect for the season of goodwill.

'I'll bring the crackers,' I say.

***

I'm barely back in the cube farm when I receive a call from Marianne De Nunes. 'I'll take her.'

'Who?' I ask.

'Michaela. Excellent candidate. She has all the right skills. We need more candidates like her that enhance diversity and bring valuable new perspectives to the team.'

'Fantastic!'

Marianne cuts the conversation short. 'Get me Graydon.'

I transfer her to Vermin and do a spin in my chair. Although I'm still struggling to fit in with normal office life, it's fulfilling finding someone a job.

'Well done, mate,' Vermin says when he's off the phone. 'This calls for a celebration.'

'Some other time.'

'I wasn't planning on celebrating with you.' Vermin walks out followed closely by Janine.

'Well done.' Cassie appears in my cube. 'A senior placement like that puts you right up this month's sales ladder. That deal is worth thousands in commission.'

'I'm splitting the fee with Vermin, not that he deserves it. He would have canned Michaela given the chance, which is out of order.'

'Still, it's enough to have a holiday back home.'

'Why would I go back?' I turn my back to her so she won't see the angst on my face. How can I go home when my mother is shaken to the core and my father helped me sneak out of a country I love? As for my brother, I miss him, but he let me down so badly I'll never get over it. He let me down and I let him down.

We should have known better.

We should have known better.

We should have known better.

Plus, family aside, it would be impossible to look Erin in the eye after turning her world upside down.

A hand touches my shoulder and I jump.

'Whatever you spend it on, well done again,' Cassie murmurs.

'Thanks.'

She leaves me alone and I plug my headphones into my computer, leaning back as the music takes over.

Iron Maiden, 'Infinite Dreams'.

The lyrics are tremendous, packed with the woes of suffocation, insomnia, and cold sweats. Bruce Dickinson is willing me to exist beyond the pain. When it finishes, I push repeat so I can hear him rasp about how we return to live again, reincarnated, to play the game:

again …

and again …

and again.

My email pings in the corner of my screen.

Vermin: *I need to sandblast Janine's lipstick off.*

Me: *???*

Vermin: *She just blew my trumpet in the stationery cupboard.*

I press pause amid a classic guitar riff.

Me: *Dude, not cool. Keep it to yourself.*

Vermin: *Just because you're not getting any.*

He's right. I'm a recluse in this cube farm. My sex life is as barren as a battery hen after a bird flu epidemic wipes out the whole flock of partners.

Chapter Twenty-Four

When I get to the Anvil, Cassie is already there dressed in a jumper with '*Jingle Bells*' across the front.

'Happy Christmas!' I give her an awkward hug and a small gold bell sewn on her jumper tinkles.

She sits back down to nurse a glass of wine. Several punters boo as the Queen starts her Christmas Day speech on the big screen.

'Worse than watching grannies on a needlework program,' one punter shouts, knocking into our table and spilling half of Cassie's drink.

'Hey, watch it,' says Cassie as she pushes her chair back to minimise getting soaked.

'I am watching it.' The man leers at her before staggering back to the bar.

I'm seething, but relieved he's gone without too much trouble. 'Men can be idiots sometimes,' I say to Cassie.

'You sound like my mum. Here, I've something for you.' She hands me a present.

I tear off the paper. Inside is a T-shirt with a yellow Mr Man on the front. 'Mr Happy?'

'That's you, right?'

'I wish.'

'So, I figured you needed cheering up.'

'Thanks. This is for you.' I pass Cassie her gift, a satire book I hope she might find funny.

50 ways to lose your ~~Lover~~ Mother.

'Priceless.' Cassie scans the blurb and grins. 'Though I thought I might be in line for that angel you bought at Dalhousie.'

'I'll get you another drink,' I say, to avoid sharing who the angel recipient will be.

'Shall we order while you're at the bar? I'm all in for the traditional roast if you are?'

'You have to have a roast in this weather,' I reply, getting up.

If my brother were here, he would have insisted we have the roast too.

Jaco is home and Ma and Pa are off work as the library is closed for the day. There's a heat wave this Christmas and we should be eating cold salads and seafood, but Jaco was hell-bent on having a roast.

'What a lunch, Ma!' My brother polishes off the last of his three meats with all the trimmings. 'Totally was worth coming home for.'

'There's dessert too,' Ma replies, glowing.

Jaco rubs his stomach. 'I'm stuffed, but I'll squeeze it in.'

I get up. 'I'll fetch it, Ma. You relax.'

She's been at it all morning; peeling, stirring, carving – so I clear the table and load the dirties in the dishwasher. When I'm done, I shove some matches in my pocket and carry out the brandy pudding and a jug of Ma's homemade custard.

'Do the honours, son,' Pa says as I set it on the table.

'*You always light it.*' *I pass him the matches.*

'*I'll do it.*' *Jaco grabs them and strikes a flame to set the pudding ablaze.*

Pa recites grace, even though he already said it once before the roast, then we tuck into the pud, pull crackers and read the jokes with paper hats on our heads.

I pull mine off as Erin comes in the garden with her surfboard. 'You ready to hit the waves? It's pumping out there.'

My face is already red from the midday heat, but it gets hotter seeing her in a see-through white sarong over an orange bikini.

'*You need any more help clearing up, Ma?*' *I ask.*

'*No, you kids go have fun,*' *she says. 'And be careful.*'

'*We will,*' *I reply.*

'*Merry Christmas!*' *Erin says.*

'Merry Christmas,' Cassie says when I get back from the bar.

'Merry Christmas,' I reply.

The Queen's royal words hum in the background, while inside I'm royally fucked up. The pretence of my life is causing a black depression barely manageable. The ups and downs of monotonous daily life saturate my days, interspersed with flashbacks rendering me unstable, sapping my rational thinking. At night, I battle insomnia until finally drifting off to wrangle with my *infinite dreams* until I wake again in a sweat. Medication would no doubt help me get back on an even keel, some kind of antidepressant like Lexapro or Prozac, but I'm too scared to go to the doctors in case they find a flaw in my identity records that gives the game away that I'm not really me. It's ironic torture. I need to go to the doctors because I don't know who the hell I am, but I can't in case the doctor finds out who I really am.

I open my mouth to share my innermost secret with Cassie,

then close it again. She will either bolt or it will bring us closer, and I cannot deal with either right now.

I get up. 'I've got to go.'

'What about your turkey?'

'I'm not that hungry.'

'Not again! You're not walking out in the middle of Christmas lunch?'

'I'm ... I'm sorry.' Picking up my Mr Happy gift, I exit into the harshest wrath of winter.

The wind pummels relentlessly as I hurry away with my head down. Gum and grime fill the cracks in the pavement. My mind is an exact replica; fractures held together with gum, grime ... blood. I have to pull it together and move on with my life. Enough is enough. It's time to yank myself up from the dirt. I need to dust myself off and find myself again.

I am not Mr Happy.

I am not Graham.

I am Simon.

Bar-L

Chapter Twenty-Five

I t's New Year's Eve and it's just me and the sofa saying a sorry goodbye to the diabolical year just gone. Diet Coke is in hand and my bare feet are propped on the coffee table with no glass. The gas oven pings, announcing my frozen pizza is now crisp and edible, or maybe it's just crisp.

The hot air smacks me in the face as I lower the oven door, like the drawbridge to Edinburgh Castle inviting me in to enjoy the wonderment of what is inside.

I could stick my head in to kill myself, but I'm unsure about the practicalities of this. A lot of hot air has just escaped, and the breeze of the winter air seeps through the edges of my single-glazed windows. I pull a ragged tea towel out of the kitchen drawer to use as an oven glove. I've only three others in there; not enough to stuff into every nook and cranny to seal a chamber to successfully die in. The low oven height is also a problem. It has a storage space underneath where Teflon-coated pots and pans are stored. Shame I'm not Teflon-coated so shit can slide off my surface. To manoeuvre my head into the grease-covered storage cavity I'll have to kneel on all fours and take my final rasping breath doggy style. I should have cleaned the oven so at least the last thing I see is pristine walls. Probably should have ordered in too, rather than waste valuable last moments cremating a frozen meatlovers thin crust.

Cause of death: Oven baked.

The incongruity of my thinking is fucked. I'm torn between pulling the pizza out to eat it or making the oven habitable enough for my head to occupy so I can avoid starting another hellish year. I slide out my dinner and pull up the drawbridge. This year has to be an improvement on the last one, granted, coming off a low base. My ancient TV crackles as the lyrics of 'Auld Lang Syne' ricochet around the flat.

'Should old acquaintance be forgot and never brought to mind?'

It's impossible not to remember old acquaintances, but I need to try harder, much harder, to make new ones, instead of isolating myself and shutting people like Cassie out. I've been forlorn and bored with my own crabby company since walking out on our festive lunch. It hasn't been the season to be jolly. It's been a time for reflection, assessing everything under the microscope to figure out what I'll do differently.

Robert Burn's words are sung in the traditional Scottish Hogmanay celebration, but for me they mark a farewell, of the man I was before and of who I am today. I'm Simon at the core, but he's embalmed inside of Graham, mummified in sodden bandages, buried in a tomb of misery.

So many people are trying to cope with maintaining even a basic level of mental fitness. Trying to avoid developing a long-term split personality disorder has made me realise how many other people might be suffering with mental health decline. Normal people who were going about their daily business when suddenly they had their world rocked. We pass them in the street. Sit next to them in the office. Push our trolleys beside them in the supermarket. Smiling family members, acquaintances, passers-by, hiding immense pain, trying to avoid giving off signals that indicate parts of them are broken and may never heal. No doubt about it, a single incident has taken its toll on my psyche, turning me into an emotional see-saw. Battling with two identities is festering like pus into tendencies of putrid anxiety and depression that seep out of an open wound I cannot seem to stitch back together. Sometimes I am fighting a force so powerful the urge to commit suicide becomes overwhelming, but I have to be a better, stronger man. I have to give Graham the chance to right a catastrophic wrong by sending back cash to those I've hurt. Simon's inner voice, constantly interrupting my best intentions with mental reminders that I have morally sinned, needs to be silenced. It's a battle between two men. Graham who wants to live and Simon who wants to die.

Cause of death: Schizophrenia.

I slap myself across the face. Hard enough to sting. To knock ten bags of sense into the here and now, an antibiotic for the symptoms of a schizophrenic. If I'm to overcome what I've run from, I have to fulfil the goal of my New Year's resolution. I have to move past what happened.

Achieving this is more difficult than it sounds. I made a mistake in thinking time and distance might be enough to fight the impulse to find an efficient and effective means to end the interminable pain. It's not. Survival instincts battle with the inescapable horror of there being no solution to my irreversible actions. I can't erase the past, but suicide would give me the ability to control my future destiny, which is an attractive proposition, albeit a selfish, sick way of thinking. My family would be devastated, although in my darkest hours, I wonder.

Would they?

Would they?

Would they?

Pa packed me off so quickly my feet didn't touch the ground. Rational thinking has me believing this was for my own benefit, to prevent any chance of being given a slow puncture. During rock bottom moments though, I wonder if shipping me off to Scotland was for his benefit too, and Ma's, so they wouldn't have to look at my face every day, reminding them of the things they would rather forget.

Warding off depression by oneself isn't going to happen on its own. It requires a strategy, and mine is to work harder. Spending all hours at TITS making placements means less time dwelling on the past and more time creating a better future. Not my own future, but that of my candidates, clients, Erin and everyone I left back home. I recall telling Cassie I'd give it my best shot, yet I've fallen short of this.

Maak elke sekonde tel.

I'll domineer the mind of Benny, possessing him in my quest to find a candidate for every job. This will require determination and persuasion, traits I've failed dismally to display before, but I have another chance. I can master them.

I'm taking the opportunity to reinvent myself.

To no longer be Simon.

I am Graham now.

I am Graham.

Graham.

Chapter Twenty-Six

During the first week back at work in January, in the midst of Scotland's icy winter, I dive back into work with a stint at the Scottish Employment Convention. The hall is jammed with temporary cubicles resembling a larger-than-life cube farm. Expo traders jostle for attention with colourful posters to make them stand out from the crowd. The TITS booth ahead is impossible to miss, flanked by pop-up signs featuring a skinny blonde model with a chihuahua peaking from her laptop case. The slogan reads:

'Are you the next IT girl?'

I don't know why a pedigree dog has been used in the advertisement; there are only mongrel recruiters wandering about with compendiums under their arms, nosing the butts of employers to sniff out jobs they can fill on their behalf. Nevertheless, I too will wag my tail, pee on my territory and growl at the competition.

Cassie is already manning the booth, looking incredible in a tailored black suit, hair wild in defiance.

'Morning.'

She ignores me and fills a bowl with Quality Streets to entice foot traffic to stop. Once a prospective client pauses at our stand, we'll encourage them to drop a business card in a giant jar for a chance to win a bottle of bubbly in return for being added to our daily spam mailing list.

'You're a good friend, Cassie.'

'I'd hate to see how you treat your enemies.'

'I know. I've been a dickhead.' There haven't been many enemies in my life but when I was last affronted by someone not on my side, to say it didn't end well would be the understatement of the century. Familiar anxiety creeps in so I draw in a hefty intake of air and remind myself I'm Graham now. When I exhale, I'm more composed. 'I had some weird shit going on. Friends?'

She shrugs. 'Quality Street?'

I take a hazelnut whirl. 'Do you fancy a coffee? If you're okay on the stand, I'll go for a quick wander and grab us one.'

She nods so I stroll around the other booths to check out the displays. It's productive work; I make a couple of decent new contacts who may have job openings they'll use an agency for. I also amass an assortment of freebies, consumed by a sense of satisfaction in accumulating useless crap, like a child going to McDonald's for the free Happy Meal character toy then getting transfixed to needing the whole set. A water bottle falls from my arms which I struggle to pick up without dropping one of the USB sticks, pens and keyrings. A man from the information booth hands me a canvas branded shopping bag to pack it all in. I refine my elevator pitch by approaching every expo trader, pretending I care about Hibs, The Jambos, Celtics and Rangers, promoting how our clients can convert contractors to permanent positions with no transfer fee. Collect their merchandise. Everyone loves a Happy Meal.

Someone gives me a free stress ball which I squeeze nonstop until I make it to the networking corner stocked with complimentary coffee and biscuits. It's a feeding frenzy of pinstripes taking a break from butt-sniffing to overdose on caffeine and sweet Scottish shortbread.

A lady with cropped blonde hair dispenses coffee from a self-service machine and dunks a biscuit into her drink. 'It's all this coffee is good for. I had one earlier and it's vile.'

'Thanks for the warning.'

'I'm Hannah, by the way.' One of her eyebrows is pierced and her fingers are adorned with funky silver rings. She's dressed in a floor-length grungy patchwork dress that's out of place amidst the suits.

'Graham,' I reply, chatting to her as I make two coffees. 'I'm from the Talent-IT stand, we're a recruitment firm, so if you ever need any staff ...'

'You might be in luck. We're hiring at the moment for the justice sector.'

I drop one of the drinks and it splashes onto her flowing dress. 'Shit. I'm so sorry.'

'It's only a drop.' Her accent is South African, but I can't focus enough to ask about it, so she chatters on. 'Judicial systems ... parole boards ... courts and remand centres ... we need a good agent.' She hands me her business card and then wanders off into the crowds.

With my bag of freebies and the one intact coffee, I head back to Cassie.

'Aren't you having one?' she asks.

'Apparently it's like piss.'

Cassie takes a glug and grimaces. 'Shame there's no Café Kamani around here. Who was that you were hob-knobbing with?'

'Hob-knobbing?'

'Sharing a biscuit.'

'A possible client.' I look at Hannah's business card. 'She runs an independent technology advisory service in the justice space, for prisons and stuff. She might have roles for me to work.'

'You should give her a call.'

'Yah.'

I slip the card into my pocket. Her justice sector isn't one I particularly wish to reacquaint myself with, but she has business I'm going to have to chase.

Chapter Twenty-Seven

A layer of silver frost dusts the trees in Princes Street Gardens, making it a pretty stroll to work as I jostle with the usual humdrum of commuters pounding the city pavement with a frown on their face. I'm still a Pinstripe Prisoner with them, but I've accepted my fate to be part of the rat-race. Meetings about meetings, number-crunching to reach a magic number, excelling on Excel reports. It's a different kind of life sentence.

When I arrive at the office, Vermin is already scrawling up a placement win. 'I've nearly as many notches here as I have above my bed.'

I survey the whiteboard. 'Great effort, but Cassie is closing the gap.'

'I know. Not a bad effort from her to bill a mil'.'

'All this time you two have been discussing my new-found success, this plant has been starting to flower,' says Cassie, so we crowd into her cube to observe the sprouting buds.

'Let me know if you want it deflowered instead,' Vermin offers.

'Shut it, Vermin,' I say. 'Nobody wants to hear your sleezy crap.'

'It's a shame you're still to get off the mark this month, Kevin,' Janine provokes.

'Kevin obviously doesn't have golden balls like me.' Vermin grabs his crotch, instigating an unwelcome flashback of my time in the Struisbaai cell.

'Seriously, would you quit being such an arsehole, Vermin!' I yell.

'Alright, alright. Keep your hair on.'

'This shit is not funny,' I tell him.

'Aye, well, at least I'm not a grumpy fuck like you,' he fires back.

I let it go and change the subject, determined to start the year on a positive. 'Did you all have a good New Year?'

'I had way too much to drink,' Lorraine says. 'I'll have to detox.'

'Why would you want to pull your face back like that?' Janine asks.

'That's botox, not detox.'

Laughter erupts. It might be a new year, but other than me consciously fighting my own depression and Vermin being a bigger schmuck than ever, nothing else has changed in this place.

I head to my cube and call Hannah.

'It's Graham. The one who spilled coffee on you.'

She recognises me immediately and although she's busy, we agree to meet after work.

***

After I leave the office for the day, I cross Princes Street and cut through the manicured gardens. I've time to kill before I meet Hannah, so I sit on an empty bench amidst the rows of cherry blossom trees. They are waiting patiently for warmer weather to creep in so they can take on a pink hue. Ma would love the landscaping and exquisite, intoxicating flowers if she were to visit in spring. I can picture her smiling as she walks a carpet of fallen flowers, petals swirling around her, caught in the wind like snowflakes. I'm suddenly lonely as people to and fro; families with children, a homeless man with bare feet that are surely blue beneath the dirt and tourists representing many nationalities. It's beyond busy but nobody sees me engulfed in solitude.

Eventually I wander to the Old Town, strolling past quaint stores on the steep slope of Edinburgh's prettiest thoroughfare, Victoria Street. There are numerous kilt stores, stocking tartans that have clothed Scottish clans for centuries, and a whisky specialist carrying a multitude of single malts from local distilleries.

A man robed in period costume stops me on the street, selling tickets for an underground tour of Mary King's Close. A shovel is in his hand and an enormous crucifix hangs around his chest.

'What's down there?' I ask.

A grave tone seizes him. 'Mary King's Close is a rabbit warren frozen in time since the seventeenth century. I'm the Foul Clenger, employed to dispose of the dead from houses beneath where we're standing. They've been left to rot in the underground city after the plague took its toll on the poor.'

'And this is a tourist attraction?'

'Haunted, they say. So many corpses.'

'Thanks, but it's not for me.'

He blesses his cross then hangs his head towards the ground as if in mourning and I flee towards my final destination in the Grassmarket.

The Last Drop pub has a traditional stone exterior. Its entrance is painted deep claret, inviting customers into a cosy interior.

I'm early, so order a Coke, and although I'm a letdown for

breweries who have no interest in the insignificant profit from fizzy soft drinks, she pushes it over the counter with a smile.

'I take it this place has been around a while.'

'Don't you know the history?'

I shake my head.

'Back in the day, the gallows used to be right outside these doors. People flocked to see the public executions for as little as stealing a loaf of bread. That's how the place got its name.'

When Hannah suggested we meet here, it had not crossed my mind that The Last Drop might mean something other than an empty pint glass. Karma has brought me to a place seeped in brutal history.

I find a booth in the farthest corner and wait until Hannah parts the crowd in an outlandish checked overcoat speckled with raindrops.

'Hi,' she says. 'It's mad out there. Did you see the street entertainers?'

I nod. Impossible to miss the array of fire-eaters, jugglers, bag-pipe players and the odd Foul Clenger.

'What can I get you?' I ask.

'A red, thanks.'

I fetch the wine and Hannah settles down and takes a gulp. Pa would tell her to first swirl it, smell it, let it breathe.

'You're South African, right? Did you ever get to the winelands back home?' I ask.

'Yah, you can't beat the vineyards in Stellenbosch. Spier is one of my favourites.'

'I don't think I've been to that one.'

'The grounds are huge with a lake, restaurants and a cheetah enclosure. There's a deli selling wine and picnic baskets for lunch. Try it next time you go home.'

Pa loves the wine regions and produce. It would be nice to saunter through the vineyards with him, but unlikely I'll be going home anytime soon.

We share more pleasantries, me from Struisbaai, her from Goodwood in the northern suburbs of Cape Town, then we get down to business about her vocation servicing the prison authorities.

'I started out as a graduate for a consulting firm. They were trying to help South African prisons transition from archaic filing systems to electronic record management, but there was no money.'

'There's definitely a lack of investment in jail systems and probably not much in the way of systematic administration.' I recall the soggy wet pen and lack of any sophisticated recording equipment in my own police interview.

'Absolutely. When my employer in the Cape went bankrupt, I packed up and left the country on a skilled visa. I worked for a global IT company before branching out on my own. It worked out though, landing me in the disruptive innovation space, shaking up Her Majesty's Prisons.'

'How exactly do you shake them up?' I ask.

'Lots of different ways. Sometimes it's implementing huge projects, other times it's simple improvements like enabling people on the outside to send more messages to inmates on the inside. The stamp and postal systems are starting to become obsolete as methods of communication continue to go through radical change.'

'Makes sense.'

'Prisoners need contact with the outside world to have the best chance at rehabilitation, but so many families have lengthy distances to cover and can't make regular visitation. We have technology like Skype and FaceTime at our fingertips. All kinds of video conferencing tools can work well if rolled out and managed safely and correctly.'

Her argument is compelling. If the opportunity had been there to chat with my brother even once in the short time I was banged up, I'd have given my right arm for it.

'There's so much red tape and prisons are struggling to cope with this new digital era erupting around them. There used to be barbed wire fences and phone calls using telephone cards. Now the mobile phone is one of the worst contraband problems being faced.'

'So they consult with you.'

'Exactly. I've just launched another pilot community program at a couple of more forward-thinking correctional facilities. It helps inmates gain invaluable IT skills for when they get out.'

'Why? What makes you want to help someone who's committed a crime?'

'Everyone deserves a second chance. It's a good feeling, helping people back into society who have served their time and want to make a real go of it.'

She exudes compassion and a lump in my throat forms as she rattles off what she needs. I concentrate on jotting down notes.

Architects, analysts, developers and testers, not only with technology proficiency, but a cultural fit too. Consultants keen to get involved in community service. The unusual specification explains why she needs me. These will be hard to fill. Geeks with a humanitarian soul are difficult to search for in Benny.

We're midway through negotiating recruitment fees when I'm taken aback to see Cassie standing next to our booth with Kevin. She gawps at Hannah who returns the stare, silently taking each other apart like mechanics stripping back a rusting old banger to its shell.

I introduce them to one another.

'We're going to share some ideas on refreshing our talent pools,' Kevin says. 'Join us if you like?'

I get up abruptly, visualising Kevin moving in to kiss Cassie. 'No thanks. Shall we get some fresh air?' I ask Hannah.

'Sure.'

'Excellent. We'll have your table,' Kevin shuffles into my warm grave before I've barely moved out.

'See you,' Cassie says.

'Yah, see you.'

Then I'm outside.

'Friends of yours?' Hannah asks as we walk to the taxi rank.

'Colleagues.'

A black cab pulls up and she gives me a hug before climbing in. Although she's a client, this social interaction doesn't feel out of place.

'Great meeting. Thanks again for taking on the open positions.'

'I'll do everything I can to fill them for you with the right candidates.'

'I know you will. You'll still have to pop out to see me first to get written terms of business signed.'

'Where should I come to?'

'Barlinnie Prison. I've an appointment later this week with the governor there. It will be perfect if you can join me to see the place and hear about their technology challenges firsthand.'

Her taxi pulls away as my heart threatens to stop.

I'd prefer to take my chances descending into Mary King's Close with the Foul Clenger.

Chapter Twenty-Eight

Donald drives along the M8 into Riddrie. 'This section of road used to be the Monkland Canal until it was filled in to convert it into a motorway.'

I've nothing to contribute to his lonely planet guide so I silently take in the view of semidetached council properties. There is a stark beauty to urban life. A sense of community in the conformity of the housing. It doesn't look too dissimilar to where Cassie lives, except Barlinnie Prison takes centre spot of this district.

We pass the local library. My mother and father, both librarians, gave me access to so much knowledge, yet not one book could have prepared me for this. I'm an illegal stowaway about to visit Scotland's largest prison.

A couple of turns later we pull into a car park overflowing with vehicles. Donald circles a couple of times before finding a space being vacated. A small bicycle is chained to a lamppost next to where I get out of the car. It has a wicker basket on the front and a pink helmet with daisies printed on it hanging from the handlebars.

This is an awful place for kids to visit, but whoever brought the bike here took time to secure it from thieves. There's love in the gesture.

'Do you know this place is known as the Bar-L?' Donald asks as we walk through the car park.

'Yah, I've heard it's notorious. People nickname it The Big Hoose on the hill too, because it houses everything from first-time petty offenders to serial killers with life sentences.' Since I last saw Hannah, I've done nothing but ask Wikipedia everything there is to know about the place. Obsessively researching what prisoners eat, how they live, the way they cope with what they have done.

'Aye, it's pretty overcrowded,' Donald replies. 'I think they designed it for over a thousand residents, but some of the cells have got two in a bunk. It's well above its quota.'

Two per cell seems like luxury in comparison to the stack of mattresses on the floor of my tiny cell in South Africa. A Victorian building with five-star facilities. 'Until a few years ago they were still slopping out in buckets and there was talk of closing it, but the Scottish executive spent millions on refurbishment. New flushing toilets, televisions and recreational sports.'

'Sounds like a holiday camp, if you ignore the fact they used to execute people in a hanging shed there.'

'They've a library too. You know my folks are librarians?'

'That's right. I remember they always loved talking about books. Lovely couple, your mum and dad. Stayed in touch ever since we met while cruising the Med. Give them my best when you talk to them.'

'Will do,' I say. 'My mother would struggle working in a prison. She favours historical romance novels with a female heroine and likes to share her recommendations with patrons. I doubt too many prisoners would share her literary taste. Her favourite book is *Fingersmith.*'

'I suspect some readers in The Big Hoose may be habitual fingersmiths more than readers of that one,' Donald laughs.

We approach the prison. Hannah is waiting at the front entrance, a crocheted bag slung over her shoulder, paperwork sticking out of the top.

'Let's go,' she says after I've introduced her to Donald.

Pressure mounts as we enter the building and the door closes behind me, strip lights doing little to improve the austere surroundings. The light blue reception walls close in. It's like being trapped inside a giant robin's egg. I want to fracture them, crack free and get the hell out of there.

'Visitors can point out where they come from,' Hannah says, nodding to a huge world map pinned to the wall. 'Not everyone speaks English so it can be hard for them to register properly at the front desk. An increasing number of prisoners come in from Eastern Europe and even remote parts of China, so the prison is trying to improve the translation of information in multiple languages.'

We approach the front desk to present ourselves to the prison officer on duty, or rather Hannah does while I lag behind.

'ID please,' the officer says, giving me a stern look.

I hand him the requisite burgundy-covered British passport and my bank card for scrutiny, then try to avoid hyperventilating by putting on my best rummy face. Hold the rest of my cards close to the thumping chest. Minimise the nervous twitch. Keep the Adam's apple still until we're told to deposit our loose clothing, bags and valuables into a locker before proceeding to an area for a pat down.

I can't fault the by-the-book security. They're thorough, making sure I've nothing hidden on my person. My crevices are clear of all foreign objects. Except there are no checks today beyond surface level, of body or the non-visual kind. Nobody questions that I'm

not who I say I am. There are certainly advantages in implementing technology enhancements that will improve the collection and
cross-referencing of visitor information on the spot.

We wait a while longer until another uniformed officer appears.
'The governor sends his apologies. There's been an incident.'

'That doesn't sound good,' Hannah replies.

'Someone tried to self-harm. Stuffed a J-cloth down his own
throat.'

It's why I took my father's advice and fled South Africa. Even
in a five-star holiday resort like Barlinnie, the desperation some
detainees feel when banged up isn't to be underestimated. Physical
wellbeing becomes compromised by mental vulnerability. In a
short space of time, side-effects of poor mental health creep in and
become permanent fixtures. I still carry the negative effects from
my short time inside, not just because of restricted freedom, but
because of what I did to deserve it. I'm battling to live a normal
life and am in a perpetual inanimate state of existence, decapitated
from the support of my family.

There may be prisoners who deserve to be locked away forever,
but others may have made one misjudgement in the moment and
that single wrong turn can end up with them in such a low dysfunctional state that they no longer want to live at all.

Who will cry if I stuff a J-cloth down my throat?

Thrusting a foreign body sufficiently deep enough between
my lips to block the pharynx corridor leading from the cavities
of the nose and mouth would be relatively simple. I could tie my
legs together first to prevent myself from running for help and
then use all manner of objects to cause complete occlusion to my
air passages. Tie my hands up in cuffs in front of me then loop
my legs through so my wrists are then bound behind my back.

Let myself spasm until this specific form of asphyxia makes me a fatality.

Cause of death: Choking.

However, I cannot get my head around the exact technique of restraining my own hands. The desire for death would no doubt be eclipsed by the overwhelming desire for air. Without a friend to assist me, like the rumoured dry-boarding case in Guantanamo Bay, where a prisoner being interrogated was first physically restrained before a material gag was crammed into his mouth and secured with duct tape, instinct would no doubt have me reverse clambering through my bound limbs to pull the foreign object back out again.

All I'd be left with is nothing but a failed attempt and a saliva-sodden J-cloth.

***

Next to the bike chained to the lamppost, we part ways with Hannah.

'We'll come back another day,' she says.

I won't be back if I can help it. It's fucked with my brain. Any open roles will be worked from the safety of the Edinburgh office. I'll be enclosed in my blue cube, still like a robin trapped in an egg, but the blue TITS colouring is far less ominous.

'This could be your big break,' says Donald as we climb into his car.

'How?'

'Not many recruitment agents get to see firsthand how IT works inside a prison, and now the governor stood you up he kind of owes you. You got him in your pocket.'

I don't want anything in my pocket other than pound notes I've earned, and I intend to smash Benny to fill them. The governor will get the resources he needs, Hannah will deliver the necessary program of work, and I'll do the grunt work for a decent pay cheque. It's a win, win, win.

'Put your foot down on the motor,' I urge Donald. 'There's still time to get back to the office so I can start searching for candidates today.'

'Love the attitude, but I need to make a quick stop,' he replies, detouring off route to halt in front of a bookies. 'You a betting man? I recall your old man was impartial to a bit of roulette.'

'Not really.'

'Watch and learn, Graham. Watch and learn.'

I follow him inside. The bookies have a handful of clientele, including a young couple both in hoodies and a bunch of men who look around Donald's age. One or two nod at Donald as he heads to the counter to place a bet, then we settle in front of one of the screens.

'God, hurry the fuck up.'

If Pa overheard Donald hurling abuse at the TV, he would tell him not to take the Lord's name in vain. My parents frequent mass every Sunday, my mother in her best frock and Pa in a freshly pressed shirt. As a child, I've been through the traditional ceremonies of baptism, reconciliation, Holy Communion and confirmation. For a long time, I thought this made me a good person, but recent events overshadow every belief I ever had. Even if there is a heaven, the entry gates will be padlocked to me.

'Donald, fancy seeing you here,' exclaims a chap wandering in wearing a tweed flat cap. He has a prominent scar across one cheek.

'The odds are not in my favour today, Max,' Donald replies as the two men shake hands. 'But I've reserved a box at the Grand National to recover the losses.'

'All in good time, old boy.'

'Speaking of the Grand National, do you think there will be space to bring Hannah along?' I ask Donald.

'Aye, we have a private coach to take us there and she's worth the investment of taking up one of the seats.'

'I'll put you in touch with someone for a loan ahead of the National if you want to score big,' Max offers.

'Who's that?' Donald asks.

'Big Mal.'

'I've heard his name around.'

I realise I'm overhearing something private so I engross myself in the poster of the week's winning lotto numbers.

'Then ye ken his reputation.' Max scribbles a number on a blank betting slip with a complimentary pencil. 'There ain't no prize for second place, unless you flutter each way of course.'

'I'm good for it,' Donald assures him as his horse sprints in last.

'Goes without saying,' says Max as Donald shreds his slip into several pieces and tosses the confetti in the air.

A wedding magazine lies open on the coffee table. Ma is thinking of buying a dusky pink dress with matching jacket, to coordinate with Erin's colour scheme.

'She'll make the most stunning bride,' Ma gushes for the hundredth time. 'I'm going to order ten boxes of the pink confetti. Is there anything else we need to organise?'

'Not until next year, Ma. The wedding is ages away and everything is booked. Tux fitting won't happen until the month before. Not just for me. For Pa and Jaco too, so there's no need to stress about anything.'

'Thanks, son. Honestly, though, you have to agree, Erin is going to look stunning. I can't wait to see her dress.'

'Yah,' I say, because it's true. Erin is the prettiest girl I've ever met. She would look good wearing a potato sack.

Chapter Twenty-Nine

I t's impossible to describe the buzz that surrounds the handicap steeplechase that is the Grand National. Spring season adds a bright atmosphere and matching fashion parade to the infamous race hype; men in waistcoats and ladies in such colourful hats they're like a flock of parrots, squawking in excitement to one another. The prelude to the race has been a nonstop barrage of music, entertainment, food and beverages, hosted in Red Rum Garden.

'Well done, Graham,' Donald says after we settle in the VIP area. 'You've pulled out all the stops to get the right crowd to Aintree.'

Our big buyers are all present. Charlie Rivers, Marianne De Nunes, Hannah. Okay, so Hannah is not a big buyer yet, but she has the potential to be.

'Why does she have to be here?' Janine hisses, glaring at Marianne bending to pick up a pen from the floor, giving everyone an eyeful down her blouse.

'I'll get it,' Vermin drops on all fours.

'Such a klutz,' Marianne giggles.

The undignified image of her knicker-less in the boardroom crosses my mind, which I disperse by tucking into a custard tart. I'm the only one eating, not as a result of my preference for baked delicacies, but because the rest of the crowd are guzzling free spirits by the treble, wine by the bottle and beer by the keg. Even if the horses fall at the first, the corporate hospitality is a winner.

'You've custard on your chin.' Cassie brushes it away. She looks cute in a lopsided fascinator and lace dress.

'And you scrub up well,' I tell her.

'She doesn't always look this good,' a drunken Charlie Rivers slurs across the table. 'First time I met Cassie she was covered in bird poo.'

He begins to regale the story but doesn't get too far before Marianne interrupts.

'You mean it landed in her hair? How grotesque!'

'I shook her hand after she touched it.' Charlie lets out a rumble that sounds like he's choking on his Veuve Clicquot.

'Are you okay?' Cassie vigorously slaps him on the back, attempting to rectify the tickle on his windpipe.

'What are you doing?' Charlie swats her hand away.

'Stopping you from choking.'

'I'm not choking, I'm laughing,' Charlie rumbles again, tears pooling in the creases above his Jagger mouth.

'I was just unlucky that day,' Cassie laughs back.

'Unlucky?' Donald exclaims. 'Don't tell me I've brought along a bad omen while I'm about to witness the most important race of the year. I thought a bird doing its business on you was meant to bring good luck.'

'Afraid not, Donald. Cassie has backed an outsider who has as much chance of first place as I have of taking Olympic gold for synchronised swimming,' Charlie jokes as the thoroughbreds line up.

'I've never been to anything like this in South Africa,' says Hannah. 'Thanks again for the invite.'

'Me too,' Charlie adds as the crowd cheers and the race springs into action. 'Let's hope nobody falls off the saddle at Becher's Brook.'

If I were to take up the job of a jockey, I'd make it a personal goal to ride at Aintree. Thirty hurdles, many larger than conventional races, make this the ultimate test to find a commendable winner. The Chair is a whopping five-foot-two-inch-high fence with a ditch right before it. I'd propel my horse forward, approaching Becher's Brook, fully committed to clearing its height. Then I might clip my horse a split second too late and we might crash into the jump, fatally snapping my neck instantaneously, in front of seventy thousand live spectators and millions of viewers at home.

Cause of death: Horseriding fatality.

Downside is I love horses and if my ride were to break a leg I would be guilty of passing on my deadly curse to an innocent animal. I'll have to think of a better way to go.

'Faster, you donkey!' Donald yells.

'Come on, you handsome beast,' Marianne screeches.

'Anytime,' Vermin quips.

The spectators roar and Cassie screams, 'I've won!'

'How the hell is your outside chance taking a share of the prize funds?' Donald slumps into his chair.

'Beginner's luck,' says Cassie with a grin. 'What happened to your horse?'

'T'was half asleep and if you snooze, you lose.' Donald summons a passing waitress and orders a scotch on the rocks.

'That's a fitting drink for you,' Charlie laughs.

Donald laughs too, but it doesn't quite reach his eyes. 'Did you know that in 1847 one of the men who built the Laphroaig whisky distillery died after falling into a vat of boiling liquor?'

This trivia fact is enough to make me reconsider my alcohol abstinence and dive headfirst into a vat too.

Cause of death: Drowning in my sorrows.

With regards to abstinence of alcohol, it's a shame Marianne De Nunes has not thought about giving it a go. She misjudges the distance leaning towards Vermin and takes a tumble to the ground.

The waitress next to us rushes off as Donald tries to hook Marianne under the armpits to drag her up.

'Gerrrrrroffffff,' slurs Marianne.

'What a disgrace.' Janine steps over her to get away from the ruckus.

Vermin kneels down. 'Marianne, you need to get up, sweetheart.'

'Fuuuuck offffff,' she says, as he tries to wipe drool from her mouth with a napkin. A volcanic eruption of vomit spreads hot lava onto his arm.

'Shit!' he recoils.

A crowd of spectators forms around us, one or two capturing the entertainment on their iPhones. I move to one side so I'm not caught on any footage and inadvertently loaded onto YouTube with the intoxicated Brazilian. The waitress reappears with two St John's Ambulance members in tow with a rescue chair. It takes several minutes to haul Marianne in, strap her down with orange velcro restraints, and wheel her off like she's a mad woman in a straitjacket.

'I'll stay with her,' Vermin gallantly offers, attempting to wipe the vomit off his jacket with more napkins before following the evacuation party.

'More fool you,' Janine shouts after him.

Alcohol has a lot to answer for.

Chapter Thirty

I get into the office early after the weekend and punch in the code to silence the alarm, which gives me confidence Vermin is not in the boardroom pounding a hungover Marianne. One of the cast-iron radiators gurgles and even though it's early April, I'm grateful it's on to take the edge off the chill.

While waiting for Benny to crank up, I chew on the life prisoners have in Barlinnie, Polsmoor and the Suid-Afrikaanse Polisiediens lock-up in Struisbaai. Inside many facilities there are no temperature control mechanisms. You either swelter or you freeze your bollocks off. In theory, if you took an average overall temperature, the conditions of global prisons would probably be deceivingly acceptable, like having one foot in icy water, the other in boiling. Every time I dwell on such absurdities, it strikes home that my mental stability may never recover from my own sorry time behind bars. The scars will always be there, maybe not as prominent as the streak down Max's face, and certainly not caused by a physical incision, but nevertheless, their presence will always remind me what I've done, where I've been and what will never be again. Once incarcerated, even for a day, the experience is with you for life. That moment basic human rights are taken away, rational thinking is wiped out and the soul is sucked dry. There may be heinous crimes for which this is a just punishment, but I've controversial reservations about a one-size-fits-all penal system and am determined to find Hannah the people she needs to improve prisons in the areas needing it most.

My cube is no bigger than the Struisbaai cell, and Benny, the only one I'm bunking down with, is malfunctioning. He's popped out an error message telling me his drive needs an upgrade. He's a lot like me.

I follow the foolproof commands. Benny notifies me two per cent of the program is installed. The installation speed is worse than watching a tortoise clamber Arthur's Seat, so I browse a print copy of *Computer Weekly*. Articles about the hottest industry trends dominate the content: cloud solutions, Apple devices, artificial intelligence. I stop on a Microsoft article about Bill Gates never being content with average performance, releasing another version of Windows even though most consumers don't use anything more complex than cut and paste. At least he's pledged to leave most of his fortune amassed from unnecessary upgrades to charity when he passes away.

I toss the magazine aside and phone The CAD. 'I need your help. Benny's face lift is taking longer than it took Wacko Jacko to get a new nose.'

'Press control, alt, delete.'

'Well, that's genius,' I snigger as Cassie wanders in. 'Whatever you do, don't attempt to upgrade Benny,' I tell her. 'You're better off putting up with his cranky old attitude.'

'I can live with that.' She throws me a smile over the partitioning.

Benny eventually reboots. He has been reinvented with a more welcoming user interface and a more responsive attitude towards Boolean searches. He ejects the details of a promising applicant who has been developing technology for various hospitals for over a decade, so I give them a call.

'Hi there. Are you free to speak?'

The question is standard practice amongst recruiters calling candidates at work. Sometimes their supervisor is hovering nearby and nobody wants to be caught hunting for another job.

'No, but I'm listening,' the man replies.

I launch into the job spec, but when I've finished, there's silence. 'I know you can't speak so if you want to go forward just nod your head. Sorry, obviously I can't see you doing this. I haven't had my morning coffee yet. Just give me a call back as soon as it's a good time to chat about the details.'

A chuckle ricochets from Cassie's cube at my gaffe.

'Bollocks!' I put the phone down.

'Priceless.' Cassie pops her head over the blue partition and laughs. 'The poor bloke is on the end of a phone line and you want him to nod his answers.'

My phone rings. 'It's him,' I mouth silently to Cassie as my target candidate tells me he now has privacy to discuss potentially submitting him.

I convince him to apply for the role and replace the phone to a thumbs up from Cassie. I'm thrilled I've my first option to submit to Hannah and want to step out of my comfort zone of average buckets to make a difference to Britain's penitentiaries.

So, I keep searching for elusive new candidates, hoping to find my old self along the way.

Chapter Thirty-One

The Serengeti shebeen is located in Leith docklands. The area reminds me of the Victoria and Alfred Waterfront in Cape Town. A hive of upmarket apartments, trendy restaurants and shopping complexes, plonked in the grounds of a historical commercial port on the Atlantic shore. Graydon reckons the Leith docks used to be crawling with prostitutes but it's getting too posh now for kerb crawling. Dread to think how he knows so much about it.

I enter the venue and it's a far cry from the Struisbaai shebeen. The lighting is a low wattage, antelope-horn-shaped chandelier under which Hannah is already seated. Animal print rugs are scattered around the mud-coloured concrete floor and portraits of the big five adorn the walls. A tea light burns in an elephant candle holder in the middle of the table reminding me I'm the man who can never forget.

'Great restaurant,' I say.

'Hope you haven't got the wrong idea about having a business meeting in a place like this. I've not been here before and have wanted to try it for ages. Thought it might be a good option, given we are both South African, but it's a bit more on the romantic side than I realised,' Hannah replies.

'It is pretty fancy.'

'Well, we deserve to treat ourselves. I've two offers for candidates you sent me today.'

'What! You only saw them today.'

'Doesn't matter. They're perfect for building a multilingual welcome app that can give the right information to visitors. There aren't too many people around with the skills we need. If you've any others, I'll take them too.'

'So, this is a celebration dinner?'

'Damn right it is.'

I scan the traditional African menu. Crocodile, kudu, oxtail and ostrich all feature heavily in the cuisine as the waiter places a bowl of complimentary biltong on our table.

I've just turned sixteen and Jaco is driving Erin and me back home from Hermanus.

The road is long, and the sun has begun to set for the day. We've a lengthy drive ahead of us, with nothing much to look at but the odd bok that sticks its head out from the fauna.

But we don't care.

Jaco is thrilled Pa has finally trusted him with the keys to his bakkie. It's pale blue and rusting badly from being exposed to so much to the sea air. It shudders, has stiff gears and regularly stalls, but to us, it's better than a brand-new Porsche.

Our bellies are full of Spur burgers topped with monkey gland sauce and served with a side of thin onion rings washed down with cream soda. We don't get out of our small town often, so we've been shopping too. Cape Union Mart for new hiking boots for Erin and the surf shop for a wetsuit for Jaco. I made him go to Woolworths to stock up with beef biltong for Pa and smoked snoek pâté for Ma too. They make the best food in Woolies.

Jaco cranks up the music and taps his hands on the worn leather steering wheel to the infectious beat of Bob Marley.

Could you be loved?

Love your brotherman.

The sound of reggae blaring from crackling speakers only adds to the authenticity of the track. I sing along to words about life's rocky roads, pointing fingers, being judged. Jaco shouts the last line about loving his brotherman and gives me a grin. I bob up and down in my seat like a toddler on a bouncy castle, then we all join forces in a crescendo for the chorus.

Erin's voice is normally melodious, sweet in tone, but she lets rip with Marley, like she's auditioning to be his lifelong backup singer.

Say something.

Say something.

Say something.

Her face is flushed. I'm not sure if it is from walking around Hermanus in the sun or from the excitement of the day.

I hear sirens above the noise and turn to stare out the back window. Blue lights blink back at me. 'It's the cops.'

'What the fuck,' Jaco replies, flicking off the music as he veers into the hard shoulder to turn off the engine.

'Be polite.' I swallow down the taste of onion rings rising in my throat as a cop walks towards us. He's young, dark-skinned, clean-shaven. Not much older than my brother.

Jaco grips the lever on the side door and winds down the window. 'What can I do for you, officer?'

'I don't know. What can you do for me?'

The cop rests his forearms on the window frame and leans right in.

'Have I done something wrong?' Jaco sits straight in his chair. His knuckles have turned white as he grips the wheel.

'Your bumper is bent.'

'My Pa knocked a tree a while back.'

'Drunk?'

'No, he doesn't drink and drive.'

'What about you? Do you drink and drive?'

'No, sir,' Jaco replies.

'I think you do.'

I bite my tongue, indignant as the cop starts to write a ticket. Many South African drivers have been behind the wheel under the influence because of the dangers of travelling on public transport, but Jaco is stone-cold sober.

'What's the ticket for?' I blurt, finding some Dutch courage that may stem from somewhere deep in my ancestral heritage.

'Dangerous driving. That bumper is going to affect your tail-lights.'

The Bob Marley lyrics from a few moments ago suddenly seem apt.

Say something.

Say something.

Say something.

Erin beats me to it. 'Officer, would you like some biltong?' She leans between the front seats and waves the Woolies family-sized packet of biltong at him.

He screws up the ticket and throws it to the ground before snatching the dried meat. 'Thanks. Drive safely.'

We jump as he whacks the bonnet of the car with his fist before walking back to his vehicle.

'You're a genius,' Jaco praises Erin.

'Everyone knows half the cops are corrupt around here.'

'*Yah, but biltong. Seriously?' Jaco adds.*

Erin shrugs. 'Times are hard.'

'*We shouldn't have had to pay him off,' I say. 'We did nothing wrong.'*

'*Boeta, it's a pack of biltong. Don't get all righteous about it now. You were useless,' Jaco replies as his knuckles return to their normal colour. 'Didn't you hear what Bob Marley said? Love your brotherman!'*

He's right. Inside I'm a cocktail of relief at Erin preventing us from being booked on our first day out in Pa's bakkie and guilt at failing to think on my feet fast enough when my brother was in trouble.

'White or red?' Hannah asks as the waiter hovers at our table to take our order.

'Your call. I gave up drinking a while back.'

'Really?'

'Yah. I'm sticking with water, but you go for it. If I were drinking though, I would probably punt for the red. Maybe try the Pinotage.'

She nods her agreement with my recommendation and the waiter scurries off.

Indecision can be a killer.

Chapter Thirty-Two

With a colourful marker, I tally my pair of placements on the whiteboard.

'No way,' Kevin says, his face deadpan.

'The Saffa immigrant is eating our cake,' Janine hisses.

'You screwing Hannah for these deals?' Vermin asks.

I ignore them all and log into Benny. We've developed a mutual understanding of one another. I'm familiar with his flaws, weaknesses and innermost secrets, and he knows exactly how to fulfil my needs. He intuitively finds me compatible options to methodically screen and I select those closest to perfection. We are the exact right intellectual blend of human meets technology. By lunchtime, I've emailed several more options to Hannah and am starving. Inside my top desk drawer is an emergency supply of nutritious grub. I pull out the instant gourmet meal of the recruitment industry. A Pot Noodle.

'You know, those things were once known as the slag of all snacks,' says Vermin as I'm about to leave my cube. 'Some marketing guru had the tagline regenerated to 'Easy Street', which is perfect. They do fill a quick hole.'

'Do you have to put me off my lunch?'

'Eat what you like,' Vermin shrugs. 'Food is food.'

Going to the basement kitchen to get boiling water to moisten the dry noodles into an edible state is suddenly a gloomy proposition. It's cramped, claustrophobic and lacking natural light down there. The intense dislike of small spaces takes hold and I toss the noodles back in my desk again and nip to the deli.

***

Around the corner, I see Donald some distance ahead, stooped, looking even older than the pensioner he is. A bulky stature steps out from a doorway and manhandles him into a side alley, prompting me to take off in a sprint. When I get to the alley, my boss is already on the ground. There's a crack as he receives a kick to the ribs, bringing a new meaning to the term lunchbreak.

'Tell Big Mal I've got the money,' Donald splutters, curling into a ball as I run up to them.

'Stop!' I yell as I approach.

His attacker throws a left hook my way. I try to dodge it, but his fist clips me on the lip and it bloody hurts.

All of the unfairness of the violence I've been drawn into as things spiralled out of control comes out vocally, in one almighty, 'Arghhhhh.'

The primeval sound from the bottom of my gut sends the assailant running, either because he doesn't want to attract attention from anyone else in the area or because he thinks I'm a total psycho.

Am I?

Am I a psycho?

I drop onto my knees, level with Donald.

'I've pissed it all away,' he murmurs. Pain and humiliation are spread across his grey pallor as a dark patch seeps through his trousers. 'No pun intended.'

'Don't stress. I've been in a far worse mess than this.' I offer a hand to gently help him up.

'I don't know how it's come to this.' He's shaky on his feet and clings to my arm for support.

'Can you walk?'

'Not to the office. I don't want anyone to see me in this state,' he says, clutching his side.

'You need to get your ribs seen to.'

'The hospital won't do anything.'

'You should still get checked out.'

'I'll strap them up myself. Just put me in a taxi home.'

'Okay, but I'm coming with you to make sure you get there in one piece.'

With some reluctance Donald agrees and we set off for Edinburgh's south-west.

'Wait!' Donald cries to the taxi driver as he manoeuvres out of the city centre. 'Pull over for a minute.'

We swerve into the curb and Donald pulls out a note from his wallet.

'Pop in there and get me a nice piece of lemon sole. Get one for yourself too. It's the best.'

I look out of the window in confusion at the fishmongers. 'How can you think of food at a time like this?'

'Still need to eat and it's the best fish in town. I'll fry it off later for dinner,' Donald adds by way of explanation.

Despite the unusual request, I follow my boss's instructions.

It's freezing inside the shop, which is a positive sign because dead fish don't appreciate decomposing in a sauna. The service is above average too. I'm given a couple of fat fillets separately wrapped in plastic, then paper, then dropped into two carrier bags. They are like Russian dolls inside all the layers.

I pay the money and don't get much change. Understandable. High overheads, what with all the refrigeration and packaging.

***

Donald's stone villa in the elite suburb of Morningside has tradition engrained in every crevice.

'Let's sit outside,' says Donald.

'You don't want to lie down?'

'In a bit.'

'Nice place,' I say, walking over natural floorboards and a worn Persian rug, to an enormous gravel courtyard out back decorated with pot plants and outdoor furniture. Low-maintenance, high-value.

Donald lowers himself gingerly into a wicker chair.

'Can I get you something?'

'Paracetamol in the top kitchen drawer. A couple might knock this on the head.' He rubs his ribcage and I'm pleased to see the hint of colour coming back to his cheeks. 'Stick one of the fish in the fridge while you're in there. Enjoy the other one when you get home.'

I leave him sitting in the spring air. It's fresh but the sun is shining, and you have to make the best of minor joys on a day like today.

Surprisingly, the kitchen is shabby. Rickety cupboard doors no longer meet in perfect joins and the scratched workbenches must have seen better days. I put Donald's Russian doll in the fridge next to the butter and locate the headache tablets. Back in the courtyard, Donald has pulled a patterned blanket over his legs, covering his wet patch. The fabric has a pretty floral design all over it.

'Was there ever a Mrs McMahon?'

'Once upon a time. She divorced me when we fell into debt.'

'You doing okay since?'

'Nope. I remortgaged a while back.'

There's a look of Pa about him during those final days in the Cape. Dishevelled clothing, sunken eyes, worry lines etched all over sagging skin. Cause and effect.

'I'll make some tea.'

'One sugar,' Donald replies, matter of fact.

I make a brew in the kitchen. Despite its shabbiness, it's airy and spacious; far larger than the office kitchen, enormous compared to a cell. I feel liberated rather than claustrophobic in here, doing something useful. A tiny, good deed won't make much of a dent on my blemished track record, but it's a gesture of kindness from the heart.

I rummage in more cupboards until I find tea bags in a tin with the King of Diamonds on the front, one man upright, the other upside down; my own world also has two topsy-turvy faces.

The tea bags have strings attached and I dunk a couple in two mugs of hot water. Donald and I are two mugs in hot water too. Shame there's no string attached to us to yank us out.

I take the tea outside. 'You need to call the authorities, Donald.'

'Thanks for the advice, but I like my kneecaps as they are.'

'Are the sharks really that bad?'

'Great whites.'

'I thought loan sharks disappeared in the eighties.'

'It's like mullet hair. There are still a few lunatics hanging on to the good old days. I'd appreciate if you keep this whole episode close to your chest.'

I remember that day at home, playing rummy, cards hugged against my beating heart. I'm good at that. 'Of course. I've enough problems of my own keeping me occupied.'

'Figures.'

'Why?'

'When I spoke to your dad he seemed pretty eager to have you leave South Africa in a hurry.'

'I never thanked you properly for giving me a job so quickly.'

'Any boy of Ronald's has to be a good 'un.'

We sip hot tea. I'm usually more of a coffee man but the sugary liquid goes down well, despite my fat lip that has been developing. The British are right in their belief that tea has medicinal qualities.

'Anything I can do to help?'

I shake my head, unable to meet Donald's eye for fear he may see the tears forming in mine. 'Likewise, if I can fend off the sharks, let me know.'

'That fish is far too big to fry. Stick to the lemon sole.'

We finish our tea in companionable silence.

Chapter Thirty-Three

Crossing the exposed floorboards, my footsteps echo through the flat. In my bedroom I swap the pinstripes for my Mr Happy T-shirt and shorts, then stretch out the day with a few sit-ups. After the workout I wander to the kitchen, fry my complimentary lemon sole, and shove it between two slices of white bread. I'm about to tear into it when my mobile rings.

'Graham, it's me, Donald.'

'Oh, erm, hi.'

'My house is burning down.'

'What!'

'The fire brigade is here.'

'I'm on my way back.'

I hang up and give my sandwich a longing look, before removing the fish and binning the bread. On my way out, I toss the fillet to the tabby in the stairwell who gives a loud meow of thanks.

***

My taxi halts beside the crowd that has gathered in the street. They're nudging each other and pointing. Someone takes a selfie with the blue lights as a backdrop. The strobes are from a police car. Panic mounts but I give myself a stern talking to. They've no interest in me. It's not my show, it's Donald's.

A fire engine is parked curb side with the hose reeled out across the lawn. My boss is leaning against the red truck with a silver foil blanket wrapped around his shoulders. I could do with one of those myself. I'm still in my shorts and the fire hasn't taken the evening chill out of the air.

'Unbelievable!' Donald exclaims. 'I dozed off while my fish was cooking.'

'Are you okay?' I ask as two burly firefighters scuttle up his garden path to enter the house.

'I'm fine. Thanks for coming over. I appreciate the moral support.'

'Do you need a place to stay? The sofa's free if you need it.'

'That would be great.'

I cast my eyes towards the house. Smoke is billowing from the one downstairs window, but the building looks intact. 'Hopefully there's not too much damage.'

'I think the firemen have it contained in the kitchen. I wonder how long it'll take the insurance company to sort this mess out. One quick snooze and the place was ablaze.'

'If you snooze, you lose.' The words roll off my tongue.

'Not this time,' Donald retorts, meeting my gaze.

He's found the perfect solution. An insurance payout that will buy him a few cheap cupboards and leave enough left over to clear his debts. The fact my boss is committing fraud should faze me, but I've done worse.

I stand shoulder to shoulder with him until the drama eases and we're finally able to leave.

***

My buttered bread with streaks of incriminating fish oil stares at us as we enter my flat, so I dispose of the evidence while Donald takes in my digs.

'You renting this place?' he asks.

'Yah. There's no way I could afford to buy a place like this.'

'You're better off renting rather than being up to your eyeballs in loan repayments.'

'That's depressing.'

It should feel weird, chatting like this with my boss who is forty years my senior, but tonight we're equals.

I sort Donald a blanket and pillow for the sofa and click on the kettle.

'No beer?' he asks.

'I don't drink these days.'

Rummaging at the back of my cupboard, I find some tea bags still in there from the previous tenant.

'You used to drink then?'

'Yah. I got drunk one night and the situation spiralled out of control. That did it for me.'

'We've all done things we regret, Graham. It's how you handle your mistakes and bounce back that make you the man you are.'

'I didn't handle them well at all.'

'There's always a way to put things right.'

'Not always.'

For the second time today, we share a few minutes of companionable silence.

199

'Hopefully you get back in your place soon,' I say between sips of tea.

Donald nods. 'The fire authorities will need to declare the place safe, but I don't expect it will take too long.'

'The sofa is yours as long as you need it.'

'Thanks.'

'If it's too uncomfortable with the sore ribs, you can take my bed,' I offer.

'I'm fine. Really.'

'You going to be alright with the sharks?'

'Aye.'

'Do you remember how much my Pa loves to play roulette?'

'Not really, but you've piqued my interest.'

'He only ever plays two chips. A long shot on a single and the other on a six with better odds.'

'Conservative with an occasional reckless streak. Unusual in a gambler.'

'It sums up his strategy in life.'

'Do you share the same strategy?'

'I've no kind of plan. I just take it day by day.'

Donald nods and I drain my mug of tea until there's nothing but dregs left in the bottom.

Chapter Thirty-Four

'Donald, I almost fell off my chair when I read your text this morning,' Nancy gushes when we arrive in the morning.

It's a wise move on Donald's part to spread his own news directly to Nancy in a controlled manner. If Nancy had got wind of it second-hand, he'd have been better off being incinerated with the fish.

As a historical form of capital punishment, death deliberately inflicted by exposing extreme heat to a bound criminal was commonly used in many societies. Sometimes large fires would encompass several prisoners at once, executing them for prohibited activities such as witchcraft, treason, incest or homosexuality. The convict would sizzle until the diminishing of the body fluids finished them off. If they were very lucky, carbon monoxide might perish them prematurely before the flames licked away their skin. If I had been with Donald in his house when the fire took hold, I could have ushered him out while I stayed on the pretence of fighting the blaze, then hunkered down in the kitchen and let the flames engulf my guilt.

Cause of death: Burned at the stake.

'You should take some time off,' Nancy admonishes Donald.

'I'm okay. I've been staying with Graham.'

Nancy looks at me like I'm a rare specimen she's wrongly classified. Thankfully I'm saved from getting into a discussion about how friendly Donald and I have become by a jobseeker arriving for an appointment.

'Morning, sir. I'm Fatima Rampal.' My candidate looks impeccable in an orange embroidered sari, neatly applied make-up and shiny gold jewellery.

We exchange pleasantries as I invite her into the boardroom. 'So, tell me more about your career,' I ask, although I already know the basics. Fatima is promising talent identified by Benny in a recent search.

'I'm a practitioner of solutions architecture.' She launches into a stream of jargon in broken English, about being instrumental in helping the police overhaul their outdated technology with modern mobile widgets such as state-of-the-art body cameras.

There would have been some gruesome footage picked up if this type of equipment had been strapped on my torso that night in South Africa. 'When did you finish working on the police project?' I ask.

'A few months ago. I've been improving my English studies and helping in my husband's restaurant while I look for work.'

Despite her heavy Indian accent, she's incredibly articulate and responsive to my questions. Her expertise is exactly what I'm seeking for Hannah's consulting firm. 'What type of restaurant does he own?' I ask, done with probing on her employment history and technical skills.

'He owns the Taj Mahal Indian.'

'No way. I live upstairs from it. Mr Rampal is my landlord. He makes the most incredible biryani.'

Fatima smiles. 'Then you should know it is my secret recipe. I make best biryani for my husband's customers.'

'Yes, you do.'

'You get me job, I tell him to discount next curry,' she says, meaning any offer I make to her now may constitute corporate bribery. 'You will help?'

'Of course. You're my bread and butter, Mrs Rampal.'

'Not bread and butter. I'm your biryani,' she corrects me.

'Biryani it is,' I say, shaking on it.

***

I get to work, manually formatting Fatima's CV into a standard template because Benny still cannot parse without mushing all logic of the text and giving me back a cold pile of sick. I type in her availability and daily rate, run a spellcheck and sit back to admire my handiwork. The admin side of the job is tedious. Making candidate details look uniform with a TITS logo worn like a badge of honour.

'Quiz time,' Vermin announces.

'Don't worry. I'll make a brew,' Janine offers. 'I'm heading to the basement ... right now.'

'The usual for me, Janine.' Vermin gets up and follows her out.

I get back to Fatima and compare her details against my open jobs. She seems a sweet match, so I email Hannah her details – with two days exclusivity to consider suitability. As my first real client, it seems only right I give Hannah a premium service, allowing time to review a submission without the pressure of multiple applications causing a conflict. Going to have a Plan B though; to make sure I do what is right by Fatima, so I scour the job boards in case there are other opportunities to submit her for if she doesn't get the gig with Hannah. I run a few more searches for companies who are advertising on their own website career pages or utilising job sites to attract direct applicants and save on agency fees. I target the ads that have been running for a couple of weeks and drop in some cold calls to offer Talent-IT search and match services. The door gets slammed in my face a few times. Job boards are fundamentally changing the face of the recruitment industry. One day they'll kill us off completely. People are becoming a commodity you can order online, like a taxi or a pizza. To stay in the game, agencies need to become more nimble, innovative, unique. There's pressure on prof-itability, performance, productivity. Everyone wants more for less.

I leave my cube to stretch the legs. Kevin and Cassie are having animated phone discussions with candidates they're attempting to woo.

'What are you pacing around for?' Vermin asks, coming through the doorway with Janine behind him.

'Stretching the muscles. Where've you been?'

'Stretching the muscles too.' Vermin flicks his eyes towards Janine and grins.

'And you didn't bring coffee back?' I ask Janine.

'I'd rather stick pins in my eyes than make coffee for you lot. In fact, Graydon, I was thinking maybe you and I could nip out to Café Kamani?' Janine asks.

'What's the former name of Zimbabwe?' Vermin ignores her and launches into a quiz.

'Did you hear me?' Janine prods.

'Zimbabwe, anyone?'

With South Africa being a neighbouring country, I know the answer, but keep it to myself as Janine's voice raises several decibels.

'Am I invisible now all of a sudden?'

'Rhodesia,' yells Kevin.

'Shit,' says Janine loudly.

'It's only a quiz,' Kevin points out.

'I wasn't referring to the question, dumbass,' she replies. 'I meant Vermin. He's a shit.'

'Milk and two sugars please, sweetheart,' Vermin demands.

'I'm not your sweetheart.'

'I'm just the one sugar, thanks,' Kevin orders.

'Make it yourself,' Janine spits. 'You're no use to anyone here.'

'Shove your brew where the sun don't shine.' Kevin stomps out.

'Is anyone ever going to make the coffee in this place without all the drama?' I ask.

Vermin tries another question while I tinker with Benny. I wish I could establish a strong social media network for work purposes. It's the best place for fishing the white-collar pool. Many of them congregate online, promoting their endorsements, referring friends in group forums and waiting for that headhunter to tap them on the virtual shoulder. People are hooked on sharing their life journey on a public stage. If I had a Twitter, Facebook or Instagram account, it would allow me to build new direct connections who could introduce me to their second-, third- and fourth-level acquaintances. The world has shrunk to six degrees of separation. Subscribing to a global social media membership would allow me to befriend Mark Zuckerberg himself. I would have the very best candidates at my fingertips.

However, if I subscribe to social media, I'll also be only six people away from being found. I'm the anomaly who doesn't want to be social and has zero desire for media in my life. I don't want to Snapchat, or happy dance on TikTok, or have someone click 'like' when I hold such 'dislike' for myself. Six degrees of separation is not far enough away from those hunting down a reason to throw me back in jail.

No.

It's just me.

Me and Benny.

***

The stairs wind down through the centre of the building and I take them two at a time until I reach the basement toilets. There are no urinals, only a couple of communal cubicles and a row of sinks. Once done, I turn on the faucet, wash my hands and splash water on my face in an attempt to recharge the batteries. Stubble is appearing on my chin, even though I shaved this morning. My red-rimmed eyes are deadpan; lack of sleep takes its toll. Turning from the mirror, I reach for a paper towel and dry myself off. Something catches my eye as I drop the wet ball into the wire wastebasket.

A white plastic contraption is amidst the mass of damp green handtowels. At first glance I think it's a COVID-19 RAT, then I realise it's a pregnancy test kit but have no idea what the two blue lines mean, so I rummage through the rubbish to find the box and instructions. I'm aghast someone would leave something so intrusive in a place where it might be stumbled upon, and even more shocked someone in the office is pregnant.

I rule out Nancy who has to be past menopause. Could Cassie …? Surely the one person I rely on to get me through the day cannot be expecting a baby with Kevin. Maybe he left her with more than a hangover as a memento of that night in Wolfie's. I throw the contraption back in the bin, give my hands another wash, and rearrange the rubbish, covering any signs of evidence with more paper towels until the cleaners have a chance to empty the trash.

Then I wash my hands yet again, like a sufferer of OCD, but I can't scrub the thought of Cassie with a child from my mind. It's a trait of mine; storing reels of film to dust off and play whenever I like.

Could Cassie …?

Could Kevin …?

Could they …?

Checking my watch, I make my way back upstairs. I've candidates to phone, placements to make, a child to feed. The blue lines have driven home a stern reminder of my own obligations in this department and the commission I want to earn to pay for my mistakes.

Maak elke sekonde tel.

Placing people into jobs and wiring the proceeds back home. That's what counts now, nothing else.

***

Although I struggle to re-establish my labour of love with Benny without thinking of babies, I keep at it. It's hard finding great candidates you instinctively know are going to be star material for your client. Candidates like Fatima who are polite, highly skilled and available. I'll find Fatima a job if it's the last thing I do. Not just to score a free curry – even though it's a damn attractive incentive – but because I need to give back to society. If I find a thousand people new jobs it won't be enough to right my wrongs, but I have to start somewhere.

I google biryani and browse images of the fragrant rice dish as a distraction from the complicated women in my life: Cassie, Hannah, Erin, Ma. My fingers tap away and before I know it, I've changed my search, zooming in on a Google Earth satellite image of home, choking up as the recognisable terracotta tiled roof appears on my screen. I click over to eBay and purchase a rare Pearl Jam vinyl to keep the classic tunes alive. The internet is a miracle.

You can also register to join a terrorist training camp, download sickening pornography if you're of a twisted mind and hunt the corners of the earth for a deserter who has fled his country under false guise.

The internet is a monster.

I'm staying away from my own dark web. Avoiding the burning desire to search the news in Struisbaai to see if I'm an Ace of Spades on the wanted list. I'm the monster staying under this bed right here.

I crack my knuckles and wonder if catching arthritis from spending too long messing with Benny is covered by the NHS. My aching fingers type in a Wikipedia search because Wiki knows even more than Nancy, The Oracle. Wiki screams back. Two blue lines means somebody at Talent-IT Services is definitely pregnant. I spin in my chair, dizzy on the carousel at the fairground, grotesque clowns laughing in my face. Getting up abruptly, my chair tips over. I leave it and storm from my cube and out of the office.

I cross the road without looking, causing a motorcyclist to barely miss flattening me.

'You got a death wish, pal?' he hollers after screeching to a halt.

My morbid brain kicks in with thoughts about road traffic causes of death …

'Graham! You okay?' I turn to find Donald has followed me from the office. With all the day's highs and lows, I'd clean forgotten my house guest.

'Sorry, Donald. Are you coming back to my place?'

'Don't worry. I've checked into a hotel tonight and should be back in my place in no time. The damage wasn't that bad.'

'How did you go with the insurer?'

'Not so good. I thought they'd send me a cheque for the damage or EFT a cash deposit, but they said they'll pay a supplier directly to do a straight kitchen refit once my claim is finalised.'

Neither of us say anything, both knowing this outcome is disastrous for Donald.

'Enjoy your evening,' he says.

'You too.'

I head off alone and get the bus home, but find company at the other end of the journey.

'Hello, Graham,' Fatima says, startling me in the street outside The Taj.

Lucky appears behind her. 'You know my wife?' Puzzlement is etched on the features visible above his beard.

'He's helping me find job,' Fatima informs him.

'You work in computers?' Lucky turns to me.

'Sort of. I'm a recruitment agent in the technology industry.'

'I always thought you were one of those computer kids. A hacker maybe. Always buying takeaway, playing rock music too loud.' Lucky chortles and the sound rumbles between the tenements like the beginnings of a monsoon. 'What are the chances for my wife?'

'Good. She has outstanding technical capability.' I give Fatima an encouraging smile.

'Then you be best friend as well as best customer,' Lucky says before disappearing back inside with Fatima on his tail.

The tabby is about to wander past, but it stops in the street and rubs itself against my leg. I'm not an island. I have friends.

Benny, Lucky and now Tabby.

I'm not such a sad bastard.

I'm sadder.

Chapter Thirty-Five

Hannah and I follow a uniformed guard to a small window-less office who then leaves us alone while he tracks down the governor and a senior government official, both who work in a team managing a significant part of the Scottish budget for areas relating to law enforcement and justice. Hannah circulated Fatima's details and my other submissions to them, generating interest across the wider corrective system in both public and privately operated facilities, not just Bar-L. The meeting today is in a different penitentiary in Edinburgh's west which houses male and female inmates; smaller, less notorious, but equally as daunting. My identification is burning a hole in my pocket, hot and illicit.

No matter what side of the bars I'm on, prison is a place where my own personal desolation festers, where wretchedness eats the flesh, peeling back the skin to expose the weeping wounds buried beneath. Coping must be a daily challenge for so many prisoners. That's why we need ongoing reform, to minimise the number of troubled criminals who eat J-cloths and prevent puny-muscled inmates from dying from a slow puncture.

Even to make it through the short time I was incarcerated takes strength. Perhaps I've underestimated my own inner resolve and the tenacity it took to take on a new identity, travel with the ghost squad and flee my homeland. This iron will to beat the J-cloth and avoid the slow puncture comes from Pa. Half my genetic make-up stems from him and he's a good man who always finds a way to overcome adversity. I wonder about the rest of my DNA. Not the intricate science of chromosomes Jaco learned about at med school, but characteristics I might have inherited from my mother. How much of her kind heart and honest soul has been transmitted to me? Despite everything that has happened and the lies I've told, I live in a constant state of regret, and remorse is my constant companion – so a tiny bit of her must've rubbed off on me. Knowing I'm not all bad gives me comfort. Perhaps there's a chance I'm on the right side of the bars today where I can make the most of the opportunity I've been presented with; to make a difference.

Maak elke sekonde tel.

My heart pounds as I compose myself while sitting in a chair bolted to the floor. I mentally count the beat like the average fella counts sheep. The rate eventually steadies, slow and even. In contrast, Hannah nervously crosses and uncrosses her arms and legs.

'You okay?' I ask.

'This is our big chance to improve the system.'

'So, we'll make the most of the meeting.' I touch her lightly on the arm. She's wearing a strange turquoise woollen suit, rough in texture, old-fashioned. It may not be modern pinstripes but the fact she's in a suit at all means she's in serious business mode. She smiles gratefully but doesn't have time to say anything else before the two men enter.

They strike me as an important pair. Sombre faces, both with grey hair. The governor introduces himself, first name terms, as Terry. His clothing is ruffled, indicating he either hates to iron, or works long hours and has competing priorities that leave him with no time to get the wrinkles out of his shirts. Deep crevices branching from his eyes are like war wounds. He's seen it all and it's taken its toll.

I stand to shake hands, mine clammy but firm, then sit back down as Hannah dives in, rattling off details of her consulting firm. Her face is animated as she describes the work she does developing technology solutions that are pivotal to transforming correctional centres, moving them into a new future era; one of safety and rehabilitation front of mind; and automation, efficiency and cost effectiveness across back of house. Terry blinks rapidly at the mention of cost-effectiveness.

'Despite the constraints we work under, our prisons are more overcrowded than ever. Tension amongst prisoners is rising,' he tells us.

I doubt Terry knows the meaning of overcrowding. A dozen to a cell with a pet blanket each isn't normal practice in Scotland. Still, he has his own dilemma of managing intake surges on a budget that is pruned more often than my mother's roses.

'We can provide you with a valve to let steam out,' I reply. 'Inmates will be less irate if visitations run smoothly.'

The governor pushes his glasses up his nose with his middle finger. They're thin wired and fragile looking, but behind them are steely eyes. His lips form a determined line that silently speaks volumes. He himself is anything but fragile. This is a man used to getting what he wants and paying no more for it than market value.

'My prison cannot ever be compromised. Whomever we appoint to do work here must be of the highest calibre. Communication channels with the outside world need to drastically improve, but in a secure way.'

'All options presented have been thoroughly screened and are prepared to undertake necessary police checks,' Hannah assures them. 'Graham has taken references and personally met each of these candidates to also check their alignment to cultural fit.'

'At this stage, I'm prepared to consider hiring one candidate for three months to assess the current state and document potential for improvement,' the governor indicates.

'Which one is of interest?' I ask.

'Fatima Rampal. She has the solutions experience needed to cover a review of our architecture. Her experience identifying critical technology risks will make it much easier to upgrade our current system stack.'

I want to do a Mexican wave instead of shaking hands, but we keep up the tradition and I grasp the palm of the governor with mine, which is still clammy and still firm. Then we're escorted back down a bleak corridor joining the inside world to the outside.

My eyes narrow as we exit, attempting to restrict the natural light my pupils allow into my eyes. The reflex is swift to adjust to the sunlight after the dim florescent lighting inside the prison. I'm thankful I'm free again to look at the blue sky. Although it's not particularly warm, the clouds have parted, and rays of sun cast alternative patterns of light and shadows between the parked cars.

The effect is checkered, a mirror image of my own life.

***

Back at the office, I call Fatima with the news.

'You'll be working for a consulting firm but assigned to projects for the prison authorities. Even though it's an initial short contract, I'm confident there's more work in there.'

'I owe you best biryani,' she replies.

'You're going to accept?'

'Of course.'

This is a huge breakthrough for Hannah and I'm thrilled to be part of something new. Maybe not groundbreaking, like discovering penicillin, but having the right resources to take prison and probation technology in a different direction is rewarding in its own way. Everything we do could help each inmate have a better shot at rehabilitation and reintegrating back into society when they are released.

'Stop by for takeaway tonight if you like,' Fatima offers.

'I just might.'

'Or bring friend to dine in. I make biryani large size.'

I wind up the call and ask Cassie if she wants to join me at The Taj to share a free curry.

'I'll come on one condition.'

'What's that?'

'I can leave my mother at home.'

Mother.

Mother.

Mother.

Is Cassie going to become one? Curiosity over the two blue lines hasn't deserted me.

'Yah, of course you can leave your mother at home,' I say, deciding that tonight I'm going to ask her if she's pregnant. If she is, I'll be there to support her as a friend.

'Put your deal up on the board then.' Cassie jolts me into action.

I wander to the whiteboard. The placement of Fatima into Hannah's consulting firm takes me to the top of this month's ladder. Adding a tally is like adding a new pinstripe onto my suit with the vertical bars representing success, not crime.

'You screwed Hannah, didn't you?' Janine accuses. 'What is it with you men fucking clients for business?'

'Do you have to degrade everything down to sex?' I ask her. 'Nobody is fucking anyone.'

'Well, we all know that statement is not true. I know about Vermin and Marianne,' she announces. 'He told me himself.'

Vermin gives me a sheepish look from his corner. 'Marianne moved in with me. I had to say something.'

'I can't believe you would screw that Brazilian witch,' Janine shouts.

'Look, things got serious after the Grand National, what with Marianne in hospital getting her stomach pumped and everything. I stayed at her side the whole time. Then her husband found my texts. Goddamn mobiles cause so much shit.'

'Doesn't mean you have to ask her to move in.'

'Stop fretting, Janine. I'm not even sure it's gonna work out. She's already thrown out my Playboy collection.'

'Screw you.'

'No need when I have Marianne,' says Vermin.

Janine sticks her finger up at him over her partition and I can't hold back from giving her a clap.

Chapter Thirty-Six

As Cassie and I enter The Taj, Lucky Rampal gives us a nod towards an empty table as he hands a takeaway bag to another patron with one hand, while on the phone taking an order with his other.

'He's pretty talented at multitasking, don't you think?' I ask Cassie. 'Landlord, restaurant manager, maître d' and waiter, all rolled into one.'

'Yup. We could do with more men like him.'

'You know, centuries ago, a heap of Indian slaves were sold to white Dutch traders and put in townships with restricted boundaries to keep them on a short leash. They were forced to carry passes, were prohibited from walking on sidewalks, given inferior or no schooling, and they couldn't vote.'

'And since apartheid was abolished?'

'Might bring equality on paper but there's a long way to go. There is still political unrest and social divides that might not balance out in our lifetime.'

Lucky finishes his call and approaches our table. I offer a hand-shake. He ignores it and throws both arms around me in a hug.

'Order anything you like tonight,' he says, releasing me from his engulfing embrace. 'You are both my guests.'

'Your wife recommends the biryani. She says she cooks it.'

Lucky laughs. It's loud and infectious. 'It's true, but I can't believe she is sharing my trade secrets.'

'This is so kind of you,' says Cassie. 'What else would you recommend?'

Lucky reels off several dishes.

'Maybe a peshwari naan and tandoori chicken?'

'How hungry are you?' Lucky asks.

'Starving,' Cassie replies.

'Then leave it with me.'

As Lucky heads off to the kitchen, I scrutinise Cassie, wondering if she's eating for two.

'What?' she asks, her intense green eyes staring back at me. 'I missed lunch today so I'm making up for lost time.'

'Yah, you were pretty busy working on sorting that contract with Kevin.'

'We got the candidate signed up in the end.'

'I'm not sure it needed both of you though?'

'We were tackling something as a team. What's the problem?'

'No problem. It's just … Look at Vermin and Janine. Luigi might not approve of inter-office relationships, that's all.'

She blushes. 'Is that why you blow hot and cold? You're worried about what Luigi might think?'

'I'm just saying maybe things are complicated?'

'Complicated for who exactly? Who are we talking about here? Me, you, Kevin, Janine, Vermin? You're making no sense.'

'Maybe it's actually about someone else,' I say, thinking of her bringing a baby into the world.

'Now I'm totally confused. You are so frustrating,' she says as our steaming food arrives.

'Forget I said anything,' I say, dishing a pile of biryani onto my plate.

'That's easy. You didn't really say anything at all.'

We tuck in and move on to small talk. We're like an unfinished Rubik's cube. Forty-three quintillion potential moves we can make, but somehow, we can't seem to align.

***

When we're finished eating, I invite Cassie to my flat above the restaurant, cringing at the dirty trainers and socks lying just inside the front door. The lingering stench of curry fumes could have done with being attacked with a blast of air freshener too. I hadn't planned for company.

'What happened to the glass?' Cassie stares at the frame of the coffee table with no surface.

'Don't ask.'

'They look good there,' Cassie admires the thinking man and the elephant displayed on a shelf.

'They remind me of home.'

'Do you miss it?'

'Sometimes.' A lump in my throat stops me elaborating.

'I love that you have records. Shall I put some music on?' she asks, browsing my vinyl.

'Go for it.'

'Do you have any Jim Morrison?'

'Doesn't everyone,' I reply, raking through the albums to find *L.A. Woman*.

Music has a way of filling the empty abyss in my life with great lyrics or a catchy riff. We sit either side of the hollow table frame and listen to every track until Jim finishes off the B-side with 'Riders On The Storm'. Cassie taps the arm of the sofa. It's an infectious beat and I sing the chorus until Cassie joins in. We alternate waves of companionable silence and out-of-tune singing until the whole album is finished.

'I should go,' Cassie declares, calling a taxi when we're done with our karaoke duets.

'I didn't even make you a drink, not that I've anything stronger than coffee.'

'When did you give up drinking?'

'Just before I moved to Scotland.'

We get up and face each other. Nothing separates us but the gap left by a sheet of broken glass, my past and the possibility of a baby.

'It's been good chilling out,' she says softly, staring at me with those eyes.

'Yah. It's been fun.' I stare back for a few awkward seconds. Pregnant or not pregnant, I want to touch her face. Cup it in my hands. Taste her. Cassie makes me want to be a better person, but I don't know where to go next, so I show her out.

When she's gone, I throw the elephant across the room, denting the wall. I'll have to patch up if I ever want to get my rental bond back from Lucky. The trunk has snapped off the elephant. I grab some superglue from the kitchen drawer and carefully reposition the trunk back in its rightful place before I return it to the shelf. The thinking man looks at the patched elephant with interest. It may be scarred for life, but it has somehow survived the trauma I've inflicted upon it. It's a shame not everything can be repaired so easily.

Chapter Thirty-Seven

Nancy hands around the cream cakes again and tuts when nobody takes one. Lorraine shuffles nervously in her chair, while Kevin taps his fingers on the table. Cassie clears her throat for the third time. The atmosphere in the boardroom is more tense than the moment before Sir Alan Sugar announces the winner of *The Apprentice* on live TV.

'Sorry, folks. I'd take you all with me if I could, but the outright winner of the sales competition is Graydon Vernon.'

Vermin cocks an invisible pistol trigger and shoots the rest of us. I flinch when he points the gun at me.

'Janine Applegate will join him in second place, and we have third place going to Cassie Walker.'

Cassie is sitting next to me, so I reach over to slap her on the back.

'I've one last announcement to make,' Donald continues. 'The business development effort within the justice consultancy arena has given our branch sales an unexpected boost and is giving us growth footprint in a new sector showing huge potential. Graham, congratulations, you've been awarded a wildcard to attend. Luigi has taken a liking to you for some reason.'

'Wow, that's great, but I don't mind letting Kevin or Lorraine go,' I offer. 'I've not been with the company long.'

'It's already booked,' Donald replies. 'And the exact destination for the trip can now be revealed. You leave for Loch Awe in a fortnight.'

'What are we going to do in the Highlands?' Vermin asks.

'It's all in here.' Donald hands an envelope to each of us attending. 'There's not much about the agenda, but I'll be presenting SPIN for one of the sessions.'

'What's SPIN?' I ask.

'It's an acronym for situation, problem, implication, needs,' Donald explains.

'Thank goodness I'm not going,' Kevin mutters under his breath.

The glum look on his face tells a different story. His eyes are deadpan and brows are furrowed. Despite the irritating way he buzzes around Cassie like a mosquito, I don't like seeing him this way.

'You should be going,' I say.

'Whatever.' Kevin gets up and storms out. My intent wasn't to patronise. He's a great recruiter who makes quality candidate calls and is precise with CV formatting, just sometimes his finger isn't fast enough on the pulse of Benny.

Donald follows him, leaving us in the boardroom as we dive into the baked goods.

'Don't any of you get fed up with this hamster wheel?' Lorraine asks. 'It's total groundhog day.'

Vermin shrugs. 'I'll never get sick of beating everyone. Benny's totally my hero. He's Pandora's box. You don't know what's inside until you dive under the covers with him.'

For once, I don't disagree with Vermin. Benny should be reclassified from a legacy to a national treasure. Until I began sending money to Erin, I wasn't conscientious about maximising my earning potential. I'd steer clear of competitive situations. This whole race up the sales ladder makes me think back to sports day in primary school.

'Hurry up, you two,' Ma shouts along the passage to me and Jaco. 'Get your takkies on.'

'Yah,' we reply in harmony.

I perch on the bottom stair of the house in my bottle-green sports shorts. It's easier to put my running shoes on while sitting down. They're brand new. My first pair with laces instead of velcro. I can't wait to wear them. Jaco, only a year older than me, has had laces for ages.

Despite being keen to show off my new takkies, I'm sick in my stomach at the thought of running in front of my parents. Ma's taken a day off work from the library. The only time she ever takes time off is for sports day or the annual school fete. She's invented a new classification system which nobody dares interfere with, so she'll have a skyscraper of books to shelve when she gets back.

'You need sunscreen on,' says Ma.

I let her slap it on me even though it's pointless. There's no need for sunscreen when you're running in the shadow of your brother.

'Have you brought the camera, Ronald?' she asks Pa.

'Yah. Let's go,' he hurries us out the door.

It's hot outside, not a cloud in sight despite living in the 'Cape of Storms'. The weather is a disappointment. A burst of rain might have meant postponement.

The four of us walk to school, winding past the houses scattered down the flora-covered mountain. At the bottom, we turn left by the grocery store, which doubles as a post office, and we're there.

The grounds are packed with other bottle-green shorts and adults with cameras. Some families have brought camping chairs and over-sized cool boxes. Ma only has a Tupperware of sandwiches, perhaps because she knows I'd be tempted to crawl inside a cool box to hide. We won't go hungry. Ever since Jaco ran in his first event we've had a nice family tradition of going for fish and chips after sports day finishes.

It seems only seconds pass before the school bell rings, but we don't go to our classrooms. Instead, we sit in rows on the school lawn, next to the overturned fishing boat the kids use as a climbing frame. I mime the school hymn while Jaco warbles at the top of his voice, then we're off.

A yellow ribbon, a green and two reds for Jaco. He's in the top three in all of his races. I place fifth in the relay. Fifth out of six is good. Better than not finishing.

The noise builds until we reach the finale; the egg-and-spoon relay with pupils versus parents.

The klaxon goes and Pa and Jaco take off, gaining a few inches to get ahead of me. My takkies cover ground so fast I can't keep up with them. My egg starts to wobble and I manage another metre or two before one of my laces turns into a trip-wire.

Ma rushes over and helps me clean the egg off my brand-new shoes.
'You've egg on your face,' Jaco laughs, brandishing another ribbon.
I want to go for fish and chips now.
Sports day sucks.

Chapter Thirty-Eight

O n the day of departure, the team heading north stand out a
mile. We are all dressed-down in casual civvies as opposed to
Kevin and Lorraine who are sombre in their pinstripes.

Our minibus is transferring us to the Highlands in the next half-
hour, but it's supposed to be business as usual until then. Luigi will
squeeze us like lemons until the bitter end to quench his thirst. Cassie
crosses my perimeter before I've time to run a quick search on Benny.

'You all packed?'

'Yah, my case is in the boardroom next to a huge pink one.'

'That'll be my luggage.'

'You need to be on anabolic steroids to lift that thing.'

'I didn't know what to pack. I know it's almost summer, but this
is Scotland.'

'I've brought Louis.' Janine crowds into my section too.

'How can you afford a Louis Vuitton?' Cassie asks.

'It's fake. I've the matching handbag too.' Janine disappears and
returns with a tan-coloured bag.

'What's so special about a Louis Vuitton?' I ask.

'Don't you know anything? Handbags are to women what cars are to men,' Janine replies. 'Performance and capacity are paramount, but exterior colour and superior interior lining add to the overall appeal. This, my friend, is the Lamborghini of bags.'

The three of us laugh. It's the smartest thing I've ever heard Janine say.

'Speaking of cars, without females the world would be full of Fords with nobody to escort.' Vermin crams into the pod, wearing a tartan kilt with a pristine white T-shirt. 'Get it? Ford Escort.' He laughs at his own gaffe as we groan.

'What's with your gear?' I ask.

'I want to do my ancestors proud.'

'What ancestors? You might lord it around here, but if you had lineage from an elite Scottish clan, you wouldn't be slumming it at TIT,' Janine backchats.

'Who says I'm slumming it?'

'How's Marianne today?' Janine spits.

'Haven't you work to do?' asks Kevin.

'Just because you flunked, don't spoil our fun,' Janine tells him.

'Don't be such a bitch,' Vermin says to her.

Janine crosses her arms. 'Better a bitch than a bitch in heat like Marianne.'

'She might well be a dog but at least I can give her a bone.' A smug grin spreads across Vermin's face.

Janine turns pale and storms off.

'You're worse than toddlers on blue food colouring. Why do you wind her up?' I ask Vermin as Cassie follows Janine. 'You don't have to rub her nose in it, you know.'

'Forget Janine. Wait till I tell you about Marianne rubbing me up in my Porsche this morning,' Vermin gloats. 'That woman is straight to fifth gear every time.'

'I'd rather not hear it, thanks, but since we have to spend a whole trip with Janine, try and be nice.'

'You're right. I could ping her for a booty call while we're away.'

'That's not what—' My phone rings, sparing me from giving a response.

'It's me. The CAD.'

'What's up?'

'I was in Luigi's office and he told me Donald's been chasing a salary advance.'

'Did he give it to him?'

'Think so. He's asked me to monitor him and made me install discreet spyware on his PC. It's borderline illegal. Think remote-controlled software and a key logger so I can monitor every keystroke and mouse click, capturing emails, bank details, whatever.'

'What are you, some kind of spook?'

'These gadgets are more common than you think. I've even heard of a mouse that has a built-in microphone and camera to let you spy on the user.'

'How long before Luigi puts a bug in the shithouse?'

'I didn't think of that.'

'Why are you telling me all of this?' I ask.

'Luigi will go nuts if he finds out I've leaked this, but he's watching Donald, so someone needs to have his back.'

'What am I, a good Samaritan?'

'I know you'll keep an eye out for him.'

The CAD puts the phone down and I vow to myself to stay close to Donald. His insurance scam has fallen flat and now he's in Luigi's pocket instead of Big Mal's.

It wasn't my intention to add the weight of Donald's issues to the boulder already on my shoulders, but perhaps this is my fate. To be slain in historical fashion by having an intense weight placed upon my person. For thousands of years, elephants were commonly used to crush people in Asia for their wrongdoing. In medieval Europe, one method of torture was to place hard stones upon the defendant's chest until they either condemned themselves or the stones condemned them. Sometimes an iron vice was even used to crush various parts of the body, including the head, turning the screws until the skull exploded into pulp like a watermelon. Although South Africa abolished capital punishment in the nineties, there are still many who would like to bring the practice back again.

Cause of death: Crushed.

Thinking of heavy burdens, if Cassie is pregnant, she shouldn't be lifting bulky items. I run downstairs and drag her pink case to the front entrance, so it'll be easy enough to pick up on the way out to the minibus. I sit on top of the case to catch my breath. Images of babies with curly auburn hair twist my mind until it's spaghetti in a tin.

Chapter Thirty-Nine

The scenic drive takes us via Tyndrum towards Oban. We wind past steep ravines and lush green valleys, through arches where the trees meet in dense, eerie silence.

'Some of Scotland's oldest clans owned land around here,' Vermin tells us. 'Robert the Bruce defeated the MacDougall clan on this grass.'

'Who nominated you designated tour guide?' Janine asks.

'You should be proud to be Scottish,' he retorts.

'Who said I wasn't proud? Just don't need to put up with you lifting your kilt to show us your own measly heritage, thanks.'

Vermin stands in the aisle and thrusts his sporran so it trampolines on his privates.

'This isn't just a jolly.' Donald turns from his seat and gives Vermin a stern look. 'We're going to embrace being sent to a serious training camp for our highest performers.'

Under his breath Vermin mutters, 'Goes without saying I'm a high performer inside of work and outside.'

Chastised, the rest of us fall into silence. High performer is not a term I'd have used to describe myself in the past, more dependable than a stand-out.

In my last job at the PC repair shop several regular customers knew the pride I took in my work. The satisfaction of taking apart a damaged hard drive and putting it back together again was enough for me. Most customers were in turmoil when their computers died on them. 'Without my machine, my life is over,' I heard on many occasions. I used to sympathise before the mighty scale of real disaster hit home.

***

We arrive at the only hotel for miles, perched on the edge of Loch Awe. It's a stone building with turrets and a view to die for. Jaco would appreciate a majestic place like this. Wish you were here, boeta.

When my brother moved to Cape Town, our town seemed quieter, like the bell had been removed from the local church tower. I never got over him leaving me in the lurch that night. Still haven't.

We disembark from the bus and the driver heaves our luggage from the hold. The enormous pink case requires muscles on steroids, so I help off-load then tug it towards the main entrance, my own overnight bag slung over my shoulder.

Cassie walks alongside me. 'I'll take that.'

'It's seriously heavy. I've got it.'

We enter the reception area which bears a lot of resemblance to Dalhousie Castle. Maroon walls, decorated with a stuffed deer above a fireplace. A hearth stacked with wood logs, ready to ignite when the weather inevitably changes from mild to freezing. The tartan carpet has a similar pattern to Vermin's kilt, except his has more prominent checks. He favours garish thick pinstripes too.

The reception desk is made of rich, deep mahogany, carved with an intricate crest of arms in the centre. A lamp to one side is shaped like an old-fashioned oil lantern. Perhaps it's the real deal.

The silver-haired receptionist checks in Donald. She has a brooch on her cardigan that looks as ancient as the hotel. 'If I tumble in the loch with that beautiful piece in my pocket, I'm a goner,' Donald says as she hands him a key hanging on a huge brass keyring.

She smiles and explains where breakfast is served and the location of the Cruachan suite.

'See you at five for the kick-off session.' Donald heads off.

For my sins I'm sharing with Vermin, and we check in next. Filling in the paperwork with my name, address and date of birth requires concentration. If I make a mistake the receptionist will be on to me, so I take care. Do it right first time. Reluctantly I part from the pink case and leave Cassie and Janine to shuffle forward. They too are roomies.

'Don't be rolling in the mud, you two,' Vermin tells them. 'This place looks like it has enough ghosts already, so we don't need you killing each other.'

They laugh but I shudder at the mention of ghosts. Me and the dead have our own history to grapple with.

I follow Vermin into the lift that has a mellow Kenny G saxophone instrumental playing and a thick-ply wine-coloured rug on the floor with 'Monday' embroidered in the middle.

'You'd better not snore,' I say to Vermin.

'And you'd better get out if I need the room for me and Janine,' he responds.

The doors ping open, and we locate our room. The colossal brass keyring rattles as I open the door and enter a spacious room with standard twin beds covered in crisp white linen. 'Wow. I was expecting chintz.'

The hotel has tastefully integrated old and new, with a flat screen plasma housed in a wooden cabinet and a sound system extending to the marble bathroom. The bath is freestanding with claw feet, a nice touch if I were on a romantic break with a girlfriend, but I don't fancy relaxing in a bubble bath while Vermin takes a shit in the porcelain toilet next to it. The lack of bathroom privacy reminds me of pet blankets and freaks me out. Heart palpitations and sweaty palms, minor stuff, nothing I can't hide.

We should have known better.

We should have known better.

We should have known better.

I leave Vermin to unpack and go onto the balcony to take in the view, gulp in the fresh air and calm my bongos.

Loch Awe, Scotland's longest freshwater loch, is flanked by the velvety ridges of the Cruachan Hills which reflect on the water. A couple of small islands float amidst the splendour, disconnected from the rest of the earth.

Am I still an island?

Cassie, the friend I keep at arm's length. Hannah, the client who drags me to the pub even though I don't drink. Donald, the boss who gambles like Pa, except Pa knows when to cash his chips in. They're all in my present. A whole era of my life has been amputated and all of my past memories are now internalised.

It's safer to remain a reclusive introvert than exposed for what I am. For what I did. In fact, I've always been something of an introvert.

It's a school fundraiser. Shiraz and Jazz night in the local church hall. Our family and the Van Der Merwes take a round table, combining our cheese platters and forces to make a team for the evening's quiz.

Erin sits between Jaco and me. We're pubescent and horny and it's hard not to stare at how her chest's starting to fill out. Erin is the prettiest beach babe in town. Always make-up free. Natural blonde. Great figure.

Pa calls our team 'No Prohibitions' which makes everyone cheer when the school principal announces it on the microphone.

There's a trivia round on food and drink. Pa and Mr Van Der Merwe get all the wine questions right. Ma takes us into first place with her recipe knowledge and literary expertise of classics like **The Great Gatsby.** *Then* **The Cats Pyjamas** *catch-up in the sports round. By the end of the last round, it all rides on a tie breaker.*

'Which famous Jasper starred in the TV sitcom, **All About Me?'**

The principal drawls on his pronunciation of Jazzzzper and I know the answer immediately.

I whisper to Erin and Jaco. 'Jasper Carrott.'

'Are you sure?' Jaco checks.

'Yah, I saw it once. It was funny, boeta. I'm telling you it's Jasper Carrott.'

'Go for it,' Erin says to me.

'JASPER CARROTT,' Jaco yells.

'Correct!' shouts the principal.

The whole place erupts.

It blares over the sound system. 'No Prohibitions' are the official Shiraz and Jazz champs.

Pa is on his feet, back-slapping Mr Van Der Merwe and giving Ma a smacker on the lips.

He moves around the table and hugs Jaco who grins from ear to ear.

'*You did it, son. You did it!*'

Jaco looks at me from over Pa's shoulder and I shrug. He knows, I know and Erin knows the glory is mine.

We're a team and I'm happy for Jaco to relish in the moment.

Chapter Forty

I'm sandwiched between Vermin and Revis Sicklemore for dinner. I'd have preferred to be next to Cassie who's at the opposite side of the circular table beside Donald, but we've been slapped with predetermined place settings. She looks amazing in a plain blue dress with sparkling straps. It skims her curves in all the right places.

'You ready for what's ahead?' Revis asks.

'Dunno. What's next?'

'It's a miracle Nancy didn't leak the program.' Revis chews on a piece of steak for longer than necessary so she doesn't have to spill the beans.

'Divin' madda,' Darren Skelding remarks from beside Janine. 'Luigi's ganna tell us all noo what te expect.'

Darren is a good-looking Geordie from the Newcastle branch, with hair blow-dried into a peak that has more height than a Scottish Munro. I strain to understand a word he's saying because of his excessive use of vowels.

'Are you still holding the Stud Muffin title up north?' Bill McGrath asks Darren with an Irish lilt. He's the bald, middle-aged branch manager of the Belfast office.

'Aye. I'm still a total stud, Bill.'

'I heard it was because you buy blueberry muffins for the girls in the office most mornings but can never find a decent girlfriend.'

'That cat's well and truly out of the bag then,' Darren says in good nature.

'And is it true what they say about you, Graham?' Bill McGrath asks.

'What do they say about me?' I snap.

'Calm yourself. Just that you have a great reputation for representing diverse candidates and are making some great placements. It's good. Diversity makes for a better workplace. I once sent a deaf man for a PC support job in a call centre,' says Bill. 'He got the job and they supplied him a phone with digitalised voice recognition software built in. It was very cool.'

This piques my interest. Equipment for the deaf that relays what's being said visually on a screen. Not useless technology or software like the invention of a smiley emoji app. I chat to him about the technology adoption in the prison service and the conversation makes dinner pass quickly.

Tummies full, we shuffle into a semicircle. Luigi assumes a commanding presence – front and centre – in a cream suit and leather loafers. Only an Italian millionaire could go for the *Miami Vice* look and still look credible.

'Welcome,' Luigi bellows. 'I hope you're enjoying the cuisine and the resplendent Highlands setting.'

He hasn't said anything rapturous, but everyone claps with old-fashioned British politeness.

'You're my prize performers. Have fun and learn from each other. Enjoy the experience and seize the day!' Luigi gathers momentum. 'Success is a ladder you cannot climb with your backside in a seat and your hands in your pockets. Leave that to your managers. Get out and pound pavement. Put the extra in front of ordinary. Catching a big fish is just as easy as catching a small fish if you develop the confidence to reel them in, which brings me to tomorrow. You will be going fishing with your team. The baiting and waiting is all about anticipation and reward.'

Fishing. This perks me up.

'Get an early night and create a team name before you meet at the loch after breakfast tomorrow. Your cameramen will be waiting there for you, but let me introduce them to you now.'

Three men appear and form a line beside Luigi.

'This is Ian, Clayton and Denny. You'll be divided into three groups and will be allocated one of these business psychology experts to record and debrief all activities.'

We split into teams. I'm with people I've already got to know; Bill McGrath, Revis, Stud Muffin, Vermin, Janine, Donald and Cassie. Our chaperone, Ian, is a sixties hippy; a printed tunic top hanging over worn jeans and a bunch of beads decorating his neck.

'Take a look at who is on your team. You're stuck with them until we leave,' says Luigi. 'They'll be your confidants to share your successes, failures and innermost thoughts with. Welcome to Loch Awe Liberation Camp.'

The delegates break into a round of applause, but I cannot share the enthusiasm. This isn't a liberation camp, it's Camp Abattoir.

If I share my innermost thoughts, it will be slaughter time.

Chapter Forty-One

I 'm up early the next morning and head down to the loch. My toes are inches from the water's edge. The ripples on the surface indicate fish are plentiful. One of my happiest memories is of Pa taking Jaco and me as youngsters to the rocks in L'Agulhas with our rods. He had a cool box full of Castle Lager and enough bait to last the day.

Jaco casts the first line and comes up empty-handed, so Pa tries next with the same scarcity of results.

'Maybe we should go home now,' I suggest as the wind picks up an unpleasant pace.

'Patience and attention to detail are the best tools to take on a fishing expedition.'

'What should I look for?'

'Telltale signs of disturbance. On a flat day, big ripples can mean a whole school of fish are close to your hook.'

Jaco goes again but comes up without a catch.

When it's my turn, I cast an extra-large chunk of squid towards the spot where two birds swoop.

The tug on my line is fervent. 'I think I've got one, Pa!'

'Keep a cool head,' he replies.

My rod jerks and I grip tightly with both hands.

'Don't let go.' Jaco starts off-loading bottles from the cool box as if he's bailing a sinking ship.

'It's a power of the wills,' says Pa. 'If you want the prize badly enough you mustn't let it escape.'

'It's heavy.'

Pa gives me a hand to reel in a waist-height catch. 'This baby is huge! Watch your fingers.'

The three of us wrestle it down, me and Jaco holding the writhing body as it snaps back at us. Pa takes the hook from the mouth and sticks a finger in the fish's eye to stop it wriggling. When he twists the head back, the action is quick; an inhumane act made more humane by speed. It's not often Pa kills a fish. Usually he tosses them back in, but this is a huge catch.

We take it home in the cool box, the enormous tail sticking out.

Pa shows us how to bleed out, behead and gut a dead fish. It's visceral work and I'm relieved when it's clean, skin side down, sweating on foil on the braai. Ma goes at it with the basting sauce. Melted butter, garlic, apricot jam.

Snoek is as much a part of the Cape Ocean as Table Mountain is part of the Cape's iconic vista. My catch feeds our whole family, Erin and her folks too. I almost burst with pride when Erin says I'm the finest fisherman she's ever met.

Cassie joins me, wearing spotty wellington boots already caked in mud. It's summer but petrichor is emanating from the ground covered in a wet dew. A layer of mist hangs over the loch bringing an eeriness to the atmosphere. It's made her hair frizz and added a sheen to her rosy cheeks.

'Stunning, huh?' she greets.

'Incredible.'

We are staring at the panorama when Ian disturbs us with the rest of our group. He has a tripod under one arm, a camera around his neck and he's sprouted a pair of sandals with socks. Sandals and socks on men in the IT industry generally represent a stereotypical nerd developing a *Pac-Man* revival in their basement that can take down *Angry Birds*. But Ian isn't here to challenge *Angry Birds,* he's here to challenge us.

'Morning all.'

We greet him in unison; a sign our team might be in sync already.

'You all know my purpose is to capture you completing certain activities. I'll also debrief you each evening, in a group and individually. During these sessions, I'd like you to be as open and honest as you can. In case you're wondering about my qualifications, I was a family counsellor before becoming a business coach.'

'All we need is a couch and a box of tissues,' says Stud Muffin.

Ian ignores him. 'You'll get out of this course what you put into it. Now, I'm going to switch on the camera and it will remain on until you head off to sleep tonight. You'll work together for three hours to catch what you can. Your fish will be weighed in later against the other teams.'

'Sounds easy enough,' Donald declares.

'But there are rules,' Ian warns.

We all groan.

'You must work out how to fish safely as a team. If at any time you're putting other team members at risks with hooks and such like, you down tools in a thirty-minute penalty.'

Being thrown in the deep end is not an issue. I can show the basics of fishing to the team which may put us at an advantage against the others if they've no seasoned fishermen in their crew.

Ian points to a boatshed half a kilometre or so along the shore beside the rowboats. 'All equipment for the teams are in there. No more than two people can travel there at once and you cannot physically carry more than two items each back in your bare hands.'

'Is this one of those maths riddles? You know, seven men had seven wives with seven dogs and how many fleas in total did they all have?' Bill McGrath asks.

Ian tells us the final rule, 'Once the fishing period is over, you then have to cook these fish for your own lunch. You'll have nothing else other than bread and wine with it, so I hope you manage to get a decent haul.'

'This is ne maths riddle. It's the last supper,' declares Stud Muffin.

Donald steps in. 'Let's come up with a team name?'

'The Studs,' Vermin offers.

'You're not a stud, you're a donkey,' Janine spits.

'And you can ride me any time,' Vermin replies.

'You think you're the king of men, but you're not.' Janine folds her arms. 'How about Donkey Kong?'

'The iconic arcade game,' says Bill. 'What a perfect name for a bunch of IT recruiters. This is guerrilla warfare. All we need now is a couple of barrels to throw at the enemy.'

We agree, Donkey Kong it is, and Ian claps to set us all going. Nobody moves.

'Let's crack on,' I say.

'Who's going?' Vermin asks.

'Not you by the looks of those member's yacht club shoes,' Bill

McGrath says laughing at his shiny loafers that he's wearing without any socks. 'Did you shop for those at the same place as Luigi?'

'I can cook,' he says, with a flamboyance suggesting his cooking skills are as bad as his dress sense.

'I'll go,' Revis Sicklemore declares.

'That boatshed could be lonely, pet. I'll gan' we ye,' Stud Muffin offers.

Revis shrugs and jogs off with him behind her.

'Are you going to leave that pair alone?' Janine asks Ian.

'You should be worrying less about those two and more about your strategy,' he replies, swivelling the camera towards us as Luigi approaches and leans against a tree to watch.

'We haven't got a plan of attack yet,' Bill tells him.

Vermin intervenes, 'Aye we do. Instead of trying to catch a load of small fish, we could catch one big fish. Ian said get the fish get weighed in, not counted in.'

I have to give it to Vermin; it's a genius pick-up. 'We'll need to go in deeper.'

'I'm good at that,' Vermin says, catching Janine's eye before she stomps off.

'I should go after her,' I say to Ian.

'Leave her to enjoy the fresh air,' he replies.

'Bit selfish of her. She's left us one short on the Donkey Kong team,' says Vermin. 'When Revis and Darren come back, two more could go for one of those row boats. A couple can go on the boat while the rest shore fish.'

Luigi claps and nods at Vermin. 'You lot have a spanner in your team.' He wanders over to the other group huddled a few metres away.

'Spanner means planner,' Donald explains. 'Let's decide who's going for the boat. Revis and Darren are on their way back already.'

'I'll go,' I offer.

'And me,' Cassie adds.

'No, you can't. It weighs a ton,' I tell her.

'So what? I'm not a total weakling, you know.'

'I didn't say you were,' I snap, driven insane between wanting to protect a pregnant friend from heavy lifting and feeling that gut punch when thinking of her with Kevin.

'I'll go with Graham,' Bill volunteers.

The camera light catches my eye. Green, like Cassie's eyes. Green, for go.

'We need to get moving,' I say to Bill as the runners approach with a fishing rod and bait box each.

Bill and I set off at speed.

'How come you're so fit?' I ask between puffs, struggling to keep up.

'My Da was killed during the Troubles. Both legs blown off 'cos he didn't run fast enough.'

I run faster.

'What's your story?' Bill asks as we reach the boatshed.

'I'm hoping Ian's camera runs out of film before I have to share.'

'Your story is worse than mine then?' Bill asks as we haul a rowing boat onto dry land. He doesn't press me when I don't answer. 'Let's load this baby with gear and leave nothing for the other teams,' he says.

'What about the rule about carrying only a couple of things at a time?'

'Ian said we can't physically carry more than a couple of things with our bare hands. We're only going to have one item in our bare hands. The boat.'

We go back in the boat shed and stare at the fishing equipment surrounding us. Half-a-dozen rods, bait, hooks and buckets.

'Just to be sure we won't get disqualified, we could row back with the stuff,' I say. 'That's definitely not physically carrying anything.'

'An even better loophole. Fucking ace,' Bill says as we supermarket sweep the place, two items at a time, until the rowboat is full.

We tug the boat to the loch and jump inside, not caring that our feet take a soaking.

'Hey, you can't do that,' The CAD shouts, approaching the shed with another colleague.

'Watch us,' Bill shouts back.

'Sorry, mate,' I call to The CAD, tugging ferociously on the oars to cut gashes through the water.

The team are up ahead, chanting 'Donkey Kong'.

'If you go with one of them in the boat, I'll rally the rest to fish from the shore,' Bill suggests.

Ian has the camera pointing at us.

'This is what you call taking out the competition,' Bill shouts as we approach and off-load a heap of kit two items at a time.

'You up for a couple of hours out there?' I ask Cassie.

'Depends on what other crazy stunts you're thinking of pulling to win this task.'

'Does it matter?'

'Don't suppose it does.' She wades in.

'Bet you didn't think recruitment would bring us here.' I grab an oar and synchronise rowing strokes with Cassie.

'Did you?'

'I just wanted to get out of South Africa.'

We both stop rowing and the boat floats in the loch. There are no ripples. The undercurrent is in the air rather than the water, and I want desperately to win back her friendship.

'If I'd stayed with my parents, my life would have been over.'

Cassie stiffens. 'That's how it is for me.'

'Your mother?'

'After Dad left, she became bitter, but I'm all she's got.'

'If you leave home, you can still be part of her life.'

'Maybe. What is it between you and your folks?'

'They were always there for me, but I fucked up. Staying there would have been a constant reminder of it, so I saved them the trouble and left.'

'Have you ever asked them if they want to be saved?'

'I didn't need to.' We pick up a steady rhythm again and out of nowhere I say, 'How are you and Kevin travelling?'

'Not by boat,' she jokes, before adding, 'there is no me and Kevin.'

'I saw you together in Wolfie's.'

'I've told you before, nothing happened. He made a move and if you'd stuck around long enough you would have seen I backed off.'

'And that night when you were out with him on the Royal Mile?'

'You were having drinks with Hannah, but it doesn't mean you two are an item, does it? Kevin is just a friend.'

'So, you're not pregnant?'

'Pregnant?' Cassie's eyes bulge. 'Did you seriously think …?'

'I found a test in the basement. Blue lines and all.'

'It certainly wasn't mine.'

'Whose was it then?'

'Not Lorraine's. Her hubby had the snip,' says Cassie.

'Janine!' we say in unison.

'Vermin's?' Cassie asks.

'Dunno. You ready to fish?'

'For more info on the Janine situation or for lunch?'

We pull our oars into the boat. 'Can I just say, I'm pretty relieved you're not up the creek and the paddle is right here.'

This gets a smile out of her.

'I should be mad at you,' she says. 'I can't believe you thought I might be pregnant with Kevin's baby!'

'No time to be mad. We have to work as a team. One for all and all for Donkey Kong.'

'You better catch one heck of a bad boy.'

'Isn't that what landed Janine in trouble?'

We chuckle and I hook my bait onto the line.

***

Donkey Kong have a trout feast to cook; six brown and one rainbow, which Ian tells us must be a random escapee from a local fish farm.

We're huddled around a gas barbecue and a table containing a bunch of parsley, salt, oil, and a chopping board and knife. The other teams are across the grass, planning how to make their measly catches stretch further.

'I recall being allocated the job of head chef.' Vermin grabs the paring knife in his hand.

'Before you cook, there are some new rules,' Ian interrupts. 'You've one hour to prepare your meal, which Donkey Kong will eat for lunch. Myself, Luigi and the other two coaches will also sample food prepared by all three teams to score your efforts.'

We groan.

'The final rule is there are no rules. You can beg, steal and borrow ingredients from the other teams as each has three unique basic food items provided.'

Bill cranes his neck to see what the other two teams have been issued. 'Nobody else has olive oil, but there's pepper and a lemon. And those lucky bastards have soy sauce.'

'Donkey Kong, your time starts now,' Ian announces.

Janine is suddenly back, dishing out orders. 'Get on with it then,' she tells Vermin, plonking the dead catch on the table in front of him.

'I'll do it.' I take the knife as Vermin dry-retches.

I make rapid work of gutting the fish while Donald wanders towards team two and chats to Luigi. While the two men talk, Donald slides the soy sauce into his jacket pocket before casually strolling back to add his prize to our ingredients.

'If you value your life, crawl back where you came from,' Bill McGrath snarls at someone he catches on all fours under the table attempting to pilfer our oil. The thief scuttles off empty-handed while Bill cradles the oil in both hands, legs apart, facing the enemy line.

'The parsley's gone!'

'How did they get past me?' Bill asks, perplexed.

I stand next to him to help protect our supplies while pandemonium breaks loose.

Three competitors surround Revis Sicklemore. 'Hey, watch you don't knock me,' she shouts.

'Rather, be careful you don't knock them,' says Vermin, staring at her chest.

'Back off,' the Stud Muffin tells Vermin.

'What?' Vermin exclaims. 'It wasn't even me who knocked her.'

'Yeah, it was,' says Revis. 'Just not with your elbow.'

'Yeah, Vermin.' Janine prods Vermin in the chest. 'And have you suddenly forgotten about poor Marianne while you are ogling everyone else.'

'What the hell do you care?' Vermin replies as Donald attempts to protect the salt but is outrun by The CAD.

'That's it.' Bill passes the oil to Cassie and storms into battle.

She clicks on the barbecue, and I drizzle the griddle with olive oil, trying not to think of the bottle in the larder next to Pa's gun.

We douse the first fish in soy sauce and throw it on the heat beside a second smeared with oil and parsley.

'What's the point of this exercise?' Cassie asks, as Bill returns from a tour of duty with a jar of marmalade.

'I'm not sure if it's to chase the big fish or to screw our colleagues.' I smear the marmalade onto one of the fish. 'This is my mother's recipe, well, kind of. She loves to use apricot jam on fish. It makes the best marinade.'

'Marmalade marinade sounds nice,' says Bill. 'There was a chilli over there, but The CAD shoved the whole thing up his fish's arse. Whoever eats that will have steam coming from their ears.'

The three of us high-five, but although we've bonded, I'm still an island stranded in the middle of the outdoor kitchen floor.

***

Inside, the conference room is set up like the last supper, with baskets of bread and our fish platters.

Ian positions his tripod so our table is framed. 'Don't eat until you're told to start.'

The judges tuck into our infused fish and score nine out of ten.

Bill rubs his bald head. 'How have we dropped a point? Our cuisine has to be better than a *MasterChef* finalist's.'

'I haven't finished yet,' Luigi replies. 'Donkey Kong, you also get three bonus points for having enough food to feed an army, making you the winners.'

'Not fair!' someone shouts as we whoop.

'Cheats!' The CAD roars.

Luigi holds his hand up to simmer everyone down. 'This team showed ingenuity in wiping you out right at the beginning with ...'

Vermin strolls in looking pale. 'Sorry I'm late, Luigi.'

'This is not a holiday camp. Maybe you don't feel the need to attend the SPIN technique presentation Donald is about to give?' Luigi unclips his cufflinks and places them on the table before rolling up his sleeves.

I've been in the thick of a fight before, but it was my takkies that got removed. Nobody lost their gold cufflinks.

'Can you present the SPIN technique?'

'No.'

'In that case, your lateness has cost your team their win. The fishing task is officially a draw.'

The other two teams cheer while Donkey Kong hurls abuse at Vermin.

'There is worse shit in life than getting slammed by Luigi,' I whisper to Vermin as we settle down for the presentation.

'I've got my own SPIN going on,' Vermin replies, as Donald launches into the marvels of using the situation, problem, implication and needs technique.

'Don't we all.' I paste an attentive face on. It's an art to physically look engaged while you're mentally elsewhere.

Donald roams around, picking on anyone with a glazed expression or a doodling pen. He approaches my table and I drop my head and make a note on a complimentary hotel notepad. He moves on to someone else.

I lapse into the self-absorbing assessment of my own unique situation, problem, implication, needs. In the absence of a textbook technique that'll turn a shitstorm into an opportunity, there's nothing for it but to live daily life in an ordinary world with every-one oblivious to my past.

Suck it up,

Donkey Kong.

Suck it up.

Chapter Forty-Two

Ian transmits the day's footage onto the flat screen and we squirm watching the playback. Janine glaring at Vermin. Darren arriving back with Revis close to empty-handed. Bill and me sprinting off. The discomfort of watching myself on screen feels surreal; an out-of-body experience, like I'm watching someone else. In a sick way, I am.

The camera moves to Cassie. 'We didn't even check if anyone else preferred to fish once we had the boat and equipment,' she says, as we wade into the water.

'There's your first leadership lesson,' Ian tells us. 'It worked out for you this time, but before you dive into a new plan, always consult your team.'

'Give them a break,' says Bill. 'Nobody else came up with a single idea, and everyone was already preoccupied.'

The footage changes to Janine and Vermin squabbling.

'Do you want to share your issues with Graydon?' Ian asks Janine. 'It might help get things off your chest.'

'Who says anything needs to come off her chest?' Vermin grins.

'That is my issue!' Janine says, folding her arms.

'You should take this seriously, Graydon. Janine is clearly unhappy with the inappropriate things you say, and your actions are not always aligned to today's business environment. That's what this session is about, dissecting your behaviour and getting feedback.'

'I think you should dissect Bill's behaviour first,' Vermin says.

'Everybody is going to have to open up at some point. This is all about self-awareness,' Ian says. 'Bill, do you mind coming up front and sitting opposite your colleagues?' Ian asks.

Bill does as asked as we shuffle the rest of the chairs into a semi-circle facing him. 'Hit me with it, Donkey Kong.'

'You've excellent decision-making skills, Bill,' I say.

'Thanks. Sorry if I come on too strong with the commands. My da was IRA.'

Everyone nods in understanding as he regales parts of his past and we discuss how his upbringing is what gave him many of his strengths, then he swaps with Revis.

We compliment her on her efficient coordination skills and her ability to support Luigi and all of his demands.

'We also all just want to know if the reason Stud Muffin does nothing for you is that you prefer muff ...'

'Out!' interrupts Ian as Revis stiffens in her chair.

'Come on. I was just joking around.' Vermin says.

'Nobody is laughing,' I reply.

'Let me tell you, this will be reported to Luigi,' Ian adds, as Vermin gets up and leaves the room.

'So, yes, I do have a girlfriend back in London, and she's amazing,' says Revis. 'There, I've said it.'

'I'm so pleased for you, Revis,' Cassie says. 'But you shouldn't feel you need to share a single thing about your personal relationships with any of us.'

'Aye, ignore Vermin,' says Stud Muffin. 'We love ye, pet.'

Revis suddenly looks radiant. 'Thanks for the moral support, Donkey Kong.'

We all clap as she swaps places with Donald.

He looks vulnerable as he pushes his grey hair back with wrinkled hands.

Cassie opens with a heartfelt speech. 'From the day I started, you've given me so much help to understand the industry. I owe all of my experience to you.'

'You're a true leader, Donald,' I add. 'You're like my old man. Conservatively hiring the best team but showing the occasional reckless streak when you hire a misfit like me.'

The rest of the group look lost at the conversation, but Donald nods. He knows what I'm talking about.

'You were the first one to steal the soy in the cooking task,' says Bill. 'Leading by example on the front line. I like that.'

'Sleight of hand,' Donald replies. 'I've played my fair share of cards over the years. Totally aced it with the Edinburgh team though. Look at Graham's prison track record.'

My jaw clenches.

'Who could have predicted those sales achievements you got with Hannah,' he adds.

Relief hits, swiftly followed by guilt. Donald thinks I'm a champion and the alternative of revealing the truth is too appalling to contemplate.

After Donald's psych evaluation finishes, I discreetly inform him The CAD installed spyware on his office machine. Some truth is better than none.

'Better not play too much online poker then,' whispers Donald, gratitude in his eyes.

I'm bundled into the hot seat and Bill goes first, telling me, 'By far, you gave the most outstanding contribution on the day for the fishing task.'

'One of my best team players,' Donald continues.

'Slow down. I'll be unable to get my head out of the door,' I joke.

Cassie is barely audible. 'I feel like today is the first time you've been honest with me.'

The deflation is not a slow puncture. It's the instantaneous balloon burst. Out on the boat I shared nothing but half-baked truths. Cassie deserves honesty, but the dirt has dried under my fingernails. I'm in so deep I can't come clean.

I'm the Pinstripe Prisoner, locked behind the bars of the facade I've created.

Chapter Forty-Three

T he schedule is relentless with little rest, before we're instructed to take a group walk through the woods. The weather is balmy; temperature in the high teens, which in Scotland is a tropical heatwave. The Donkey Kongs peel garments down to short sleeves, and the sun gently toasts the hairs on my arms as we forge past the trees into a clearing where a khaki tent is set up with a contraption suspended in the trees above it.

Two wires have been strung from a single tree, forking out in a narrow V-shape. The other ends of the wires end a couple of metres apart on different trees. A rope ladder snakes up the tree, ending on a platform next to the starting point of the wires.

A man is hanging in a harness from one of the wires, messing about with a carabiner.

'That there is Nelly, our safety expert,' Ian informs us.

'I've got the wrong shoes for this,' Vermin says, slinking into the tent.

'There's an urn and tea bags in here,' he hollers from inside.

He's been much quieter since getting a warning from Ian. 'Save us a jam scone,' I shout back.

'As this task obviously involves heights, I understand if anyone else wants to sit this out,' says Ian.

Janine glowers towards the tent. 'I do, but there's no way I'm going in there for a scone and tea with that idiot.'

'Stay here then, on the ground, and give Donkey Kong some moral support,' Ian suggests. 'This task isn't as easy as it looks.'

'I'm also happy to give it a miss,' says Donald.

'Okay, everyone else pair up,' Ian instructs.

Revis and Stud Muffin shuffle towards each other and I move to Cassie's side.

'Looks like it's you and me, Bill. Are you okay going first so we can give everyone a demo?'

'No bother,' replies Bill.

Ian positions his tripod, pointing towards the wires, as Nelly lowers and unclips himself to kit the pair of them out with a harness and helmet.

'We have to walk along the two wires, using only each other for support,' says Ian. 'When we get up there face me and take my hands, then we inch along on a wire each until they get too far apart and we fall. There's nothing to worry about. We're in harnesses.'

We cheer as Ian scales the ladder, followed by Bill.

'You ready?' Ian asks from the platform several metres above ground.

'Ready as I'll ever be,' Bill replies.

They edge out, one foot each, onto their respective cables. Ian puts his second foot onto the cable with Bill mirroring the move, then the two men stop hugging the tree and join both hands, leaning in towards each other, wobbling as they let go of the tree. We wolf-whistle from below as their bodies form an arch between the two cables.

Ian takes command. 'And take a step.'

They shuffle along.

'Again,' says Bill, taking control.

The gap between their bodies widens as the cables split further apart. Eventually they're leaning so far in Bill slips and drops between the cables, dragging Ian with him. We cheer as they swing onto their harnesses.

'You guys were quick,' Ned says, lowering them down.

Bill claps Ian on the back. 'My da taught me well about who I can trust.'

Stud Muffin looks at Revis. 'Piece of cake. You ready?'

She nods and Nelly gets to work with their harnesses.

'It's pretty high up there,' Bill says as they begin their ascent.

Stud Muffin pauses halfway up the tree. 'No shit, Sherlock.'

'Keep going. One rung at a time,' Revis says, continuing her climb.

'If ye can de this, so can I,' Stud Muffin replies.

We fall silent as Revis cajoles him to keep moving up the rungs.

'Fuck me,' Stud Muffin pants as he reaches the top. 'Why are we doing this stupid shit?'

Ian calls up the tree. 'This exercise has all kinds of benefits. It can foster trust and help you overcome fear. These tasks enable you to also say no. You can say no.'

'I wish I'd learnt the lesson about saying no before today,' Janine says as Revis tries to persuade Stud Muffin to put a foot onto the cable.

'I can't de it.'

'I'm doing this and so are you,' Revis replies.

He seizes her hand and they move into action.

They're slow as they move along the cable to the midway point, but their chat is nonstop.

'Keep going,' Revis pushes, until suddenly they slip.

Stud Muffin roars as they fall. Revis chortles as Nelly lowers them down, and they strip off their kit and engulf each other in a bear hug.

'You're amazing,' Revis tells Stud Muffin.

'And you're a pure nutter.'

'And that's what I call team building,' Ian gloats.

Cassie's green eyes widen. 'This is it, Graham.'

'There's nothing to be nervous about,' I say, stepping one leg through each loop of my harness. Nelly fastens the clips across my chest and gives it a tug to make sure my balls are not in a vice.

'Do you want to climb first or second?' I ask Cassie as we reach the tree.

'If you don't mind, I'll go first.'

'I'll be right behind you.'

She grabs the ladder. 'This thing wobbles.'

'You'll be fine. It took McGrath's weight.'

She scales the ladder quickly and I join her on the platform.

'I thought it best to get the climb over with as fast as possible,' she says, her word formation cracking. Her arms wrap around the tree like a cat on its ninth life.

'We don't have to do this.'

'I want to.'

'You've nothing to prove to anyone.'

'I want to prove to myself I can make it.'

She unfurls one arm from the tree. 'Let's go together on three.'

'Okay.'

'One. Two. Three.'

Our fingers fuse together and the cable sinks as my whole weight is shifted onto it. Cassie tightens her grip on my hands. We push against each other, entirely dependent on one another as we use our weight to balance us.

'One. Two. Three,' she counts, then we take the step.

'One. Two. Three,' she says again.

Her eyes never leave mine as the distance between us increases. The quiver of the cable increases as our arched arms start to spread. Our bodies are further apart, but our hands are so intertwined they feel like they've been soldered together.

Encouragement is coming from Donkey Kong below. They know we're not far from falling. My eyes stay on Cassie, not because I'm afraid to look down, but because I'm afraid to look away. She's put her trust in me, yet I've been untrustworthy since the day I met her.

'We might fall on the next step,' I say softly. 'Or we could jump, then we know what to expect? We can control the decision when we fall.'

'On three. When you jump, I jump,' she says.

'Isn't that a line from *Titanic?*'

'Yup.'

'Didn't it sink?'

'Exactly. We are going down together.' Cassie blushes.

I give her hands a squeeze one final time. 'Do you want to count us in?'

She nods. 'One. Two. Three.'

We step off the cable and our hands slip apart as we tumble. The loss of physical contact feels immense.

We swing in our harnesses for a couple of minutes, then Nelly lowers Cassie down inch by inch, then me.

On the ground we don't say a word as she hugs me tight, and I hug her back so hard I can feel her heart beating against my chest. Or maybe it's mine beating against hers.

'You two are so boring, planning to jump like that,' Janine complains. 'It really was like a scene from *Titanic.*'

'There's nothing wrong with planning ahead with someone,' Ian remarks.

My arms flop to my sides, and I back away from Cassie. I can't plan ahead with anyone. My future has only two routes it can take. A life spent using a false identity or one banged up in jail.

***

When we enter the tent, Vermin is slouching on a wooden bench.

'I can't believe you didn't even bother to watch your team,' Janine criticises.

'He's useless in those pansy shoes,' Bill McGrath ribs.

We grab paper cups and make ourselves a brew from a tepid urn of water, then sit, surrounding Vermin.

Ian sets up the camera in a corner of the tent and hands each of us a sheet of paper and a pencil. 'You're not done yet, Donkey Kong,' he says.

We groan.

'De ye have to have your camera in our face every five minutes?' Stud Muffin asks.

'It will be turned off after tomorrow's individual debrief sessions with me, which you're all having before you go home.'

'What exercise are we doing now?' Bill asks.

'Each of you spend ten minutes drawing your childhood, your present and your future. Matchstick men and matchstick women are fine.'

The task needs no further instruction as pencils begin to skim surfaces. Ian looks over my shoulder at my blank paper. 'If you can't illustrate your childhood then draw your present and future.'

'I thought we were meant to be empowered to say no.'

'Try. You don't want to be the only one without a picture.'

'Fine.' I scribble on my page, not wanting to attract attention by avoiding such a simple task. I sketch me, Jaco, Ma and Pa; my family as it was in childhood. My pencil hovers above the paper as I think of Erin. It's impossible to draw the fragmented family as it is today so I sketch me in a pinstripe suit instead.

The present.

I start to draw myself behind bars, the future and the past colliding in one stupid matchstick sketch. I scribble it out frantically, over and over again until a hole appears in my paper. Everything is a blur as my pencil drops to the ground.

I'm jammed between Cassie and Janine on the bench. Pushing my way out isn't an option. One is pregnant and the other sets my skin ablaze if I so much as brush against her.

'You okay?' Cassie asks as she slides out to let me pass.

The answer forms in my mouth but I can't utter the word 'no', so I silently leave. Outside the tent, I lean on a tree while my tear ducts overflow like gutters in a freakish storm. The light of the camera blinks. My feet move towards it, and I grab Ian by the scruff of his neck.

'Easy, mate,' he says. 'I've turned it off.'

I let him go and sink to the ground.

'Do you want to talk about it?'

'No.'

'Unpacking the baggage might seem daunting, but it's weighing you down. You need to off-load some of the stones.'

'I can't.'

'You can pack the backpack again, but it will be lighter.'

'Leave me alone.'

'Okay, but tomorrow we talk.' He leaves me there amongst the dead twigs to naturally blend in, as there's no more substance to me than a matchstick man.

'I wondered where you got to,' Cassie says, emerging from the tent.

I wipe my face and get up.

'You okay, Graham?'

'I'm fine.'

'You're not fine. Sit with me a minute.'

She climbs onto a fallen tree trunk, its branches amputated. To one side is a stream of water flowing over several large boulders.

I climb up next to her, our legs swinging in the breeze. 'You were right what you said about me. I'm full of shit.'

'You wanna tell me about it?'

'No.' Sweat runs down my back, perhaps not all from physical exertion.

'I've never been this far north. It's pretty.'

'Yah.'

She catches me looking at her. 'What?'

'Nothing.'

Cassie's nails scratch at the tree bark and I put my hand over hers to stop the movement.

Janine suddenly appears. 'Look at you two love birds.'

My hand shifts back to its own zone.

'Mind if I join you?' she asks, letting out a loud sniff as she clambers up next to Cassie. 'I'm pregnant,' she blurts.

'We know,' I say, as the leaves rustle around us. 'I found a test kit in the office bathroom. Is it Vermin's?'

She nods, crying in earnest as Ian muscles up again, this time without the camera.

'Just checking on you all. Are you okay, Janine?' Ian says.

'Leave me alone!' Mascara trickles down her cheeks, leaving tracks through her foundation like rubber marks scorched on tar by a joy-rider.

'Sorry, just doing my job.' He disappears again.

'Have you told Vermin yet?' I ask.

'Aye. On this trip. That's why he looked pale and was late for the SPIN session. I told him just before that. He wants me to have an abortion.' Janine squirms like she's caught on a huge fishing hook. 'And I agree with him.'

'Don't make any rash decisions,' Cassie says kindly as we jump off the tree to start the walk back to the hotel. 'Take your time to absorb everything.'

'I'm done thinking,' says Janine. 'And thanks for listening, but I don't need advice from either of you.'

This is a relief since I'm the least qualified person to give anyone advice about having a baby. Erin was eight months pregnant when I fled and left her alone to bring a child into the world.

Chapter Forty-Four

O ur final night on Loch Awe is spent in wigwam accommodation, positioned around a firepit in a field overlooking the loch.

'We could chant Kumbaya just to add to the ambience,' Bill McGrath says, sticking a marshmallow on a stick and poking it into the fire.

Cassie has a blanket over her knees, which she's sharing with Janine who is sitting next to her. Stud Muffin hands Revis Sicklemore a beer. There's comradery and acceptance of each other's flaws, except for Vermin's attitude and his leather loafers, which can't be overlooked.

The loch is black and formidable at night, the surrounding mountains cocooning us while we're transformed. Luigi's goal is for us to emerge as stronger salespeople who have found our wings to fly, but Ian probably hopes we'll simply be happier, better people.

'One last exercise tonight,' our coach says. 'I'll give you an envelope soon and inside is information about two candidates, both waiting for life-saving brain surgery. This operation is costly, so you need money which you're going to earn.'

'I'm good at making money,' Vermin says.

'You're good at nothing,' Janine snarls.

'There are two physical tasks to the exercise, each with a time limit of thirty minutes, and if successfully completed will earn you enough to pay for surgery for one patient. Therefore, each task you fail may result in someone being refused their brain surgery.'

I'm struggling already. Brain surgery, medical expenses, saving lives. 'Why give us such a stupid task?'

'You don't even know what the physical tasks are yet,' Ian replies.

'I mean the brain surgery.'

'It's theoretical.'

Cause of death: Brain 'hypothetically' shot to pieces.

'It's dumb.' I stand and walk to the fire. The flames are soothing. The smell of burning wood, the crackling, the flashes of red, orange, yellow in my eyes.

'What's up?' Cassie reaches my side.

'Nothing.'

'Enough, Graham. This constant weirdness with you is not nothing. You're talkative one minute and a brick wall the next. Your mood swings are impossible. Sometimes I think you might actually like me and other times you're downright rude and horrible.'

Cassie's hands are dug in her pockets. Her cheeks are red and her hair chaotic, with tiny bits of ash billowing around her. She generates more heat than the fire.

'I do like you, green eyes,' I say.

'Well, that's a start.'

'So, you want me to do the rest of these tasks?'

'Let's go.'

***

We're challenged to put together an enormous three-dimensional jigsaw of Edinburgh Castle.

'You're such a big puzzle yourself, this task should be much easier for you to figure out,' Cassie says to me.

Donkey Kong go straight at it, putting together sections of the iconic castle, but it's so crooked the structure is unfit for anything other than bulldozing.

'You're useless,' Janine snaps at Vermin as we tear it apart.

I pick up a piece and slot it into Cassie's.

'That bit next,' Bill points.

'Now what?' Donald asks.

'We need a strategy,' says Vermin.

'Pfffftt.' The sound comes from Janine.

'Let's halve the team and pieces, and spend a minute putting them all upright. It should be easier,' Cassie suggests.

We separate out, and the jigsaw quickly begins to take shape. We're two pieces away from completion when Ian calls time. The groan is loud.

'You do realise someone is left without a brain,' Vermin says.

'I know we can't give someone a new brain!' I yell.

'Chill, mate. I was just saying, one dead, that's all.'

Janine's hands fly over her tummy.

'We've got a second chance, Janine,' I say, hoping to distract her from whatever turmoil she's in. Hoping to distract myself too.

'Divin't worry aboot the results,' Stud Muffin adds. 'We'll improve on the next task.'

'And we will be skiing for that,' Ian announces.

'There's no snow,' we babble, following Ian to an area behind the wigwams.

Two wooden parallel planks await with ropes across the width for us to slot our feet into.

'I know how this one goes.' Bill slips his feet into the makeshift skis.

We line up on the planks behind him.

'Use the rest of your time to make it to the field boundary. Each time a foot touches the ground you begin again,' says Ian, capturing our efforts on camera.

'We've got this, Donkey Kong. On the count of three, left foot forward.'

'One, Two—'

'Did you mean we step on the word three, or after the word three?' asks Revis.

'On three, left foot forward,' Bill replies.

'I'm sitting this one out,' Janine declares, unhooking her feet. 'It looks dangerous.'

'What happened to team spirit?' Vermin asks.

'I'm fed up with you and your strategies.'

We topple over and I land in Cassie's lap, my limbs wrapped in hers.

'Did you ever play *Twister?*' she asks as we untangle ourselves.

My hands are on red, my butt in the air, legs spread across yellow and green. Erin is pinned underneath me, half on blue, the other half jostling for my red circles. Jaco is on the perimeter, untangled, both hands on the two spots in front of him.

'I'm gonna win this hands-down. You two are useless,' Jaco gloats.

'And you're twisted,' I say, my head hanging upside down looking at Erin.

Jaco laughs. 'No, I'm not. That's why I'm gonna win.'

Erin laughs. Our faces are so close we could kiss.

'Your turn, boeta,' says Jaco.

I take my turn and attempt to get out of the mess, even though I'm quite happy right where I am.

'I used to play *Twister* as a kid,' I reply. 'Great game.'

Bill gets us back into the rhythm and we shuffle forward inch by inch.

'Time is running out,' Ian announces when we're scarcely metres from the end point.

We shuffle faster.

'Time,' he calls, a second after we stumble against the fence.

'Get in!' Stud Muffin yells.

'We get to save someone!' Bill triumphs.

Ian hands me an envelope. 'I need a team decision in ten minutes on which of these two candidates you'll save.'

We head back to the fire and I read the note inside the envelope. One male, one female. The male is young with all the signs he'll recover well from brain surgery and live a long healthy life. He's nice to his parents and to most people he meets, but he has spent time in prison. There's no data on what offence he's committed.

The female is older, a model citizen who has helped thousands through her charity work with the Cancer Council. At best, she's a less than fifty per cent chance of survival if she has an op on a recently diagnosed brain tumour.

'Save the woman,' Revis suggests.

'Pointless. She won't make it,' Vermin counters.

'You're not God, you heartless bastard,' says Janine.

Jaco studied stillbirths, cot deaths and the deplorable custom of female infanticide. In China, as a result of sex-selective abortions, the population imbalance may be as many as forty million more males to females, but the number is difficult to quantify because of the concealing of illegal children in a country practicing a child quota policy. I wanted to retch when Jaco told me in feudal times baby girls were cruelly murdered by being held underwater, strangled or suffocated. Barbaric servants would sometimes place the newborn inside the chamber-pot overflowing with blood and water from the birth, to die in a deplorable fashion.

Cause of death: Infanticide.

'I'm not going to decide who lives or dies. You lot figure it out,' I tell Donkey Kong before throwing the envelope and instruction card into the fire. The flames rocket, consuming the accelerant with hunger, like my clothes that day at Meisho Maru shipwreck.

I go to my wigwam. It's the tiny sanctuary I need, with a futon bed taking up the whole space. When I lie down, I can still reach the coned ceiling.

'Can I come in?' Cassie's head appears between the slits of my door canvas.

'Bit tight.'

She wriggles in anyway and lies down beside me. 'We saved the man.'

'If pressed, he would have won my vote too.'

'Why didn't you say so?'

'Dunno.' Unable to take her stare, I roll on my side, my back to her.

I don't know how long passes before we spoon and her arm snakes around my waist. Her breath hits my neck in warm little bursts as I drift off.

I sleep deeper than I have in all the months I've been in Scotland, right here in a wigwam.

Chapter Forty-Five

I t's a bright sunny morning when I enter the MacArthur suite for my private session with Ian.

'Apparently the MacArthur clan used to own half the land around here. They were supporters of Robert the Bruce and fought at the Battle of Bannockburn,' Ian says, by way of explaining the decadent decor.

Green and blue tartan has been used for the curtains, matched in the carpet pattern, and gilt-framed art contains historical portraits of kilted men with eyes that follow my every move. I hope there are no dead spirits haunting this place.

Technology ruins the ambiance. Ian's camera wire feeds into the TV screen like an umbilical cord I want to cut.

'This is a safe environment,' Ian soothes.

One day you can be huddled in a comfort blanket, and the next it's swapped for a pet blanket to cover your modesty while you take a dump.

'Nowhere is safe,' I say.

'Everything you share here is confidential. The camera isn't recording anything. It's only here to replay footage.'

I'm on screen scribbling the matchstick drawing, getting angry in the woods and burning the envelope in the fire. Ian rewinds and shows more clips. Me and Cassie on the rowboat, cooking our catch, falling from the treetop cables and toppling on our shared skis. He pauses on Cassie disappearing inside my wigwam.

'It's not what you think.'

'I wasn't thinking anything.'

'We're just good friends.'

'So, if you can't talk to me, why don't you talk to her?'

'Maybe I don't want to talk to anyone.'

'You seem to have a really good rapport there. Be open with her.'

'No.'

'Then be open with me?'

'I can't.'

'I can sense you're supressing something significant. Talking about it might really help.'

I fold my arms, but he ignores my closed body language.

'Mindfulness is important to survival, Graham. You need to face whatever is wearing you down. Will you at least try to open up to Cassie?'

'Maybe someday.'

'Make it someday soon.'

'I'll try.'

'Life is too short to mess around.' He shakes my hand and I walk out. 'Don't let your future be overshadowed by your past.'

The realisation Ian has made an immeasurable dent in my armour is profound. I'm still the Pinstripe Prisoner, but maybe it's time to reach between the bars and see if there's a key somewhere to unlock me.

***

It's lunchtime when we regroup for the conference finale. Luigi is behind a lectern sharing a history lesson on the journey of floppy discs to thumb drives.

'Technology will never stop evolving.' He launches into a speech about the population's scramble to digitalise, automate, innovate and disrupt. 'We must capitalise, not just on the insatiable demand of consumers who want the latest applications to make them smarter, but on the fundamental basics like IT security too. There are sophisticated ransomware criminals and hackers that can bring a corporation to its knees.'

'Faster than Monica Lewinsky did with the leader of the White House,' Vermin whispers too loudly. 'If you want to make it in this industry, you need to grow a set of balls.'

Revis Sicklemore glares at him before calmly picking up her bag and leaving the room.

Luigi looks perplexed, then clears his throat and clicks on the projector to open a presentation outlining his latest revelation, *The Overseas Campaign*.

'We're going to attract unique skills from … Saaf Africa. You lot can demand astronomical margins for filling the unfillable with planeloads of Saaf Africans,' Luigi says, glancing my way.

The room erupts. We are a colony of clapping seals, freshly trained on how to catch more fish.

The thought of capitalising on a South African recruitment campaign generates a sense of excitement, but it also brings patriotic discomfort at the thought of my country being raided of their educated talent to service another government's labour shortfalls. It will be easy to attract people who are fed up with the huge influx of uncontrolled illegal squatters in a country where unemployment accounts for more than a third of the 'known' population.

The ability to present South Africans – many underprivileged – the opportunity to work in the UK outweighs the thought of stripping the country of their talent. I join in the clapping.

Fuck me, I need a black leather compendium.

Chapter Forty-Six

Nancy rushes into the cube farm in such a frenzy her scarf has come loose. 'Kevin has resigned.'

'What?' I reply.

'He's in with Donald now. I just took them coffee and heard Kevin telling him how dejected and humiliated he felt after being excluded from the Highlands trip. And that's not all. Revis Sicklemore has also quit.'

'What? Why?' I ask.

'I heard it's because of you, Graydon, and all the inappropriate comments. Apparently, your attitude towards women is too much for her. Is it true?' Nancy asks Vermin who is looking our way.

'I spoke to Luigi about it. She's just hypersensitive,' he replies.

'Vermin, you can't keep commenting at other people's expense. Everybody has had enough, not just Revis,' I tell him.

'It's not that big a deal. Luigi paid her out so it's not going to court,' says Vermin.

'That doesn't make it okay,' I reply. 'You need to learn some respect.'

'Who's been paid off?' Kevin asks, reappearing.

'Forget it,' deflects Vermin. 'What's happening with you? We heard you threw the towel in.'

'Gardening leave.' Kevin beams as we crowd into his cube. 'Four weeks' pay to stay at home.'

'Why can't you work your notice while Donald finds a replacement?' I ask.

'Don't be simple,' says Nancy. 'He could download everything from Benny and take copies of all the records to a competitor.'

'I'd never do that,' replies Kevin. 'But I'm not sorry to be going. We're nothing but battery hens and I'm not laying one more egg in this cube for Luigi.'

'You're scrambling instead,' says Janine, getting a laugh from us all.

'Who are you joining?' asks Nancy.

'I'd rather not say for now, but it's a better gig. They're giving me a golden handshake to tide me over financially while I build up my client base. Plus, I don't need anything from Benny. Their database is state-of-the-art. Automatically parses CVs and everything.'

Vermin nods. 'Working here is like being dropped in Iraq with a bergen filled with shit equipment.'

'I'm actually quite fond of old Benny,' I tell them both.

'And there was me thinking you only have eyes for Cassie,' Kevin says.

Cassie blushes as Kevin empties his desk contents. A rusty can of deodorant goes in the bin, a pack of tissues go into his pocket and a pile of customer business cards come out of an ancient Rolodex.

'You can't take those.' Janine steps towards him in an already overcrowded space.

'They're mine.'

'Client information is our intellectual property.' Janine snatches at the business cards, causing them to scatter across the desk. 'This is why Donald is putting you on gardening leave.'

Nancy reties her scarf tightly with a double knot. 'I'm afraid Janine is right, Kevin. I'm going to have to ask you to leave.'

Cause of death: Chiffon strangulation.

'So that's it?' Kevin asks.

'That's it,' Nancy replies.

'Hey, wait!' Cassie disappears into her cube and returns with her pot plant to hand to him. 'Mine grows better than most of the others. It will bring you luck.'

Kevin's lower lip quivers, but at least he has tissues handy if he can't hold back the tears. He waves his free hand and heads off with his plant in the other.

When he's gone, Janine makes a beeline for the vacated desk. 'Check this out. When did he get a new calculator?' She snatches it along with the business cards.

I'm stunned Kevin's departure has ended in such an impersonal, abrupt manner, but then something catches my eye and my fingers extend to grasp my prize of a black leather compendium embossed with the TITS logo.

***

At lunchtime, I head to a traditional barber on Rose Street. Judging by the long ponytail and bristles on the owner's face he doesn't practise his trade on himself, but he's a dab hand with an old-fashioned cutthroat razor. When he's done on my short back and sides, he hands me a hot towel and angles a brass mirror so I can admire his handiwork. Strange to see something resembling my old self stare back. A recruiter with a purpose instead of a rebel without a cause.

It wouldn't be professional to look unkempt while I take copious notes in my compendium and pitch for an international campaign.

My motivation to succeed is not just down to wanting to support Erin. Donald doubled down on his debt, borrowing from Luigi to pay off Big Mal then he took another loan from the shark on his clean slate. Pa bailed me out of hot water. If I sell a single international campaign, it will pay at the premium end of our commission structure. I can bail Donald. I've been mapping stakeholders in my target market and trying to better understand their business challenges, all with the help of Fatima Rampal.

It's an interesting recruitment phenomenon, the way well-treated candidates become informants. Seeding the right person into an account where they establish insider trust enables them to discreetly sniff out workforce opportunities. Establishing a good supply chain should be in the new starter training manual; next to instructions on how to reel in a big fish. Fatima is my human asset. Every time I go to the Taj I walk away with a takeaway of mouth-watering biryani and new information about challenges across detention, parole and probation. She is well-versed in procurement buying patterns. She compliments Benny's efforts, whom I've sweat like a vindaloo addict of all the local candidates I can find to help the Ministry of Justice achieve transformation and improve service delivery through upgraded technology, business process re-engineering and improving reform and care for men, women and youths caught in a destructive cycle of crime and incarceration. I make a mental note to ask Hannah what her vision is for extending services to support victims and their families and how we can better manage staff attrition in a tough, often confronting industry. Thinking about South Africa as a potential new candidate pool to fulfil the endless resource demands means my surfing techniques take on a new lease of life. I ride the waves of Google, tunnelling through useful information about advertising costs in the Cape, pound to rand exchange rates and the intricacies of South African justice systems.

The memory of being incarcerated in a cell surfaces every once in a while, but I practice self-discipline, channel the energy and keep on task. Researching everything I can develops my knowledge about mobile applications the police can use to report crimes in the field, the benefits of body cameras and the latest electronic tagging systems.

I'm certainly thankful I wasn't tagged when I was released from jail as I've strayed a long way from home.

Chapter Forty-Seven

'Stress remedy?' Donald pulls a glass vial from his pocket with a pipette for a lid.

I pause from rehearsing my dry-run presentation to squeeze more than a few drops under my tongue, grimacing at the sharpness of the medicinal flavour. The miniscule amount of alcohol in the mixture is the first to pass my lips on Scottish turf.

Donald takes some too. There is a kindred spirit between us, both wanting the upcoming meeting to go well so he can keep his front teeth intact, and I can repay my debt for what happened after I knocked someone's out.

I continue practising my lines aloud until Hannah appears at the boardroom door. 'Erm, hi,' I say, spotting her.

'Keep going, Shirley Valentine,' she replies.

Donald offers her a seat. 'Nancy's gone to buy cakes so there's nobody on reception.'

'That's okay, I'm early. You two look impressive.' Hannah nods at our immaculate suits and starched shirt collars. In contrast, she's in denim drainpipes and a jumper knitted more of holes than wool.

We talk through how we've tailored a solution to secure the best resources, until Nancy enters.

'Sorry for interrupting.' She places a pack of chocolate biscuits on the table with a pot of English tea. 'The bakery was closed so I bought you Penguins.'

Hannah reaches out for the pack of biscuits and breaks it open.

'P-P-P-Pick up a Penguin ...' Hannah mimics, munching on a chocolate biscuit as the next PowerPoint slide transitions in.

It's a picture of Boulder's Bay, one of Cape Town's iconic beach coves, which is populated by wild penguins. Hundreds of them have made their home on the sand and rocks, happily cohabiting with the tourists and sunbathers.

'I love that place!' Hannah exclaims. 'I must've been there a thousand times when I was a kid.'

'We're going to source a whole team from there.'

'It's genius,' she replies as we celebrate with more biscuits. 'I'm confident it will work with you out there to run this campaign smoothly, Graham.'

My heart plummets. 'Can't we deliver it by video conference?'

'You always get a better cultural fit if you meet candidates face to face.'

'Janine's far more experienced at screening candidates. She would be best placed to get the results we want.'

Donald glares at me. 'We can discuss our talent acquisition team later.'

I lean in with a handshake. 'Thanks again, Hannah.'

'Have you fallen off the wagon?' she asks. 'You have a vague scent of booze about you.'

'No way. I just took too much herbal stress remedy.'

She chuckles. 'Good to know you take my business seriously.'

Then she's gone.

'Don't screw up,' says Donald. 'This is your campaign to lose.'

'I won't if you don't.'

We dip a chocolate biscuit into our tea and seal our pact.

***

I take Janine to Café Kamani to discuss what we need to do, and we both order a glass of milk.

'You're still a teetotaller then?'

'And you're still as witty and observant as ever,' I reply.

Janine smiles. 'Good on you for getting this far with selling a campaign.'

'Bumping into Hannah at the recruitment convention was a lucky break.'

'You make your own luck. I saw how you built her trust, learning about market salaries, retention rates and replacement ratios.'

'I s'pose. I've spent endless hours spent with Benny so I can source the perfect match for a job. Sometimes I batter his keys so hard he could file an abuse claim.'

Janine grins and takes a sip of milk. 'Crikey, think of all those references we need to take, and the work rights, tax and bank details to sort out. The contractual paperwork and onboarding workload will be massive. You know how much hand-holding some candidates need just to move jobs in Scotland, never mind relocate to a new country at the same time. I know you moved halfway across the world without so much as blinking, but it's a pretty major transition for some people.'

'It wasn't so easy moving for me either, trust me. I know the whole campaign will be a challenge,' I say, 'but we just have to tailor things to everyone's individual needs and provide the best support possible.'

'That's why you're perfect to run this thing.' Janine suddenly grimaces. 'Graham, get me a taxi.'

'Are you okay?'

'I don't know. I need a doctor. I think the baby could be coming.'

'What?' I try to remain calm as I help her outside. The sky drizzles on us as we flag a cab. Janine slots her hand between the seatbelt and her abdomen to minimise friction. 'I think I just properly realised how much I want this baby.'

'That's good, Janine.'

'It's not. Something's wrong.'

'We'll be there soon. You're going to be okay,' I tell her over and over, until I see the hospital ahead.

We pull up and I pay the fare then link Janine's arm and help support her walking into the hospital. The place is heaving. I find a nurse who gets her a wheelchair and directs us to maternity.

'Will you wait?' Janine asks when we get to the right ward.

'I'll be right here.'

'Hopefully I won't be long.'

'Take all the time you need.'

Janine gives a watery smile before disappearing into the bosom of the NHS.

***

Darkness has fallen by the time Janine resurfaces, her ashen face sagging towards the linoleum of the hospital floor. Without a word, I know the baby is gone.

'It'll be okay,' I say as Janine approaches.

'I'm being punished for considering an abortion.'

I open my arms and hold her tightly.

'What kind of person am I?' she sobs into my chest.

'A better one than me.'

'I know Donald wants me to go, but I don't think I can travel to South Africa,' she says. 'I need some time off.'

'Don't worry about anything except looking after yourself.'

We head into the night air and I escort her home. It's a quiet journey; her, no doubt thinking of the baby she's lost; me, thinking about the one born in South Africa.

Chapter Forty-Eight

Donald clears his throat to address the whole team in the board-room. 'It's with great delight to announce Graham has managed to secure our first order for a South African recruitment campaign.'

'I'm just a lucky underdog,' I say as my peers clap.

'An underdog with willpower is an unstoppable force,' Donald says with a kindness that reminds me of Pa.

The day I get my exam results from school, I arrive home to find Ma and Pa sitting at the dining table covered in the sunflower tablecloth. Judging by the smell of a roast cooking in the oven on a weeknight, their expectations are high. Ma's roast with all the trimmings is the business.

I take out the sealed envelope and sit beside them to open it. I've passed every exam, but with only the one distinction. The rest of my results are middle-of-the-road grades. Even though I've no illusions of myself being some kind of academic genius, the disappointment is unexpected.

'Well done,' Pa gets up to hug me.

'I'm sorry I didn't do better.'

'Why? You passed them all with decent marks and you certainly

don't need a piece of paper full of straight-As to make the most of your life, son. The underdog often achieves unexpected wonders.'

Pa knows me well. I'm hurting like hell I didn't achieve grades matching those of my big brother.

Donald continues. 'We had planned on Janine going to Cape Town as she has such extensive experience and would be great at running that side of the operation, but she's had to take some personal time off, so I've had a chat with Graham and he's going instead. Obviously, being a native, he knows Cape Town very well and we're confident enough candidates can be sourced from one major city. But the effort needed to fill every role in a short space of time is huge, so I've decided to send one of you with him.'

Donald flicks on the projector to show an Excel spreadsheet populated with the number of jobs we're all working on and our whiteboard scores.

'Based on the data, the person I'm sending to South Africa is Cassie.'

She throws me a bewildered look.

'Fantastic. We work well together so the campaign is in the best hands.' I smile at her, but inside, my stomach is doing flips.

Despite the problems the country has faced, I'm honoured to show anyone the rustic vibrancy of my homeland. However, I turned my back on my family to save my own skin, so the thought of being back in South Africa fills me with dread. I'm terrified of what awaits on home turf.

My bloodstained clothes burning beside the Meisho Maru.

The Suid-Afrikaanse Polisie.

A game of rummy.

And a bottle of wine.

Chapter Forty-Nine

C assie wants moral support to break the news of another work trip to Margarita, so I accompany her home.

This time there are no glue sniffers around as we approach the flat, but the dreariness remains. A teenage mother drags a crying toddler past me, cursing at the child to shut her trap. They disappear into a door, its paint peeling like an onion slowly losing its skin. It's enough to make the eyes water.

We find Margarita in the kitchen, opening a tin of corned beef which she layers with mushy peas and mashed potato.

I don't have a chance to greet her properly as she goes to answer the phone ringing in the hallway.

Cassie dishes for us. 'It's panackelty. Basically, just think of it as Michelin star corned beef hash.'

We sit at a couple of bar stools in the kitchen and tuck in. I'm pleasantly surprised to find the bizarre concoction is tastier than it looks.

Margarita comes back into the kitchen. 'George has met someone else!'

'Oh, no,' Cassie gasps.

'The scumbag. I'm going to be out of a job.'

'Has he fired you?' Cassie asks.

'No, but how am I meant to concentrate at the auctions while George is on a platform in front of me with a hammer in his hand?'

'Then get another job,' Cassie replies.

'Who's going to employ me?'

'Go to the competition. I'll help you put a CV together before I go to South Africa.'

'What do you mean, before you go to South Africa?'

'I'm off to Cape Town with Graham to help run a huge recruitment campaign.'

'You've put her up to this, haven't you?' Margarita glares at me, hands on hips.

'It's nothing to do with him,' Cassie intervenes.

'He's taking you for a ride. All men ever want is one thing. Look at George.'

'He's not taking me for anything. I'm going over there to work.'

Margarita glares at her. 'Who do you think you are, with your upmarket job and your fancy boyfriend?'

'I'm proud of my job and he's not my fancy boyfriend.'

'I think I should probably leave,' I mutter to them both.

Cassie's voice cracks. 'Graham is just looking out for me, which is more than you do.'

'How can you be so ungrateful, deserting me after I've looked after you all these years?'

'Firstly, I'm not deserting you. Secondly, serving tinned food and frozen dinners isn't looking after me.' Cassie puts her plate next to the sink with a clatter. 'When do you ever ask what I want in life? All this drama doesn't wash anymore. I'm going to South Africa and that's it.'

'But George has just left …'

'I'm sorry about the timing, but I'm going.'

'I don't know what's got into you, Cassie?'

'A bit of courage. I love you, but I want to live my life without all this negativity and if I can't do that here, I'll find somewhere else to live.'

Margarita sits with a thud at the table and starts sobbing.

'I'll get some tissues.' I get up and disappear to the bathroom.

There's a spare toilet roll inside a crocheted cover with a frilly lilac trim. When I return to give the roll to Margarita, they're still arguing.

'Nothing I do is ever good enough and I'm sick of it.'

'You're just sensitive, Cassie.'

'I've been trying my best for as long as I remember, and you just keep putting me down.'

'I never meant to.'

'But you do. Everything is always about you.'

'It's been hard all these years on my own,' Margarita mumbles.

This sets Cassie off crying. I take the toilet roll back from Margarita, unravel a handful and pass it to Cassie.

'Your dad walked out and sometimes you remind me of him, that's all.' Margarita reaches over the table to place her hand over Cassie's.

Cassie pulls her hand away and gets up from the table. 'You can't keep treating me like this just because Dad left.'

She gives me a stare and I follow her down the narrow hallway.

Margarita chases us. 'Don't leave me on my own.'

'I'll be at Graham's. I just need some space.'

We step outside and Cassie wipes away her tears as we walk past the peeling-onion-skin door.

287

***

My flat is freezing even though we're still in the latter half of the summer months, but there's no point getting uptight about chattering teeth. At least I've got all mine. More than I can say about the bloke who got my fist to his mouth in Maxwell's. I think about him a lot. Regret lashing out. Replay how it unfolded. Wonder about ways I could have avoided the punch-up.

I press the boiler ignite button to boost the gas flame back to life and listen to the radiators gurgle into action. Cassie paces the lounge while I rake through the contents of the laundry cupboard and pull out a blanket and a towel that is stiffer than cardboard and frayed with age. I shove it back and rummage again until I find a softer one.

'Thanks,' she says when I return with full arms. 'The sofa looks comfy.'

'You can sleep in my bed.'

A blush creeps up her cheeks.

'Don't worry. I'll crash here,' I say.

'I don't want to put you out.'

'You're not.'

She sits on the sofa, still in her suit. In her haste to leave home, she's brought nothing with her.

'I'll be back in a minute.' In my bedroom I find a pair of tracksuit pants, plus, remembering she likes The Doors, my favourite T-shirt. I return with her sleepwear. 'Might be a bit big, but probably comfier than sleeping in your work gear.'

'They're perfect. You're a good friend.' She takes the pile and disappears to the bathroom then comes back looking sexy as hell in my Jim Morrison top. She sits next to me on the sofa and curls her bare feet underneath herself.

'You okay?'

She nods. 'My mother has always had these raw nerves that tip into a hot-headed anger. I've always been scared I'd set her off, like that day with the doll incident when Dad left. Maybe that's why I've put up with her crap all these years.'

'It wasn't your fault he left, Cassie.'

'I know.'

'You've done okay for yourself. You should feel proud.'

'You're doing okay too.'

'Not really.' I don't elaborate. This is Cassie's time to unpack her baggage, not mine.

She talks a while longer until eventually we fall asleep on the sofa, sharing the blanket and soft towel. When I wake, I'm refreshed because it's the first night since the wigwam I've not tossed and turned through the night. I make us toast and tea while Cassie is still sleeping. When it's ready, I nudge her gently. Her hair is wild, partly covering her face. She pushes the curls to one side and stretches.

'Morning,' she croaks.

I place her tea and toast on the floor since the coffee table still has no glass. 'I'm glad you're coming to South Africa with me.'

'Me too,' she says, picking a piece of fluff off Jim Morrison's face.

I ache to touch her, but can't, so I sip my tea and eat my toast, enjoying just being with her and living in the moment.

Maak elke sekonde tel.

Maak elke sekonde tel.

Maak elke sekonde tel.

The
Tablecloth

Chapter Fifty

I t's a Sunday and we are enjoying some downtime five days into the campaign. It's a beautiful winter's day, a far cry from the bleak Edinburgh weather I've become accustomed to. The skies are cloudless, save for one enormous white puff hovering over Table Mountain.

'You can see the revolving cable car from here going right to the top. Look.'

Cassie lowers her sunglasses to check it out from a distance.

We're across the ocean from the mountain, on one of Cape Town's top beaches, surrounded by upmarket apartments with resident swimming pools and gated security entrances.

'This view is spectacular,' says Cassie.

'This area is called Bloubergstrand, which literally means Blue Mountain Beach in Afrikaans.'

She's sprawled out on a striped beach towel, propping herself up on one arm. 'I bet the views are incredible from up there.'

'Yah. The wildlife too. There's this weird creature called a dassie that's been endangered by eagles. They're like a cross between a squirrel and a huge rat.'

'I vaguely remember getting the ferry on holiday to Rottnest Island in Western Australia when I was really young. There's a similar native animal there called a quokka.'

'We'll have to climb the mountain sometime to compare it. There are so many awesome places to show you, we'll never have enough time to fit them in.'

'We definitely underestimated the manpower needed to get through the applications. It's surprising so many people want to leave a stunning place like this.'

'South Africa is struggling post-apartheid. Trust me, people with a chance of getting out will grab it with both hands.'

'Is it really that bad?' Cassie asks.

'The crime rate is one of the highest in the world, third behind only Venezuela and Papua New Guinea. This is a nation still struggling to reduce massive poverty and inequality. The shift won't happen overnight just because the law changes.'

'I know I've only been here a few days and haven't seen that side of things, but I've loved every minute. It's sad really, seeing all this talent wanting to flee such an amazing country.'

'Yah, it is beautiful. I still miss living here. Most of our candidates just want to move to a safer place without the racial tension.'

We've become relocation advisors to applicants from a variety of backgrounds. Some are university educated with penthouse apartments and maid service. Others, despite first-rate skills, are still trying to claw themselves out of the townships. We also have the red-eyed, genius, mumbling mammals, who cannot string a sentence together unless it's written in code. They all need nurturing through the process.

'Did you know the job would eventually bring you to this point?' Cassie asks.

'I didn't think it would be this rewarding, being able to give people the chance to follow their dreams. I mean, in this country do you know how easy it is to end up in jail? It could have been me, you know.'

I stare towards The Tablecloth over the mountain and think of the sunflowers once covering Ma's dining table.

'What happened?'

I change tact and nod towards Robben Island, visible across the ocean. 'Mandela was imprisoned for years over there.'

Cassie doesn't probe. Instead, her hand covers mine and we bask in the sun until I drift into a nap on the soft sands of Blouberg.

***

On the drive back to our hotel in the hire car, we detour into Canal Walk for an impromptu shopping trip to find a gift for Donald. It's a spacious mall with marble floors reflecting the natural light coming through the glass roof. We wander around boutique retailers before ending up in one of the megastores.

'What about this?' Cassie picks up an electronic chess game. 'Donald can compete against the machine instead of playing online cards.'

I pool my cash with hers to pay for it. It's the perfect widget for Donald and makes me think about my own relationship with technology; immersing myself in its positive impact on society through the prison work, and I love useful gadgets with a meaningful purpose, like a chess set designed to intervene a gamblers' habit. Yet, there are the technophobia headbutts when I dwell on its darker side. The internet, social media, mobile phones; they shrink the earth so people can connect, make new friends, reconnect, be found. I don't want to be found. I want to hide beneath The Tablecloth. Pull the enormous cloud over my mountain of pain. Yet these days, nowhere is off limits.

Even in the *cloud* technology is thriving.

Chapter Fifty-One

My hotel room style is minimalist, neutral shades of brown and beige with built-in cupboards with sliding doors. I'd love the chance of a sliding door moment. To go back to Maxwell's. Take another path where I can enjoy the full monopoly of a life in South Africa where I am not marched off to a new home.

Do not pass Go.

Do not collect $200.

Do not go to Jail.

There are no other sliding doors though. However, there is a convenient door connecting my hotel space with Cassie's, which she has pushed open.

'I've caught the sun,' she announces, coming in.

Her nose is burned red raw in the middle of her pale skin. 'It matches your hair,' I say as she gives me a playful punch.

Her curly locks are wet and she's in the hotel robe, white and fluffy. Way fluffier than the home towel we shared as an extra blanket. She plumps up a feather pillow and props herself up on the bed beside me. Steam comes off her and it's not from the shower.

She's hot.

Has she always been this hot?

Why did they torture me by giving us connecting rooms?

She flicks through the TV channels until she stumbles across an Australian flick about an awkward woman called Muriel who wants to get married to a South African swimmer, so she can get a visa to escape her small seaside town.

'I love this movie,' Cassie gushes.

I could save Muriel a whole load of trouble by sending her to a tik dealer in a Struisbaai shebeen who could get her fake papers overnight. 'Shall we get room service while we watch it?' I ask.

Cassie nods and I order us a couple of club sandwiches.

'I do wonder sometimes what life would have been like if we had moved back to Australia,' she says. 'I don't remember that much about Fremantle, but we were always at the beach.'

'You should go back there someday to see for yourself where you were born.'

'It's so far to travel to Australia. Why bother? You can take me to the beach here again.'

'I'll take you to another good spot before we leave.'

'You'd better,' she replies.

Although being this close to Cassie is making me want her, and I don't want to want her, I'm deliriously happy living this simple existence; watching old movies and eating room service. The downside is when the credits roll and she closes that door between us, the terror comes back as I slip in and out of a fitful sleep.

I peel off my T-shirt that is soaked with sweat. The sheets are damp too. Squeeze my eyes closed. Open them again. Sit up and rub them so

ferociously phosphenes form on the insides of my eyelids, creating circles of vivid colours like I'm trapped in a twilight zone. I don't bother
waiting for my eyesight to adjust to the dim light as I pull off the necklace threatening to choke me and throw it across the bed. Apart from
my vision, everything is clear to me now I'm back on home soil. There
is no getting away from it. I'll have to see my family before I leave, and
if I go back to Struisbaai, I know Erin will also come to see me.

I retch so badly the noise reverberates around the room. The
sound is intolerable to my own ears, like listening to rampant sex
through anorexic walls. I knock over the bedside lamp before stum-
bling into the bathroom, where I slump over the toilet for several
minutes, clutching the porcelain as my stomach contracts.

Eventually, when I've nothing left to give, I get up from all fours
and splash my face with icy water. When a knock comes at the
connecting door, I don't even care I'm only in my boxers.

I swing open the door and Cassie is there, still wrapped in her
fluffy hotel dressing gown.

'Are you okay?' She puts the bedside lamp upright again and
switches it on, then guides me to the bed and lowers me onto the
edge. She raids the minibar for a bottle of water for me to sip. 'I
want to help.'

I reach across the throw and retrieve the tooth-and-leather
memento which I slowly put back around my neck, and we sit side
by side in silence until I can't bear it any longer. Then the whole
sorry story spews out like the bile I've emptied into the bowl of my
five-star hotel bathroom.

Moenie kak praat nie, poephol.

I remember those last words to Jaco, and how since then, I try
to consider more carefully what I say. With Cassie, I start with the
punch-up at Maxwell's and don't hold anything back.

'The bouncers took forever to break the fight up. There was two. They took their smoke break together, or maybe they were watching us, enjoying the entertainment. I don't know.' Still in my boxers, I shiver, cold, inside and out.

Cassie gets up and pulls my gown from the closet which I pull on.

'Looks good on you,' she compliments.

'Looks good on you too.'

She sits beside me again and waits in silence until I'm ready to continue.

'If someone had stepped in before it escalated into a testosterone showdown maybe things might have turned out different.'

'I'm sorry.'

'If I hadn't drunk so much, I wouldn't have knocked the guy playing pool which started the fight.'

'It's not all on you, Graham.'

Her hand is back on mine, but I pull away and veil my eyes from her stare.

'I don't know how to say it.'

'Say what, Graham? You can tell me.' She reaches out and locks her fingers in mine.

'My name isn't Graham. It's Simon.' My hand squeezes hers hard.

She gasps. If Jaco were here, he'd say, 'Moenie kak praat nie, poephol,' to me now, but I'm not talking shit.

Finally, I'm telling her the truth.

Chapter Fifty-Two

I t comes back to me in great tidal waves; a tsunami churning
everything in its path, leaving the aftermath of destruction.

*'Jou mofgat,' Jaco goads me in the kitchen after the fight in
Maxwell's. After I call him a poephol.*

'I'm not soft.'

*'You are. Look at you, quaking at the knees. You've got no balls. We
can take these bastards out.'*

*We jest constantly, but it's out of character for him to be this callous
in his ridicule, so I remain silent, not wanting to wind him up further.*

'Let's go back there.'

*'It's not worth it. I thought we were going surfing early in the
morning.'*

*There's a madness to his stare. 'You're just going to let them get away
with messing with the locals?'*

'Who cares?'

*'I care. They'll not be so quick to pick a fight if I take this, will they,
boeta.'*

Pa walks in on us and Jaco turns and brandishes the pistol towards him. 'Jaco!' he yells, his eyes wide.

'Leave us alone, Pa. What, do you think I'm gonna do, pull the trigger?' Jaco retorts, swinging the gun around to the side of his head. The blood from the fight has now congealed and crusted like mud in his eyebrow, but a glistening of sweat dribbles down his left cheek. 'I've brains in here, you know,' he says.

I flinch as Jaco taps the barrel against his temple. It's the same movement I've seen him use to chip the top off a soft-boiled egg in the morning, to dip buttery fingers of Ma's homemade bread into the centre. Worse than the tapping is the stillness when he stops, leaving the metal pressed against his skin.

The terracotta tiles on the kitchen floor are a gulf between us.

'Stay the fuck away from me, boeta,' Jaco warns as I take a step to cross the distance.

I halt in my tracks. The sound of the fridge-freezer pulsates loudly, matching the beat of my heart threatening to explode in my chest.

'Son, give me the gun,' Pa says gently. His palm opens as if waiting to collect change from buying his daily tabloid in the newsagents. He looks skeletal, his cheekbones protruding, accentuating his age.

'Get out of here, Pa. This is between me and him.' Jaco turns the gun towards me.

'Please, Jaco, stop,' Pa begs.

I look my brother square in the eyes, silently pleading with him as the haze of the alcohol in my system evaporates and my senses rush into focus. My desperation to turn back the clock is overwhelming. I want to play another round of rummy, order a pepperoni pizza from Mr Delivery and sit with my feet up in front of the television, enjoying a quiet night in, laughing at the antics of a sitcom with Jaco chuckling beside me. Where's my Tardis from the childhood camping holidays when I need it? But there's no time machine. I've never been Doctor Who. I'm just an average small-town bloke, standing in front of the oven watching my brother wave a pistol around as if it's the national flag on display to support the Springboks in a World Cup final. I'd give my front teeth to be somewhere else. One is conveniently loose from the fight anyway. Has my mouth been bleeding like the guy I punched in the face?

I'm immobile with indecision, unsure of whether to back away, fall to the floor, or gradually inch in.

Jaco distributes the tiniest amount of pressure from his forefinger. In a panic, I dive towards my brother to shove the firing line away from me. From him. From Pa's path.

'Stop it!' I bawl as we both fall to the floor. I grapple with him as I try to reach for the weapon and manage to knock it from his grasp.

It clatters and slides across the tiles, hitting the edge of the dish-washer. Jaco and I both dive for it. My fingers reach it first, wrapping themselves around the weapon to snatch it away to put back in the cupboard next to the extra-virgin olive oil. But then Jaco is beside me, swinging at my arm, taking me by surprise as he dislodges the gun from me.

He scrambles to his feet. 'Back off, boeta.' He taps his temple again with the firearm.

I don't back off. I get to my feet and grab at the gun. My hand and Jaco's on the trigger.

'Son, leave it!' Pa screams.

But he's drowned out as a single shot rings out and blood splatters across the room. There are no toothpaste eruptions, no monarch butter-fly flutters, no need for a defibrillator.

Cause of death: Gunshot to the head.

Chapter Fifty-Three

My mood is morose as we drive along the notorious N2 towards Sir Lowry's Pass, not because our departure is imminent, but because our arrival is. We're going home, me, to face the music; Cassie, to prop me up while the tune plays.

She's riding next to me in the passenger seat of our hire car for these final days on the African continent. Even though she now knows I'm a liar, she's stuck with me, a man who assumed another man's name.

I've told Cassie about all the moments when I nearly slipped up. Being asked for my identity documents by the ghost squad, opening a bank account in Edinburgh, the moment I met her when I almost introduced myself as Simon in the rain. Immense shame engulfs me over the deceit, on top of remorse and culpability. My cargo is larger than Ian could ever have envisaged during the Highland's shrink session, but lighter now it's been shared. Whatever happens when I get to Struisbaai, I'll never forget Cassie has stood by me.

We spot a herd of ostriches in a field as I pull into a petrol station to refuel. One separates out, running to cover ground. Jaco and I could have done with lengthy ostrich legs to sprint from Maxwell's that night instead of hanging around to get a kicking. I'd rather have been labelled a coward than have Jaco end up as angry as he was.

A farm stall and gift shop are attached to the garage, and we go inside so Cassie can browse at the painted ostrich eggs and bumpy ostrich leather purses. Takeaway ostrich burger is on the menu – which I'd order if the majestic birds were not so blatantly enjoying life outside of the window. I'm about to comment on this ironic predicament but Cassie is so excited by seeing an ostrich for the first time I quietly pay for fuel and a packet of Simba chutney crisps instead.

'This place is incredible,' she says, her make-up-free face animated as we walk back to the car.

She looks pretty in a floor-length gypsy dress with sandals on her feet, no socks. Ian didn't influence the Donkey Kongs as much as he might have liked.

I'm overjoyed our pinstripe suits are packed away in our cases and we've finished the campaign work. We've screened, assessed, shortlisted and interviewed so many candidates, my experience as a recruiter is now comparable to Bill Gate's knowledge of computer software. Our schedule has been demanding, hooking Hannah into out-of-hours calls to make final offers, selecting the team that will inject fresh perspective into prison technology.

I've been thinking about the judicial problems since being back in South Africa, perhaps because I'm closer to the cell that I was locked up in. My thoughts are invaded with chilling flashbacks of eating pap with my back against the wall.

'Prisons really have the opportunity to transform with technology,' I say, driving off.

'I assume you're not talking about giving every inmate access to Facebook or making a holiday camp out of their sentence.'

'I'm far more conservative than that. Improving productivity through automation and better document management of inter-view paperwork and prisoner records could have a positive outcome across the whole service. There are so many ways we can improve deficiencies through the use of devices that will really help prison-ers, wardens and visitors. Maybe then, more time can be spent on rehabilitation or expanding victim support programs.'

'Why do you care so much?' Cassie asks.

'Prisoners may well need to be held accountable for their crimes, but there are some who have genuine remorse and want to take the right path. They just need more support.'

'I know there are.'

'Maybe a second chance isn't always deserved, but surely the system has an obligation to provide hope, otherwise we might as well hang the guilty in a noose outside The Last Drop. Plus we have to keep doing what we can for the victims of crime and their families. I can tell you, my family crumbled and there was no net beneath them to break the fall.'

I speed up on the open road and leave the running ostrich behind. They're flightless birds, able to run but not fly, burying their head in the sand when they are afraid. If I'm ever to be any-thing other than an ostrich, I need to stop running. Face my fear. Pay a visit to the Suid-Afrikaanse Polisiediens.

'Are you nervous about seeing your parents, Grah—?' Cassie starts. 'Sorry, I still can't get used to calling you Simon.'

'Nervous, yah, you could say that.'

To hear my real name come from Cassie's lips is going to take some adjustment. My new identity is so deep-rooted, it's like pulling out a wisdom tooth and leaving an enormous crater in the gum that needs time to heal.

Graham was an easy name to remember, but one that delivered a blow to the heart every time it was spoken.

My brother, Jaco *Graham* Coetzee.

Chapter Fifty-Four

During more positive moments, I've imagined arriving in Agulhas and seeing Eleanor, my mother, pushing the hospitality boundaries for her son returning home, with a warm hug, fresh handtowels in the bathroom and snoek grilling on the outdoor braai.

And my father, Ronald, a strapping fellow, with a booming voice, and an even bigger heart, rolling out the red carpet for his youngest boy, back after his trip to the land of stuffed intestine delicacies and men in skirts. We would tune in to the sports channel, shoot the breeze over the cricket results and mull over the latest rugby team selection.

'Did you watch the ashes, son?'

'What do you think about the Bok's scrumhalf change?'

'How useless is the new coach?'

I've envisaged a welcoming committee that is free of undercurrents, joking over trivial matters like the lack of phone calls and non-existent letters. In my dreams, I've melted back into my family, losing myself in their affection and easy conversation.

Instead, as I park in the drive, Erin appears by the garden gate with a one-year-old girl in her arms who has the curliest blonde Shirley Temple hair I've ever seen.

My breath comes in short gasps as I suffer from one of the panic attacks I so often try to ward off.

'Breathe, Simon,' Cassie says, handing me the empty crisp packet I threw on the back seat. 'Do you want to use this?'

I'm no scientist, but the thought of sticking my head into a foil bag to sniff in crumbs seems like a ludicrous conundrum, so I shake my head. She's only trying to help ease my predicament any way she can. Looking in the rear-view mirror, my own dark-rimmed eyes stare back. I will myself to pull my shit together and get out of the driver's seat, but I'm frozen, hands still gripping the wheel.

A knock on the windowpane makes me turn. Cassie is standing there. I'd not even realised she'd climbed out.

She opens the door for me. Offers a hand. 'I'm here.'

'It's okay. I'm fine.' I rub the sweat from my palms onto my khaki shorts as Monique peeks towards me. She's pink and chubby, with emerald eyes – just like Erin's. Cassie's too, and the green grass at Newlands.

Monique sends my senses reeling as I drink her in. Her jawline and forehead are strong, a determined shape, which is a duplicate of my own. It's also a mirror image of Jaco's face, and why wouldn't it be?

She's his child.

***

No matter what negative feelings I've had about coming home, it's impossible to dispute the beauty of the Western Cape shores. Rough waves provide the backdrop to the house, foaming at the mouth, producing spray like a thousand elephant trunks who have not forgotten a thing. I sense the energy flowing through the water, wiping out the novices, begging for experienced surfers to master the current. Jaco was a master of the surf as much as he was a master of medicine. Just by looking at the horizon, he could estimate the wave amplitude, wavelength and frequency.

I miss him.

Every day.

Boeta.

God created the ultimate country that is South Africa. Behind the politics, corruption and crime that has seeped into its crevices, he did a fine job. There is no place on earth like it. What bothers me is how HE, with all of his unlimited talents, can leave a destructive trail of shattered dreams and miracles repudiated.

I walk towards Erin on shaky feet, knowing I've taken everything away from the woman I grew up with. She was engaged to be married when she fell pregnant. My mother was going to wear dusky pink to the wedding. My brother was ecstatic with happiness, desperate to be a good lover, a husband, a father. I left a bride-to-be with nothing ahead of her but ineffable grief, and left this girl with the gummy smile without a father.

When I reach Erin, she nods, face straight and eyes free of emotion, but she makes a move to hand my niece over to me and I take her into my arms. Monique snuggles into my embrace and I squeeze her as if there's no tomorrow.

Sometimes there isn't.

Erin reminds me my parents are inside and although I've no desire to give up the innocent child and the scent of baby shampoo, I reluctantly release her.

'Oh, I nearly forgot. I bought you this back in Scotland.' I reach into my pocket and hand Monique the small carved wooden angel I bought months ago at the Dalhousie Christmas market.

As the little girl gives a small squeal of delight, Cassie echoes the sound. 'Oh, wow. I remember when you bought that. It's the most thoughtful gift ever.'

'I nearly bought one for you too since you're my other guardian angel, but it seemed a bit silly at the time.'

She smiles, then I do the polite introductions to Erin and Monique, affording me a few more seconds to compose myself before going inside.

I walk up the garden path. Ma has been diligently pruning again; I'm glad she has her roses to tend to. Letting myself in, I step inside the doorway and immediately smell my mother has been baking. The whirring noise in the background adds further intensity to the wave of nostalgia. The ancient top-loader washing machine always reverberates throughout the house when a load is on.

I'm home.

Cassie is still chatting to Erin about baby behaviour, so I leave them in the hallway. I'm lost without her by my side as I walk into the lounge alone.

Sitting on the chintz sofa is Ma, hands clasped over her legs. A home-baked gateau is next to her favourite delicate teapot she always uses for visitors.

Is this what I've become?

A visitor?

My father is in his faithful worn velour chair, a scatter cushion placed in the small of his back, which has seen better days. Jaco and I clubbed together a couple of birthdays ago to buy him a leather Lay-Z-Boy with a pouch for the remote control. It's been used as a clothes horse in the corner of the master bedroom ever since.

'Hello, son.'

'Pa,' I croak before breaking into tears. Ma gets up to wrap me in a hug, stroking my hair like she did when I broke an arm when I was six, falling from a tree in the park. The contents of my nose gorge a path down my chin and the release of emotion feels good.

I cried the night Jaco died, in the back of the van after the cops bundled me in to transport me to the lock-up. I blubbered during that short journey more than I ever thought possible for a man. And again, when I saw my father shaving in the bathroom the day of the funeral, same as he's always done before a visit to church. There was no accusation, just a blank stare, but I felt the culpability which sent me into a heap beside the ironing board, which Pa hauled me up from. I rearranged my features until they were hardened in place after that.

During the funeral service, I held it together out of respect for my brother. Jaco was always tougher than me. The lump in my throat snowballed as the town came out in droves to pay their respects. It was like a hundred crows decided to roost in the church, all dressed in black, with caws coming out of them like nesting mother birds whose eggs have gone.

One of the worst moments to endure was seeing Pa collapsing onto his knees as the priest said his final words of respect. Seeing him doubled over like that was more distressing than scrubbing my brother's brains from my hair. Pa was always there for us as a pillar of support, encouraging us to embrace life, and I caused his pain by sending his eldest to his tomb.

I perch on the edge of the sofa as Ma cuts me a slice of triple-layer gateau.

'Your father bought me a new KitchenAid,' Ma says as I take a mouthful.

I struggle to swallow the delicious buttermilk icing as my throat grabs onto it like it's coated with velcro.

'How was the journey?' Ma asks.

'Alright. The drive wasn't too bad except for passing roadworks by Houw Hoek.'

'The traffic's been piling up there for weeks,' Pa says. 'Workers aren't what they used to be anymore.'

The carriage clock on the mantelpiece counts away the seconds, the ticking louder than an IRA bomb about to detonate in Canary Wharf.

'I'm sorry, Pa.'

'It wasn't your fault, Simon,' Ma chimes in.

'I should never have played the hero by trying to disarm him.'

'You had no choice.'

'I was too hasty. He mightn't have pulled the trigger if I'd backed off.'

'It was a split-second decision,' says Pa. 'There wasn't enough time to think about whether you should back off or not.'

Pa makes a lot of sense, but it's still senseless. I don't know what made me tackle Jaco when he had a gun in his hand: alcohol, angst, anger, jealousy, love or love lost …

It's hot in bed. So hot I can't sleep. Haven't slept a wink. Outside, the sun is rising. I left my blinds open last night so I wouldn't miss the orange glow streaming in the window and onto my face. No way I was going to sleep in today. It's Wednesday and Erin always surfs before school on Wednesdays.

I get up and pull on clean boardies. Wetsuit pulled up to my waist. Will zip up later. Put a bit of wax in my hair, even though it's a waste. Hair products say they are for waves, but they should say, 'excluding those in the ocean'.

It's quiet in the house as I creep past Jaco's bedroom. Told him I was skipping the surf today. I feel bad about lying, but just this once I want to head to the beach alone.

My surfboard is waiting for me. Pa was going to buy me a new one for my birthday, but I love this old orange squash tail. It's familiar and comfy. Manoeuvres like a dream. Tuck it under my armpit and walk as fast as I can to the sands.

I can see her down at the water's edge on her own. This is it. I'm finally going to ask her out. Maybe a burger in the dorp, or we can go walk around the Arniston caves. Explore around the rocks a bit. They're not that big, but they're dark and quiet. I can hold her hand. Feel a bit sick in case she says no.

Do it.

Do it.

Do it.

It's low tide and the sand is wet for a good stretch. She still has her back to me. Gonna surprise her. Haven't been hitting Wednesday morning surf since school hired the new principal and made midweek assembly way earlier.

I start to walk, then stop in my tracks. He's coming out of the water.

Jaco.

WTF!

I duck behind the flora. He'll be pissed if he sees me after I told him I wasn't coming today again. Realise I should also be pissed because he said he wasn't coming either.

My heart stops as he goes right up to her and wraps his hands around her waist. He's kissing her.

Jaco is kissing Erin.

Erin is kissing Jaco.

I can't believe he got to her first. Why didn't I tell him I liked her?

Why didn't he tell me he liked her? I could kill him for not saying anything. I can't watch. Got to get out of here. Can't ever tell either of them about this. That would be embarrassing.

I scratch my leg on the flora as I run away. Prickly sucker. Realise it's not the bush that's a sucker.

It's me.

Depending on the impact location of a bullet, a small percentage of gunshot wounds to the head can be endured. If a low-velocity bullet, fired from a low-calibre weapon and from a distance, enters the skull through the forehead, the victim may feel like they are staring death in the face, but they'll have a greater chance of surviving because it may only superficially damage one hemisphere of the brain. It might leave motor and sensory impairments, or memory loss, but it also might leave a pulse. My boeta though wasn't wearing a helmet when he caught a missile at close range. It entered one temple and exited the other, crossing several parts of the brain. The perforating wound was so horrendous it sprayed his brains all over me and Ma's treasured KitchenAid. I'm glad Ma made coffee cake whisked up with a new appliance that had no remnants of my brother lodged inside its parts.

What's stuck with me is not only how much blood can come out of one head, but the smell of death too. That faint metallic odour and then the whiff of faeces from one second of trigger pressure.

Maak elke sekonde tel.

I wish I could take back that second. The moment when I fragmented my brother's skull and ripped away his life. And even though it was for my own good, to avoid slow puncture, my South African roots were ripped away in that second too, when Pa prescribed exile, which was both a punishment and a gift.

Staying at home wasn't an option. I had to go. I killed a decent man. We had the odd brush-up, just like all brothers do, but aside from the night at Maxwell's, there are no recollections of Jaco transforming into a suicidal brute to be feared.

I'll always remember him as the kind of person who would pick up a spider and return it to the underside of a rose bush.

Chapter Fifty-Five

I n the kitchen, Ma sinks into a ball, clutching her head into her knees as if protecting herself from a quake on the top end of the Richter scale, her body shaking as if the core of the earth has shattered. She's in her favourite nightgown, and her feet are bare. No time to put slippers on when the blast of a gun explodes in your house. The sound coming from her is primal. Pa crouches next to her, rubbing her back. I'm close enough to Jaco to rub his back too, but it would be futile.

'We need to call the police,' I say.

'In a minute,' Pa answers as Ma starts to crawl to Jaco. 'Don't, Eleanor,' he says, but she's already on top of my brother, stroking his hair like she always does whenever we get sick.

She reaches for his hand, feverishly whispering the Lord's Prayer.

Feeling like an intruder, I back away to give her space to say goodbye.

'Give me your clothes and go and take a shower as fast as you can,' Pa orders. 'I don't want the police knowing you were anywhere near that gun.'

'No!'

'Do it!' Pa shouts. 'You know what happens to people like you in jail?'

'Listen to him, Simon,' my mother instructs in-between asking God for our daily bread and asking him to forgive our trespasses. 'I don't want to lose a second son.'

She's feral. Wild-eyed and alien to me. I don't know how she can have so much blood streaked down her face, arms and garments. Then I look down at my red, wet, sticky self.

I kick off my shoes and tear off my clothes, losing them swiftly like I'm about to lose my virginity. In some ways, I am. This is a first for me.

Pa yanks the tablecloth off the dining room table and gently removes the gun from Jaco's hand, using a corner of the tablecloth to wipe it clean. When he's done, he deftly puts the gun back into my brother's hand and bundles up my clothes in the sunflower material. 'You didn't touch that gun, Simon. Do you hear me? Now go clean up.'

Shivering in my boxers, I do as I'm told; trooping to the bathroom to take a hot shower, to scour my skin, scrub my hair, clean under my nails. The tiles look inviting. I rest my forehead against them as the jets hit my back. The wall has a coolness that should benefit the hothead that landed me in this mess, but it doesn't. I bang my head, gently at first, then harder and harder until it hurts.

When I'm done taking a layer off my skin, removing all traces of the tiny little pieces of my brother, I pull on fresh jeans and a sweater and go back to the kitchen. My blood-spattered clothes wrapped in the sunflower tablecloth are nowhere to be seen.

'The police are on their way,' says Pa. 'Just remember, you were nowhere near him when that gun went off. I told them he shot himself and we all rushed in here after we heard the gun go off.'

Ma is clutching Jaco's hand, weeping and moaning. There's a primitive need somewhere deep within me — part of me in denial — that maybe he's still breathing. I try to avert my eyes from what is left of his head, but it's impossible. Blood has pooled around his head. The bullet has torn through his hair, scalp and muscle, projecting itself into his skull with such brutality the high velocity has split his skull wide open and sprayed its contents everywhere.

I start to vomit and choke it back again, not because I'm afraid of leaving unwanted evidence at the scene of a crime, but because I don't want to defile what's left of my brother with oxtail potjie.

'I'm so sorry, boeta. I love you. I'll see you soon,' I whisper hoarsely.

The goodbye will never register with him. Jaco's filing cabinets are sealed closed, unable to store memories of my apology.

Pa is beside Ma, trying to help her onto her feet. I move to help him.

'Stay back,' Pa says. 'We don't want you to get blood on you.' He supports Ma as we move away from Jaco's lifeless body to the front room. I take Pa's favourite chair while he sits next to her on the sofa, rubbing her arm while waiting for the police to arrive. His voice dips in and out of my sphere, telling me how Jaco has been troubled with the pressures of a medical career and how he didn't take it well, coming off worse in the fight in Maxwell's.

'Simon! You need to focus.'

I try to tune into the channel, rehearsing my lines for the police while Pa adds Polyfilla to the cracks.

The doorbell rings and I wring my hands as Pa lets in a pair of officers, affirmative action visible in the mix of one black, one white and familiar. The older officer is Pa's good friend, Nick Boshoff. They walk straight past the doorway to the lounge to enter the kitchen.

Immediately, they dive into asking pertinent questions. Pa tells them my brother shot himself as they gawk at his body obstructing the route to the kettle, preventing Ma from getting up to offer them a cup of tea and a gingersnap.

Nick takes Pa out into the passage and talks to him alone for a few minutes. I hear him call in more help on the radio, then I tune out again. Don't hear if it's an ambulance, a coroner, the television crew of Carte Blanche *who will have a field day investigating this event for M-Net viewers to enjoy.*

The other cop paces. He rubs at his moustache so often he may be inadvertently shedding hairs all over the crime scene. Ma flinches as he paws one of the silver photo frames on the sideboard, of Jaco in school uniform with a bad haircut, then puts it back down in the wrong place. Ma is particular about her photos.

'Do you mind if I sit?' He doesn't wait for an answer as he pummels the cushions before settling on Pa's favourite chair. 'I see your knuckles look raw,' he says, staring me down.

'My brother and I got into a bar fight at Maxwell's. It was nothing. We came back here afterwards.'

'What happened when you got back here?'

'My parents were in bed. Jaco was infuriated about being thrown out of Maxwell's after we got pulled into some stupid fight over nothing. I went to the bathroom and heard the shot from there.'

He doesn't write down any notes, perhaps because my brevity is making it easy for him to recount later.

Pa comes back in with Nick. Takes over. 'We all ran into the kitchen,' Pa tells him. 'Me and Eleanor at first. Jaco behind us. Eleanor knelt down to try and help him while I called you, but he was gone.'

The cop fingers his moustache again and nods. 'Thanks, Mr Coetzee, but I need Simon here to come down to the station.'

'Why is that necessary?' Pa challenges.

'We have more questions for him, that's all.'

'What kind of questions?'

'Did you fight with your brother?' the cop asks me.

'No. There were some out-of-town idiots who gave us a hard time. He was on my side,' I reply.

'How did you get home? Did you drive?'

'Jaco drove.'

'You sure?'

'I told him not to,' I mumble.

'And you had been drinking?'

'You can't charge my dead son with drink driving!' Pa shouts.

The cop ignores him and stares at me. 'We can talk more at the station.'

'Leave him out of it,' says Pa. 'This has nothing to do with him.'

'He's intoxicated and been in a fight involving both of your sons. We need him to come with us.'

'It's okay, Pa.' I follow them outside to the van. Pa nods as they bundle me in, wordlessly reassuring me that everything will be okay.

But my hand was wrapped around the barrel of the gun that killed my brother, and that very same barrel has been wiped clean by my father using the tablecloth covered in sunflowers.

I'll never be okay.

Jaco will never be okay.

We will never be okay.

Chapter Fifty-Six

M a fiddles with the crucifix around her neck. There's always been religion in the family; church every Sunday, grace at dinner, prayers before bed.

'When I was in that cell I wondered over and over again why God didn't intervene,' I tell her.

'Don't lose your faith, son,' she replies. Her hair is dull and thinning and she looks hunched and frail.

When I get home after almost twenty-four hours in jail and a drive to the Meisho Maru, Ma is on her knees, hunched and frail over a bucket of soapy water. She's scrubbing the pieces of Jaco off the floor that are never going to make it to the coffin.

'Let me help.'

'Don't touch!' she snaps, smears forming as the cloth struggles to erase the crimson liquid.

'Do you want me to get the maid in?' I ask.

'No, I want to do it myself. I'm going to make bobotie tomorrow for dinner. Will you eat bobotie? You like bobotie. I need to get this kitchen

clean so Pa can paint it before the funeral.'

She averts her eyes from the blood-spattered walls as she prattles and scrubs.

Prattles and scrubs.
Prattles and scrubs.
Prattles and scrubs.

Her hands are red raw, eyes matching, while I hover helplessly in the doorway.

'My faith has long gone, Ma. Most days, I just want to die.'

'Stop it.' Her stare warns me I've overstepped the mark. 'Only God can decide when we move on. Just because we've lost Jaco, it doesn't mean we've lost God, and you don't get to decide when I lose you.'

'If anyone is to blame, it's me, not you and not God,' Pa adds. 'I left a loaded gun in the house. Your mother never wanted it there in the first place.'

I turn to meet Pa's gaze for the first time since taking away his firstborn. My mind is awash with confusion, but slowly, like a snake uncoiling itself after months of hibernation, recognition takes over. He feels as responsible as I do for what happened. Both of us have condemned ourselves, claiming the guilt and treasuring it as our own.

I'm stranded, as shipwrecked as the Meisho Maru in front of me as Pa gives me a flight ticket from Cape Town to Amsterdam in my name, and another departing Amsterdam to Edinburgh in a name that is horribly familiar.

'Graham?' It punches me hard. 'You want me to take Jaco's middle name and use his date of birth?'

'Graham Coetzee. It's perfect. If you get stuck, you can use some of Jaco's other paperwork and just let people know you go by your middle

323

name. We have his original birth and baptism certificates and a few other documents you can take with you.'

'I know, but every time someone talks to me, I'm going to be reminded of him.'

'If we had more time, we could go with a whole new identity, new passport, new birth cert, the works ... but we have to sort your new ID tomorrow. Using your brother's middle name is the best option given the short notice. That way, we only need the passport done.'

The waves roar around my ears, almost as loud as the sound of the gunshot. My hands are numb and I warm them on the fire burning my blood-splattered clothes to ashes.

'Maak elke sekonde tel.'

'Why don't we come clean with exactly what happened?'

'I panicked, son. Things were done in the spur of the moment. None of us were thinking straight and I couldn't take a chance you'd be blamed for this. There's no way we can tell the police now that you and Jaco were in a struggle. About the clothes we burned.'

'It was an accident.'

'Nobody in Maxwell's is going to talk to the police; people see a uniform coming, they run for cover, even when there's nothing to hide. The police saw your injuries and Jaco's and they suspect the worst. If there's even the slightest chance you'll end up in prison, I'm not prepared to take it.'

My voice shakes. 'They'll find evidence.'

'The evidence is gone, Simon. That mongrel in your cell even took your takkies. That was a blessing. The cops did you a favour not intervening there. I don't know why I didn't think to destroy them when we got rid of your clothes at the shipwreck.'

'It was Nick Boshoff who let the guy in my cell take my takkies.'

'Nick is a good man,' says Pa. 'He told me at the house when it happened that he would do everything he could to look after our family.

'But Pa, I can't keep hiding like this. I'll be okay if they punish me. I deserve to go back to jail.'

'Maybe you don't.'

'My finger was on the trigger, Pa. Jaco's was on top of mine, but my finger was on the trigger.'

'So maybe he pulled. Maybe you pulled. It doesn't matter.'

'What if I hated him more than I ever realised? Because of Erin. I never told anyone, but I always liked her, Pa, and I was so angry when they got together.'

'Yah, me and your mother guessed you liked Erin, but it was a long time ago and you loved your brother, Simon. It was an accident. I won't let you go to jail, and neither will your mother.'

My fate is to run from my mistakes. I'm under no illusions I'm still a suspect in my brother's shooting. My father knows it too, and although it hurts to have him so readily ask me to leave everything I know, he's doing it for me. Willing me to escape. To blend into a new country with a new identity, without fear of a slow puncture every day spent behind bars.

I look at the wreckage of the Meisho Maru. Neither floating, nor sunk. Stuck forever in limbo.

I am the Meisho Maru.

I am Bar-L.

I am The Tablecloth.

'Listen to you both,' Ma scolds with the sternness of a head-mistress addressing two disobedient scholars. 'I've been tending to my boy's grave and praying for him to rest in peace. God forgive me, it crossed my mind too why he would be taken while so many other monsters walk the earth.' She crosses her shoulders and chest in a sign of the cross. 'But Jaco is gone because God needs him in heaven. Only the Lord knows why Jaco had to go early, but who are we to question his judgement?'

Shame takes over at the demise of my faith when tragedy has only intensified my parents'. For the first time, I realise venting anger on myself has been a mechanism for coping, and to prevent me from not being so mad at Jaco for being a drunk poephol and checking out. Faith trickles through my soul, drop by drop at first, then gushing, pulsing with energy as it courses through my veins. The life of my brother hasn't been snatched in a twist of evil cruelty. Jaco is the chosen one, selected to stand by the side of the Almighty Father in heaven. While I was being greedy, wallowing in textbook deaths and bathing in my own sorry self-pity, my mother should have had my moral support. As for God, He who has the power to create heaven and earth deserves my trust. Ma is right; everybody dies when it's their time. There's no excusing my suicidal behaviour. I've been a selfish bastard.

'You're right, Ma, but I'll always wish I'd never gone out with him that night.'

'He was his own person, the way God made him,' she replies, matter-of-fact. 'If I'd seen Jaco brandishing a gun in your face, or your father's, I'd have tried to take it from him myself. You mustn't torture yourself.'

'I just don't think I can keep hiding though, Ma.'

Her eyes widen and there is fear in her eyes.

'Have the police been back around since I left?'

'Twice to look for you. The same cop, Peterson,' Pa answers. 'But he's not been back for a few months now.'

'I'm going to go and see them.'

'Son, please, go back to Scotland,' Ma begs. 'You can't take a chance.'

'I have to, Ma. Answering to *Graham* is a constant reminder of what happened.'

My father gets out of his chair. 'I never thought about how it would be overseas for you, Simon. I just didn't want you in jail.' He holds his arms out and hugs me as if it were the first day at school when he dropped me off into the care of a strange teacher. I cling to his shirt and great heaves of raw emotion ebb from us both. 'Lord knows, you did the right thing that night,' Pa sniffs. 'Nobody blames you. I was about to go for the gun myself.'

Relief floods through me, like I'm sitting on death row and hear the lethal injection being ruled inhumane in the name of Christ, Our Saviour.

Eventually Pa releases me and I return to the sofa where I take Ma's hand in mine. The veins feel more pronounced than I remember and her hands are dry. She always used to smother them in hand cream, a ritual after washing the dishes, pruning, baking. I'm ashamed. Every opportunity should have been taken to call and check on my folks. I give her calloused hand a squeeze and silently say my thanks for being given a second chance to make my parents' later years more enjoyable. My father wipes his eyes with a paisley handkerchief as he pours himself a cup of tea and cuts a piece of gateau. That's how Cassie finds us; sitting together, licking buttermilk icing off our fingers, talking about the culinary difference between a British fish and chips dinner versus an African boerewors roll with Mrs Ball's chutney.

Chapter Fifty-Seven

I drive along the main road of Struisbaai until I pass the fishermen's cottages and reach the Suid-Afrikaanse Polisiediens.

The lock-up attached to it is even rustier than I recall. It would be great to tear it down eventually. I don't ever want to see the place again.

Inside, the tiny front desk is unmanned, so I ring the bell. It takes an age before someone finally appears with a steaming mug of coffee in hand. A young officer I've not had the pleasure of meeting before.

'How can I help?' he asks.

'I'm just back from overseas and want to check how my brother's case is going.'

'What's your name?'

'Simon Ronald Coetzee.'

'And your brother's?'

'Jaco Graham Coetzee.'

I give him the date of the incident and he puts down his cup to tap the keyboard with a speed likely to turn his coffee cold.

'What is it you want to know?' he enquires.

I'm hyperventilating as I hold on to the desk with both hands. My voice comes out like a squeak.

'I just want to check the latest on the case.'

'It was closed three weeks ago. Suicide, it says here.'

'Are you sure? There was a cop, Officer Peterson, who questioned me after it happened, but I've been out of the country.'

'Peterson left a couple of months ago. Transferred to Cape Town. This one was closed by Officer Nick Boshoff.'

'Is Officer Boshoff around?'

'He retired three weeks ago with not a single case outstanding.'

'How come nobody told my folks the outcome?'

'We're short-staffed. It must have been overlooked.'

It would be easy to think the case was closed so a retiring officer could leave with tidy paperwork and an impeccable record. South Africa has been on a massive drive to keep crime stats low too. Suicide is better than murder for tourism. But Nick Boshoff had integrity. Was one of the best officers in town. Kept the streets pretty safe around Struisbaai, which in a place like South Africa, takes a lot. At worst, maybe he let my blood-splattered trainers walk out the door because he knew my father, me, Jaco, our whole family. Maybe it was a genuine oversight. In any case, I'm awash with relief. He waltzed out a hero with a clean rap sheet and a tidy pension, and I can leave here a free man.

'Mr Coetzee.'

Fear bubbles to the surface. 'Yah?'

'Where were you overseas?'

'Scotland.'

'Isn't that where William Wallace lived?'

'Yah.'

'I'm sorry about your brother, Braveheart.'

My heart isn't brave, but it beats again.

***

Before we leave, Erin takes me for a drive to Struisbaai Plaat with Monique strapped in her car seat. We're alone on the beach road. Not even a puff adder has slithered down from the mountains to bask on the tar, but as we reach the car park, Monique babbles away excitedly.

'Dada. Dada.' She points a chubby finger towards the ocean, and I know Jaco is out there at one with the waves.

Leaving the car behind, we trek through the sand dunes in silence. It's windy and sand billows around us, but Monique doesn't care about the weather. She's comfortable resting on her mother's hip, sucking her thumb. The beach is empty as far as the eye can see. Even the fishermen don't feel like casting a line from the shore in this weather. As we reach the wet stretch of sand running parallel to the surf, Erin stops and puts Monique down to roll up the bottom of her trousers. I follow her lead and roll up my own jeans. She's about to lift Monique back up again, when she takes a tiny step and falls into the sand.

'Oh wow, that's her first step!' Erin exclaims.

'Incredible!' I say, helping Monique up.

'Maybe it's time we all take our first steps,' Erin says.

We take one of Monique's hands each and walk into the ocean, lifting her over each wave as it rolls in. She squeals in delight and the sound fills me with hope.

'How have you been?' I ask Erin as we splash around in the shallow water.

'Don't get me wrong. I miss Jaco, but I've met someone else.'

I try to hide my surprise. Erin and Jaco were inseparable growing up. I was always the third wheel tagging along with them. Playing *Twister.* Swimming in the lagoon. Sharing Spur burgers in Hermanus. I knew on prom night when Erin came to our house, dressed to the nines. Jaco told her he loved her the second he saw her, tied a corsage to her wrist. He wore his heart on his sleeve after that. They made a great couple.

'I wasn't expecting to move on so soon. It just sort of happened.' Her voice cracks. 'I'll never forget him though, Simon.'

'I'm delighted for you. You deserve another chance at happiness.'

'It's not right for me to take your money any longer.'

This crushes me. Providing for my niece is all I've left to link me to my brother. She's been the only reason I get up in the mornings to drag myself to work. 'Let me provide for her, Erin. I took her father away.'

'No. It's over now and we're doing okay, but I'd like one last favour.'

'Anything.'

'Will you be Monique's godfather?'

'Dada,' Monique gurgles, sitting to play with a shell she's picked up.

The lump in my throat means I can only nod my acceptance. I'm soaring so high my hair is probably tickling Jaco's feet. No matter what obstacles lie in my path, I'll always be there for Monique. She is my tik.

I take off the tooth pendant necklace – a souvenir from the dead sand shark Jaco and I found washed up by the tide once – and hang it around Monique's neck.

Erin nods. 'It's what Jaco would have wanted.'

I hope so.

Chapter Fifty-Eight

K*aapstad*, the capital of the Western Cape Province, lies on the south-west tip of the Cape Peninsula, infecting it with charm – perhaps because it was founded so long ago, in 1652. Cassie and I hit the roads early, so the traffic is low enough to be on cruise mode, enjoying the scenery as we drive. It was easier to get up at sunrise and say goodbye quickly to my folks than drag out a long day of emotions, knowing I would be leaving at the end of it. Despite rebuilding bridges with my family, I'm going back to Scotland. The decision was a hard one to make but I've a plan in mind for the future – both mine and theirs.

Driving back through the metropolis is a pleasure. A journey framed by the Table Mountain range on one side and the ocean on the other. It's a clear and sunny winter's day. The Tablecloth has lifted, exposing the three-kilometre level plateau of the mountain peak.

'Legend has it The Tablecloth is attributed to a smoking contest between the devil and a local pirate called Van Hunks,' I say to

Cassie. 'When the cloud hovers over the landmark, it symbolises a contest is underway.'

'It's nice to see it's gone today then,' Cassie replies, staring out of the window.

It pleases me too. In the last few days, I've lifted my own table-cloth to confront the festering devil underneath and have a clear view ahead for the first time since Jaco died.

I veer left towards the Victoria and Alfred Waterfront, an enormous tourist attraction in the renovated part of Cape Town's historic docklands. I'm normally not one for visiting places that attract the masses, but any experience with a maritime connection is worth a detour. One of the things I love most about it is the changing nautical backdrop of a working harbour that caters for the fishing industry and a wide range of vessels and yachts.

The vast number of retail shops around the perimeter, as well as attractions like the craft markets, aquarium and cinema complex, are still closed, but I park close to the Clock Tower. The restored Victorian Gothic style clock is a national monument which is in keeping with the Waterfront character of old mixed with new.

We stroll towards the original Bertie's Landing site, passing by the Robben Island Museum and Nelson Mandela Gateway ticket office. Twenty million people a year pass through the Waterfront, not least because Mandela and his time on Robben Island continues to fascinate and inspire the world. I've always loved the vibe around Bertie's Landing. Way back, before they built a new swing bridge, a penny ferry used to transport guests between the two sections of the harbour. It's still retained some of the original architecture in many of the buildings. This respect for heritage is what makes Cape Town such a unique place.

We find several seals lounging on the platform amidst the reclaimed tyres lining the quayside.

'Don't they have a great life?' Cassie observes as the huge mammals stretch out to bask in the morning sun. She leans over the fence to watch them while I stand next to her, enjoying the strong smell of the ocean and its creatures.

The restaurants start to pull up their shutters, and Cassie chooses a quaint place selling coffee and traditional South African plaited koeksisters. We order the syrup-infused donuts and tuck in at an outside table.

'I dig this place,' Cassie informs me. 'It's so diverse and I can't get over how amazing the food is. I honestly had no idea.'

'I'm glad you got to see the best of Cape Town. Everyone knows it's got a bad side which can overshadow the good, but South Africa will always be under my skin.'

I reflect on the country, its people, my parents, Erin and Monique. Their hospitality to Cassie has been overwhelming, and their willingness to welcome me back into the fold is such a godsend I could throw my head back and bark like a seal in thanks.

***

Before we go home, I've one final place to take Cassie.

Simon's Town.

It's a one-hour drive from central Cape Town, but as it's one of the most scenic spots in the area it's well worth the petrol. We make a brief stop in the beach-side suburb of Muizenberg along the False Bay coast, where we take a walk and talk about my childhood.

Jaco and I are on holiday. It's Easter and we've eaten a mountain of chocolate, after the egg hunt in our chalet. Ma and Pa are having an afternoon snooze, but we're close to the beach and Jaco is a teenager now; thirteen – thinks he's thirty. Ma's holiday rule permits him to go to and from the beach with me, but we always have to be back for dinner.

It's not that she's over-protective, simply cautious. The great whites drift along the coast and creep in closer at dusk, so she worries about us surfing within feeding range.

We tug on our wetsuits. Mine is getting tight. I've sprouted since moving into high school and am only an inch off being as tall as Jaco. Barefoot, we carry our boards underarm to the long stretch of sand. It's a pretty beach with a row of Victorian bathing huts painted in bold primary colours.

The shoreline is packed with children eating ice creams and building sandcastles, while their parents grab a few rays. We jog past them and hit the water. It's ice-cold, making me gasp despite the wetsuit, but we paddle out and wait to catch a wave.

We recognise a couple of girls out on their boards from the day before. The surfing community is friendly, even for hormonal teenagers, and they give us a nod before a perfect long wall of water sweeps Jaco into the zone.

He demonstrates a good frontside snap manoeuvre, the one he's been practising all week as he progresses from novice surfing to more radical moves. He's riding frontside with his back to the shore, gathering speed as he gets his balance right when cutting back into the white water by turning his head in the opposite direction ready for the snap. He partially turns with a quick blast and the snap displaces water off the back of the wave in an impressive spray. His technique is improving, with a strong pivot and smooth body adjustments.

There is a wobble; too much pressure on his back foot, and then he wipes out.

I swim towards where he went down but can't see him surface. I freestyle faster, my lungs bursting as I cut through the water, and then he pops up.

'Awesome, boeta,' he pants, blowing his nose on his bare hand to clear the mucus. 'I almost hit the seabed.'

We paddle back out. As we get closer to the girls back out in the surf,
both give him a smile.

I take my wave but there's no frontside snap in my repertoire yet.

My moves have never been as quick as my brothers.

'You liked Erin a lot then?' Cassie asks.

'Aside from Jaco, she was my best friend.'

'And you two never dated?'

'Nope. I nearly asked her out once, but Jaco got in first.'

'And you don't have feelings for her now?'

'Not like that, no. Once they got together, I moved on.'

'She's a great lady.'

'Yah, she is. So are you, you know.'

'What?'

'A great lady.'

Cassie smiles and I smile back.

We move along the coast to Simon's Town, passing South
Africa's largest naval base to reach the compact Boulder's Beach.
The car park is busy. It's a popular spot even though an entrance
fee applies. The main boardwalk to the beach is crowded so I take
Cassie on a minor detour onto the unmarked boardwalk to the
right of the ticket booth. We keep walking through a wooded area
until we stumble on several penguins in the shrubbery.

'This is unbelievable.' Cassie whips out her phone to fill her
storage space with hordes of penguin snaps. One of them is sitting
on an enormous egg and another waddles past, brushing her shoes
as it disappears between two bushes.

'Oh, I want one. They're too cute.'

'I'd get one for you if I could. Which one would you pick?'

This sets me off, regaling the story of Nancy bringing chocolate
biscuits to a boardroom meeting.

'PPP … pick up a penguin,' we say in unison.

We reach the end of the boardwalk, laughing. The view over the water here is much more enjoyable. There are no crowds in this spot, only me and Cassie, here, in Simon's Town. I stare at the water. It dawns on me I've been sluggish on the uptake my whole life. In egg-and-spoon races. Taking frontside snap manoeuvres. Asking Erin out. I'm not going to be slow on the uptake again.

I turn to Cassie. Her green eyes stare at me, bright with hope and passion. They close as I lean in and kiss her.

Chapter Fifty-Nine

I'm jet-lagged when I get back to the Scottish office. Vermin has his head in hands, looking glum.

'What's up?' I ask, although I'm not in the mood to be an agony aunt.

'Nothing's up. That's his whole problem. He's not getting any.' Janine gives a loud snort from inside her cube.

'Marianne walked out,' Vermin elaborates. 'She's gone back to her husband.'

'Unlucky for him,' Janine hollers.

'You know, you used to be fun once, Janine,' he replies.

'I lost our baby. What do you expect?'

'Best thing for it.'

I wait for the cube farm to detonate but Janine is silent.

Vermin lifts his head off his hands. 'I'm just saying, we should get back to our staple fix, Janine.'

'You want your staple fix, do you?' Janine says, peeking over her partition at Vermin.

He nearly trips over himself to rise. 'Stocktake?' he asks.

Janine nods and follows him out of the room. I shake my head and log on to Benny.

I register every applicant from South Africa, making Benny groan as he uploads the data. Then I call each of the new recruits, check their flight options and confirm everything is progressing smoothly with their visa processing and relocation. I answer queries about schools, the best residential suburbs, and setting up bank accounts. I'm delighted with the appointments we've chosen and their commitment to a new life as an expat.

I'm about to call Hannah to give her an update when Vermin arrives back, clutching his scrotum. 'The bitch fired a staple into my bloody privates in the stationery cupboard,' he squawks.

Janine grins from behind him, clutching a staple gun. 'You asked for a staple fix, Vermin, and I aim to please.'

'I'm sorry, Janine.'

'You're a waste of space. Even Marianne saw sense.' Janine disappears back in her cube, head held high, as Vermin shuffles back to his corner.

I leave them swirling in tension and head downstairs to the boardroom to place a private call to Hannah.

'Everything is in order,' I tell her. 'We've staggered the arrivals over the next eight weeks.'

'What a success. I've four different departments all interested in progressing with teams to deliver similar technology modernisation plans.'

'I'm thinking of resigning,' I blurt.

'What! I need you.'

'A bit presumptuous, I know, but I figured you might need a team leader to drive all these improvements into the prison service.'

'I would love you on my team!' says Hannah.

'There are a few things I need to tell you first.'

'Oh?'

'My name is Simon Coetzee, not Graham.'

'What are you talking about?'

'I tried to stop my brother from shooting himself or taking a shot at me or my father and I was responsible for the gun accidently going off. It killed him.' My voice breaks and Hannah waits while I compose myself. 'They locked me up overnight. It was so horrendous I fled before they could properly charge me with anything. I used my brother's middle name and fake passport when I left South Africa. I was scared I'd be sent to prison long-term.'

Hannah remains silent, so I ramble on about prison conditions in South Africa. About how easy it is for prisoners with no education and extreme unemployment issues on the outside to lose their way. Inmates are frequently homeless, and joining a gang is a way to feel like they belong. Most become institutionalised after being banged up with no means to establish themselves in society.

'I genuinely want to make a difference to the system,' I say with heartfelt sincerity. 'Nobody cares about the overpopulation of South African prisons. It creates an inhumane living environment. Bunks are at double or triple capacity, sometimes worse, and attempts to segregate gangs keep failing.'

I tell her about some of the research I've done. The limited outdoor time convicts get in the enclosed courtyards and how exercising is frowned upon by the gang leaders. Instead, drug smuggling is the rampant pastime between some of South Africa's most dangerous inmates, and corruption is rife with some of the wardens. Resources are scarce and improvement programs launch but often they are underfunded or left unfinished.

'Tell me more about your thoughts on the technology,' Hannah finally interrupts.

'General lock-up security is tight, which limits ways of escaping, but IT security is way behind where it should be. Technological advancements in correction facilities are reshaping the system, but not fast enough.'

We chat about developments in handheld scanners that are able to more easily detect hidden weapons. New devices able to pinpoint cell phones. Needle-free medication to reduce the need for syringe injections, reducing the spreading of infection.

'Do you know globally there's an evolution of identification badges through biometrics?' says Hannah. 'Swipe passes are becoming obsolete as new retina and fingerprint recognition technology tells officials exactly where inmates and employees are located at any given time. Radio frequency identification tracking has been specifically designed for the corrections industry, reducing time and effort needed from guards in finding out an individual's whereabouts. The demand for tech skills with law enforcement industry experience is on the rise.'

'That's pretty cool. I want to be a part of it, Hannah. I think I knew it the minute I saw that kid's bike chained to the lamppost at Bar-L. Maybe we can start even thinking about innovative ways we can help keep children connected to their parents who are detained. It could help with rehabilitation. Maybe around education as an example. Shared learning apps so their parents can support their schoolwork from the inside. That kind of thing.'

'We need to talk more about your ideas! This is all timely. I've already been thinking about expanding the new team we've recruited to break into new territory in England as well as Scotland.'

'I know a loyal administrator on the market I can put you in touch with. She might be able to support you establishing more business down south. Her name is Revis Sicklemore.'

'I might take you up on that, but let's get back to you.'

Hannah launches into a question-and-answer session so intense it's like I'm being interviewed for a management position comparable to Dame Stella's old rank.

Then she makes me an offer.

Chapter Sixty

C offee in hand from Café Kamani, I head to share my news with Donald, but his office is empty, so I go back to reception. Nancy is busy chatting to a couple of contractors.

'Graham, these two men will be upstairs upgrading our wi-fi today. We'll finally have improved speed and bandwidth.'

'Fantastic. Luigi is splashing out on the Edinburgh branch. We must be in the big leagues now we've sold an international campaign. Where's Donald?'

'In the boardroom with Charlie Rivers. He won't mind you interrupting him.'

I pop my head around the door.

'Graham, just the man. Come in,' Donald orders as Vermin follows me in. The bank CIO is next to Donald.

'I've been talking to Charlie about the success you've had in South Africa tackling skills shortages here,' Donald brings me up to speed.

'It's an interesting concept,' Charlie acknowledges. 'Donald, if it's

343

okay with you, I'd like Graydon to leave this discussion. We can have a more open discussion on how South African financial institutions don't have too many synergies with our technology platform.'

'I don't understand?' says Vermin.

Charlie puckers his lips. 'You present extremely well, young man, but Marianne De Nunes will not proceed with you leading this campaign. She intends to hold firm on this matter and I support her wishes.'

'But ... but ...' Vermin stutters.

'No buts,' says Donald. 'I'm afraid our customers and the rest of our team come first.'

'I'll talk to you later about all of this,' Vermin says, getting up to leave.

'I will meet with you later for a broader discussion of this matter,' Donald replies, his face stern, then he looks to me. 'Now, about you, please share more about the recruitment you have just done in South Africa with Cassie.'

I dive in, walking Charlie through the benefits of a campaign.

'South Africa is not the only option to consider sourcing candidates from,' Donald says when I'm done. 'Several banks in Australia have virtually identical systems to your bank, Charlie. You will be able to get a whole team from there with the experience you need to take the bank forward.'

'If I want to go ahead with a large number of highly skilled hires to fill some of our long-standing open vacancies, who would fly to Australia to meet applicants face to face?' he asks. 'I certainly don't think it's appropriate Graydon goes given the circumstances of his relationship with Marianne. I regularly play golf with her husband at St Andrews. He's an old friend of mine and he's devastated by the behaviour. I'm so glad they are making a go of their marriage again.'

'I was thinking we could send ...' Donald says, before a bang above us interrupts him reaching the end of his sentence.

'It's just the contractors installing our wi-fi,' Nancy says, peeking around the door.

'Charlie, I was thinking more along the lines of sending Cassie and Graham. Both have experience of running this type of recruitment drive, and Cassie is Australian by birth. It makes perfect sense.'

Charlie's nods. 'I remember Cassie. The girl who wiped the poo from her hands on my topiary trees.'

'That's her,' I reply. 'She's also the lucky one who won at the Grand National.'

'I like your attitude. You and Cassie will do a good job on this,' Charlie beams as a piece of ceiling plaster falls on top of him.

'Oh, shit,' I say as the CIO coughs beneath a blanket of dust.

'Sorry mate,' a workman in a florescent hi-vis shirt hollers through the gaping hole.

'You okay?' I ask as Charlie dusts himself off.

Charlie puckers again. 'Let's hope the workmanship is more superior in Australia than it is in Edinburgh.'

'That's what we call bringing the house down,' I joke.

Charlie laughs, then we delve into the details while I ponder on how Donald is going to take the news of my departure, given this turn of events.

***

It's late in the day when I finally get a chance to talk to Donald alone. He's at his desk playing electronic chess, and I'm proud to see him move his white knight to corner the king into check.

'You beat it yet?'

'The gambling?'

'The electronic chess master.'

'I still have the odd urge to blow some cash on the horses, but this chess machine is the best distraction ever. It's like an irritating nicotine patch that just takes a while to get used to. I'm determined to beat it, but it's a damned good player. Whoever programmed it is brutal.'

I smile. 'Glad you like it.'

'Well done on this next campaign.' He looks down again as the chess set flickers, considering its next move. 'Before today's mess, I thought maybe there was a chance I could still use Graydon to help coordinate things from this side, but it's not to be.'

'Donald, I hate to say it, but he is beyond inappropriate. It's not good to keep ignoring his behaviour in the workplace.'

Donald nods. 'I didn't want to say anything, but we will be parting ways. I'm just carefully managing timing his exit to mini-mise damage and risks to the clients he manages.'

'Graydon is really leaving?'

'Too many complaints. This needs to be one cohesive team and I can't have one bad apple disrupting the dynamics, no matter how good of a recruiter he is.'

'Donald, dare I say it, but it's the right decision. We can manage without him.'

'You were out getting coffee, but he's already aware and I've let a few of the team know that he will be moving on. I don't know why he wandered into this meeting. I think it was a last-ditch attempt to show his client relationship skills with Charlie, but it didn't pay off.'

'Does Cassie know?'

'Client visits. I'll fill her in later.'

'I don't know how to tell you this, Donald, but since you are talking about bad apples ... there's something I need to tell you.'

'There's nothing you can say that will stun me,' Donald replies as his opponent instructs the black king to retreat.

'My name isn't Graham, it's Simon.'

Donald ignores the electronic chess despite the fact he has checkmate on the next move.

'Too blunt?'

'Sledgehammer.'

'My brother's middle name was Graham. We were pulled into a bar fight, and he was so furious he got out my Pa's gun, and I tackled him. It went wrong and he got shot. I fled after a night in prison and changed my identity before I came to work here so the cops wouldn't come looking for me. I killed my brother, not intentionally, but he's dead. I'm so sorry. I remember saying once I wouldn't let you down.'

Donald looks at me. 'Let me put you straight on this. We all make mistakes. I pissed my pants after loan sharks got hold of me and I burned down my kitchen to try to pay them off. You have not let me down. Luigi has given me an advance for the campaign commission I'll be due, even though it's only due in a month. I'm in the clear because of you.'

'You going to stay off the horses?'

'That's the plan.'

'What if the batteries run out on the chess?' I ask.

Donald laughs. 'You'll be flush enough to buy me a ten pack of Duracell.'

'That's not all,' I say.

'Oh?'

'I want to hand in my resignation.'

'You're joking, right?'

I shake my head. 'I'm going to join Hannah's company. They

need someone to manage the new team there and I'm pretty sure they'll be growing the headcount soon. The government are keen to push ahead with some ideas she's floated with them.'

'You're not joking?'

'I know this might leave you understaffed, especially with Graydon going, but it's the right move for me. After what happened with my brother, I've developed a massive passion for helping drive transformation of correctional services. It's the perfect industry for me.'

'I suppose it makes sense. When I leave here, I want to become a jockey,' he jokes. 'You have to gallop after the dream so might as well do it from the saddle.'

'Damn, I'll miss this place.'

'I support you all the way, but there is just one request.'

'Anything, Donald.'

'I want assurance you'll use Talent-IT to recruit for anyone you and Hannah need.'

'Of course. You know, Hannah has just recruited Revis Sicklemore to be her gatekeeper so Graydon wouldn't have been allowed at any of the meetings with her company either.'

'Sounds like I'm best rid of him.'

'If it's Cassie working on her recruitment, I can't see Hannah having an issue. You said it yourself, she knows exactly the skills we're looking for after all those South African interviews.'

'Which brings me nicely on to another request. I still want you to go to Australia.'

'With Cassie?'

Donald nods. 'The bank wants an army of programmers from there and I don't want to let them down.'

'I know.'

'I'll push Charlie to get procurement underway as quickly as possible if you can give me a couple of months' notice instead of one.'

'Done. I'll talk to Hannah, but she'll understand I think.'

There's no other way I'd rather depart than on a high, delivering a second successful campaign with Cassie. Her inheriting Hannah's account from me is also a bonus. She'll be my point of contact as the account manager at Talent-IT, but this is preferable to working together every minute of every day where our relationship would have to stay under wraps or be relegated to sneaky trysts in the stationery cupboard.

'I'd better get out of here. If the team already know about Graydon going, then they are already out there thrashing it out over who will get his hole punch. I can share the good news that they needn't brawl over it. Mine is up for grabs too.'

Donald comes around the desk and hugs me.

'I might still pop around sometime for a fish supper and a cuppa,' I say to Donald.

'You do that,' he says.

Chapter Sixty-One

Cassie and I step off the bus at the stop on the Fitzroy Estate, outside the grocery store that's a central congregation point for local youths. The group of teens hanging there are smoking a joint and passing around a bottle of cider, reminding me of the Cape Flats. Some of these estates, on the murkier side of Edinburgh, are not too different from the Cape Flats. They're breeding grounds for gangs, crime and drugs. But there are good kids caught up in it all, looking for an outlet, needing a break in life. The cogs in my head turn, wondering how technology initiatives could also reform youngsters; to keep them off the streets before they take the wrong path to a sentence behind bars. I'm excited by my new prospects with Hannah and the opportunities for life-changing innovation.

Cassie takes my hand and one of the underaged drinkers wolf-whistles, loud and shrill. I reach out for her palm and we continue walking past, hand in hand. Since returning from South Africa, our relationship has been developing in a manner which is low-key but intimate. Another kiss when I left her at the airport, lengthy phone calls at night, and now me accompanying her to break the news to Margarita that she will be flying overseas for a second time, this time to run a campaign in Australia. There's been no awkwardness or shyness – only a cautious approach on both parts – while we're still colleagues.

'You excited about going home?' I ask.

'I can't wait. We have to go to Fremantle. It's been so long since I lived there, I hardly remember it.'

We reach Cassie's place and she lets herself in, where we find Margarita watching a game show on television.

'Cassie! I've been offered a new job for another auctioneer pay-ing much better money,' she announces when she sees us.

'Congratulations,' Cassie says.

'George will be livid. Every time he's on the circuit, he's going to spot me with a competitor. Serves him right.'

'Forget about George and just enjoy the moment.'

'I can't just forget him, Cassie. He was just like your father, leaving me like that after promising the world.'

'I didn't come back to open up old wounds. Me and Simon just came to share a bit of news about work, that's all.'

'Simon? Isn't his name Graham?'

Cassie looks at me and then back at her mother. 'It's a long story. I'll tell you about it some other time, but I'm just going to come out with the work thing. We're heading to Australia to run another campaign.'

Margarita turns to stare at me. 'You've manipulated her into this, haven't you?'

'No, Mrs Walker.'

'I'm not Mrs!' she yells, before turning to Cassie. 'That's it, isn't it? You're going to look for your father.'

'No. He walked out and never came back. I've never forgiven him for that. This isn't about Dad. Everything isn't always about Dad.'

'So why go?'

'It's an amazing career opportunity.'

'I need you here, Cassie, not swanning off abroad again.'

'For what?'

'It doesn't matter what for. You're not going.'

Cassie opens her mouth and then closes it again. She takes my hand for the second time this evening and pulls me to her bedroom. When we get there, she's in tears.

I use my thumb to wipe her cheek.

'If I'm to salvage my relationship with my mother, I have to get out of here,' she says, 'for good. I love her though, Simon. Please don't judge me.'

'Who am I to judge anyone? I get it. You're like this beautiful conflict diamond in an inner-city war zone.'

'That's the nicest thing anyone has ever said to me,' Cassie says with a watery smile.

'I know it's out of the blue, but move in with me,' I blurt. We're still facing each other, in the middle of her petite bedroom that's no larger than my cell in South Africa. She bites her lip and I kiss her to distract her from the angst.

'We've barely just got to first base, Simon. It's still a worry it doesn't work out. Working extensive hours in the office and seeing each other at home isn't ideal.'

'I've something to tell you.'

'What?'

'You won't see me every day at the office.'

'Why? Where are you going?'

'I'm resigning.'

'What?'

'I spoke to Hannah and she's agreed to take me on in a team leader position. I approached her after I realised in South Africa it's what I want to do. I just didn't want to share anything about it until it was locked and loaded.'

'Why do you want to leave?'

'Well, no offence, but I don't want to work with you anymore. I want to be with you, together, you know, not as colleagues. Plus, I think it has always been my destiny to be linked with prisons forever. I don't know, Cassie. I can see the flaws in the system and I want to improve them. I honestly wanted to die when I was locked up. Maybe I can make them a better place.'

'So, this is like a serendipity moment?'

'I guess so.'

Cassie stares at me and I drown in those deep green eyes; so like Monique's. She cups my face in her hands and kisses me again. I pour everything I have into the embrace, because when it comes down to it, all a person has is love and life.

When we unlock, I know she's made the decision to come with me.

'Even though you have your differences, you'll still need to visit Margarita. Tell her when you leave, that you love her. It will soften the blow.'

'I will, but you need to do the same, Simon. Visit your folks and Monique more often.'

'Deal.'

'I'm going to tally it on the whiteboard as a win.'

'I totally won the day I met you,' I tell her. 'My brother brought me to you and I'm going to dive headfirst into whatever lies ahead.'

Cassie pulls out a suitcase to transfer the contents of her wardrobe. 'First things first. Give me a hand packing, will you?'

'I'm serious. I'm going to maak elke sekonde tel with you,' I say, when she has finished packing her pinstripe suit.

'What does that mean?' she asks.

I kiss her. 'Make every second count.'

'Say it again.'

Maak elke sekonde tel.

Maak elke sekonde tel.

Maak elke sekonde tel.

Acknowledgements

This book has held me prisoner for so long, chained to the laptop for precisely fifteen years. It started as a maternity leave project, drafted about a year after my daughter was born, when I was a novice writer living in Cape Town. A bubble-gum office romance. A flurry of artistic experimentation. It ended up a gritty book about the impact one unfortunate incident can have on the mental health of an ordinary man.

Life changed.

My concept changed.

I changed.

They say patience is a virtue; it's true. My extraordinary publisher, Karen Mc Dermott, you are yet again my guardian angel for sticking with me to get this book into print. For gently nudging me along with professional encouragement, indulging me with unwavering support, and every now and then, scheduling a much-needed video call to kick my ass back on track after I digressed and ran the risk of losing my mojo forever. Thanks are extended to your broader group of KMD, MMH Press, Serenity Press and EPA writers who provide an encyclopedia of knowledge and invaluable cheerleading.

Lusaris (a literary imprint of Serenity Press), I am beyond excited to have *The Pinstripe Prisoner* in your fold. Without your talented crew injecting care and expertise into design, editing, production and distribution, this manuscript would have remained locked away for ever. Dylan, your book cover and creative vision was spot on, and Eleanor, thank you for your keen eye which sought out and eradicated many pesky gremlins.

Clive Newman, I will never forget our first coffee meeting in Fremantle when you agreed to represent me as my literary agent. You instantly understood my raw perspective and dark humour, tirelessly going to town to find the right publishing house to get this baby born. Thank you for having faith in me before I had faith in myself.

This book is nothing like its original form. For those in Scotland who read the earliest, very premature baby, you deserve a medal … yes, that's you, Grace Hilditch and John French. That initial rough copy made it into the trash can (John … the Anvil pub somehow survived and made the cut!). A few years later, a couple of characters resurfaced and muscled their way back into my notebook, bringing multiple points of view and a fundamentally different, darker, psychological vision. This time a handful of readers did the honours, namely Anna Moolman, Margot Wood and Kevin Alexander, a cohort who politely gave feedback before the pages went back into my top drawer to incubate under another layer of dust. Like many prisoners, the words eventually got tired of being banged up indefinitely, so after pleading for release, I decided to give the manuscript another chance, but not without substantial reform consisting of yet another full rewrite.

Several people can be attributed to the iterative evolution of this novel. Thanks to my network in the outsourcing, workforce solutions and technology industry, who have been instrumental in my corporate career progression and have given me anecdotes to mould into material. More often than not, fact is stranger than fiction. Joanne Fedler, your sensitivity check and knowledge of South African political undercurrents gave me balance and an invaluable different perspective. Tess Woods, I am still indebted to you for slotting me in last minute to your Wales writing retreat, for your ongoing friendship and the golden introductions into the publishing community. Laurie Steed, coffee with you way back was filled with the richest beans, giving me those important early nutrients needed for growth. Luke Johnson, hats off for making sure I injected the right amount of male testosterone when the fight scenes needed a bit of oomph. As a by-product of the 'Authors for Fireys' bushfire disaster appeal, additional story input was also provided by Kimberley Atkins, editorial director at Hodder & Stoughton in London, and freelance book editor, Catherine McCredie.

Appreciation to the police officer who allowed me off-limits access into a cell in Struisbaai and answered endless questions about criminal behaviour as part of my research into South African prison life. I extend my deepest respect to those working tirelessly every day to keep guns off our streets and those transforming the police force, correctional facilities and justice system for the better.

Katharine Susannah Prichard Writers' Centre, endless gratitude for awarding me the coveted First Edition Fellowship, supported by the Western Australia Department of Local Government, Sport and Cultural Industries. The residency in the Perth Hills afforded me the much-needed time and space to edit this book, and the mentoring sessions provided by the Fremantle Press team were what

I needed to refine my rookie skills as a fiction author. Appreciation also goes to my one-to-one mentor, author Annabel Smith, who holed up with me in the KSP library to give in-depth feedback and constructive guidance on how to tighten up early sections of this manuscript. Gratitude also to the Society of Women's Writers NSW for granting me airtime at your events, and in particular to Rita Shaw, for chasing me for late submission material.

From a PR perspective, it is always incredible to have a spotlight on my literary shenanigans. For the coveted radio slots, thank you Alfie Joey and the production team at *BBC Radio Newcastle*, Barry Nicholls at *ABC Radio Perth*, and Karen Sander at *Radio Northern Beaches*. There are too many newspapers and magazines to call out, but each of you has made a difference to my career progression. A special thanks to Sonia Sharma at the *Newcastle Chronicle*, *Journal* and *Sunday Sun* in the UK, Rosamund Burton for your article in *Pittwater Life Magazine,* and editor Nigel Wall for your forgiveness of my media faux pas and giving me a double-page feature regardless. Thank you also to Nivashni Nair and *The Sunday Times* in South Africa, and *The Suidernuus* team in Bredasdorp, South Africa. Ongoing hugs to Lisa Gal Bianchi and Kelly Smeath for gifting my books to numerous Hollywood superstars … hello Robert DeNiro's hotel suite!

On a journey this long, friendship is essential fuel. Without my global network, I would be navigating alone in the wilderness and that is no fun at all. Special kudos to the WA posse of Laura and Stuart Nisbet, Jacquie Campbell-Howard, Jackie Rafter, Verity Wilson, Karyl Treble, Steve Mann, Bill and Mas O'Neil, and the Liwara and SHC parents. To the inner circle who collaborated with me on various literary festival mental health programs, you make me smile on the rainy days: Michelle Weitering, Danielle Aitken,

Skylar J Wynter and Susan Wakefield. To East Coast roadies Ben Tobin, Fraser Gordon, Miki Ikari and Donna Carter, who trundle along midweek to cheer on my live boom box, you are very bad for playing late on school nights but very good for giving me priceless moral support. A quiet whisper to the humane heroes in my forever alumni for teaching me to speak out with courage when it matters most and standing by my side when trying to create a more inclusive world for all. Good things come to those who fight for what is right. To book sellers, bloggers and readers, without you, I would still be trying to break out with no parole in sight.

To my extended family of the Van Nelsons, Doubells and Hendersons, as always, you are my sanity. Without the chats, I would be Shirley Valentine, talking to the wall. Roy and Sandra, eternal love for welcoming me into your home in South Africa back in the nineties, sorting out a shotgun wedding on Melkbosstrand beach without blinking an eye at impulsive young love and treating me as a daughter ever since. I am blessed to have you in my life.

Imani and Kayin, love you to the moon and back. You have both been with me every step of the way. You will be relieved to know I can finally sleep a full night far more easily now the never-ending scribbling and editing has finally made it over the finish line into a beautiful book. Together we live fearlessly, chase our dreams and never give up.

Shaun, you took me over the waters (down the dangerous rapid route), opened my eyes to the vibrant beauty of South Africa, smoked me out with my first braaied snoek, shared a cold one at shipwreck and pushed me up the last few metres to the summit beneath The Tablecloth. I've lost count of how many times we have packed up the bags and detoured off the beaten track. Adventure junkie moments keep the head straight. Absence makes the heart grow fonder. Home is where the dog is. *Maak elke sekonde tel.*

Mental Health Support

I acknowledge many people have been impacted directly and indirectly by challenging life events and circumstances. You know who you are. If any of you are reading, I thank you from the bottom of my heart and wish you the brightest light at the end of the tunnel.

If you are struggling with anxiety, depression, are at risk of self-harm or have suicidal thoughts, reaching out for support and getting treatment will help in your steps towards recovery. There are many trusted sources of information and assistance available around the clock that provide mental health care in a crisis. In Australia, these include, but are not limited to:

- Beyond Blue aims to increase awareness of depression and anxiety and reduce stigma. Call 1300 22 4636, chat online or email, 24 hours a day, 7 days a week.
- Lifeline provides 24-hour crisis counselling, support groups and suicide prevention services. Call 13 11 14, text on 0477 13 11 14 (12pm to midnight AEST) or chat online.
- Kids Helpline is Australia's only free 24/7 confidential and

private counselling service specifically for children and young people aged 5 – 25. Call 1800 55 1800.

- Headspace is the National Youth Mental Health Foundation, providing early intervention mental health services to 12-25-year-olds. Visit www.headspace.org.au

About the Author

Kelly Van Nelson is a contemporary author and poet from Newcastle upon Tyne. She lived in London, Edinburgh, Cape Town, L'Agulhas and Perth, before moving to Sydney, Australia. Her poems, short stories and articles have featured in numerous international publications and she regularly appears on radio and television discussing current issues prevalent in society. She is represented by The Newman Agency.

Graffiti Lane, her powerful debut poetry collection, showcased at the London Book Fair and became an instant number-one bestseller, raising awareness and influencing change around bullying, mental health and suicide. *Punch and Judy*, her second bestselling poetry collection, puts the spotlight on domestic violence, generating much-needed conversation. Her third bestseller, *Retrospective*, explores the underbelly of urban life. She is also the author of *Rolling in the Mud*, a short story collection, and the curator of *Globalisation: The Sphere Keeps Spinning*, an anthology featuring several international poets. Her books are frequently gifted to Hollywood celebrities, music icons and Academy Award winners.

Kelly is a 'KSP First Edition Fellowship' recipient; an AusMumpreneur 'Big Idea - Changing the World' gold award winner for her creative use of the literary word as an antibullying advocate; a double-gold 'Roar Success Award' winner for 'Best Book' *(Graffiti Lane)*, and 'Most Powerful Influencer'; 'Social Media Star' silver award winner, and bronze winner of the 'Making A Difference' award. She is also a 'Telstra Business Women's Award' and 'CEO Magazine Managing Director of the Year' finalist.

Kelly is the mum of two children, wife of her soulmate of more than two decades, TedX speaker and managing director on the executive board of a global organisation. In the spare time she doesn't have, you can find her hanging out on the open mic performing poetry around the world. In short, she is a juggler.

www.kellyvannelson.com

Lightning Source UK Ltd.
Milton Keynes UK
UKHW021157090922
408533UK00001B/15